DEAD HEADS

A Gloomwood Novel

R Young

Copyright 2013 Ross Young

All rights reserved.
No part of this publication may be reproduced, stored in a retrieval system, stored in a database and / or published in any form or by any means, electronic, mechanical, photocopying, recording or otherwise, without the prior written permission of the publisher. You heard me.

To Ruth

Table of contents

Chapter	Page
1	1
10	33
20	79
30	140
40	179
50	213
60	247
70	281

01

Ralph Mortimer shook as he reached out towards the matte black doors in front of him. Making a fist with one quivering hand, he let out a sigh, and rapped his knuckles against the solid dark wood. He shuffled his feet and glanced behind him as he waited for an answer. At the bottom of a short flight of stairs, a woman frantically gestured at him to go inside, waving her manicured hands. He shrugged and knocked again.

"Just go in," the woman whispered.

"You go in. I'm not barging into his office. What if he's doing something?"

The woman folded her arms and glared. "You're the third assistant to the manager of the O.D. I'm just a secretary. You should be prepared to barge in. What if something happened to him?"

Mortimer turned around. Even though he was standing a step above, the woman loomed over him. "You're not just a secretary. You're *his* secretary. You probably go in and out of his office a hundred times a day. Why did you call me?" He held his arms out and waited for an answer.

The woman waved a finger at him. "You, well, you—" She made a noise like an exasperated horse. "I've never been in his bloody office and I never want to go in his office." Grabbing a designer handbag off her desk, she began throwing items into it. "I don't need this. I'm highly qualified. People should be working for me. Greatest honour, blah, blah, blah, and you, you… well, I could just bloody, well, no, in fact, I quit!" She swung her bag over her shoulder and stormed away.

Mortimer stumbled down the stairs after her. "Wait, you can't just quit and walk out like that."

"Why the hell not?" she shouted as Mortimer caught up to her.

"Don't mention hell." He winced as he said it.

"Oh, sod the bloody O.D. and its rules too."

"Wait, I, just wait, please?"

"What?"

"It's just, well, that's not actually your stapler."

She let out a wail of fury and threw the stapler at his head. He ducked, and when he looked up, she was already out the door.

He scooped up the two halves of the stapler and made a poor effort of reassembling it before he placed it back on the desk and turned to look up the short flight of stairs towards the doors. His hands were damp, and he rubbed them against his cheap suit jacket as he walked back up the steps. Glancing behind him to make sure no-one was watching, he muttered under his breath, "Please don't chop my head off, or my arms or legs. I can't afford to get any decent parts at the moment. If only we hadn't bought the fancy shed."

The sound of his knock, timid as it had been,

reverberated down the corridor and he waited a full two minutes before taking a deep breath and saying loudly, "Sir, I'm coming in."

His hand was trembling as he gripped the handle and twisted it. The lock clicked, and he gently pushed open the door.

"Sir, I'm very sorry to interrupt. It's just that… sir? Oh… oh dear, um."

He backed out of the room and pulled the door shut. Letting out a strange bleating sound, he sprinted down the stairs and along the corridor, away from the room.

02

The Damned University is an educational establishment of the highest order. Being the only place of learning for the dead, it is filled with all manner of people who declare themselves experts in the most obtuse, bizarre, nonsensical and, in some cases, macabre of fields.

Of particular debate is the question of where exactly the land of the dead exists. This is in itself unanswerable because every point of reference conceived begins in the land of the living, and thus is largely irrelevant to the workings of anything, either within the land of the dead or outside of it. Unfortunately, the same argument has been posed many times with regard to astronomy and space travel. For this reason, and this alone, it is still a subject worth debate.

Enter the Head of Necrogeographics, who begins his first year lectures with the following diatribe, "If we were to draw life as a race, the human race perhaps, then there would be a clear finish line. The object of the race would doubtless be to arrive at the finish line as slowly as possible. Any sensible person would choose not to be in the race or to run the race in the opposite direction and so our theoretical model falls down. Let us hypothesise for a moment that the race takes place on one of those moving walkways prevalent at airports, and that the walkways are incredibly crowded by people with large suitcases and screaming children. If the walkway is moving inexorably towards the finish line, it is impossible to avoid the end, which is the sole purpose of the walkway. Now, when we reach the end of the walkway and cross the line, we enter duty free. Here there is a huge range of shops where we can spend the remaining change we have left over from being alive. So we have time to pick up some whiskey for our great-great-great-great-grandfather, or maybe even a few hundred cigarettes now that they really can't harm you any more. Then we have the departures lounge and finally we have the place you arrive at: Gloomwood."

This fairly absurd introduction to understanding the position of the land of the dead is unfortunately the most clearly explained and easy-to-understand description of what actually happens when people die. Well, when people die and end up in Gloomwood, at least.

It was with this theory in mind that Angus Ableforth, an early contributor to the industrial revolution who had died while attempting to break the land speed record on a steam-powered tricycle, decided to try to fight against the moving walkway. He did this by sending a message from beyond the grave to his great-great-great-great-grandson, informing him that he and his family should jump over the side.

Misinterpreting the message, James Ableforth found himself in Gloomwood only three hours later, having jumped over the side of a cross-channel ferry on its way to Dover. His family were not stupid enough to follow him.

Bitterly disappointed by the actions of his many-times-removed grandson, Angus Ableforth sought him out to ensure his deceased kin understood how foolish he had been. Upon finding James, he was shocked to learn that the younger Ableforth blamed the elder for his death and so ensued a great battle between the Ableforths Senior and Junior. As a result of this scuffle, the first death of a dead person took place, and henceforth, the expunging of a dead person was known as Ableforth, in honour of Angus Ableforth, the victim.

Describing it as murder is, of course, an over-simplification, as the victim was certainly already dead. All the same, his existence was snuffed out and Ableforth Junior was sentenced to Death without parole, a sentence he was already serving. As an aside to this, the university decided to suspend the head of Necrogeographics until he had designed a new basic introduction to the subject and all communications between the land of the living and dead were banned. Those breaking this ban are punishable by incarceration equal to that received for committing Ableforth.

03

When Augustan Blunt died, it was not with anger or fury. He didn't battle or rage against the dying of the light. Not that he had lived that way, at least not for a long time. He didn't die with a sense of fulfilment or duty, nor did he die safe in the knowledge that his family and friends were cared for, for he had none that were living.

At the time of his death, he wasn't filled with remorse or a bitter sense of injustice, although he did have the right to feel this way. There wasn't a sense of relief that finally he had reached the end of the line. He did not wish the end would come sooner, but neither did he wish for a few more seconds of life. At no point during his demise did he ponder the question, why me?

He felt indifferent. As the life flowed out of him and he felt his physical self growing colder, emptier, and further away from the familiar comfort of being alive, he had no feelings one way or the other. Death was inescapable—he was well aware of that—and having no true belief or opinion on the matter of an afterlife, he chose to ignore the possibility entirely.

If you had asked him what he thought happened when a person died, he would not have divulged his thoughts on mortality. As far as he was concerned, the shifting of a mortal coil was irrelevant, a meaningless inevitability. He would not have spewed forth a bilious attack on religious belief because he neither agreed nor disagreed with the concept of a greater being or a grand plan. Although if you had asked him what he thought he amounted to in the grand scheme of things, he may have told you he was insignificant, which in itself might be considered some form of belief.

His past did not appear before his eyes and he did not reminisce, however briefly, on the stages in his life. He did not look back fondly on times gone by, and he did not consider all the things that he would never experience. When he finally choked, coughing out his death rattle, he felt no need to whisper some poignant final words.

When Augustan Blunt died, he did it without style or panache. He did it without making a statement. There were no tears as he died, from himself or those close by. It is important to note that his death wasn't businesslike either. He did not believe that his life had a limited period and that, like some contract, his period on earth had ended with no hope of renewing it. At no point did he wonder if his body was a vessel to carry his non-corporeal self, a vessel which had simply broken down the extended warranty period over only a day before.

He did not wish that he had lived one more day, or that in the past, he had lived his life to the fullest. He did not believe that he was soon to be transported to some higher plane with cherubs playing harps and half-naked women simply waiting to inflate his ego.

It was not his belief that he would be pulled down into the fiery torment of hell where he would live out every cruel injustice he had inflicted on others for all eternity, although there was a distinct possibility of it happening.

He did not desperately—with his final vestige of strength remaining—reach towards the sky and try to grasp at what was not there. There was not music playing in the background and there was not the panicked work of doctors or paramedics trying to keep him alive. He did not consider that he might be missed or fondly remembered.

At no point did a partner burst onto the scene, wrap their arms around his body as the life dripped from him, and scream "NOOOOOOOOOOOOOO!" into the air, furiously raging against the injustice of it all.

With his dying breath, he didn't claw at his weapon, or manage with his last reserves of energy to lift a gun, firing off one last shot to kill the man who took his life. He didn't carry a gun.

None of this happened.

When Augustan Blunt died… he simply died. It is what he did after that changed him.

04

Petal held the drug in his hand, breathing in the musky odour that reminded him of cut grass and a gym bag filled with damp, sweaty clothes. In his mind, it was the scent of life; a pungent mixture of things lost when he had exited the land of the living.

He only took a little of it in. He knew having an addled mind while he was dealing would be a mistake. The neighbourhood that served as his patch was little more than a slum, and a slum filled with the dead was not the kind of place in which people blossomed. Misery and bitterness had burrowed themselves deep into the consciousness of the community, and with it paranoia and crime had insinuated themselves. The drug was a release that these people needed desperately; he was merely providing them with what they required.

He leant against the door frame of his meagre dwelling, the wood groaning under his weight. The terraced houses in the neighbourhood had seen better times, but that was before Petal had arrived, and he'd been in Gloomwood for over a hundred years. Time was neither important nor a consideration for most citizens. It was as relevant as the risk of disease. They were dead, and that was not going to change.

Looking out, he watched an old man and a young boy, who in life would not have been more than seven, walking haphazardly across the street. Their eyes were still bright. It was drunkenness that had taken them rather than Oblivion.

"Petal!" the child cried across the street. "Oi, Petal, you big bastard, sell us a snip."

The demi-god sighed. Any other dealer would have torn the boy's head off for being so obvious, but Petal was forgiving.

"You gone deaf?" the child asked.

"Show some respect, old man." Petal's voice rumbled like a dozen rusty anchors in a cement mixer.

"Piss off, Petal. We're old friends here," the boy said.

"Who's this?" Petal asked.

"This here's Malcolm. Only died couple of days ago, but he's already heard of Oblivion and I told him I knew someone who could help him out."

"Hmph." He flicked the solid purple cube he'd been holding out onto the road and watched the boy scrabble after it.

"Don't just stand there, Malcolm. Pay the man," the child barked over his shoulder as he desperately grabbed at the purple crystals in the middle of the road.

The old-timer's appearance was deceptive. Age was something that affected you when you were alive, when the skin was still capable of stretching, hair and nails still grew, and bones and muscles could still change. Out of Petal, the boy, and the old man, it was the one who looked the most worn, who was by far the youngest.

As the man handed over the last of his cash, a truck came screeching around the corner. The child barely had a chance to look up into its headlights before he was caught up in the wheels of the automobile. His body twisted as it was half crushed beneath the massive tyres. Brake pads squealed in protest as the driver slammed his foot down, dragging the wheel, causing the rear end of the truck to kick out wildly, brake lights glowing red like the eyes of a snapping serpent.

Petal gave the accident a brief glance, but was more interested in the money the man was supposed to be paying. Finally, the truck ground to a halt, leaving the child's body mangled with a leg still trapped beneath the rear tyre.

The driver climbed out and rushed to the back of the truck. "What the hell were you doing?"

"You blind bastard," croaked the distorted body on the ground. There was no blood around the corpse. Petal was only mildly surprised that the child could still speak, but beside him, the old man's face had betrayed every emotion you would expect from a living person witnessing such a nightmarish incident. With a gentle groan, he collapsed to the ground in a heap. Petal reached down and plucked the money out of the old man's pocket. He turned and stepped back into his house, ducking and turning sideways to fit through the doorway. The door closed behind him with a thud.

05

"What is it, Mortimer?" His boss fixed him with a glare that said a lot more than "This isn't a good time." In fact, it said, "This is a very bad time and if this isn't important, I'll probably have you fired and publicly humiliated after which I will have your final moments depicted in a mosaic mural for the city to enjoy for all eternity." It was an impressive glare.

"Er, perhaps I best tell you in private, sir." The man held a piece of paper in his hands, nervously turning it over and over. It was blank.

His superior, Crispin Neat, had the air of an undertaker. It's unfair to say that he looked like an undertaker. It's fairer to say he looked how an undertaker would look if they did fit the strange stereotype that people have of them. He was tall, slender, and sombre. His suits always fit perfectly and his shoes were polished to a shine that you could see your reflection in. His hair was slicked back from his prominent forehead, and his eyes seemed far larger than a person's should be.

He stood up from behind his desk, opposite which two slightly less terrifying but equally sombre people were observing the exchange with curious interest. "If you'll excuse me for a moment," Neat said, forcing a smile. His face reacted badly to the unusual arrangement of muscles and contorted into a disturbing grimace.

The two men slipped through a door, and Neat

closed it slowly. He whirled around on his subordinate the second the latch clicked. "This had better be important."

"It is. I would never intrude upon a meeting if it wasn't." Mortimer said.

"Stop simpering and tell me."

"Well, it's him."

"What about him?"

"He's not with us any more."

"What do you mean he's not with us any more? You bothered me just to let me know he's gone home?"

"No, I mean he's gone, well the important bit."

"What? Spit it out, man!"

"Well, for want of a better word, he's headless."

"What's that supposed to mean?"

"Somebody appears to have stolen his head." Mortimer desperately shrugged, already struggling to find any other way he could state the facts. His suit jacket refused to return to its previous position, leaving a hump on his back.

"Don't be ridiculous. No-one could harm him."

"Well, someone has, sir."

"Have you lost your mind? No, you're far too

dull for that. You're serious... how could this happen?"

"Well, I..." Mortimer sighed pathetically. "I don't know..."

Neat began rubbing his temples. "Who knows?"

"Right now, just you and me. I went to get his signature on the renewal contracts, and his secretary said he hadn't come out of the office all day and wasn't taking his calls. She made me check on him."

"So she knows?"

"No, she quit before I checked."

"Good, no-one else must know. We'll carry on as if it hasn't happened until we know all the facts. I need the list of people who came in and out of the building today."

"Yes, sir."

"No, wait. That's a bad idea. When the public gets wind of this, the fallout will be catastrophic."

"Yes, sir."

"We'll need to tread carefully; everyone in the building is a suspect. We're talking, I mean, is it Ableforth?" Neat's eyes narrowed as he glared at Mortimer.

"No, no, I'm sure it's not Ableforth. He—well, his body—was moving when I saw it."

"That's something at least, but it makes even less sense now." Neat turned away from his subordinate and faced the wall, his face contorting as he considered the situation.

"Shall I call the police, sir?"

"Don't be an idiot, Mortimer! We can hardly expect that bunch of fools to do anything other than cause panic."

"Sorry, sir, I just thought, what I meant was, well I—"

Neat, bored with Mortimer's hesitant pandering, waved the man into silence. "Whoever did this is probably long gone by now. They'd be as stupid as you if they were still here. Everyone in the whole damned city is a suspect."

"But surely not everyone would want—"

"Of course they would. Whether people admit it or not, they still blame him for them being here at all."

"I don't think that's true, sir. The people love him." Mortimer felt the door at his back. His feet somehow had shuffled him slowly away from Neat.

"Love him? They fear him, Mortimer, and with good reason. People grovel at his feet not out of love or respect but out of pathetic terror, and it's the way it should be."

"But then, who can we trust?"

"Not even each other. We need someone from the other side. It's the only way we can be sure they weren't involved. If he's gone, the city could crumble beneath our feet. The city and everyone in it will be in turmoil. There's no telling what could happen. Then there's the fact that this could happen at all. Even if we resolve it, people are going to realise that he's vulnerable, that he isn't indestructible or infallible. They'll ask how it could happen, who was responsible for ensuring it didn't happen. We need someone to fix this, someone dispensable."

"But surely we want our best people on this?"

"Are you questioning my judgement?"

"Ah, no, sir, of course not."

"We need someone coming in soon."

"A policeman?"

"Yes, a real policeman. Do you have any idea how many genuine policemen end up in Gloomwood?" Neat asked.

Mortimer shrugged. "I can find out. It's all filed away."

"Almost none, Mortimer. A policeman. We need a genuine detective…"

"I think there's a private investigator—"

Neat held a hand up, silencing Mortimer. "No, I remember now. We have an ex-police officer—a detective—coming in soon. We can rush his arrival, find him and bring him here quick."

"But who am I looking for?"

"His name was something like Tool, no, not Tool. It begins with a B."

"Bucket?"

"Don't try to help, just get the file of anyone who fits the description to me as soon as possible."

"What if I can't find him?"

"You had better, Mortimer, or you'll have me to answer to. While you're at it, get me Mandrake."

"Mandrake? But you said we can't trust anyone. Why would you want him?"

"Just send him to my office, Mortimer."

"Do you think it's a kidnapping? We should expect a note."

"We'll worry about it as it happens. Another thing, Mortimer, you'll be this detective's case officer."

06

"Whoa! Fella, you sure picked a messy way to go."

"Don't just stand there! Help me!" Blunt shouted through fog, actual thick grey fog.

"Bit late for that, mate. You're a goner," the voice said, getting closer.

"How can you stand there watching a man die?" Blunt asked, choking and coughing through every word.

"Hah, all part of the job, mate. Isn't the first time I've done it, won't be the last time either. 'Course you're making a bit of a meal out of it. I mean all that writhing about in agony and stuff, unnecessary really."

"What? What did you just say? Unnecessary? I'm dying. What would you like me to do? Whistle a happy tune?"

The voice went quiet. "Whistling a happy tune while your lungs fill with blood probably wouldn't be the most fun in the world. No need to get touchy. I'm just saying you needn't carry on so much. You're dead. Accept it."

Blunt couldn't contain his fury any longer. Unfortunately, unconstrained, it was no more effective. "I'll accept it when I'm dead, you bastard."

The voice sounded hurt. "I'm not a bastard, and

even if I was, there's no need to go getting personal. You're a liar, anyway."

"What? How exactly am I a liar? What the hell are you playing at?"

"You said you'd accept it when you're dead. Well, I reckon you've been dead for about a minute now and you haven't accepted it, so you're a liar."

"I'm not dead yet. How could I be having a conversation with you if I was dead?"

"Ah-ha, and there we have the answer to proving you're dead. I'm dead too, been dead for ages I have. Anyway, enough of this. Get up. We've got to go."

Blunt thought about arguing for a moment and decided it was useless. "Okay, I'll get up as soon as I stop bleeding and suddenly regain my health by some miraculous magical spell."

"Great! Come on then."

"Listen, you insignificant little tosser."

"Hey, there you go, getting personal again. Anyway, I'm six foot two, hardly little. As for insignificant, well, it all depends on your perspective. For instance, right now I'm extremely significant to you. Without me, you're in real trouble. Now get up because I'm running out of patience. It may help if you attempt it, oh and will you look at that, it must be a miracle. You're not bleeding or, in fact, injured any more. Some might say you've magically regained your health, 'cept you haven't. You're dead."

Blunt realised he wasn't in pain at all, nor was he

wallowing in a pool of his own blood. The gaping wound in his chest had healed, or at least disappeared. He pushed himself into a sitting position and looked around. Staring down at him was a gangly teenager in a black hooded jumper and baggy black jeans. His boxer shorts were on show and these too were black. "You bloody kids, you scared the crap out of me. I suppose you think this is funny, walking around in your hoodies terrifying people. Well listen to me, sunshine. You just messed with the wrong guy." Blunt leapt to his feet and went to grab the teenager.

"You old geezers are all the same: see someone wearing a hooded jumper and all of a sudden they're criminals and reprobates. You're ageist and hoodiest."

"What? Hoodiest? Does that mean you have a bigger hood on your jumper than everyone else, or that you're more of a hoodlum than everyone else?"

"Maybe it means I'm more committed to the neighbourhood than anyone else; I care about my 'hood. Therefore, I am the hoodiest."

Something in the fantastic clockwork of Blunt's mind seemed to be trying to grab his attention and then, as if a spring had suddenly shot out of the finely tuned, well-oiled machine that was the main power behind his investigative powers, it broke free. "I'm dead, aren't I?" He stopped short of grabbing the teenager's clothes and left his hands hanging in the air.

"Yes, now are you ready to go?" The teenager asked from behind his hood, without the vaguest trace of smugness or pleasure. Just as quickly as he said it, he turned and began walking away.

"Okay," Blunt said as he caught up with the youngster, aware that for some reason the fog was more dense the further away from the teenager he was. The candle in the teenager's hand flickered for a moment and Blunt had an ominous feeling that he didn't want the flame to go out. He didn't ask where they were going.

"Follow me." And with that, the teenager walked through a door that hadn't been there before. Blunt looked at the door; it didn't seem to go anywhere, which in a way made sense. A door that wasn't there before wouldn't really lead anywhere. It was made of something black and shiny, like vinyl, and had nothing written on it. As he tried to look around the edges, which didn't seem to exist, a hand reached out of the door and yanked him through.

07

On the other side of the doorway, there was a route marked out by velvet ropes that zigzagged into the distance. Otherwise, there was darkness as far as the eye could see. The teenager who had pulled Blunt through the door was standing next to him.

"Okay, Detective Blunt, welcome to immigration. Do you have your passport with you?"

Blunt's mouth hung open as he stared past the teenager. There was a huge archway in the distance. The only blot on the black velvet landscape. Just in front of this was a little box. He guessed it was a desk, although from the layout of the place it might have been a tiny confectionery stand at the world's biggest cinema.

After the teenager repeated his name a couple of times, he finally caught Blunt's attention. "Passport Detective?" He asked.

"No, I was a private detective. I think the correct term is immigration officer anyway," Blunt replied on auto-pilot. He'd made the same joke a hundred-times when going through airport customs.

"Do you have your passport?"

"Um, no, sorry. Didn't bring it with me," Blunt answered, still awestruck.

"It was just a joke. No such thing as a passport here, ha, ha. We, um, try to lighten the mood a little. This can be quite traumatic for a lot of people. I mean, it's the big D and everything."

"Big D?"

"Death, Mr Blunt, the big D, the final curtain, the end, kicked the bucket, gone to the other side, gone to a better place, bought the farm, not coming to visit anymore, and all that."

"Er, right, yes, so I'm dead. You're dead too?" Blunt asked. He looked around at everything and nothing in particular.

"Right. Don't worry about how you're feeling at the moment, Detective; it's quite normal to feel shell-shocked by the whole experience. Even I took a long time to come to terms with death. 'Course, I was more surprised I was dead. Got my head stuck in a toilet and drowned. Would you believe it? It sounds impossible, but somehow I did it. Oh well, easy come, easy go and all that. I do still feel sorry for the plumber though, and the guy who was in there before me. Can you believe that some policeman actually got it into his head that it might have been cannibalism, that the poor bloke had eaten me whole, then relieved himself of my entire body in one go! Still, there's always one, hah. They probably said that about me, kid who dies with his head stuck in the toilet. Well, there's always one."

Blunt was ignoring the chattering teenager. In front of him, there was a confused woman talking to herself. "What happened to me? I was just walking the dog. Where's the damn dog gone?" It was then that Blunt noticed other people in black hoods; one of them seemed to pop up out of nowhere to escort the woman away. With every step they took away from Blunt, they seemed less real, less solid, until they simply weren't there anymore, faded away to nothingness.

Blunt turned to the hooded teenager. "Who are you?" He asked.

"Oh, well, you've probably broken a few records there, Detective. No doubt that's why you're a detective. Very perceptive. I'm a reaper. Reapers are the people who collect people who have died from the land of the living and bring them here. It's far more complicated than that, but you don't need to know the details. My name's actually Philip, and I'm looking after you specifically today as you're something of a VIDP."

"A what?"

"Very Important Deceased Person."

"Okay, why am I so important?"

"How should I know? You should be grateful. You're going to get to cut through very quickly. Some people have been in this queue for years. 'Course, priority is given to some people over others, but not normally like this. You must be important."

"Don't ever tell me that again."

"Tell you what, Detective?"

"Tell me to be grateful. You said that I should be grateful. Don't ever say that again. I'll be grateful for things I'm grateful for and not for things people think I should be grateful for. What other people anyway? There's no-one here," Blunt said, puzzled. Where there had been people, there was now nothing but an empty expanse. The velvet ropes were still there, but everything else had gone.

"Okay, Captain Cheerful, whatever you say."

"Philip."

"Yes, Detective?"

"Where's everyone else? Where did that woman go?"

"She's, well it's quite hard to explain, but I guess it's like she's behind a pane of glass, but the glass can't be seen through."

"Isn't it just a wall then?"

"Um, yeah, so it's like she's on the other side of a wall. Only really, it's a slightly different phase in time."

"Right." Blunt paused, considering whether or not it was worth pursuing the conversation further, and decided against it. "Can someone die here?"

"Hmm, not really. I mean, you're already dead, but that'll be explained later."

"Can people be hurt here?"

"Yes, unfortunately they can be."

"Then stop being so bloody cheerful or I'll hurt you very badly."

"Detective," the hooded teenager said, with an unmistakable tone of dwindling patience.

"Yes Philip?"

"If I hadn't been ordered to take care of you, I'd have left you on the other side. You're a bastard."

"That I am, Philip, that I most certainly am," Blunt said, starting to feel more like his old self again. "Now if I'm a VIDP, how about skipping this queue a little?"

"We are. That's why you can't see anyone."

Blunt nodded. Maybe being dead wasn't so bad. He moved to step over the velvet ropes.

"STOP! What are you doing?"

"Well, there's nobody in the line. I'm not going to walk all the way around the bloody ropes. It's not like they're a seven-foot wall or something."

"They're there for a reason, Detective."

"Yeah, so that more space is available when there's a really big queue," Blunt said, reaching forward to unclasp one of the velvet ropes, but the hooded teenager reached a hand out to stop him.

"Don't touch that rope. We have to follow the route."

"Why?"

"Because, Detective, that's why they are there."

Blunt scowled, but he could tell this wasn't an argument he could win. "This is ridiculous," he muttered as he began the long, circuitous walk.

08

The lean figure of Crispin Neat strode down corridor after corridor until eventually he stopped in front of the most inconspicuous of doors. He knocked twice and a wizened old man opened it a crack.

"It's me."

"I can see that," the old man snapped, and the door was drawn open. "Is the detective coming?"

"He's on his way now," Neat whispered, flicking his head from side to side, looking for anyone who might be listening; he looked like a lizard catching flies.

"Come in, Crispin. You look terrified. Tell me exactly what's happening."

Neat ducked beneath the door frame and into the little room. Inside, there were hundreds of vials of strange coloured liquids lining shelves that covered the walls. "Still no luck with your experiments?"

"There never will be until you find me gone, Crispin. You and I both know that. But still it pleases me to try. It keeps me busy."

"Yes, apparently so."

"Nobody saw you come to visit me?"

"Of course not. I wouldn't allow it. Even if they did, what would it mean to them, anyway?"

"True, so tell me everything you know," the little man said while pulling himself up into a chair. He settled into a comfortable position with his feet dangling above the floor, shoes precariously balanced on the end of his toes, and his wrinkled hands folded across his stomach.

"Well, early yesterday, Mortimer came and interrupted me in a meeting. Actually, now that I think about it, that was quite brave of him. Anyway, he told me… well, you know what he told me."

"Afraid to say it?"

"Aren't you?"

"Yes, I am, but I thought maybe you… never mind, continue."

"Well I decided, in order to ensure there was no chance of corruption, we needed someone who was new to this side."

"A good idea, but surely skipping the transition will just make their job so much more difficult."

"No doubt it will, but we have nobody we can trust who will be able to deal with this. Mortimer will be their assistant, hopefully helping with any differences between there and here."

"Yes, you're right. That's the best course of action. What of the investigator?"

"His name is Augustan Blunt. He was a policeman, and then he became a private investigator. He's solved many crimes, but nothing for quite some time. I don't know if it was the best we could have done, but he's not famous and he's not a resident here yet."

"We couldn't have done any better?"

"People don't die whenever you need them."

"I know, Crispin. We just can't afford mistakes."

"I've read his file, and he's not exactly what we need. He won't just solve the case; he'll also make sure everyone knows he's looking into them. He's as subtle as a brick, but it doesn't matter. He's a detective and we need one. From what I've read, he's good at his job but lacks social skills."

The old man nodded sagely, "As always, you're right on top of things."

Neat smiled and then reached across to a small table in the corner of the room. On top of it was a chess board. "Where were we?" he asked.

"I believe you were about to lose the game."

"Nonsense, it is you that's about to lose."

"Well, there's a first time for everything."

Neat looked the old man in the eye. "Yes, there certainly is."

"I must ask Crispin, and please don't take offence. Did you do it?"

The corners of Neat's mouth shifted upwards for the briefest moment. "No, although it might end up benefiting me in the long run. The truth is, I believe this to have been the crime of someone quite insane."

"If it wasn't you, then I agree, and that is most

concerning."

09

"Four hours it's taken. This is ridiculous; what if there was an emergency or something?" Philip asked, tugging his hood forward.

"What, like everyone dying?" asked Blunt.

"Good point detective," Phillip said. The word *detective* had become some kind of cuss word. Every time it was said, there was more bile dripping over the letters.

"If we'd just stepped over the ropes, it wouldn't have taken this long," Blunt said.

"For the last time, they are there for a reason. If everyone simply stepped over them, the whole system would be chaos."

Philip had gone from good-natured to more bitter than a bag full of lemons in unsweetened lemonade. He'd even begun poking Blunt in the back when he wanted him to move, rather than speaking to him.

"Right then, de-tec-tive, you need to fill this in."

Wonderful, Blunt thought to himself. Now even the gaps between the syllables of the word *detective* were becoming saturated in venom. The surly teenager thrust a piece of paper into his hands, and Blunt had to resist the temptation to grab a wrist and twist it around the skinny brat's back until he apologised.

The piece of paper was fairly straightforward. It asked for his name, place of birth, date of birth, date of death, and method of death (examples in the brackets included motor accident whilst driving, suicide by hanging, murder by cricket bat, choking on a squash ball, bitten by rabid garden mole, etc.). Blunt wrote, "Murdered by pig-faced, druggy little cock goblin with a knife through the chest whilst unarmed."

When Blunt finished writing, Philip trotted towards the counter. The woman behind it was the first person other than Philip who Blunt had seen since the brief glimpse of the woman who had lost her dog. She asked him some questions regarding his form.

"Is this how your name is spelt on your birth certificate?

"Yes."

"In full?"

"Yes."

"And is there any doubt as to the date of death?"

"Um, no?"

"You didn't die near midnight and weren't flying over any time zones at the time of death?"

"No."

"Did your murderer actually have the face of a pig?"

"Not the actual face of a pig, no. It wasn't a

human-pig hybrid; it was a man who looked like a pig."

"And when you say druggy, did you observe him over the course of his entire life or is that judgement based on one particular incident or scenario?"

"Well, I suppose it is based only on my brief interactions with him."

"I see... What is a cock goblin?"

"I... I don't know."

"Okay... a knife in the chest whilst unarmed?"

"Yes, that's correct."

"So, the knife was somehow contained in the pig-boy's chest? Did he hug you?"

"No, I was unarmed when he stabbed me in the chest."

"Right, but you were definitely murdered?"

"Yes."

"Okay, sir, you can carry on, but if you could please take more care when filling in forms in the future? After all, I'm sure you're not a cock goblin, are you, sir?" the woman said without a flicker of humour.

"Well, I don't know if I am or not. I think we've covered this."

"Good day, sir."

Blunt shook his head and walked through the gate

where Philip was waiting for him.

The reaper was checking some kind of notebook when he noticed Blunt approaching. "I know I've been moaning, but that was actually really quick. It took me four days, and that was considered speedy. Of course, most people in the line have no concept of how long they've been waiting. Time's a little messed up in the terminal. You've had a very unusual journey. Next stop is orientation, except for you it's going to be very brief."

Blunt didn't say anything; Philip had irritated him to breaking point, and he knew his own temper well enough to realise that conversation needed to be kept to a minimum. The teenager seemed to realise that the detective wasn't in the mood for idle banter, and instead simply nodded and began walking.

Seemingly from nowhere, neon signs hung out of the air, giving directions to various locations. They indicated duty-free shops, restaurants, toilets, departure terminals, baggage collection and other places Blunt associated with airports.

A large sign with the word *orientation* written on it in bright green letters loomed in front of a shop selling an extensive array of ties and luggage. Blunt couldn't help wondering who would want to buy anything right now, or with what. His only explanation was that, as with airports in the land of the living, these shops were specifically designed for the purpose. Luggage ones were the worst. Who wants to buy luggage once you're at the airport? You've already checked your suitcases in and yet the shops remain, presumably immovable objects.

Blunt deliberately concentrated on thinking about anything but the situation he found himself in. Yes, he was dead, and he couldn't possibly disagree with the fact that he was being led through what appeared to be an airport for dead people, which probably meant he was in the process of leaving life behind, but why in God's name would somebody choose to run a tie and luggage shop here? Quickly finding his own imagination incapable of providing sufficient subject matter to give him a diversion, he decided to bring Philip into his web of distraction. "Philip, why do they have these shops here?"

"So people can buy things, obviously."

"But who's going to want to buy anything here? It's the same with airports. The whole thing's stupid. This is a dream, isn't it?"

Philip stopped walking in the direction the sign pointed. "Finally, we get some sense out of you. No, it's not a dream, but it's about time you asked that. It's all real. You're dead."

Blunt swatted away the teenager's words with a wave of his hands. "Never mind that, I want to know why the hell they have these shops, especially ones that sell luggage."

The teenager hesitated for a moment, holding his breath. "Fine, I'll tell you the answer. Then you have to agree to get a move on."

"Fine."

"The tie shops and luggage shops are an elaborate con by the companies behind them. They find a suitable site for an airport, then build the shops. Once they've done that, the airport gets built around them. If the shops aren't there, then there can be no airport. It's very clever and all to do with preventing people from arguing about having an airport nearby. The airport planning committee request permission to build two shops. The locals shrug and say 'Yeah, why not?' and then when nobody is looking they build an airport around the shops," Philip said, as he shrugged and turned smartly on his heel, heading away from Blunt.

"That's ridiculous. If you don't know, why not just say?"

"Fine, I don't know. Stop dragging your heels and get a move on," Philip said over his shoulder as he led Blunt to the far end of the terminal to a small video screen.

"Right, watch this video. Should only take about ten minutes and then we can get moving."

"And this video tells me what?" Blunt asked, a hint of suspicion creeping into his voice.

"Everything you need to know now that you're dead." Philip actually smiled as he said it; consequently, Blunt's right eye began to twitch.

"A ten-minute video will tell me everything I need to know about being dead."

"Well, it's more of a brief summary. Here we go," he said as he clicked his fingers and the screen lit up.

A familiar actor appeared on the screen.

"Hello there. If you're watching this, you probably recently died. Well, congratulations and welcome. Being dead means a few changes, but don't panic. It's not the end of the world." As the actor said this, text scrolled across the bottom of the screen. "ALL STATEMENTS TRUE AT THE TIME OF PRODUCTION, PLEASE CHECK WITH YOUR NEAREST REAPER SHOULD THE END OF THE WORLD HAVE TAKEN PLACE."

"To try to help you adjust to the changes you're currently going through, our psychological experts have put together this video montage," the actor said through a grin as he faded away and was replaced with a bunch of balloons. The next five minutes of the video were filled with the balloons journeying over various landscapes. Eventually, they began to lose air until they fell to the ground and were popped by the thorns on a bunch of roses. Text filled the screen: "You're dead. Die with it."

The actor walked onto the screen again with a smile on his face. "Well, I hope you're feeling a little better after that video. Let's talk about some of the things that have changed," he said. A plush arm chair materialised behind the actor. He sat down and crossed his legs.

"Now, we can't explain everything about death, just like no-one could give you the answer to the great questions of life, but we can tell you this much: being dead can be a lot of fun."

"Here are the three most important rules about being dead. First, you're on your own. Nobody is responsible for your actions except you. Second, you're not indestructible. You can't die, but you can still be injured. Be careful. Injuries can be a fate worse than death. Of course, anything bad that happens here is a fate worse than death. That'll take some getting used to. It's also worth pointing out that while you can't die as such, you can be Ableforthed. Don't worry too much about it though; Ableforth is very rare. But just so you know, it's the final, final curtain. Your existence, even in the land of the dead, is over. Finally, you will probably never meet anyone you knew in the land of the living."

"That's often very disappointing for people, but there's a simple reason for it; not everyone comes here. You've come here, and probably with good reason. What it is, I don't know. Only the Grim Reaper has the answer. That's not a joke, by the way; there really is a Grim Reaper. I've met him. He's quite nice, really."

"Okay, so we're talking a lot about death, so it will please you to know, you will be dead forever. There's no going back, no reincarnation. That may sound quite daunting, but it means that you can really do whatever you want. There's no such thing as a mid-life crisis in the land of the dead."

"Now I've got to go, but here's what will happen next. Someone in a black hood will collect your group and you'll be escorted through to the arrivals area. If, while you were alive, you believed you could bring personal belongings with you, then you may be able to collect these belongings in the baggage department. Good luck and remember, always look on the bright side of death."

Credits rolled across the screen to the sound of the Kinks' "Sunny Afternoon."

"What the hell was that?" Blunt spun around and glared at Philip, who was beaming from ear to ear.

"Brilliant isn't it? We just added the induction video to the whole setup. Since we brought it in, we've found the number of people who lose their ability to function has dropped by one percent, which is pretty significant." Clearly this was a monumental achievement, as the teenager was completely oblivious to the rage on Blunt's face.

"It's a complete waste of time."

"Exactly. Once you're dead, there's a lot of time to waste."

Blunt shrugged. There wasn't a lot he could argue about until he understood what was going on. Instead, he fell back into his usual mode as an investigator. "What is the percentage of people who can't function properly?"

Philip looked around nervously to make sure nobody was listening, which was pointless as there was nobody there. "Since we've brought in the video, it's about two percent. We're hoping to bring it down further," he said, his voice almost a whisper.

"And what exactly does not being able to function mean?" Blunt had the feeling he was uncovering things he shouldn't be. A sense of anticipation and pleasure washed over him. If it hadn't been for his morals and a real lack of any kind of artistic temperament, he'd have become a paparazzi photographer.

"Not being able to function means they get placed in care." Philip was barely audible over the background noise of the near empty terminal.

"Care?"

"Yes, care. We're almost through now, detective, just around this corner."

"Philip, what exactly is care? Is it that Ableforth thing?"

"Ableforth, oh no, I mean, we would never condone Ableforth for any reason, and certainly not just because someone struggled to function. In the land of the living, do you kill people because they're a bit out of step with reality? I think not. Anyway, I really shouldn't be discussing this—"

"Explain, and while you're at it, explain what not being able to function actually entails."

"Detective, I understand your desire to get as much information as possible, but really, why don't you worry about yourself before you worry about anyone else? I'm sure none of this is relevant to you, anyway. What did you spend your free time doing when you were alive?"

"Listen, you snot-nosed little brat, I'll ask the questions." The truth was that Blunt hadn't really done anything with his free time. He'd normally attempted to find a comatose state as quickly as possible. He was a great explorer in that sense, having discovered more comatose states than he'd imagined had existed. He'd planned to write a guidebook. Of course, it was a little late now, as he'd found the final, ultimate Oblivion.

Philip drew himself up to his full height, his hood obscuring his face completely. "Speak to me like that again, Detective, and you may find yourself in a non-functioning state. You've been ungrateful since I brought you here, and I really don't need the hassle. Get a life, man."

"What? What did you just tell me to do?" Blunt asked.

"Sorry, bad use of words. You're still a jerk."

"You—"

"Shut up," Philip said, turning his back on Blunt and walking towards the exit.

"You—"

"Hey, I don't need this. I don't have to deal with you. We're here, so how about I just leave you to fend for yourself?"

"I was trying to tell you that you seem to be going kind of see-through."

"Oh right, well thanks, Detective. There's a man waiting for you. I've really got to run. Guess I will leave you to fend for yourself. Good luck." With that, the teenager vanished before Blunt's eyes. Feeling a bit nauseous, Blunt pushed open the glass doors in front of him and stepped out onto a concrete pavement.

10

Blunt looked around, filled with expectation. Behind him were the doors he had walked through. In front there was a road, across which was a staircase. Above this hung a sign saying, "This way to buses." The sign didn't glow, and it was slightly skewed. The man who was supposed to be waiting for him was nowhere to be seen.

There were pieces of paper being blown across the road which was otherwise empty save for a row of black hackney cabs, beside which stood bored-looking figures waiting for a fare.

He couldn't help marvelling at how real everything looked, probably because it was real, just not real to a living person. No, wait, that didn't make sense. It was real. Everything here was actually happening. He decided to sit on the pavement. As he placed his hands on the ground, he took deep breaths. He was dead. He was actually dead. And this is where he was. Somewhere on the other side. He was in the land of the dead. Worse still, it was where he belonged. Panic started to take hold. It was getting harder to breathe, and a feeling of suffocation was taking hold.

He couldn't get enough air into his lungs. Every time he took in a breath, he felt like he desperately needed to breathe out, but every time he did, his lungs felt desperately empty. His breathing sped up, and he knew he was hyperventilating. A childhood memory floated to the surface of his consciousness, and he remembered the last time he'd had a panic attack.

The fair ground, a Ferris wheel, and those machines that slide back-and-forth trays of coins. He was five or six and lost. He recalled tugging on a familiar-looking dress to be confronted by a woman with more hair than face. He remembered running desperately between people's legs and finally being spoken to by a man in a blue uniform who had a strange, gruff accent. His mother had eventually found him, but by that point, he had calmed down. The man in uniform received a lecture from his mother, which—now that he remembered the event—was a little backward, but typical.

The memory didn't stop the panic that gripped him; getting lost was very different from realising you're dead. It felt like someone was wrapping their fingers around his throat and squeezing his windpipe closed. As he began to feel dizzy, he heard a voice. "Detective Blunt, excuse me, sir, but are you Detective Blunt?"

He desperately tried to see the face looking down at him, but everything was blurred. Then, just as quickly, the fog lifted, and he could breathe again.

"Ah, I see, you appear to be having your first attack of a little thing we call the Glums," a deep voice said. The man in front of Blunt was short, so short Blunt could almost look him in the eye without standing up. His skin—what could be seen of it—was covered in some kind of tattoo. It looked like a map covered with spidery writing. Across the top of his head, the point at which Blunt found he could best see, were written the words, "Beware ye who trespass, here there be monsters."

"Well, thanks, I think," he said while desperately trying to catch his breath. "What the hell are the Glums? Sounds like a miserable children's television show."

"Not really sure. Happens less and less the longer you're dead, though. Probably something to do with the residual feelings you associated with being alive. You were a biological entity, so there's a good chance the Glums are actually a reaction to the soul adjusting to its new container. At least that's what some people might say. Personally, I think it's because most people can't deal with being dead. I had them for a while and I was never a mortal in the traditional sense, so couldn't really tell you either way. Anyway, I'm your driver today. You better get in; they're waiting for you."

"Who's waiting for me?"

"Office of the Dead sent me. Come on. Despite what you might think, we haven't got eternity. Welcome to Gloomwood."

"Gloomwood? Sounds lovely."

"There's not much that's lovely about this place, Detective, although by the look of you I'd imagine you're not one for loveliness."

Blunt nodded and give a quick smile. "I try but I don't seem to mix in lovely circles." The man didn't say anything and instead opened the door of the taxi and ushered Blunt into the back seat. It was only then that he noticed the temperature, or more importantly, that the sensation of temperature had returned. Throughout the terminal, he hadn't noticed any sensation. He hadn't noticed a lack of it either, but whatever hadn't been there had definitely returned.

The taxi pulled away from the curb and Blunt watched the building he'd left disappearing. It was much smaller than he had realised. It was too ridiculously small to contain everything he had seen, no bigger than a petrol station on the side of the motorway.

Blunt was trying hard not to think about what was happening. The hope that he was in a coma or having some kind of reaction to the drugs the paramedics who had been called to the scene of his attack had pumped him full of kept running through his mind.

He'd never heard of a place called Gloomwood, never imagined that death could lead to a place so depressingly matter-of-fact and grim, but he'd never really thought about death in the first place. Dying was what old people did, or sick people. As much as he hated to admit it, that's what he really thought. There were plenty of times he'd been put in a situation that could have led to his downfall, but he'd always made it through. Somehow he'd begun to imagine that he always would, that he was just lucky.

Escaping by the skin of his teeth was what he was good at. He couldn't be dead, shouldn't be dead. The concept was ridiculous, but he didn't have a choice. If this was a dream, the afterlife, or something else, then he didn't have any option other than to get on with it.

"Funny weather we're having," he ventured to the taxi driver.

"Weather's always miserable here, Detective. You might have noticed no temperature in the deathport. It's in some kind of temporal vortex thing. Out here in the real world, it's pretty much miserable all the time. Sometimes it rains, sometimes it doesn't, but it always looks like it's just about to. It's pretty rubbish in general. You'll notice people still talk about it like they did before you died. Don't know why they bother, personally."

"Quiet at the deathport today," Blunt said, aware that his opening gambit on the weather had been shot down in flames.

"Always quiet there, sir. not like we get floods of people in. You'd think that we did, but it's more of a steady trickle, two or three people a day. Sometimes they'll order a minivan when a cluster come through together, never more than six at once, mind you. I guess most people have got better—or worse—places to go. City grows slowly. We lose just slightly less than we gain."

"You lose people? I thought people couldn't die here."

"Course they can't, already dead, aren't they? Can't die, but they can end up in the library or just go walking, or on rare occasions we have an Ableforth." The man shuddered as he said it.

"What does that mean?"

"You'll find out soon enough. Gonna take us an hour to get to the city. You must be exhausted. How long did it take you to get through?"

"I think about four hours, not including orientation."

"Hah, four hours, you lucky beggar. Took me three weeks. I was near mad when I got out, had to sleep for a week to recover. Even then, I was pretty loopy for the first couple of months, but you get used to it. Guess you're a special case. You've got a meeting straight away, unusual that, bound to be something important."

"I guess I'm lucky then?"

"You're dead, Detective, so I wouldn't try to pretend you've had a good day so far. What did you do then, fall off the edge of the world?" the strange man asked and Blunt sensed a small amount of hope in the man's question.

"Um, no, I was stabbed. Do you ever get people who've, you know, fallen off the edge of the world?" Blunt couldn't help himself. He knew he was wandering down a dangerous path, but he had to push on.

"No, damn selfish bastards, haven't had someone falling off the edge of the world in a long time. Apparently, people decided to believe the edge of the world didn't exist anymore. Then what happens to the poor bastard who was the end of the world, eh?"

"I'm sorry, I don't understand."

"Not your fault. I suppose people knew the world was round before you were even born. Well, they must have or I wouldn't have been here to give you a lift, would I?"

"You've lost me, I'm afraid."

"My name's Barry by the way."

"Nice to meet you, Barry."

"Wasn't always Barry, mind you. I took that name when I arrived here. You won't know much about this place yet. They don't tell anyone anything, just expect you to learn it by yourself. I was pretty important before I came here, you know. Real big time, I was."

"Well, I suppose it changes for everyone."

"'Course it does, but for me—and the others like me—it's harder," the man said, with no small amount of venom in his voice. It wasn't directed at Blunt, but at the same time it didn't exclude him.

Before Blunt could question him, the man continued, clearly on his favourite topic of conversation. "See, I was the fact, or the idea, depending on how you look at it, that the world was flat. When some smartarse decided to go and find proof that the world wasn't flat and everyone else started to agree with him, it was the end of the line for me. I died pretty slowly, but it was inevitable in the end. I mean, honestly, the world being round? It's ridiculous."

"Hang on, are you trying to tell me that you were the idea that the world was flat?"

"Exactly, hence the map all over me. There're others like me, all sorts here, Detective. You'll learn soon enough. Best get some shut-eye while you can though."

Blunt closed his eyes and surprised himself by falling asleep almost immediately. The last thing he remembered was wondering if dead people dreamt of dying.

11

The Marquis of Muerto Lago rested his finely sculpted chin on his well-manicured hand and sighed as he gazed down the table which stretched the length of the room. He glanced at his wrist, at the delicate yet gaudy watch he had chosen to wear to breakfast, and paused as he caught his own reflection. He reached up and moved a single golden-blonde hair less than a millimetre before checking the time.

He had to mouth the calculation to himself, as the foolish designers hadn't the decency to put numbers on the watch. Instead, they made do with diamonds placed at twelve equidistant points around the watch face. Time had always been a struggle for him to come to terms with. He couldn't understand why people took any notice of it. The living, well, time controlled them, but the dead had no need for such trivial things. He sighed as eventually he calculated the time: twenty to eleven. He was going to be late.

He grimaced as he took a sip of steaming-hot coffee and made a mental note to fire whoever had allowed it to arrive at such a high temperature. Time, pain, being late. It was always in the mornings that these things disturbed him like angry gnats, reminding him that he was the same as everyone else. Except, he told himself; he wasn't. He was better than everyone else.

The Marquis had once been a near-insignificant demi-god of a tiny tribe living in the Amazon rainforest. He was the god Plap, and had represented for them a kind of party god. He died out when the tribe was assimilated into a larger community. The god Plap became a joke before finally the last vestiges of belief faded. Those who had worshipped Plap quickly switched allegiance, and he was doomed. Not that he cared. The Marquis was far more powerful as a person in Gloomwood than he ever was as a minor deity.

Still, he did wonder if the last person who had the smallest belief in him as a god really needed to take a trip to Scunthorpe before dying. Would he have ended up in Gloomwood if they'd stayed in the Amazon?

As he bit down on a piece of toast smothered in the finest honey in the land, he heard an eerie sound that sent a chill through his bones. A strange singing floated through the room, and filled him with an irrational dread.

"*She'll be loaded with bright Angels when she comes.*" A voice, a strange hollow-sounding voice, echoed through the cavernous dining room.

The Marquis, who was blessed with an ego so monumental that he considered anything not of his own design and choosing to be meaningless and nothing more than an inexcusable annoyance, pushed his food away from him and stood up, ready to berate whoever had so rudely interrupted his meal. They had spoken. Worse still, they had sung, and nobody was allowed to do more than whisper before noon at the earliest.

At the far end of the table, her back to him, sat a

small girl. In one hand, to one side of her, lay a teddy bear. The bear was ragged and battered, a well-loved but poorly cared for sign of childhood. On her other side was a black bag. It was from this that the singing came. The girl wore an old-fashioned red dress. Even the Marquis could tell it was out of date, and he was no expert on children's fashion.

The girl's head nodded gently from side to side in time with the singing, "*She will neither rock nor totter, when she comes...*" The Marquis, a man unaccustomed to children, pushed his chair away and strode down the side of the dining table towards the girl, his face a mask of fury and disbelief. Which one of his servants would have been foolish enough to allow one of these people into his house?

His footsteps were loud on the marble floor, and they punctuated the singing, out of time with the song, "*She will run so level and steady, when she comes...*"

As he drew nearer, he hesitated for a moment. The song ended, and the girl stood up and strode out of the far door.

The Marquis yanked the door open and threw it against the wall. A doorman jumped as it crashed against the marble. "Everything okay, sir?"

"You there. Why was there a child, well one of those people anyway, in my dining room? Your job is quite simple. Are you not capable of maintaining a secure room for an hour?" his face was inches from the doorman's.

"Sorry, sir, they must have slipped by as I went to

the toilet, sir, I can't apologise enough."

"No, you really can't. You're fired."

"But—"

"I'm sorry. Who are you? Because you don't work for me. Trespassing on my property, are you? Well, maybe I'll call the police."

The guard, terrified, watched as the Marquis closed the door gently behind him. He was worried, but only of anybody overhearing the Marquis' words. The man was well aware the Marquis had almost no memory for the faces of his staff, which was the main reason they had to wear ridiculous uniforms.

In his dining room, the Marquis was having similar thoughts as he wandered back to his seat, and considered whether he should follow through on his words. He took a sip of the wine and shook his head, deciding to forget the matter entirely. "*She will take us to the portals, when she comes...*" The voice came from the floor by the side of his chair. He leapt to his feet and looked down in horror. A large black sack lay open on the floor and inside it, glaring out at him, was a skull. "*Oh hello,*" the skull said before the Marquis felt a sharp pain in his neck and darkness swallowed him.

12

Ralph Mortimer was running, well he was trying. He careened around a corner and bounced off a corridor wall, a corridor wall that hadn't been there yesterday. After dusting himself off, he broke back into a trot.

He'd worked in the Office of the Dead for years, but in an effort to prevent staff becoming stale, the management had long ago decided that the building would need constant refurbishment. This led to the layout of the building changing on a constant basis. It was a clever concept, but it was inherently hazardous to staff members. There were frequent cases of staff working late and finding themselves in offices that no longer had a door, not that it made much of a difference to their workloads, which were automatically topped up by an infernal system of self-filling in-boxes.

Mortimer passed by an open door. After walking another five metres, he turned back around. He popped his head around the frame and peered into the room. Inside, two large women were cackling over cups of coffee. One of them spied him as he stepped into the room.

"Hello ladies, how are we this fine morning?" It was not a fine morning; there had never been a fine morning in Gloomwood.

The two women giggled. Mortimer wasn't a ladies' man. Far from it. Instead, he had cultivated a kind of persona that he used in uncomfortable situations, and unfortunately, he nearly always felt uncomfortable around women.

"Fine, thank you, Ralph. What can we do for you?" The larger of the two usually did the talking for both of them, but Mortimer was used to it.

"Well, ladies, I have a bit of a favour to ask you, if it's not too impertinent of me." The women shook their heads in what they imagined was a coquettish manner. They looked like two Great Danes waiting for a ball to be thrown. They also had no idea what impertinent meant.

"Fantastic. What I need you to do is to travel over to one hundred and eighty-five Pale Avenue, Flat 4B, if you could give it one of your brilliant once-overs. We have a newbie coming on short notice and haven't got time to get a standard clean-up crew." The look on both the women's faces suggested they weren't keen on the idea, and Mortimer was beginning to turn red.

He knew that one of the two women had been a promise in the land of the living, the promise not to eat the last biscuit, but he was never sure which was which. They were notorious for arriving seconds before cake or other snacks were produced for the office staff. They'd even been known to hover over the shoulders of staff just as they opened a packet of crisps.

"Of course, ladies, this will count as overtime. We'll pay you double for two hours' work each. I completely understand if you don't want to do it, but we really could use your help with this one." That did it. Mortimer was supposed to negotiate with them, but he didn't have the stomach for that kind of situation. Besides, this way, the women would still be friendly to him.

The women, on the other hand, would have done it even for normal overtime, but they knew Mortimer well enough to know he was a pushover. A stern glance or even simply losing their over-the-top smiles was always enough to put him under pressure. Other members of management would have dealt with the union before they'd even considered time and a half, but not Mortimer; he was soft.

The women left the little coffee room whistling. They would go and clean the flat thoroughly and would even make a special effort, leaving some flowers for the new guest, because Mortimer had asked them nicely. It was a happy arrangement. Mortimer got what he wanted, and they got what they wanted.

That was the funny thing about Ralph Mortimer, third assistant to the manager of the Office of the Dead; he always got things done and people still liked him. Other people would have argued for an hour to save a few pennies, but Mortimer thought of people as well as people. In the long run, he saved money for the office by giving in quickly, reducing overheads by minimising the time in negotiations, where, of course, everyone needed to be paid. Still, he had a reputation as a dogsbody. It wasn't his job to organise cleaning of anything, but then it wasn't his job to do anything specific.

He made himself a cup of coffee and trotted

out into the hall. The coffee slopped over the side of the polystyrene cup and scalded his hand. He had to run back into the coffee room to pour cold water on it, and in the rush, he spilt most of the rest of it down his suit. In the end, he gave up on the coffee and tried to tidy up. When he glanced at his watch, he realised he had a couple of minutes to get to the manager's office, which was bad because he wasn't sure how to get there.

Running back in the direction he had come from led to him meeting a dead end with considerable force. He had to jog back with a slight limp. Just as he saw the staircase he needed, the wall around it began to grow over. He dived through the closing gap and ended up with his tie caught in a wall where once there was a corridor. There was no way he could remove it. By the time he arrived at the door to the manager's office, he was tie-less, limping, and covered in coffee. When he went to knock on the door, it swung open and he ended up on the floor of the office, looking at the feet of Detective Augustan Blunt.

13

"Ah, Mortimer, glad you could join us. I was just about to send someone for you." Neat was sitting behind his desk, one of his special looks on his face that told of a long, painful torture scene involving the slow removal of parts of Mortimer's anatomy.

"Sorry sir, I was in a hurry and I spilt the coffee then the refurbishment started to happen–"

"Enough, Mortimer. I'd like you to meet a newcomer to our lovely city. Some of our residents refer to it as the rotten apple, ha, ha." He directed the second half of the sentence to Blunt.

Detective Blunt had watched the entrance of Mortimer with disinterest. Now that he was being confronted, he decided to fall back on an old policeman technique he'd learnt as a youngster; it had served him well over the years. "Very funny, sir," he said, being careful to remove any sign of sarcasm or irony from his voice. This tactic usually worked well to placate superiors, clients, and occasionally pompous or arrogant suspects. It worked like a charm on Neat. His ghoulish smile stretched even further. Mortimer, meanwhile, pulled himself to his feet and attempted to dust himself off.

Blunt did a rapid assessment of the two men before him. Clearly, the mousy-looking man was the subordinate. He was a nervous man who no doubt spent most of his working day running around doing errands for anyone and everyone who spoke down to him. As with most men of the type, he was probably incredibly honest and didn't even realise how little people thought of him.

The man behind the desk was a different story entirely. Often people would make the mistake of describing a man like Neat as a shark. Sharks are devious killing machines with nothing but a predatory instinct to hunt. Neat had all the features of a shark, but he had the ability to control and manipulate situations, a trait that would make him more successful. A shark doesn't have the ability to set a trap for its prey to make its hunting more successful and waste less energy. Neat wasn't a shark—he was smarter—but Blunt's experience told him that whatever a person may seem on the surface might not be what they were underneath.

"Nice to meet you, Detective Blunt. I'm Ralph Mortimer." Mortimer reached out a hand. Blunt only hesitated for a moment. It was the first time he'd touched the flesh of another dead person. He felt his skin crawl as he touched the man's palm. It felt normal and Blunt almost felt silly until he realised that his hand was dead, too. Could he actually feel anything?

"Pleasure to meet you, Mr Mortimer."

"Please call me Ralph."

"Thanks, Mr Mortimer." Another old trick; accept their offer of friendship gratefully, but spit it back at them at the same time. It shows they're weak for offering, but you appreciate the fact that they've raised you above them in the pecking order.

"Ahem." Neat made no attempt to fake a cough. He actually spoke as he interrupted them. "Now you know each other, perhaps I should explain to you why you've been asked to meet with me, Detective."

Blunt shifted his gaze slowly to the man behind the table and said, "I'm listening."

"Mortimer, close the door, will you? Now, Detective, I think you'll find we've gone out of our way to get you here as quickly as possible, and soon enough you will realise why. First, I'm going to explain one or two things to you about Gloomwood."

Blunt smirked. The man was enjoying this, and Blunt didn't mind playing along. Doubtless he was one of the big fish, and at the moment Blunt was a sardine. He knew it was going to take time for people to realise he was more of a puffer fish; inedible and a pain in the arse.

"First, a very brief history lesson. Up until about one hundred years ago, this town was never bigger than three, maybe four thousand people, but things have picked up and we've grown. Once upon a time, all the criminal activity could be taken care of by the big boss. In case you didn't realise, that's the Grim Reaper."

"Kind of like a one-sheriff town?"

"Exactly, Detective. However, I think we only had two instances of crime in well over four-thousand years. The threat of the Grim Reaper was more than enough to dissuade anyone."

"Yes, well, you can imagine, the mere thought of

it, although in reality he was perfectly nice," Mortimer interrupted.

"Shut up, Mortimer. As I was saying, we had no real problems, and then came the great expansion. I'm not quite sure of the reasons behind it or when it began exactly, but Gloomwood rapidly swelled in population. I wouldn't be surprised to learn it bore some relation to the industrial revolution, world wars, etcetera. There was no real crime, at least nothing that affected the government of the city. As a sign of goodwill to the people, we did set up a small police force. They're really just a bunch of thugs who break up bar fights and the such-like. They have no remit to investigate crimes."

"Right, so you've got a problem you can't go to the police with?"

"Not exactly. We have other organisations. A city this size can't get by without some other organisations."

"Just a guess, Mr Neat, but when you say organisations, I'm assuming you mean government-sanctioned organisations who work in the best interests of the city?"

"Exactly."

"Like a secret intelligence service."

"I couldn't possibly comment on that, Detective."

"I understand, and these forces that you can't comment on can't handle whatever you're about to ask me to do."

"It's of a very sensitive nature."

"You think these forces may have something to do with whatever it is then, and you believe that I, as someone who is freshly dead, am able to work in a more objective manner, and clearly I couldn't possibly be involved because I have no allegiance to anyone at the moment. My demise has been very convenient for you."

"The death of a man is not always unfortunate and regrettable, Detective. In your case, your death could be one of the most celebrated this city has ever known. You see, there's been an incident, a highly sensitive incident."

"Really? I'm shocked," Blunt said, displaying less emotion than a wooden spoon.

"Yes, unfortunately it is rather high profile."

"Let me guess, Mr Neat. The Grim Reaper has been murdered and you would like me to investigate," Blunt said.

"My word, Detective, you are truly a man with great insight, but there's no such thing as murder here. The word, if it was the case, would be Ableforth, and that hasn't happened. The Grim Reaper was attacked in his office here in the buildings of the Office of the Dead. This building is the oldest in Gloomwood. It's somewhat akin to number ten Downing Street, or the White House in America. I hope that gives you some perspective on the case as it is. Similarly, imagine the murder of a president, prime minister, King, or the Pope even. There are many who will benefit, but of course he has not been Ableforthed. Instead, we will refer to it best as abduction; his head has been stolen from him."

Neat had another one of those smiles on his face, but Blunt was impervious to subtleties. "Mortimer here will be working with you. Consider him my liaison. I cannot stress enough the need to keep this as quiet as possible, for this will quite definitely shatter this world, Detective. We're talking civil war, not some tabloid exposé." The smile had completely faded. All that remained was a stare that could have cut through steel. "If you find me the kidnappers and the Grim Reaper's skull, we might be able to quell the situation, but things are still going to be bad, Detective. I'm not going to lie to you; whatever is going on here is probably to do with a power struggle between the most powerful people in this land."

Blunt held up a hand, cutting the severe man off. "Mr Neat, I have to stop you there and ask if you already know who is responsible. Is this an investigation or am I here to pick up the person you plan to pin this on?"

Blunt's interruption was something Neat didn't seem to know how to deal with. The bureaucrat pursed his lips and waited just long enough for the moment to become uncomfortable. "I see where you're going here and you're quite correct. This is your case, and it's best you start it from a position of complete impartiality. If there is anything I can do to help let Mortimer know, he'll contact me. I'm aware that at some point I will be on your list of suspects and plan to keep my involvement to a minimum. In the meantime, Mortimer will show you the scene and fill you in on the case. Good day, sir."

Neat suddenly picked up his pen and began working on something unrelated. Blunt knew a curt dismissal when he saw one, but he wasn't finished. "You didn't answer my questions. I'd suggest we start there."

"I have my suspicions, Detective, but it is in the best interests of everyone if you find your way there, or not, on your own. Now, as I said, I bid you good day."

14

On the way to the crime scene, Mortimer talked incessantly about nothing and everything. Blunt barely listened to a word of it. Small talk wasn't his forte and, more importantly, there was a crime to solve. That was all that mattered. Being dead could wait until later.

The office itself was situated on a floor of its own. A flight of stairs made of obsidian marble led up to palatial black doors with huge, grotesque gargoyles sitting on either side of the entrance. Mortimer shuffled along in front of Blunt, frequently gesturing for the detective to follow.

At the bottom of the stairs, they passed a desk with a broken stapler scattered across it and a large inbox overflowing with paper.

"Very grand," Blunt said.

"Well actually, this monument was built with a very specific purpose. It's one of the few things that doesn't ever get moved," Mortimer said as he stood at the top of the stairs, fiddling with a complicated system of locks on the door.

"Moved in what way?"

"Nobody explained that? No, I suppose they wouldn't. It's really not very relevant to you. I doubt you'll be spending much time here. The building rearranges itself periodically and all the rooms transform and move around. Doorways disappear, new corridors open, you get the idea. That's why I've got no tie. Never mind, it's not important. The main entrance never moves—actually the whole of the ground floor remains pretty much the same, although the number of cubicles in the toilets does change for some reason—and then this room is always found here."

"And this room is where the alleged crime took place?"

"Yes, this is his office."

"Well, that explains the grand entrance."

They stepped through the ornate gates and arrived in front of a very tall mahogany door. The door suddenly made a loud clicking noise and very slowly it began to open. "It may be a grand entrance, Mr Blunt, but inside is really quite cosy," Mortimer said.

Blunt grunted with surprise as the massive double doors opened up to reveal a very modest office. A desk that was clearly purchased for its functionality rather than its appearance was covered in neatly organised stacks of paper, on top of which sat an assortment of paperweights, snow globes and tiny porcelain animals. A simple wooden chair sat behind the desk and on the wall there were pictures of a skeleton in a hood and cloak shaking the hands of famous figures throughout time. There was one with Kennedy, a man Blunt presumed was Caesar, Albert Einstein, Winston Churchill, a very old picture of a man with long hair and a beard, Elvis Presley. The detective gave them a perfunctory glance and began peering around the rest of the room. A sticker on a filing cabinet in the corner read, 'You don't have to be dead to work here, but it helps.' Blunt barely batted an eyelid. On the floor there was a chocolate bar wrapper and next to it several more of the chocolate bars that hadn't been opened.

He turned around and pushed the doors shut, leaving himself and Mortimer standing in the room. On the back of the door was a calendar with pictures of puppy dogs in various poses throughout the year. Beneath the calendar a huge scythe was buried in the door, the long handle of it stretched backwards into the room, ending inches from Blunt's face.

"Where's the corpse?" he asked Mortimer without looking at him.

"It's in the chair, sir, and sir, I think corpse may be an inappropriate word to use. After all, aren't we all corpses really?" he said. The man looked more nervous than ever now that the doors barred their exit.

"Mortimer, there's nothing in the chair but a piece of black cloth and, what's this?" He lifted the black cloth up, quickly realising it was probably the cowl the Grim Reaper usually wore. With the sound of an amateur xylophone player tentatively playing a few dud notes, a pile of bones fell to the floor. "Oh, I see, and this is it, is it?"

"Yes sir, such a shame sir, the man always had the best intentions, wore his heart on his sleeve, always turned the other cheek, never lay a hand on anyone."

"Mortimer, where is his heart, his hand and his cheek?"

"Well really, it's a little unfair to make fun of the dead, sir."

"So I can't make fun of anyone?"

"What do you mean?"

"I'm going to count to ten, Mortimer. In that time you're going to remember that we're all dead, that I am only just dead, that I don't tell many jokes, and that any question I ask you requires a full answer or you will pay the forfeit of having my foot buried up to its ankle in your backside. One, two, three–"

"Sorry, Detective. The Grim Reaper was a skeleton, sir. I thought everyone would know that."

"Really? Well, I know he was always portrayed in that fashion, but he really was a skeleton. Interesting. Why aren't you a skeleton? Or everyone else, for that matter, and more important still, where's his head, Mortimer?"

"Um, well, it's gone, sir. That's how he was found."

"What? So if your head is removed you die, I mean cease to exist?"

"No, but, well, if you then destroy the skull, crush it into powder, I guess there would be no coming back. Or if you shattered the skull into many pieces. It's pretty much about splitting the skull into as many fragments as possible. We call it Ableforth."

"And that's been done, has it? Or are we assuming? In my experience, that is always a stupid thing to do."

Mortimer shook his head gently and said, "If you'll

look beneath the cloak again."

Blunt nervously lifted the black material away from the bones and stared at them. "What am I looking for here?" he asked

Mortimer was standing as far away as possible from both Blunt and the chair. "You'll see," he said.

"What the?" Blunt exclaimed. He had to resist the urge to scream as he stared at the bones. "Ralph, are these things supposed to move?"

"That's the point, you see. Unless someone has been removed from existence, you know—the thing we call Ableforth—their body should still have, for want of a better word, life in it, or energy I suppose, even if the head is separated."

Blunt looked from the bones to Mortimer and back again. "So he's alive?"

"Well, no, but then neither is anyone else," Mortimer said. "Better that we say he still exists, somewhere."

Gingerly, Blunt reached down into the bones and withdrew a skeletal hand, the bones somehow holding themselves together. He placed it on the table. The fingers tapped the desk in a manner that seemed to show impatience. Blunt frowned at them and asked, "Could the body tell us where his head is?"

"Not really, it doesn't have a brain, and it didn't see anything; the head did. It shouldn't really be moving at all. Normal people's bodies only really move if the head is close, but then he was the Grim Reaper, so who knows? It probably doesn't really apply to him."

Blunt looked at Mortimer, taking in the way he was nervously folding and unfolding his arms and trying very hard not to brush up against anything. "Have you looked for his head?" he asked.

"What?"

"His head, have you actually looked for it?"

"Oh, yes, I mean, of course I have. I've searched this entire room from top to bottom. No sign of it."

"You did it yourself?"

"Yes, yes, nobody else can know. Perhaps it's best we get you some food and talk about things before we go rushing off."

"We can eat?" Blunt asked, surprised.

"Yes, Detective, shall we?"

15

Constable Jeremiah John Jacob Johnson sat behind a desk at West Mourning Police Station, a slightly ostentatious title for a corner shop that had been converted into an office. His desk stood next to a rack filled with greeting cards that, for some reason, hadn't been removed with the rest of the paraphernalia from the shop.

He'd been with the force for three weeks and was the new hopes and promises liaison. Having never had much to do with the police force before he had arrived in Gloomwood, he was finding it difficult to integrate himself into the department. It didn't help that he was the first hope to join the force, part of the equal opportunities programme that had been put in place by the Office of the Dead.

Other officers hadn't exactly welcomed him with open arms. There was only one previous non-mortal in the force, and he'd been a god before he'd passed over to Gloomwood. Gods in general were held in high regard in Gloomwood. They were low in numbers, but their natural arrogance and self-belief had led to a number of them rising to high status within the city.

Hopes and promises, on the other hand, were generally looked down upon. A reminder to the mortal population of what they had missed out on. Even ideas and theories were above hopes and promises in the social pecking order.

Constable JJJ Johnson had been aware that he was going to find it tough, but he hadn't been prepared for the animosity from the other officers. They felt he had been allowed into the force purely because of what he was and not who he was or what he had proven. He'd passed the entrance exams with the highest results ever recorded, but being able to calm down a fight using diplomacy wasn't something that happened in practice, nor was dealing with distraught people after something had happened.

He had shown his knowledge of police procedures and techniques to be above and beyond some of the most well respected officers in the city and had completed the obstacle course in record time. His threshold for pain had been tested and found to be massively beyond that which was necessary, but that was more because the officers testing him quite enjoyed their jobs. He could recite the entire of the criminal justice guidebook from memory—all four pages—and he had the best-kept uniform in the force.

Unfortunately, none of that mattered. Once he had been brought on to the force, he was immediately told to forget everything he had learnt. The only thing you needed to know how to do was take care of yourself in a fight and how to make sure you hit the other bugger before he hit you, and no matter what happened, make sure there's someone else to blame.

He tried hard to put procedure in place, to follow the rules, but the other officers resented him for it. However, it was when they had found out the details about who he was that they had really made an effort to ostracise him. JJJ Johnson was, unfortunately, the hope that this season the sporting team you support will actually win something, and the fact that he was in Gloomwood meant that for enough people in the land of the living, that hope was dead.

When the word had got out, he'd been shoved into the corner of the office and given work to do that was purposeless. The hopes and promises liaison job was quite straightforward. He wasn't there to fix anything but simply to try to calm down the growing unrest and discontentment from the parts of the city that were populated mainly by his fellow hopes and promises. Most of the day was spent reading letters of complaint about the treatment of his people.

For the first few days, he had passed on anything that had sounded like it might have needed looking into, to his colleagues. He'd found all of his notes in the bin one morning and decided that it was pointless. He was a crushed Hope, devastated that all his hard work would come to nothing because the majority of the force didn't care. No, it was worse than that; they didn't believe his people were important enough. He'd spent the day in silence, deciding that it was up to him to do something about it.

When he had arrived in the office, the same day Blunt arrived, he had found his desk covered in football scarves. Some bastard had carefully selected a variety of scarves from the teams recently relegated from the various leagues in Gloomwood and draped them over everything on his desk. That wasn't just a witty joke; it was a carefully thought-out, malicious attack. He'd grinned and pretended to find it amusing when the others in the office had made a spectacle of him. He was pretty sure they didn't even know how offensive they were being. When it had died down, he'd swept the scarves up and placed them in a drawer of his desk. Beneath them on the desk had sat an envelope.

So there he sat, staring at an envelope that had his name written on it in spidery handwriting. It was a cheap envelope, and it was crinkled and battered. Below his name, there had been another address that had been scribbled out so the envelope could be reused. He sighed. Another letter from some poor soul living out in the slums, probably about how their landlord demanded more rent every month despite there being a hole in the ceiling that he called a skylight.

He was right: the note was from a promise, but it wasn't about the landlord. After he had read the note, he folded it up and put it in his pocket. This was serious, but he couldn't ask for help because the case would be taken away from him and then it would be consigned to the bottom of a pile of cases deemed more important because they concerned people other than hopes and promises.

He grabbed his coat, checked that he had his baton, and strode out of the building.

16

Blunt and Mortimer sat in a diner. The term *greasy spoon* could have been coined for the place, although singling out spoons might have been a little unfair. A film of grease seemed to linger over every surface, including the fat man who was pushing a greasy mop across the floor. Outside, rain fell in heavy droplets the size of golf balls and the sky was as grey as a single white sock in a load of dark washing. Behind the counter, a woman stood pouring coffee and chewing gum like she was trying to get a bad taste out of her mouth, which, given the smells emanating from the kitchen, wasn't unlikely.

A cup of hot coffee sat in front of the detective as he stared moodily at the surrounding scene. "Okay, Mortimer, enlighten me," he murmured to the man opposite him. Mortimer was just biting into a jam doughnut. As Blunt spoke, he jumped a little and strawberry jam dripped onto his already coffee-stained shirt.

"Um, okay, I suppose a crash course in the history of the place would help." He dabbed at the stain with a napkin as he spoke. "Time's a bit funny here, so history isn't quite as linear as back on the other side, but here we go."

He took a deep breath before he started speaking. "Death wasn't always a requirement of life. In fact, there wasn't always life. In the first place, there was just existence. Then someone invented life and everyone was really happy. All the animals, birds and trees were really chuffed."

Mortimer glanced at Blunt to make sure he was listening, then looked down at the table before continuing. "Then people began to evolve and think more deeply about things and someone realised that if there's life, there must also be something that isn't life, so the concept of death was born. Of course, not everyone could get their head around the concept of death, which was good because it meant it didn't really need to be dealt with. With me so far?"

Blunt took a drink from his coffee cup. "You're saying that when life came into existence, there wasn't any death until someone realised the equation didn't add up, so death was invented."

"Exactly, detective. So death was invented, and people weren't too happy about it, so religion was invented, and there were hundreds of ideas about religion and there still are. It's changing all the time. This place, Gloomwood, isn't part of that," Mortimer said. He stopped and looked at Blunt expectantly.

"Yeah and?" the detective asked.

"Oh, well, it's just that most people are really shocked to hear that. Sometimes they just flip out."

"Well, I'm okay with it. Carry on."

"You're sure you don't want to take a mouthful of coffee and spray it everywhere in surprise?"

"Will it change anything?"

"Might make you feel better."

"I'll admit the thought of spitting coffee all over you does make me feel all warm inside, but I'll be all right for now. Maybe I'll save it for later."

"Err... okay. So, as I was saying, death was invented, and then religions were invented almost in the same moment, so people had places to go when they died. Really, it's all about real estate, but I'll explain that another time. In the moments between life being invented and religions giving people a place to go after life, there was a gap, a void in time and space where people were discarded like so many rotten fish heads."

"So basically there was a build up of dead people?"

Mortimer continued. "Yes, detective, that's a fair analogy, but somebody fixed the problem. Now we're getting to the interesting bit, the bit that explains why you're here and I'm here and every other poor soul's here instead of elsewhere."

Carefully, Mortimer took a sip of his drink before slowly putting it back on the table. He blinked, then seemed to remember where he was in his story. "The first person to die was killed. He was murdered. He was skinned alive and before he was completely dead, his flesh was consumed by fire. Pretty nasty, but not the worst either of us has heard, I'm sure. Anyway, he had nowhere to go and nothing to do after he was dead, and he ended up in a void for the longest length of time until one day into that void floated a piece of black cloth, and using the power of his spirit, which he was able to hone over time, he managed to make the cloth into flesh for himself. Then he returned to the land of the living, but it didn't work out because he wasn't alive, and so it all went a bit wrong and they tried to kill him. You get the picture."

"Sounds pretty terrible, but weren't there lots of people this was happening to?" Blunt asked.

"Yeah, there were loads, but this guy did something special. He created his own afterlife, carved it out using his mind when he was already dead."

"And that's tough, is it?"

"Are you kidding? He had to believe in something, put faith in something that would be there after he was dead, even though he knew there wasn't."

"I'm confused. Is this really important?"

"Yes, listen. The Grim Reaper died and had no afterlife, so even though he was dead, he created a religion that meant there was an afterlife, and that he was in that afterlife already. He tricked his own mind; he completely bent and twisted time, space, existence, and non-existence to create this world."

"So? The other religions did that too."

"No, they didn't. They followed the natural order. Afterlives are created by people while they are alive. When someone's alive, they believe in something, so when they die, it happens. When the Grim Reaper died, there was no afterlife. He shouldn't have existed, but somehow he did, and so he created an afterlife around himself."

"Right, this is all existentialist crap, isn't it? When

are you going to explain why he's been kidnapped or why his skull being gone means big bad things?" Blunt asked as he tried to get the attention of the waitress to top up his coffee.

Mortimer had given up on cleaning his shirt and was fiddling with the salt dispenser as he said, "Oh, well, who could possibly separate the Grim Reaper from his head? I mean, he's the all-powerful Grim Reaper." He smiled weakly to show he was finished and looked at Blunt, waiting for the detective's next question.

"Right, good point. Doesn't everything you've said pretty much make him a god or something?"

The salt dispenser fell over and the contents of it stuck to the parts of Mortimer's shirt that were still damp from the coffee and jam. He replaced the top and pushed the container away. "Yes, well, that's one of the major concerns. I mean, he's looked on as some kind of all-powerful ruler."

"Really good at measuring things, always straight."

"Very funny, but you get the idea, and because of that, there hasn't been any serious problem with people trying to take over Gloomwood. People have been trying to get rid of the Grim Reaper since the beginning, and it's got worse over time. There are a thousand crazies out there who want him gone for religious reasons. Then there're businesses who want him gone so they can be free from legal requirements, criminals who've been waiting for the reaper to disappear so they can take control, and politicians that want to take control, not to mention the personal vendettas people have against him. Then we've got all the problems about where people came from, like the dead gods, the broken promises and lost hopes, the discarded ideas and ideals, and us norms."

Blunt waved Mortimer into silence; it was all getting a bit much. "You can say what you like, but until we have proof that his skull has been pounded into dust and there's no fixing it, we should be looking at kidnapping. You told me we know he's alive somewhere, so what I want to know is who took his skull?"

"We just don't know. You saw the scene, and nothing's been moved since it happened. The only people to go in or out are me, you and Neat."

"What about forensics?"

"What's that?"

"Crime scene analysis, scientists, specialists in finding clues."

"No such thing here. Why would we need it? The police stamp on things as they happen and don't really do anything except act as a kind of heavy mob to stop things going too far."

"I don't know how I'm supposed to run this, Mortimer. You've given me nothing to start with. I'm supposed to work in secret, or at least under the radar, and I haven't got any support. This is bullshit."

"Well, we know somebody chopped his head off and ran away with it."

"Really? Thanks, Mortimer, that's brilliant. I'll just go and speak to the nearest headhunter."

"Sarcasm isn't going to help, Detective."

"Well, it's all I've got. You've got to give me something to go on, some kind of lead to follow up."

"You're the detective. You should be the one finding leads."

"I don't know enough about what's normal and what isn't here yet. If I follow up everything I think is strange, I'll be looking up things that are a waste of time. Can't you see that? I need more help and you better start working on it."

Mortimer quickly retreated to his normal position as grovelling underling. "We already have an office and apartment for you. What else do you need?"

"Someone needs to be at the office all the time, and if I have to be dead, I'm not going to be stuck making my own damn coffee. I need someone who knows how things work here and I need someone who can do some basic forensics work."

Mortimer looked at Blunt, already worried about the repercussions from Crispin Neat. The investigation was getting out of hand, and it hadn't even begun. "I'll make some calls. In the meantime, what are you going to do?"

Blunt nodded and grabbed a napkin. "I'm going to take a walk to this office you've got me. Draw a map on this," he said, shoving a napkin under Mortimer's nose and tapping his fingers on the tabletop as he waited. As soon as Mortimer finished, Blunt snatched the napkin out of his hands and stood up. "I'll see you at the office. How long will it take to walk?" he asked.

"Probably about an hour, maybe a bit less. It's raining, you know."

"I know that. See you in an hour," Blunt said. The detective finished his coffee, grabbed a doughnut and walked out of the door.

17

The streets of Gloomwood are grey, the people are grey, the roads are grey, even the lights give off a grey glow. The spectrum of colours in the land of the dead is significantly reduced; the whole city is washed out and tired, just like its people.

Gloomwood draws people from all walks of life, people who fell through the gaps or turned their backs on everyone who could have helped them. Often it's the kind of people who died and were never mourned, the kind of people who are found weeks after they pass away or are never found at all. Eleanor Rigby would have fitted in well in the land of the dead.

Poverty is rife; a massive divide between social classes has produced an underworld that is ignored by those in power. Dead people don't matter, and if everyone is dead, nobody matters.

There is a canal in the city that runs in a circle. Quite how it works isn't understood, but it provides a circular ferry service that carries people to several stations in the five different quarters of Gloomwood. Nobody understands why there are five quarters, either. It's just one of those things that people accept. The buildings are all old; nearly everything in Gloomwood is ancient and decrepit. Even the things that are new are built out of old and worn-out parts.

Gloomwood has a tourism department. There is no reason for it, but it keeps some people busy, and now and then bored residents will take a tour of their city.

The city's coat of arms features a scythe and a laughing corpse hanging from a noose. Its colours are grey: light grey and dark grey. The city uses the phrase *Secundum nex vita plumbeus est* (After death, life is dull) as its motto, a clumsy and unfortunate choice.

Most people work in the land of the dead. It is quite possible for a person to stop doing anything, but eventually they would calcify; their bodies would lock up and they would become a statue, their minds simply disintegrating through a lack of stimulation. So, people work, and most people fall into the same mindset that they had when they were alive, with the same petty issues and disputes they struggled through in life.

A starving person can't die, but their mind will tell their bodies to fall apart, to lose mass and eventually cease to work. They could carry on without eating indefinitely, but eventually they would be locked in their skulls and their minds would fade. It is the same for most functions they had in life; they need them now to die.

Scholars at the university have studied the alterations that people endure due to the change in their mortal status and have, in the great majority of cases, discovered that nothing at all really changes. People had a psychological requirement to meet their basic needs, and because of that, they still needed to achieve the most basic of functions: eating, drinking, socialising, working, maintaining some kind of stimulation.

The great library in the centre of the city contains

thousands upon thousands of poor souls; the ones who convinced themselves they could survive without doing the things they had while they were alive. Nothing but skulls filled with information, fact without opinion, their minds reduced to little more than reference books for scholars to pore over. Ending up in the library is a poor fate for anyone, so people work, just as they always have.

As Blunt walked the city of Gloomwood, following a map written on a napkin, he tried to get a sense of the city. He used to walk the beat when he was young and he fell into the easy gait of a man who spent his days walking the minutes away. He saw the things he expected to see in every large city in the land of the living.

Poverty sat right next to shops only the rich could afford. Haggard-looking people wandered around, grabbing cups of coffee and sandwiches before they returned to their places of work. Posters and billboards offered products and services from companies he'd never heard of, but it all amounted to the same consumer-driven economy he had left behind.

There were new things; of course there were new things. People stood on street corners shouting about the damnation of people, but their arguments had changed. There were even people who crowed about God and lectured pedestrians on the reasons for their damnation and how, even after everything, they could still be saved.

Strange-looking men and women mingled with what Blunt assumed were the norms. They stood out to him because of their unusual appearance, but quickly he realised that they were actually quite common, these creatures. Some with inhuman bodies were probably the other things Mortimer had mentioned: ideas, hopes, dreams, gods, even.

He kept an eye out for the sort of person he could use, someone who would be useful to him in gaining a picture of what the streets were really like. Not that he believed his investigations belonged on the streets, but he knew that streets had a way of learning secrets that found their way into the mouths of people who listened for them. After the first half an hour passed by, he realised he was halfway to his destination and he hadn't found out anything particularly useful.

The part of town he was in appeared to be some kind of strange subsection of the city. Street signs in garbled text adorned the shops and stalls, and vendors sold bizarre items from their vans and stands.

An eight-armed woman with snakes in her hair desperately shouted about a two-for-one offer on jewellery. Blunt looked around her and saw that the only person nearby who might benefit from the offer was the woman herself. A miserable-looking old man in red sat by an assortment of toys, drooling into his beard as he stared out from his hood, occasionally laughing in a booming voice at something nobody else could hear. As Blunt walked past, the man grabbed his coat. "Hello there, young gentleman. Have you been good?" he asked, the stench of alcohol seeping from his every pore.

Blunt pushed the man's clawing hands away, trying hard not to be disgusted while at the same time feeling his skin crawl. The man thrust something wrapped in brown paper in his direction, and Blunt muttered, "No thanks, fella," trying to extricate himself from the awkwardness of the situation before the sense of discomfort became overwhelming and his guilt kicked in enough to force him to take action. The old man quickly turned to another passer-by and Blunt sighed with relief, feeling that he was free of any responsibility he might have taken for not helping the man.

It quickly began to dawn on him that he wasn't going to have the time to learn what he needed to know about the city. It was a complicated place, even if it had been a normal, living city; it would have taken months for him to get up to speed. Here he was in a city filled with things he didn't understand, social structures, a whole new way of existence. He was going to need a short-cut or two.

He opened his coat and took his hat off his head as he walked into a large building that looked like a train station. It was glamorous in an old-fashioned way. Pillars held up the ceiling, which seemed much higher than it needed to be. People in suits scurried back and forth, reminding Blunt that whatever else was going on, this place was still a city. All these dead people had joined an even more futile and meaningless society.

In amongst the crowds, there were things that caught his eye that he tried to ignore. A man carrying a box full of what appeared to be feet nearly walked straight into him, and Blunt felt a toenail snag on his coat.

A young boy of about eleven years old brushed up against him. Blunt whirled as soon as it happened and grabbed the urchin by the back of his shirt. The boy struggled, but he was no match for Blunt, who pulled him back.

"Hand it over," he said in his sternest, you're-messing-with-the-wrong-guy voice. The boy glared at him with more ferocity than he had ever seen in a child's eyes, and for a moment Blunt was tempted to let go.

"All right, buddy. Nice catch. Here's your stinking wallet. Feels empty anyway," the child said while nonchalantly throwing the wallet in the air. Blunt caught it with his free hand. It was ragged and worn, and definitely empty, just as it had been when he'd stumbled out of the off-licence half a day ago, when he'd still been alive.

"Don't get cocky with me, sunshine. How about we go and see your parents?" Blunt asked, a sneer on his face.

The boy glared at Blunt. "Love to, buddy, but as I've been dead for eighty years, I reckon they'll be a little surprised to see me. If I were you, I'd get your god-damn hands off me before something bad happens." Blunt recognised the look he'd seen on the boy's face. It was the look of a career criminal who'd been caught by a bunch of snot-nosed kids.

"What exactly might happen?" Blunt asked, and the second he said it he knew he'd made a mistake. The boy grinned at Blunt, then moved far more quickly than Blunt thought he could. The next thing he knew, he was on the floor with his hands between his legs. An explosion of blinding pain hit him, and he tasted bile at the back of his throat.

"See ya later, granddad," the urchin said before he spat down at Blunt and strolled off into the crowd.

Blunt remained on the floor for a minute, trying to catch his breath and willing the pain to go away. Eventually, the screaming agony faded to a dull throbbing, and he struggled to his feet, wincing with every movement.

He stood still for a moment to collect his bearings and felt a heavy hand on his shoulder. "Excuse me, sir?" a voice asked from behind him, its tone heavy with the sound of indifference. He didn't need to turn to know it was either a security guard or a policeman. He turned and took a step backwards.

The voice had come from a strange creature. The word *Minotaur* floated up from somewhere deep within Blunt's memories, and he recalled something about Greeks and a maze. The creature wasn't particularly terrifying. Blunt had a couple of inches on it, and it was painfully skinny to look at. A worn blue uniform with the word *security* printed across its shirt pocket told him all he needed to know.

"I noticed you were on the floor for a moment there. Everything okay?"

Blunt knew the thing didn't want him to say no. He could tell the question was tinged with a hopefulness that stemmed from reluctance to get involved. "Yes, everything's fine. I just fell," Blunt said.

"Sorry for bothering you then, sir," the creature

replied. It had the head of a goat and Blunt knew that it shouldn't have been able to speak, but despite appearances, the creature was perfectly coherent. Before Blunt could say anything else, the creature had nodded a curt goodbye and disappeared into the crowd as if it had never been there.

Blunt reached into his pocket and pulled out the napkin with directions on it. He was a little lost. Mortimer hadn't bothered to draw the station, so he looked above the crowd, trying to find a booth marked '*information*.' A glowing sign with a question mark above it hinted at help, and he attempted to push his way through the crowds towards it.

18

Mortimer was getting frustrated. He'd done his best to recruit a scientist, but there weren't a lot of people involved in that sort of work. Almost everyone who fit the bill was already gainfully employed at one of the prestigious pharmaceutical firms in the city. There was the Damned University, one of the most unsuccessful educational establishments ever conceived, but being the only one in the land of the dead, it was the last port of call.

The only problem with the Damned University, other than its unfortunate name, was that nearly all the staff were teetering on the brink of entering the library, and some of them were actually on loan. Finding someone to take on the position of forensic scientist was proving difficult.

The unenviable task of explaining to Neat that Blunt had demanded more resources was lurking on the bottom of a never-ending to-do list. Mortimer hadn't forgotten that one of the reasons Blunt was selected was because he wouldn't require resources.

He glanced at his watch, a gift from work for thirty years of service. Almost everyone at the office had one of the same. It wasn't often a member of staff decided to leave. There just wasn't much point. It was twenty to four. He had twenty minutes to give answers to Blunt, and he had to be honest: the man scared him. He scared him almost as much as Crispin Neat did.

It was the way the detective looked at people as if everyone was an idiot or a criminal, or some other kind of pond scum. It wouldn't have been scary if it was a natural arrogance; Mortimer was used to dealing with arrogant people. It was more that Blunt didn't seem to have any higher an opinion of himself than he did of everyone else. His every movement and his general demeanour were a clear demonstration to everyone of his thought processes. Loud and clear, Blunt's face sent the message, "You're a turd on the foot of the slug that floats upside down in a basin of vomit in the rubbish skip of eternity, and I know that because I am too."

Mortimer was running out of options. He'd even considered offering a temporary internship for a student, but the university had pointed out that the student wouldn't really be learning from anyone. He pushed his hand through his already ruffled hair, then picked up the phone on what was to be Blunt's desk and pressed zero.

"Hello. Operator."

"Hello, can you put me through to Sarah Von Faber at the National Museum of the Dead please?"

"Certainly, sir."

The phone went silent for a moment, then the operator returned. "Sorry, sir, but there doesn't seem to be a Sarah Von Faber listed at the museum."

"That's fine. Can you put me through to reception, please?"

"No problem, sir."

Mortimer waited on the line; he was fiddling with a pen in the phone cord and managed to flick himself in the eye while he was waiting.

"International Museum of the Dead, making history dead. How can I help?"

"Hello, this is Ralph Mortimer, third assistant to the manager of the Office of the Dead; I need to speak to Sarah Von Faber," Mortimer said. There was rustling in the background, and Mortimer wondered why it was called the International Museum, given that Gloomwood was all there appeared to be.

"Um, I'm afraid we have no-one of that name working here."

"I know that; she's an exhibit. Can you put me through to her?"

"I think you'll have to speak to my supervisor."

A supervisor, a manager, and the curator followed. Mortimer managed to get past them via a mixture of begging and repeating his job title over and over again. Nobody knew what it meant, but they all heard the words *manager of the Office of the Dead*, which immediately made them think of the next highest official, one Mister Grim Reaper, and there was no higher authority than that.

"Who the hell is this and what do you think you're doing calling me at work?"

"Sorry, Miss Von Faber, my name's Ralph Mortimer. I'm the third assistant—"

"I couldn't give a damn if you were the Grim

Reaper himself; you better have a good reason for this."

"I need a forensic scientist."

"Really?"

"Yes, really, can you get out of work soon?"

"Where do you want me? I'll be there as soon as I can."

Mortimer gave the address, and the phone went dead. He put his head in his hands and whispered, "Why me?"

Sarah Von Faber was a prodigious scientist who, once upon a time, was considered one of the greats of the land of the dead. Then she had a massive breakdown when she attempted to find a way to return to the land of the living. She wasn't the first person to attempt it, but she was the only one capable of speaking about it. As a result of the experiment, she seriously damaged herself, suffering from an affliction previously unheard of in the entire realm of the dead: she was neither here nor there.

Instead, she spent her life fading in and out of existence, but never disappearing completely. It meant at any given time her body, or any part of her body, could fade until it was invisible and, in some cases, intangible. Objects would fall through her, and she would vanish from important meetings only to be discovered in the basement of a building after falling through floor after floor. The whole experience drove her quietly insane until eventually, through a stroke of genius on her part, she decided to submit an exhibit to the museum: the fantastic disappearing woman.

Being installed in the museum as an artefact allowed her certain privileges; she was well cared for and left to her own devices most of the time. She also earned a substantial amount of money. The museum paid the owners for the hire of any artefacts that they wanted to put on show, and in this case, Sarah received the money herself. The funding allowed her to conduct a range of experiments in the laboratory, but none of them took her to the dizzying heights of brilliance she had once reached.

Over time, she had fallen out of love with experimental science and craved the reality of fieldwork. When she had been alive, she had been one of the first pioneers of forensic sciences and since she'd died, she'd craved a return to this kind of work and hadn't kept it a secret.

The loss of some of her faculties had left her estranged from the science world, but she still regularly released articles and papers which were published by obscure journals and periodicals. There was talk of releasing a book of all her papers since the accident as a novelty present, the kind of thing that self-important scientists would have set on the cistern in their guest bathrooms.

Mortimer wasn't scraping the barrel by asking for her help. He was taking a far greater risk, for returning the woman to the general population was potentially dangerous. He was just glad he wasn't in Blunt's shoes.

19

Crispin Neat was sitting back and letting Blunt do his job, though it was risky to leave this kind of operation in the hands of a bumbling detective and Ralph Mortimer. The finely balanced political situation in Gloomwood took a lot of work to maintain, and the disappearance of the Grim Reaper wasn't just going to cause a few ripples in a small pond. He wasn't a man who worried very much. In fact, Neat spent most of his time worrying about other people; he just hoped his faith wasn't misplaced.

Back in the old days, when Gloomwood was a hamlet that slowly grew into a village, then a town, things were easy. Everyone knew everyone, and it was straightforward enough to go and knock on a person's door if there were problems. If the Grim Reaper had vanished then, they would have simply voted a new government into power. True, there would have been considerable problems in renegotiating the deals with the reapers, the various unions, and of course the deceased population as a whole, the various origins of the people notwithstanding. Then there was the concern that the fabric of reality in the land of the dead would begin to unravel.

Things were far more complicated now. There were the large pharmaceuticals, the Mayor's office, the unions, and, of course, the union workers' union— they could be extremely difficult. There were all the institutions: the library, university, museum, the church, the city works, the Office of the Dead, the Governor's office, and, of course, the media. The mass media of Gloomwood spent nearly all of its column inches on celebrity gossip and sporting rumour, but no doubt a race to rule would prompt a feeding frenzy.

Then there were other components. When the city had grown large enough, there began to be a rise in disputes between the different parts of the population. The deceased gods and demi-gods considered themselves more important than anyone else. The ideas and theories believed they were equal to the gods, but the gods disagreed. The norms–people who were simple people when they had been alive- didn't believe they should have to associate with anyone at all. They made up a large amount of the population and were seen as average because of their high numbers. Then there were the others: the lost dreams, discarded hopes, fears that had been overcome, and the broken promises, who were for the most part innocuous enough and generally kept themselves to themselves, or would if certain groups didn't hold such a low opinion of them.

Those things weren't really problems, though. They were just part of the rich tapestry of death, just the normal things that come with large populations concentrated in small areas. The real problems were the egos, the big names that could cause trouble. In reality, they were the people who wanted the power for themselves; they were also the most likely suspects in this whole scenario. The only problem was that Neat couldn't confront anyone, nor could he investigate openly. He couldn't even investigate secretly for the simple reason that he had to be a suspect. Any half-decent investigation would have him top of the list, so he needed to remain completely uninvolved.

Of course, that left him with a huge dilemma because another crime that was doubtless related to this one had just been reported, and he hadn't done anything about it yet. The trouble was that the Grim Reaper was the person to deal with this sort of crime, and he wasn't around. Neat couldn't investigate, since people would ask questions. That left only one possible answer: Blunt would have to be made official, and he'd have to work both cases.

Neat ran his fingers through his hair and picked up the phone. The operator put him through to Blunt's office, where the phone was answered quickly by Mortimer. "Detective Blunt's office. Ralph Mortimer, third assistant to the manager of the Office of the Dead, speaking. How can I help?"

"Mortimer, it's Neat. Never answer Blunt's phone like that again. It can't come out that I have any involvement in the case. I'm sure you were aware of that already, unless you are a complete idiot?"

"Sorry, sir. Force of habit."

"Well, force it out of habit."

"Yes, sir."

"I'm making Blunt official. His new title is Chief Investigator. He works for the city now."

"You're making him chief of police?"

"No, he's an investigator, not a policeman. Is that clear?"

"Yes, sir."

"There'll be a press release in an hour. Warn him. Officially, he'll be working on one case at a time. There's to be no mention of, well, you know what isn't to be mentioned. His first case is to investigate the disappearance of the Marquis of Muerto Lago."

"The Marquis has vanished?"

"Yes, well, the important part at least."

"He's been headhunted?"

"That's as good a word as any. You and Blunt must start investigating immediately. The press will want to know why the Grim Reaper isn't dealing with it in person."

"Okay, we'll think of something."

"Don't be ridiculous, Mortimer. I've already thought of something. The Grim Reaper has decided that the time has come for this city to begin to police itself to a greater extent. His involvement in criminal justice is taking up too much of his time, so he has created the role of chief investigator. It has nothing to do with the police. That is crucial. The police are here to sever and react. Blunt will deal with matters of high-profile investigation only. Once he has solved a case, the police will finish the job in their usual brutally efficient way. I'll send you over the press release before it goes out."

"Thank you, sir."

"Mortimer, don't mess this up."

"Of course, sir. So shall we put the Grim Reaper case on the back burner?"

"Don't be stupid, Mortimer. Sometimes I think you must have died because you were too much of an idiot to go on living. Tell Blunt if he can't work out what is going on for himself, he shouldn't be the chief investigator. Speaking of which, what's the news?"

"Um, well, I've hired a forensics expert and we're looking for a secretary."

"What? We're supposed to be using minimum resources. You'll draw attention… Never mind, actually that fits with the chief investigator's angle. What's Blunt doing?"

"He's taking a walk, sir."

"I hope that's a euphemism for working his fingers to the bone on some awe-inspiring, brilliant conclusion to this whole debacle, Mortimer."

"Yes, si-" Mortimer was cut off as Neat slammed the phone down.

A press release arrived in Neat's first assistant's hands within minutes. This was passed to the second assistant, who, in turn, passed it to his assistant. This assistant passed it on to the manager of the typing pool, who passed it to the supervisor of the typing pool, who passed it to the typing pool team leader, who passed it to the typing pool's team supervisor, who passed it to Marge, the typing pool's typing champion or head agent. She then typed it out again (it was already word processed) and it was passed to the mail room, where another chain of managers, supervisors, team leaders, and head operatives dealt with it and posted it. At this point, it was delivered to a delivery company where a similar personnel-heavy team passed the letter into the hands of the receptionist at the Daily Obituary, the largest newspaper in the land of the dead.

Again it was passed through the paws of many people until it reached the hands of Miss Leighton Hughes, reporter extraordinaire, or she had been when she was alive. Now she was stuck typing up press releases. Investigative reporting was only encouraged if it involved a long-lens camera and two or more of the celebrity crowd.

She briefly wondered how many hands this message had been passed through and how many times it had already been typed before she began tapping keys. Once she finished, she sent a paper copy to her editor, who typed it up again, and then he sent it down to the copy room, where it was typed up a further three times. Then the printers put the document into the massive printing press and it was released in the evening edition within an hour of it first being committed to paper.

It read as follows,

Offal ointment to the settee of Groomsword of Augustine Blune to the portion of Cheap Invertebrae as by official disease of the Grime Leper.

Today a nude position was creature to Gloomwood. Flowing the groaning perculation of Gomword, it wus decicated today that the office of the cheek intestine world be put into offal service.

The orifice will work on ann individed basis begging buy inter-venous the exhalation of the Markus Merde Lager.

A retraction was to be made the next day and the official document would be produced correctly. Despite this, sales of Merde Lager went up by thirty percent.

20

The information desk at the ferry station was manned by an extremely morose woman who seemed to take Blunt's presence as some kind of personal affront. He asked for help and when he sighed, due to his own frustration and without directing any of his anguish towards the woman, he was berated brutally for his prejudice towards all hopes and dreams. Something which he could honestly say was not at all his intention, nor had it ever crossed his mind.

Following a liberal amount of remonstrations, protestations, and supplications, the woman snatched the napkin out of his hands and scribbled—in as rushed and uncaring a manner as she could manage—a few extra details. She handed it back to Blunt, folded her arms, and looked at him pointedly.

"Thank you very much, that's very kind of you," Blunt muttered, as he carefully walked backwards, not unlike a zookeeper tiptoeing away from a hungry tiger. When the crowds of people had conveniently filled the space between him and the woman on the desk, he opened up the napkin. Further details had been added to it, along with a less-than-friendly note regarding Blunt's ancestry. Armed with the note, he strode through the station with a sense of purpose and a strong belief that he should hurry before something else happened that would only serve to confuse and bewilder him further.

When Blunt arrived at his new office, he was

greeted by Mortimer. The little man appeared to have aged a few years in the hour or so they had been apart; his moustache was more grey than it had been and his spectacles appeared to magnify his eyes to an even more disproportionate size.

Without saying a word, he took in his surroundings. His new offices were a massive improvement on the one room bedsit/office he'd left in the land of the living. For a start, his office was separate from his living space, albeit by just the one door that didn't appear to want to shut properly, but it made a huge difference. Then there was the fact that he had a bed and an entirely separate kitchen. To a man used to eating, drinking and sleeping inches from his desk, which more frequently served as a storage site for unwashed dishes, it was a sight for sore eyes, which was convenient because what he saw next was an entirely disturbing vision.

"Hello. Chief Investigator Blunt, I presume?" The thing—as that was the only way he could describe it—in front of him spoke from some invisible orifice.

"Mortimer... what's that?" Blunt's voice quivered.

"Ah, may I introduce Sarah Von Faber. Are you okay, Chief Investigator?" Mortimer asked, with an odd smile on his face.

Mortimer was enjoying watching his reaction, but there wasn't a lot Blunt could do about it. The strange creature in front of him said nothing and seemed, as far as Blunt could tell, completely uninterested.

"Miss Von Faber, it's a pleasure to make your acquaintance," Blunt said as he reached out a hand. To his surprise, it was steady. He wasn't sure what he was expecting, but out of nowhere, a woman's hand appeared and firmly gripped his hand. He had to fight back a girlish scream and attempted to cover his discomfort with a cough, a ploy that was neither clever nor believable.

"Pleasure to meet you too, Chief Investigator. Mortimer set me up across the hall. Due to my unfortunate predicament, I'm a little difficult for some people to look at. I'm glad to see you have more about you than that. Would hate to think I was working for someone so feebleminded. Speaking of which, I'm not in complete control of my faculties, so if I go a bit loopy on you, it's best just to lock me in my lab."

Blunt was nodding; he was expecting a head to appear at some point, but it never surfaced. The thing in front of him seemed to hang in the air. In another life, he would have called it an apparition. No, he wouldn't; he'd have called it a ghost. Then again, even when he'd been alive, he didn't really believe in ghosts. Not that he'd ever really contemplated their existence. He was too practical for things like that. If he'd found a ghost in his house, he would have read it its rights and arrested the bastard for breaking and entering, or at least trespassing.

Now he was dead though, and ghosts were supposed to be dead people who were trapped in the land of the living, so he was pretty sure this wasn't a ghost. It was a person of some kind; body parts and clothing kept appearing and disappearing, seemingly at random. Most of the time it seemed to be a disembodied torso wearing a red jumper, floating in the air, but occasionally they were joined by a functional-looking pair of black trousers, and once they were briefly visited by a single red shoe that quickly vanished, clearly having just popped in to say hello.

Seconds ticked by in uncomfortable silence until Mortimer seemed to think that Blunt had suffered enough. "Well, Sarah, I imagine you want to finish setting up next door. I've got a few things to discuss with the chief investigator. Then I'm sure we'll be heading to our first crime scene."

A pair of eyes appeared out of thin air as the woman answered, "Yes, well, it's a bit of a mess in there, so I'll get to it. Just give me a knock when you want me." The disembodied body parts floated to the door and down the hall. Blunt quickly walked over and closed it as quietly as he could. Then he whirled on Mortimer.

"What the hell is that? No wait, first tell me why you've been calling me chief investigator, then give me some money and tell me where the nearest bar is."

Mortimer was grinning, and Blunt was sorely tempted to beat the smile from his face with the nearest heavy object.

"That was Sarah Von Faber, your new forensics expert. She was the best I could do. Here's seventy nails. It's all I've got on me." Mortimer grabbed Blunt's hand and began pouring rusty iron nails into it. "I'll have your bank account and everything else sorted out soon enough—"

"Nails, you're giving me nails?"

"That's right. Think about it, Blunt. What's really worth anything when you're dead?"

"Nothing."

"Correct, but in the old days and in religions all around the living world, people are buried with the things most precious to them, and they get to carry them through to the land of the dead."

"And I get nails?"

"We all get nails here, Blunt. They're the only thing most of us are buried with, the nails from our coffins. Of course, they aren't literally the nails you were buried with. It's more of a symbolic thing. Anyway, there you go. That should be plenty to keep you going for a few days. As for the chief investigator stuff, well, you better read this first."

"Um, couldn't I just tear apart all the furniture and supply myself with plenty of nails?"

"Ah yes, that caused a few problems at first, especially with sofas. People always believe they've dropped a few nails down the back of it, and next thing you know, the sofa falls apart because all the nails have gone. No, those nails are very specially made. You used coins in the land of the living?"

"Yes."

"Well, would any old circular disc have been accepted?"

"I get the point."

"Anyway, here you go," Mortimer said as he passed Blunt the piece of paper with the correctly written announcement about the newly appointed chief investigator on it and then wisely bolted for the door, "Important news, I'll wait out here."

As he stood on the other side, he heard Blunt unleash a torrent of expletives. The sound of breaking wood followed, then eventually everything faded to silence. Mortimer held his breath as he turned the doorknob and tentatively poked his head around the door. A shoe hit the wall inches from his head and fell to the floor.

Inside the room, the shattered remains of a wooden chair were scattered like a carcass after feeding time at the lion exhibit. Blunt was standing at the other side of the room, staring out of a window at the street below. In one hand, he held a bottle of some unknown liquid.

"Um, right, so I see it wasn't the news you were hoping to hear?"

Blunt didn't answer. Instead, he lifted the bottle to his lips and took a long swig of the contents. "Um, I'm sorry, sir. I realise this isn't the best of situations for you, but there isn't a lot we can do about it." Mortimer had his best subordinate's voice on, but it wasn't helping.

The sour-faced man took another massive swig and turned around slowly. "What have you done to me? I died today, you know? I died and came here and then had all manner of crap dumped on me and now this. What are you going to do next?"

"Nothing compared to what that floor cleaner is going to do to you if you have any more."

Blunt spat the cleaner he had in his mouth onto the floor and started coughing.

"Relax, Chief, it's not going to kill you. I'll go get something to counteract it from Sarah. Just wait here and calm down." Mortimer said. "Oh, and you might want to consider how you're going to manage this case with the Marquis."

After Mortimer had left the room, Blunt sat down on the floor, where his chair had been previously, feeling sorry for himself. He'd died, entered an entirely new world, and now he'd been put in charge of something he didn't even know about. Things were very bad. It was beginning to dawn on him that he might be in hell. Chief investigator? He'd never even been a Sixer at Cub Scouts. This was very, very worrying.

He had two high-profile cases, one of which was being conducted in secret. He didn't have a single lead on either one, and now he was going to be under a magnifying glass. The city was completely unfamiliar to him, and he didn't have any idea how the infrastructure worked. He couldn't call in any favours, and now that he was part of the establishment, people weren't going to want to talk to him.

How the hell was he supposed to investigate the Grim Reaper's demise without arousing suspicion? If this world was anything like the one he'd left, he was going to suffer from the public limelight. It never helped an investigation, and he really needed some help.

Help. Now there was a word that he didn't want to think about. At the moment, the only help he had in the world came from two people, only one of whom was a full able-bodied adult, and that was Ralph Mortimer, hardly the most powerful ally.

If he dwelled on things, he knew he'd sink into a serious depression. The thought of turning into a disembodied skull hidden in the depths of the library began to appeal to him. Then he remembered what he enjoyed doing, which for the most part was drinking, and he realised that if he had to be dead, he might as well be dead and working, or dead and drunk.

Mortimer returned with some kind of liquid to counteract the effects of the floor cleaner. Blunt still felt odd, but that might have just been the fact he was dead. Once he'd swallowed the last drop of the foul-smelling liquid, he turned to Mortimer and said, "Right, thank you very much, now I'm going for a drink."

"Ah, no rest for the wicked I'm afraid."

Blunt growled as a deep and primal rage reared its ugly head. "What did you say?"

Mortimer paled as he spoke. "Just a saying, really, sorry. Completely thoughtless. This isn't hell, really it isn't."

"I hadn't really been worrying about that part, but now you mention it... so, this Marquis?"

Within minutes, they had left the building and were on the way to the Marquis' home.

21

Neat walked down four flights of stairs before opening a door into a cavernous hall filled with pillars. He counted under his breath until he reached the pillar he was looking for, then knocked three times. A previously invisible door opened up to reveal a ladder inside the pillar. He climbed it and came out into another corridor, at the end of which was a single door. It opened at his knock.

"You should be more careful. The door wasn't even locked."

"I unlocked it when I heard you coming."

"How did you know it was me?"

"You have an unusual walk: swish stamp, swish stamp. You drag your feet, then try to compensate by stamping down. It's almost like you don't want to get here."

The room was exactly the same as the last time Neat had been there. The chess board had the pieces laid for the start of a new game.

"Never that I don't want to be here, just worried about what I might find."

The little man finally turned to face Neat, chuckling. "Well, they'll never put me in the library if that's what you're worrying about."

"That doesn't worry me. What worries me is what's

going on out in the real world."

"The real world or the world of the dead?"

"To me there's only the world of the dead."

"Ah, Crispin, to be as narrow-minded as you must be wonderful. I understand you've appointed the detective as chief investigator. He won't like that."

Neat had long since given up on trying to find out how the man knew so much about what was going on. "If he doesn't like it, he'll have to deal with it. The Marquis has met the same fate as the Grim Reaper."

The little man smiled and said, "I have no hand in this."

Neat's eyes opened wide. "I never suggested you did."

"Nor would you. You're far too wise a man to make that mistake. But truthfully, I had no hand in this, and I don't know who did. That's why I'm so worried about this detective. So much rests with him. Shall we start a new game?"

The old man shuffled slowly across to the chess board and glanced up to Neat expectantly. "Crispin?"

"Yes, let's play. You caught me contemplating the situation." Neat leant forward to examine the state of the board, despite there not having been a single move made. "How does it work?" he asked.

"The device?"

"What else?"

"It's complicated. Suffice it to say that it does

work… I'd be more interested to know what kind of mind can build it and, worse still, use it."

"Could you build it?"

"Possibly, but I wouldn't. It's your move."

Neat looked down at the board again. Somehow, the old man had moved a pawn without him noticing. "Do you know who could?"

"No, not now that he's gone. If I did, I would tell you. They need to be stopped. Whatever has been done, it is serious. I can't imagine someone wanting to do anything with his skull—and the Marquis' as well—that wouldn't lead to disaster. What of the Marquis? Not as much of a shame that he's gone, but it must make you nervous."

"Indeed it does," Neat murmured.

"I'm sure it will work itself out."

"I'm glad you're confident. I wish I was."

"The detective will lead the way."

"So far I am unimpressed with the detective."

"His ability is irrelevant. He is merely a tool. Sooner or later, whoever is behind this will be forced to move upon him. In doing so, they will reveal themselves."

"I would not fall for such a simple ploy."

"Of course you wouldn't, Crispin, but you have learnt to temper your arrogance. Whoever has done this is overconfident."

"This is a gamble."

"This is what must be done."

"I have taken steps."

"I know you have, but where you are unimpressed with the detective, which is a good thing, I am impressed by him."

"Ridiculous. The detective will be relieved and he will be viewed as a hero, something he never really had the chance to experience while he was alive."

"If you're sure," the old man said, his fingers interlocked before him.

"I am."

22

"Now presenting Augustan Blunt, chief investigator for Gloomwood, and Ralph Mortimer, third assistant to the manager of the Office of the Dead," the doorman announced as they entered the majestic mansion that had been the home of the Marquis of Muerto Lago.

They stepped through the doorway into a room full of people dressed in ball gowns and dinner suits. Mortimer glanced around and sheepishly tried to pull his coat more tightly around his coffee-stained shirt. He was painfully aware that he didn't even have a tie on.

Blunt was dressed as he always dressed, his all-purpose suit beneath his all-purpose coat, that had for some reason travelled with him from the land of the living. He appeared completely unfazed by their introduction and the silence that fell upon the room as they entered. He looked upon the guests, who had doubtlessly paid a small fortune for their dresses and suits, as if he was disappointed in them that they hadn't made more effort. He, on the other hand, wore his clothes as if they were just there to please everyone else.

"Take me to the Marquis," Blunt barked at the doorman, who panicked under Blunt's gaze. He seemed torn between leaving his post and obeying Blunt.

The relief was clear on his face as a woman

holding a mask over her face said, "Allow me, Chief Investigator." Her voice had that husky quality that reminded Blunt for some reason of sticky toffee pudding. She wore a dress that covered every inch of her body from her neck down, but still left very little to the imagination.

"And you are?" Blunt asked with the same tone of voice he used for everyone: sharp, impatient, disdainful.

"Why, Chief Investigator, surely you've heard of me? I'm none other than Lulu Devine," the woman said as she lowered her mask to reveal her face. She wasn't the sort of woman Blunt ever expected to meet in person; she was the kind of woman who only exists in magazines after photographers have been at work with their airbrushes. As beautiful as she was, Blunt wasn't the sort of man to be swayed by a pretty face.

"I'm new to these parts. It's a pleasure to meet you. Now, are we going to make small talk, or will you take me to the Marquis?"

For a second Blunt saw a glimmer of surprise in the woman's eyes. She was clearly used to people being in awe of her, no doubt pandering to her every whim. "Of course, if you'll follow me, we haven't touched anything. I believe that's normal procedure in these situations."

It was Blunt's turn to raise an eyebrow. He hadn't put much hope in people sticking to procedure in Gloomwood. After all, procedures are a way to deal with things that are likely to happen, and somebody being beheaded wasn't a common occurrence. Not that he personally believed strongly in procedures. It was just nice that other people did.

"That's correct, Miss Devine. Very astute of you to realise."

Her smile grew at the compliment, and there was a clear reaction from around the room, not least from Mortimer, who was staring adoringly. "Well, Chief Investigator, shall we?" She spun on her heel, a move she had clearly perfected, as her dress swirled around her dramatically, and headed straight through the crowd that parted before her. Blunt walked after her, with Mortimer following swiftly on his heels.

The crowd drew together again as they passed, and there was whispering on either side of them. People kept their masks to their faces and made an effort to step away from Blunt as he walked by, as if he carried some kind of disease: the evil scent of common. It was impossible to tell who was who, and Blunt felt some annoyance at the fact that he wouldn't be able to recognise anyone later. They walked through a pair of ornate double doors that were shut behind them by another pair of ridiculously dressed doormen.

The room beyond was extraordinarily flamboyant. The walls were carved out of marble and reflected the light from a chandelier, lighting up the room like a disco ball. There was very little furniture other than a huge dining table that stretched into the distance. At the far end, there was a throne-like chair with a body sprawled out of it and over the table.

"This is where it happened. We're not sure exactly what took place. As far as we were aware, he was in here alone. That's the way he always took his breakfast."

Blunt nodded carefully as he surveyed the scene. "I'll need some time alone, but I'll have some questions afterwards. I'll need to know his movements for the past twenty-four hours and anything you can think of that might have caused people to want him dead. Mortimer here will need to bring in our forensics expert, but it might be best if they came back in a way that is a little more discreet."

Lulu Devine looked down at Blunt in horror, her words conveying her disbelief. "I'm sorry, chief investigator. I don't normally deal with that sort of thing, but I will pass your requests on to the head of the household staff, whom I'm sure will accommodate you. How long will this all take? You may have noticed we're having a get together in honour of the Marquis. Of course, the main event will be the parade down Main Street, but that's for everyone. This is not."

"Then perhaps you'll tell your guests that the Marquis' skull is missing? We plan to find and return it to him, so sobbing into serviettes is a tad hasty. Now, from what I'm led to believe, this place is always having a gathering of some kind. How did you know the Marquis?

"We were friends. Nothing more."

"Really? I find that surprising."

"I don't mean to be disrespectful of the, well of the Marquis, but you, sir, give him too much credit and me too little."

"Maybe I don't think very highly of either of you."

She gasped at his audacity and turned to leave, but something changed her mind. "Chief Investigator, perhaps we got off on the wrong foot," she said as she turned back towards him. "It's a tragic loss to everyone in the city, but particularly to those of us who knew him well. He was, despite rumours to the contrary, a good man, something he was deservedly going to be rewarded for next week. I just want you to know that I had nothing to do with his accident."

Blunt answered sharply, "I very much doubt it was an accident. Pretty difficult to accidentally cut your own head off, then hide it. Maybe he slipped while buttering his toast."

"Fine, whatever happened to him, believe me: I'm not happy about this."

"How does it affect you, Miss Devine?"

"I'm a shareholder in Marquis public relations. This isn't going to do us any favours."

"But your share in the company will increase?"

"I have no idea if it will or not, but my lawyers are looking into it. The truth is that it's more likely to go to the government. It's not like the land of the living, Chief Investigator. It's not like we can declare him presumed dead. We already know he's dead, just like the rest of us. Unless Ableforth is proven, his shares—just like the rest of ours—are in limbo. Now, I really must attend to the guests, but for the last time, how long will this take?"

"It'll take as long as it does. A man has been decapitated in his own home," Blunt replied coldly.

The woman's smile faltered then fell completely, her face suddenly a black hole for happy thoughts, sucking them out of everything she looked at, like some vicious vacuum that fed on joy, leaving behind only misery. She made a point of looking at Blunt. "Very well, I shall wait in the east hall," she said as she turned and stalked out in stark contrast to the rehearsed manner with which she had led them to the dining room.

"Go and get Sarah, and stop looking so stunned. That woman is a bitch. Don't be fooled by a pretty face," Blunt said as he knelt down to look beneath the table, where the Marquis' foot was gently tapping out a rhythm. Without saying a word, Mortimer shuffled out of the room.

The upper body of the Marquis was spread out across the table. The remains of whatever he'd been having for lunch were trapped under him, but in one hand, he still held a piece of toast. His arm would occasionally wave it around in the air, seeming to expect a waiting mouth to take a bite. Blunt walked closer and peered at the toast. It was smothered in a thick honey that had clearly congealed since he had been attacked; it was unlikely to have contained poison, too obvious and no guarantee that he'd eat it. Besides which, the distinctive lack of a head was the most likely cause of his collapse. There was liquid on the floor. Blunt inspected it and risked dipping his finger in and licking it: red wine. He was glad; it could have been something disgusting.

He stood back and looked at the body. A heavy blow to the back of the head could have knocked him out. He wouldn't have had a chance to struggle, and then someone could have sawn his head off. The question was not *how*; his head was clearly gone. The question was, *why*? The doorway was some distance away, so for an assailant to have entered the room and made their way behind the Marquis, they must have known him, or perhaps they were simply not seen as a threat. A man who lived like the Marquis did was likely to be more than a little arrogant. Looking at the distance between the throne-like chair and the wall, it would have been a tight squeeze to get behind the Marquis, probably not enough room to swing something heavy. That meant someone very strong, but Blunt discounted it. The power required would mean someone bigger than could fit in the space available.

So not poison, and not a heavy blow to the head. Blunt contemplated the scene. He was looking at the incident as if it had taken place in the land of the living. In this place, it wasn't how the victim was decapitated that was central to the scene; it was who they were. It was an interesting problem and one that got Blunt thinking. He couldn't rely on a weapon or type of assault, which would be down to Sarah's forensics, although now he was pretty much convinced that the Marquis was attacked by surprise, his decapitation instant, or instant enough for him not to react. Instead, he had to investigate the suspects without any real knowledge of how the crime was committed.

The layout of the room suggested that if someone had to be there in person to extinguish the Marquis, then he would have to have seen them coming. Blunt hadn't moved the body—he'd been waiting for

Mortimer and Sarah—but he crept behind it to get an idea of the Marquis' view. The lack of a head made the exercise very simple.

The table stretched away from him, a long way from him, and at the end were the big double doors. The only other entrance to the room was for the serving staff, half way down the room. Blunt hadn't noticed it when he first walked through, since the door was flush to the wall with a barely perceptible outline. It just happened that the light hit it from this angle to make it visible. The detective grunted when he noticed it. The room was probably set up so that the only person who could see where the door was, while it was closed, was the person at the head of the table.

If, as was most likely, he was attacked with a blade of some kind; it was likely the Marquis had never seen it. If he had, he would have reacted. Blunt sat down in the chair next to the body and waited for the return of Mortimer, with Sarah in tow. He was only certain of one thing: foul play was afoot. A man didn't have his head removed, then hide it for fun; at least he didn't think they did.

23

Constable JJJ Johnson was back in his old neighbourhood trying to find the person who had sent him the letter he'd received at work. There had been a time when he could walk through the neighbourhood and be warmly welcomed by people. Ever since he'd joined the force and moved to the outskirts of the area, things had changed. Now people only saw the police uniform. He was part of the thin light-bluish-grey line. In the slums of Gloomwood, the area people knew as Coffin Town, the blue-grey uniforms of the police were looked upon as a warning. Nobody in Coffin Town had a good word to say about the police. They were feared, the uniformed men that came when they were least expected and indiscriminately punished the hopes, promises, and dreams for existing.

The sad fact was that the residents of Coffin Town really did know how the police operated. They weren't investigators; they were a small army of thugs whose sole aim was to find someone to persecute. With some help from the media, they had managed to make the population of Coffin Town, and the place itself, the root of all the problems in Gloomwood, so when the police needed to justify their existence, they took a trip into Coffin Town and arrested anyone stupid enough to get in their way. In an area of the city inhabited by the poverty stricken, they were unlucky to arrest someone who wasn't involved in some criminal activity, or who couldn't be stitched up for an unsolved crime.

In Gloomwood, there were no family ties. People occasionally married, but families didn't exist, since reproduction for the dead was an impossibility. They were dead, and so, just as they didn't have an actual need to feed, breathe, feel, move, or shit, they also didn't reproduce.

Whereas neighbourhoods in the land of the living might still have family members living nearby one another—aunts and uncles, cousins, siblings, and in laws—there was nothing. No firm solid relationship or grounding in an area, no such thing as a nostalgic location, a place to return to if things got too much. People in Gloomwood were never asked where they came from; everyone came from the land of the living.

Constable Johnson surreptitiously checked that his truncheon, a thick piece of dark wood attached to his belt, was still there. He knew that if he was out of uniform, he wouldn't be at risk, but that wasn't the job.

He had looked at the crumpled envelope in his hand for a return address. The street name was illegible, but there were only two streets in the city that started with an X, and the other was Xylophone Avenue, which the word clearly wasn't. He was on Xe street, struggling to identify which one of the horribly decrepit yet oddly uniform mishmash of houses he needed to go to. On the envelope it looked like a number three, but the scribbling made it difficult to read. It could just as easily be an eight. Worse still, it could just be part of the number. It was all he had to go on, so he shrugged his shoulders and walked towards a door that had a three painted on it in dark grey paint.

The houses in Coffin Town were run-down. Rooms were rented out to two or three people at a time. On certain streets there could be fifteen people to a building. Occasionally a particularly strong gust of wind would blow and instinctively people would look up, hoping that they wouldn't be unlucky enough to end up crushed beneath falling tiles.

Nobody answered his knocking, but that didn't come as a surprise. The front door creaked open. Whatever locks that might have existed were long since stolen—the only thing of worth in the houses. The floor was bare of any carpet and the wooden boards were old and frail. He stepped carefully, well aware of the accidents that were common in the unmaintained, decrepit terraces. The house appeared abandoned, but Johnson knew this didn't mean it was uninhabited.

He approached the narrow stairs and reached for a grip on the banister, but the wood crumbled away beneath his fingers. There were missing steps all the way up the stairs, and those that remained looked unsafe. The whole building was an accident waiting to happen. He decided to make sure the lower floors were empty before risking the upstairs.

A door lay on the floor in the corridor and he walked around it, conscious that it might cover a gaping hole beneath. There was a room to the side. As he stepped through, the air filled with a thick stench that burnt his nose hairs. They'd had training for this, but it was experience that won out. The smell was the scent of Oblivion, high grade narcotics that had a destructive effect on users but which, it was said, for a moment made you feel alive again.

Johnson wrinkled his nose in disgust; he'd seen enough of the effects of Oblivion to know it wasn't something he wanted to be around. The poor souls who used it were quickly addicted, and more often than not, they rapidly lost control of their habit, going to darker and lower places in their desperate quest for another hit.

In the corner of the room, beneath a pile of blankets, Constable JJJ Johnson saw what he'd been dreading. A woman was sitting on the floor cradling a bowl. She hadn't even noticed Johnson enter the room. She was lost in the swirling colours that danced in the shimmering liquid within the bowl. This was Oblivion. She had brewed it like tea to drink. The drug was a substance so potent that once the user began taking their trip; they were unable to separate themselves from it until they collapsed into a near comatose state.

He knew better than to interfere. There was little doubt in his mind that this woman had sent him the letter. Sprawled about her feet, he could see the previous attempts to write the note that had made him seek her out, each one a slight variation on the next, but every single one with his name printed at the top with the same spidery handwriting. Knowing that interrupting the narcotic experience could be more damaging than letting it run its course, he sat down to wait, shuffling through the notes the woman had made for some kind of clue. She knew who he was and had sought him out on purpose, but who was she, and what did the letter mean?

24

Blunt watched as an ashen-faced doorman tried, unsuccessfully, to hide his discomfort at being in the presence of Sarah Von Faber. The woman had half a face. Blunt, who had prepared himself for her appearance, was pleasantly surprised by the half he could see. She was an attractive lady, not much younger than Blunt had been when he'd died. It was the missing half of her head that was terrifying the doorman. Blunt, given his own initial reaction, felt some compassion for the man and waved him away.

"Well then, Sarah, if you're feeling up to it, we've got a crime scene to examine. Mortimer, don't take this personally, but you're standing watch. I'd be surprised if we weren't interrupted, and nobody forget that the perpetrator nearly always returns to the scene of the crime. There's a whole load of psychological mumbo jumbo to explain that, but basically it comes down to them being idiots."

He knelt down and peered under the table. His voice echoed in the cavernous room. "Okay, Sarah, I think you might want to start by constructing a step-by-step search. Given the size of the room and the available space, I reckon we'll do a spiral moving outwards from the victim. We might get interrupted at any time and at the moment, I don't think we actually have any legal jurisdiction. I've contaminated some of the area already, but it couldn't be helped. Shouldn't be a problem though, as my footprints can be easily eradicated and I haven't left any fingerprints." He waggled his gloved hands in the air and nodded towards Sarah, who took a pair of latex gloves from her pocket.

"I don't mean to be rude, Sarah, but can you see properly? You're not going to miss anything?"

"You can't see me, Blunt, but believe me, I can see everything. It's difficult to explain. I can talk to you even though you can't see my mouth. Well, I can also see even though you can't see my eyes." She said it without any tone of annoyance.

"Right, well," Blunt hesitated, searching for words that didn't exist. Something from his school days told him that it shouldn't be possible that Sarah could see, but he pushed it aside. "Anyway, we need to get an idea of who has been in and out of here in the last few hours and then eliminate as many of them as we can. We know he was killed between ten and one o'clock. Once I've spoken to the staff, I'll probably have the time of the attack down to a few minutes, so don't worry about trying to figure a time of death, unless you think it will be different."

"I should imagine it was very different; he's been dead a very long time," Sarah said, being careful not to put any kind of undercurrent to the words.

"Bollocks, of course he has, but you know what I mean."

"I don't think we'd have any way to work that out, I'm afraid." She pursed her lips as she spoke.

"Fine, fine, okay then. Do you think you could work out how his head was severed?" Blunt asked, peering at the body.

"With a very sharp instrument. The flesh is already dead, of course, but if we look closely…" Sarah said. She moved over to the body and poked at the neck with a pencil while staring at the edge of the wound. "Yup, no signs of burning, and the removal wasn't as clean as it appears. There were actually two cuts, very close to each other, so it isn't easily spotted. The weapon, I'd go for a large pair of scissors, or maybe a pair of sharp blades."

"Like a pair of rapiers?"

"No, that would be ridiculous. Something heavy like a broadsword—maybe that's too large—but big and sharp anyway," she said.

"Scythe?" Blunt asked.

"Hmm… unlikely. A scythe would not normally require two together, although the blades were curved like a scythe. It's more likely it was intended to look like a pair of scythes, or at least one scythe."

"Why would they do that?" Blunt asked.

"Really now, you're the detective. I'm just a scientist. My first guess would be dramatic effect. I mean, the thought of a murderer—sorry, headhunter—running around with a scythe in each hand is scarier than a man with some curved garden shears."

Blunt stared at the half woman but had to concede the point. He was the detective and his investigative sixth sense told him he was missing something. "Mortimer," he called towards the doorway where

Mortimer was attempting to look like a man, 'on watch', "who, other than the Grim Reaper, uses a scythe?"

"Some of the reapers carry them, but they don't often venture into the city," said Mortimer.

"The reapers, well, I can imagine there are plenty of people who would want to implicate them," said Blunt

"Not really, most people quite like them," Mortimer replied, having now abandoned any pretence of being a lookout.

"Really?" Blunt cast his mind back to his encounter with the self-important Philip. "Well, it doesn't matter. Making it look like scythes implicates the Grim Reaper and the reapers. Presumably if people believed the Grim Reaper did this, they would want answers, and if it was a reaper, what would be the general reaction?"

"No idea. There are around two hundred reapers. It could be any one of them."

Blunt fell silent. He needed more information. He tapped his foot, then stopped when he realised that his tapping was in time with that of the Marquis'. "We need to start interviewing people," he said.

"Wait, there's something here," Sarah said. She was kneeling on the floor by the body of the Marquis.

"What is it?"

"A button, a single black button. It appears to have come off something with brown fibres on it."

"So we're looking for someone in a brown coat?" Mortimer asked.

"No, we're looking for someone missing a button off something brown. We don't know it's a coat yet," Blunt replied. "Anything else, Sarah?"

"This is going to take a while; there's not much conclusive evidence. Pity they couldn't just leave a business card."

"Mortimer, when she's done, I want you to bring in the person who served him breakfast. Find out if there's anything here that wasn't before, or if there's anything missing," Blunt said as he walked down the long dining hall towards the main doors.

"Where are you going?" Mortimer asked.

"To speak to the staff. Am I right in thinking the reapers only wear black?"

"Yes."

"And the Grim Reaper too."

"Always."

25

Blunt strode into the main hall where the guests were mingling with each other, and a small number were dancing to music provided by a string quartet. By the main entrance, a man with a long moustache and several tentacles was serving drinks. Blunt ignored the rest of the party and stormed straight to the bar. "What are you serving?" he asked.

The man's moustache rose slightly at the corners as he answered. "Whatever you should require, sir, and may I add, sir, that your attire for this evening is most inventive. You have clearly constructed the best mask of all by coming as you are."

"If you are trying to suggest that I look slightly out of place, just say so. Convoluted attacks on my general appearance will only serve to annoy me. Then I'm likely to lose my temper, and given that you are the person standing between me and a drink I've been needing since I died, you don't want to make me angry," Blunt growled as he drew himself up to his full height, which was not as considerable as he would have liked. He leant towards the man over the bar and said, "Now, about that drink."

The man nodded. "Something to take off the edge. May I recommend a Tombstone?"

Blunt hesitated before saying, "I doubt I got one."

The man shrugged indifferently and pushed forward a glass into which he poured a large measure of a thick grey liquid. In a vicious-looking font on the bottle's label was the word *Tombstone*. Without a second's hesitation, Blunt picked up the glass and knocked it back in one.

It was strong stuff and frighteningly foul to taste, which left Blunt with little doubt that it was very expensive. He suppressed a shudder and calmly placed the glass back on the table.

"Thank you," he said, unable to avoid the way his words came out as a wheeze. He spun away from the bar and once more examined the room. Talking to the guests was likely to be an exercise in futility. He had little doubt that anything they'd have to say would be irrelevant. Giving people the attention they so craved was only going to irritate him past the point of caring.

He glanced at the doorway and saw the man who had let them in. He was dressed in a white shirt and a purple mourning suit. His hands were clasped in front of him, the white gloves he wore marking him as a servant of some kind. Being careful to avoid conversation, Blunt walked through the room, nodding and offering short, civil, yet final greetings to those who tried to engage him in conversation.

He reached the man in purple and offered a hand while introducing himself. "I'm Augustan Blunt, here investigating the Marquis', um, predicament. Who might you be?"

The man, who had clearly observed Blunt moving towards him, still feigned surprise. "I'm sorry, sir. I believe you're looking for someone else."

Blunt, his hand still held in front of him, looked

the man in the eye. "How could I possibly know that if I don't know who you are?" he asked.

The man shot his hand out, and they shook hands quickly. "My apologies, sir. I will be of whatever assistance I can. My name is Toby Richards. I'm the household coordinator."

"Excellent. You are, in fact, exactly who I wanted to see. Now, Toby, can we get out of this room and have a little talk somewhere? Being around this many people can make it difficult to have an honest chat," Blunt said.

Richards waved a sombre-looking man over and whispered something in his ear. The man nodded and took up a stance exactly the same as Richards' by the door. "How about a beer in the kitchen?" Richards asked Blunt.

"Sounds wonderful."

Richards turned out to be exactly what Blunt had been looking for. As soon as they had stepped out of the ballroom, his entire demeanour changed. His shoulders dropped and his walk became almost languid. He grinned at Blunt. "Well, I guess you can spot someone who's out of place. Bloody hell, that lot in there are a bunch of pretentious vultures. You know, I haven't even seen half of them before. God knows—pardon my religious reference—what they're doing here. So you want the skinny on the Marquis, a little info on his royal arseness?"

Blunt laughed. "In one. But I've also got to ask if you did this."

"Really, is that how you're going to catch the bastards, by asking everyone, 'hey buddy, did you cut off the Marquis' head?' Well, good luck with that," Richards said.

"Yeah, something like that. You know I've got to ask, so did you? You must've had reason. I mean, he was your boss, wasn't he? And from what I hear, a pretty crap one at that."

Richards opened a door and Blunt was blasted with heat from inside. The smell of roast potatoes and slow-cooked pork wafted out. "Come in, grab a pew and a beer."

Blunt sat down on a stool at an aluminium-covered table spattered with drips of gravy. The surrounding clamour took a moment to get used to, and the frenzied activities of the kitchen staff slowly turned from chaos to the smooth workings of a complex machine as he watched them.

After Blunt had watched a pastry chef somehow construct a swan out of meringue, Richards reappeared with a beer in each hand. "This'll take away the taste of the drink Neville gave you, you know the lad with the tentacles. He's alright really, but can't help serving up some god awful—excuse my religious reference—drinks to newcomers." He handed Blunt a bottle opener.

"Thanks," Blunt said as he popped open the bottle and took a long hard pull on the drink. He felt the bubbles filling his mouth, and the taste of malted hops made him stop and savour the mouthful for a little longer than he should've. "That's lovely," he said, holding the bottle in Richards' direction.

The man in the purple suit nodded. "Bloody well should be, for how much it costs. Still, we can't help it if I dropped a few bottles while moving them. Accidents will happen. Now, about the Marquis. First off, yes, he's a class A knob. Nobody will say otherwise, well nobody honest anyway. Thing is, he was also pretty much as thick as pig shit. Nobody—and I mean nobody—would dare tell him to his face, but really, there isn't a soul in the staff of this place who would do him any harm. Oh yeah, he fired people left, right, and centre, but nobody actually lost their jobs. I just shuffled things around a bit and we carried on happy as Larry. The pay is good, the hours are whatever we organise between ourselves, same goes for holidays, and he buys so much crap that our homes are all decked out as well as his is. Most of the time he just tells me to get rid of stuff however I want. Talk about an easy time of it. No sir, right now I can tell you that nobody—and I mean nobody—on the household staff would have done this. Come on, look around. We're all terrified we might have to get real jobs."

Blunt took another look around. The staff did look haunted, nervous even, but there was no guilt about them. "You want me to discount everyone on the household staff just like that? Can't be done, but I appreciate what you're saying. What I'm looking for is a personal vendetta against the Marquis."

Richards took another mouthful of beer and swallowed it. "Well, there'll be a few of those. I mean, like I said, he wasn't or isn't a good guy, but killing him doesn't do much good for any of us on the staff. I mean talk about a golden goose."

"Okay, fine," Blunt said, "why don't you just tell me about what happened building up to the incident and I'll back off here until I have reason to do otherwise."

"Deal," Richards said, smiling, and then he poured out the Marquis' every movement, building up to his beheading.

The Marquis had spent the day leading up to his decapitation the same way he spent most of his days. He'd woken and had breakfast at around noon. He took his time over it, reading the papers and sipping wine. After this, he'd spent an hour in meetings with a perfume company who wanted to use his name to sell their latest product; the Marquis had declined as he didn't like the fragrance. There was no animosity from the company; he'd agreed to put his name to another product within the next six months, provided they made one he liked. He was not interested in being involved in the design of the fragrance; he and the company agreed that something like that was beneath him.

Following this meeting, he'd spent two hours getting ready to make an appearance at an art gallery exhibition. He was ready by four. From four until five he picked up his date for the evening, a Miss Fleur Devallier. His dates were arranged by the public relations company that bore his name.

He attended the art gallery for three hours. The guests at the exhibition noted nothing unusual about the Marquis or his partner at the event. Afterwards, he left with his date, who was immediately dropped off at home.

Blunt spoke to Miss Devallier and discovered there were no romantic entanglements between her and the Marquis. The date had been arranged for the sake of the photo opportunities. The Marquis' firm represented her, and it was good for both of them to have their pictures in the papers. Blunt learned that the majority of pictures of the Marquis in newsworthy situations were staged. It was a fact that most of the public were aware of but chose to ignore, preferring the fictional version of events, a bit like pretending that professional wrestling is real. That is to say that some of the events might actually happen and the majority of people involved were highly skilled, but that, in general, it was a farce.

The Marquis travelled home to have dinner with some guests in the evening. A fight did break out between some guests, but the Marquis had absolutely no involvement in the argument or even in resolving the matter. After dinner there was a party, as there was almost every evening at the Marquis' house.

There were over a hundred people at the party, but it was small compared to the scale of his normal events. Blunt had spoken to the guests quickly, unable to waste time grilling them individually. Each one had told him when they arrived, who they arrived with, and what they saw of the Marquis. Surprisingly, few of them spent time with their host. He spent a great deal of the evening in the DJ booth; the Marquis liked to play his own mixes, which meant nothing to Blunt.

The Marquis was in view of nearly everyone for most of the night, even if he didn't do much mingling. At around three in the morning, he retired to his room in the company of four women. Blunt interviewed them individually. Each one told the same story, or at least similar stories with varying degrees of graphic content. Throughout the conversations, Blunt found himself feeling increasingly uncomfortable. It was clear the women had absolutely no qualms about regaling Blunt with their adventures with the Marquis. Three of them had already sold their stories to the papers, and the fourth was writing a book. Blunt was left with no reason to believe any of the women would have wanted the Marquis to disappear, although none of them seemed particularly bothered that he had been beheaded. If anything, they all seemed a little disappointed that they had rushed out and signed deals that, had they waited, would have been worth considerably more.

Following the night of debauchery, he was woken by his housekeeper, the sombre gentleman who had taken up Richards' post after Blunt had taken him aside. He was a gentleman with next to no personality. Blunt couldn't help but wonder if this was what people became like when they began to be considered for internment at the library. The housekeeper had laid out the Marquis' breakfast clothes and put the women into taxis. Then he had ordered the food to be prepared. It was delivered to the Marquis' table by the chef, who prepared it, so there was no opportunity for anyone to interfere with the meal before it was put in front of the Marquis.

Richards had called the chef over while Blunt was sipping his beer and going over the timings with him. During the brief interview, Blunt picked up on a number of signals, which made him believe something was being hidden. Upon questioning, the chef broke down, revealing that he had been over-ordering food and wine and selling it on the black market for a profit. He wasn't actually present at the time of the attack, as he was meeting some of his customers.

The room fell silent at the revelation, and Blunt made his excuses to leave. As he stepped through the door from the kitchen, he heard Richards' voice. "You selfish bastard, Jones, we've got an agreement. Everyone gets their cut."

Blunt shook his head, wondering why the most honest people always end up being the least trustworthy.

The only thing throughout the entire set of interviews that had sparked the slightest glimmer of curiosity on Blunt's part was the mention of drugs, specifically something called Oblivion. The Marquis' himself wasn't a user, but he was happy for his guests to partake if they wished. Richards' revealed that the household staff refused to supply drugs to the Marquis and that it was part of their contracts, one of the few parts of it they actually upheld.

It was the Marquis himself who insisted on the rule. Richards explained that the man had a huge fear of losing control of himself, of slipping into some kind of drug-fuelled rage or pharmaceutical coma. It was the household coordinator's opinion that the Marquis was terrified that he might lose some part of himself and return to the strange omniscient realm that he had come from when he was a god. Apparently, it wasn't uncommon in deities who had passed through from the land of the living. Being an individual was far preferable.

It didn't mean much to Blunt though; drugs were drugs. In Blunt's experience, narcotics tended to come from unsavoury types, the sort of people who might viciously hack off someone's head. It was an unlikely lead. Even if the Marquis had drugs at his events, it was clear the man could afford it. He was probably a long-term customer and with the money he had at his disposal, it would be a shame to lose him.

The drugs were probably not the reason for the attack. They certainly wouldn't be a reason to attack the Grim Reaper, who was known for his aversion to any kind of intoxicating substances. It was more likely that the drugs were controlled by some kind of syndicate; organised crime in Gloomwood. Taking out the Grim Reaper could be an attempt to overthrow the government. Taking out the Marquis might be a warning to other high-powered individuals who might think about standing in their way. Unfortunately, all Blunt really had to go on was a body without a head and a button.

The key was finding the link between the Marquis and the Grim Reaper, and so far there was only one, something people referred to as 'The Changing of the Keys.' It seemed unlikely there could be a pair of greater opposites; the Marquis was a parody of himself, a strange kind of uber-lothario, while the Grim Reaper avoided companionship, the public, the press, pretty much everyone. If there was a link, it was in their public personas. Both of them were instantly recognisable and in their own ways they were considered leaders of the city, hence the upcoming award ceremony which everyone seemed a little in the dark about.

He needed to give himself some time to mull over the facts, so he walked back through to the scene of the crime.

The dining room was covered in pieces of string and what appeared to be tiny traffic cones. Mortimer was standing by the side of the room, holding one end of a piece of string, while Sarah, what there was of her, held the other piece above her head as she stood on the table.

"What are you doing?" Blunt asked.

"Well, there are two entrances to the room. We know the Marquis' kidnapper didn't leave through the main entrance because there was a guard, which only leaves the second entrance, except how could the Marquis not see someone enter? He's got the best view." Sarah wandered down towards where the Marquis' body was sitting as she spoke.

Blunt tiptoed his way towards the dining room table and stood beneath the string. "Okay, I understand your point, but what's with the string?" he asked.

"Reflective angles," Mortimer said.

"Yes, exactly right, Mortimer. We're trying to work out if there is a way a mirror could be used to hide the fact that someone was in the room. Kind of the reverse of the door; the outline can only be seen from a certain angle," Sarah said.

"Okay, so with a mirror someone can?"

"Go stand behind the chair," she said.

Blunt did as he was told and looked towards the door, trying hard to avoid the occasional flailing piece of toast that the Marquis' arm kept waving in his direction. "What am I looking for?" he asked.

"Mortimer, tilt the mirror in the direction of the string."

One moment the door was there and in the next it had vanished, the wall apparently smooth, "Very clever, very, very, clever, but pointless," Blunt said.

The beaming smile of self-congratulation on the half of Sarah's face, that was visible, collapsed. "Pointless?" she asked. "It's how the attacker got to the Marquis without him seeing them."

"No it isn't. I can see for myself how they got that close to him. You can see it as well," Blunt said as he pointed at the tiny cones around the room. "There's a bloody clear pattern!"

"Yes, well, explore all avenues."

"Not once you've got an answer! Look. Brown fibres, yes?" Blunt stooped to the feet of the Marquis and lifted a fibre.

"Yes. Following that there are several others, a piece of some kind of foam, and some black threads, none of which came from the Marquis."

"Could they have been left by the staff?"

"No, one of the few plus sides of the garish outfits he makes them wear is that none of them are as mundane as black or brown."

"So it is safe to assume," Blunt strode back to the main doors as he spoke, "that the phantom guillotine salesman entered through this door."

"Yes," Sarah answered. Mortimer lowered the mirror to watch Blunt's analysis of the scene. His head seemed to hover in mid-air.

"Mortimer, please put the mirror to one side. I've got a body without a head and Sarah to contend with already. No offence, Sarah."

"None taken."

"Right, where was I? Ah, through the main doors we said, but the problem we have there is that the main doors were guarded." Blunt looked towards Sarah, waiting for her to provide an alternative solution. She wasn't forthcoming, so he continued, "What if the axe-wielding maniac was already in the room?"

"That's a bit unlikely," Mortimer said quietly.

"Is the room guarded all day?" Blunt knelt down as he said it, his question directed at Sarah.

"No, it was only guarded when the Marquis was in here, and even then the guard admitted to disappearing for a few minutes to relieve himself."

"Ah-ha! I also spoke to the guard who said that during breakfast the Marquis had popped his head out and, in the guard's own words, gone a bit mental. I believe that someone entered the room while the guard went to the toilet. The Marquis challenged them and they left before the guard returned, but as soon as they left, they ran to the hidden entrance and waited. Now, even though I have never met the Marquis, I think it would be fair to say he's not a happy chappy in the mornings, so he will have then chosen to berate the guard. At this moment, the attacker will have entered through the side door and hidden under the table."

"So theoretically someone could have snuck in and hidden themselves under this ridiculously over-sized table and waited for the Marquis to come and join them for breakfast." As he said this, he waved Mortimer and Sarah towards his position on the floor. They dropped the string and joined him.

Blunt pointed towards one of the chairs that was pushed under the table, on top of which sat a piece of paper. Being careful to make sure he didn't corrupt the evidence, Blunt reached forward with one gloved hand and retrieved it.

The paper was old and had been folded many times. When Blunt finally managed to open it, he read it slowly, because that's the way he read things. His lips moved as he followed the words. "It looks like some kind of shopping list. Listen: eggs, milk, bread, something very sharp, shoe polish, a ladle, punch bowl, twenty cigs, head of the Marquis, sugar, spice, pretty decorations, birthday candles, chocolate ice cream."

Mortimer shrugged and said, "sounds like they're having a party."

"A birthday party, though?" Sarah said.

"What's wrong with that?" Blunt asked.

"People don't celebrate birthdays after they're dead. There's nothing to celebrate any more. If people celebrated them after then, we'd say things like, 'My great grandfather is two hundred this year.' Then you'd say, 'Wow, two hundred, that's old.' Then I'd say, 'Yes it is, but he's been dead a hundred and seventy years.'" Sarah spookily switched the visible sides of her face as she played the different characters in her conversation.

"Right, you didn't need to do that. You could have said birthdays aren't celebrated in Gloomwood and have been done with it," Blunt said. He blinked several times, then folded the list back up and placed it into a clear plastic evidence bag. "Let's get back to the office and see what we can come up with."

Mortimer raised a hand above his head and looked back and forth between Sarah and Blunt.

"Mortimer," Blunt glared at him and said, "are you actually putting your hand in the air to speak?"

"Um, yes, I thought it would be, um, polite?" The man seemed to get smaller in stature with every word.

"Don't put your hand up, for crying out loud, Mortimer. Grow some balls. Oh forget it, what are you going to say?"

"Well, it could be for the celebrations."

"What celebrations?" Blunt asked.

"Well, the keys to the city celebrations, of course." Mortimer smiled as he said it.

"The celebrations? People mentioned them before.

Changing of the keys. What the hell is it?"

Extract from the Guidebook to Gloomwood by Ralph Thaddeus Mortimer:

If you're lucky enough to visit Gloomwood on its centenary, then be sure to attend our fabulous Changing of the Keys. Once every hundred years, the City of Gloomwood rewards its six most influential people by awarding them the keys to the city.

As Gloomwood is a land where nobody dies, the previous holders of the keys must hand over their keys to the new bearers of this most prestigious award. Of the six keys, one is always held by the Grim Reaper, as nobody could be more influential than the creator of our great land.

The ceremony itself is presided over by the Master of Ceremonies, a man who lives in solitude and watches the city with absolutely no involvement to ensure that his judgement is as fair as possible. Once every hundred years he announces his chosen six to the city, and a great parade takes place. Presents are given to those closest to us, and all is filled with friendship, compassion, peace, and harmony on one of Gloomwood's few national holidays.

26

Blunt fell asleep in the car on the way to the office; they'd tried to wake him but he slept, unsurprisingly, like the dead. So much so that Sarah and Mortimer had to struggle to carry him to his bed.

As he slept, he dreamt of being alive again. It was an unpleasant dream, as if the drink he had consumed wanted to punish him. Once he'd been married. He'd had a daughter, and they'd been happy. Then his world had crumbled around him.

The police had been good to him for a while. They had a heavily mortgaged home with two incomes and friends who they liked, and then things went wrong. On their way back from a trip to the beach, there'd been an accident. The other driver was drunk. Blunt had been careful, kept to the speed limit, and watched for erratic driving, but he couldn't do anything about it. The driver of a Mercedes had flown across a junction, hitting their family sedan at over eighty miles an hour. Both cars landed in a ditch, the Mercedes on top. His wife, a striking figure of a woman, was gone instantly, her life taken from her before she knew what had happened. In the back, his daughter Susie had cried out for her mother once when the cars first collided, but when they slid into the ditch, the roof of the car collapsed and she was gone a second after his wife.

Blunt had been left in the car for hours before the ambulance and policemen arrived and dragged his badly injured body from the crash. He'd spent four months in a coma, and when he'd woken up, he'd already been found guilty of dangerous driving. The driver of the Mercedes had been the son of the Speaker of the House of Commons, and Blunt was warned that if he tried to pursue matters, things would get worse for him, but he couldn't leave it alone. The system turned its back on him.

The friends they had quickly deserted him as they became convinced that he was drunk, that he was responsible. The harder he fought to disprove it, the faster those above him moved to block him. The names on the breath tests were switched, and the court found him in contempt when he refused to accept their verdict.

In the end, he attended his wife and child's memorial in handcuffs. He'd never recovered.

He awoke to the sound of car horns and sirens outside, and for a moment he thought he might be alive again, that the nightmare wasn't over. Then he opened his eyes. The office didn't feel like home yet, which Blunt saw as a good thing. The last place he'd called home was a sty, home to an ex-pig.

Dragging himself from the bed, he noticed several things at once: he needed the toilet but he wasn't panicking about it, his aches and pains, while still there, were considerably duller, and most importantly he didn't have a headache for the first time in a long time despite the strange drinks from the night before.

There was nothing to eat or drink in the apartment, which annoyed him, but then everything annoyed him. He hadn't been in a good mood since… he shook off the thought and moved on. Minutes later, still hungry, he was knocking on Sarah's door.

When it opened, he was greeted by a face he'd only seen half of before. "Sarah?" She was prettier with both sides of her head. Brunette, her hair cut into a short bob, she smiled brightly as she greeted him.

"Morning, Chief Investigator. I've got my face back. No idea how long it will last, but enjoy it while you can. Anyway, no time for small talk. I've made an interesting discovery," she said as she opened the door revealing the lab. It was half morgue and half hi-tech laboratory. Blunt only recognised one thing in the whole room, and until yesterday he wouldn't have recognised that.

"Ah, I didn't realise you had company," Blunt said. "How rude of me. I didn't think you'd be into the playboy type." Sarah was not amused, but Blunt was warming to his theme. "Well, he's not much of a talker, but I imagine it's his body you're interested in." The scientist, who was only missing her legs, floated away from Blunt towards the table, a scalpel in her hand. Blunt followed, still spouting idle chat. "Strong, silent type, is he? Brings a whole new meaning to the term *stiff one*. Hmm, maybe that's a little crude. Technically, I suppose most of these work for everyone in Gloomwood."

As Blunt paused to ponder on the thought that he was dead, Sarah got to work. With her scalpel, she cut down the centre of the Marquis' chest. Blunt made a strange gurgling noise as she pulled with all her strength, producing the sound of snapping bones and tearing sinews as she opened the rib cage. She reached in and pulled hard, twisting as she did it. In one gore-covered hand she withdrew the heart; a dried-up, prune-like thing. "Now, Chief Investigator, he's a heartless bastard," she said, chuckling as she placed the heart into a metal dish. If Blunt had eaten, he'd have been in serious danger of throwing up. As it was, he felt a kick at the back of his throat, the signal that he was close to retching.

"You've made your point, Doctor. It is *doctor*, isn't it?" Blunt asked.

"Yes, it is. Now I wanted to tell you about my discovery," Sarah said. "I think you'll find it interesting." She was digging away with relish while Blunt was trying not to watch as bits of dried-up flesh fell to the floor. She kept talking. "You see, the fingerprints you asked us to gather?" She gestured over to a wall that was covered in pieces of clear tape stuck to black paper. Each piece of tape had a white fingerprint trapped beneath it. "Well, I tried to tell you at the time, but you were in a hurry; we don't have people's fingerprints on record."

"Surely you've got known criminals on record," Blunt said, looking at Sarah as if she was losing the plot.

"If the police catch a criminal, which is almost unheard of, they lock them up, give them a severe beating, or put them in the library."

"Okay, fine, fingerprints are irrelevant. What have you found?"

"Several things. Firstly, I wasn't sure until I took out the heart, but I can now say he's still alive."

Blunt looked horrified at the wreckage of the Marquis' body. "What the hell are you doing, woman?" Blunt shouted. "That poor man." He moved forward, desperately looking for something he could do to help.

"Of course, when I say still alive, I mean still dead, in that his head has not been destroyed. Had it been, then his heart would have turned to dust, as would most of the rest of his internal bits and pieces. He is not physically attached to his body though, and will not be feeling any pain." She finished the sentence through gritted teeth as she yanked a scalpel out of the detective's hands.

"Okay, sorry," he said as he felt his heart rate returning to normal. "Explain it to me. I thought we knew that because his body had been moving at the crime scene. He was tapping his foot and waving about bread." Blunt looked away from the body to the floor of the lab, his emotions somewhere between horror, embarrassment, and relief.

"Well yes, that pretty much means he's definitely not Ableforthed, but I read in a journal about a body that was once kept moving by clockwork. Nearly allowed the attacker to get away with it, took them weeks to realise he was Ableforthed. Fortunately, they caught the attacker winding the body back up."

Blunt grinned and said, "Brilliant, it was a proper wind-up then."

Sarah didn't smile. "You may find this more interesting. It's a closely guarded secret, but pharmaceuticals and the big plastic surgeons link the body and minds of their high-profile clients. It prevents body robbery. You know, someone knocking you out and stealing your limbs," she said.

"Like black market organ dealing," Blunt said.

"I don't know what that is. Must be after my time. Basically, it means someone can steal a part of you and sell it and you'd be buggered."

"What? Why would they bugger you?" Blunt asked. "I mean, that's really kicking a man when he's down."

"I didn't mean that they literally bugger you, Blunt. You knew that." She pointed a scalpel at him as she looked down at the corpse.

"It is black market organ dealing, so because of this problem, people have links to their bodies. So can we trace the Marquis?"

"Possibly. The devices are supposed to trace bodies, not heads, as there is no profit in stealing a person's head, at least no simple profit. Normally the body company takes the head in, wires it up, and it tells their computer where the body is via some kind of radar."

"GPS?"

"I don't know what that is."

"Global positioning system, it's—"

"It doesn't matter. We don't live on a globe, so no, it isn't GPS. It uses clairvoyance."

"Clairvoyance?"

"Yes, you know, like those people who find water,

dowsers or something."

"It doesn't matter. Carry on."

"Anyway, it locates the body, and the head and body are reunited. Problem is, this time we have the body and not the head."

"I think we need to pay a visit to the body company."

"I agree completely, but before we do, there's something else. Something that Mr Mortimer said made me think."

Blunt made a face of mock surprise. "Something Mortimer said?"

"Very amusing," she said as she waved him over to the side of the room where a metal dish was sitting. Inside, covered in what appeared to be rags, was a single gold key.

"Let me guess: a key to the city?"

"Exactly. You catch on quick, don't you?"

Blunt didn't even crack a smile before he spoke. "He was due to be at the ceremony and so was the—"

"So was what?"

"The, uh, the press. So were the press. Him not being there has ruined a fantastic photo opportunity, which in turn will have some effect on his PR company. On top of that, he won't be around to hand the key over, so maybe, and this is pure guess work, maybe he planned this himself so he could keep the key." Blunt was sweating as he spoke, desperately trying to backtrack.

Sarah paused and slowly put the scalpel down on the surface next to the metal tray. "If that were the case, wouldn't he have kept the key? And are you forgetting that he was pretty much the bookies' favourite to receive the keys to the city this time round? After the Grim Reaper, of course. I hope you've got better ideas than that, Blunt."

"It was just a thought. Anyway, where did you find the key?"

Sarah was lost in thought. She looked up and remembered he was there. "Oh sorry, what was that?" she asked.

"The key. Where did you find it?"

"Oh, it was on a necklace. I think the only reason it didn't come off was because it was held so tightly to his chest by his shirt."

"Well, good work. It gives us something to go on at least. Was that everything?"

"No, no, certainly not," she said, waving him further along the bench. Sealed within two plastic bags were the button and the shopping list retrieved from the scene. "I'm sure you recognise the list of items and the single black button complete with brown threads attached."

Blunt nodded his head slightly and grunted.

"Well, it turns out that the hairs are very specific, not from a coat at all, as you told Mortimer off for assuming. The button is not traceable, but the threads come from a very specific manufacturer, one that has been out of business for some time, a toy manufacturer." She looked at him expectantly.

"And?"

"Honestly, Blunt, think about it. How well do you think a toy manufacturer is going to do here in Gloomwood, the land of the dead?"

"Surely that depends entirely on what sort of toy they make. I mean, board games are played by people of all ages; look at chess. Technically, toy makers make chess, draughts, and all those other board games that I won't mention due to copyright infringement."

"Hmm, I suppose so, but I meant your traditional toy bears, train sets, that kind of thing. The point is that, now and then, somebody starts up a toy shop and then realises there aren't really any kids in Gloomwood."

"Well?"

"The fingerprints."

Blunt shook his head and said, "I know, you don't have them on record, completely useless, etc. Thanks for the reminder."

"Not completely useless. They're unusual in one crucial aspect."

Blunt glared at her and blew air out, making his cheeks inflate. "Spit it out, woman," he spluttered.

"Thank you for reminding me I work with someone who would actually speak to me like that. You're a misogynist."

"I don't care. Tell me what it is you have to say."

"The fingerprints are small. Smaller than an adult's fingers would be."

"So they're a child's prints?" Blunt asked, puzzled.

She shook her head. "Not a child's prints."

Blunt held a hand up to stop the conversation. "Now hang on, I might be new to this whole corpse-life thing, but I'm pretty sure a kid tried to mug me just yesterday," he said.

"Well, there are people who look like children, Blunt. Of course there are because there are people who die as children. They don't stay children forever though, maybe in appearance, but that's more by choice than anything else."

"So that was an adult who chose to appear to be a child? Actually, that makes more sense than I thought," he said, remembering the child shouting about his parents being dead for eighty years; it hardly suggested a youthful outlook on life.

"We're getting away from the point. The brown fibres—"

"—yup, brown fibres, I'm with you."

"Good. Now the place that made these went out of business about twenty years ago. It only stayed open about six months, and that was mainly because of its novelty value. It was the first toy shop in about ten years. Anyway, the hair comes from a speciality line of handmade brown teddy bears."

"So the murderer had a teddy bear?"

"That's right."

The two fell into silence, neither of them sure how to continue.

Eventually, Sarah broke the silence. "Shall we look at the shopping list?"

Blunt nodded, grateful for the change of subject.

"Well, it's an odd list, that's for sure. I mean, apart from the Marquis' head and possibly the words' *sharp object*, we could call it fairly normal. I was thinking about this last night, and I don't think it's for a birthday, or at least I can think of an alternative."

"Let me guess, the Changing of the Keys, just like Mortimer said?"

"In one, Detective, well done. I've also done an analysis of the handwriting, and it too suggests that it was written with a child's hand."

Sarah ran a hand through her hair. As she did it, her hand vanished. It was an eerie thing to watch. After taking a deep breath, she spoke much more quietly than she had before. "There are children here. Plenty of children arrive here. I mean, not as many as adults, but still a fair few. Most of them, after a while, decide to have changes made to make them appear like adults. A few people decide they shouldn't ever change."

"So we go visit them, and one of them is our killer."

"Yes, on the surface of it that would be the answer, but they still count into the thousands and, well, most of them live in one part of town." She said it with a grimace.

"And…"

"Well, we aren't usually welcome in those parts as, well, adults."

Blunt shrugged. "I'm the chief investigator. I don't like it, but I've got to do it and I'll go where the investigation is. I couldn't give a toss what a bunch of snot-nosed brats have to say about it," he said.

All appearances of politeness disappeared from Sarah's face, and then her entire head vanished. "Being reckless isn't going to help you here, Blunt. The part of town we're talking about isn't even entered by the police. It's run by the Youth Order. They're serious trouble," she said, though Blunt could no longer see her speaking.

"I'm dead. How serious can they be?"

"Nothing's been proven, but the rumours suggest that they're skull crushers."

"What?"

"The only way to eliminate someone from Gloomwood completely is to destroy their skull. I'm trying to tell you that if these guys are involved, the Marquis isn't coming back. They, well, Ableforth, Blunt. They deal in… no, it's worse. They condone Ableforth."

Blunt looked at Sarah and raised an eyebrow as he spoke. "I'm not expecting the Marquis to come back; I'm expecting to find the criminals who did this."

"Before you go calling anyone a criminal, I'd make sure you had your facts right."

"I'm a detective, Doctor. I know how to investigate a crime, thank you," Blunt said. Then he turned and shoved the door hard. It rattled against the door frame, so he grabbed the handle and pulled, opened it, and walked out of the room.

"What are you going to do?" she asked, chasing after him. "You don't even know where it is."

Blunt didn't even turn around. "I'm calling Mortimer. He's got to be useful for something."

"Look, before you do that, what about the body company?"

Blunt stopped and asked, "What about them?"

"Honestly, you're running around without thinking things through. You don't have a clue about Gloomwood. The body company should be the first stop. They might have a lead for you."

Blunt turned slowly, "Really? Why thank you, Miss Von Faber, that's very helpful. Any other helpful bits of advice from the woman who literally can't find her own arse with both hands?" Before she could answer, he ducked out the door, slamming it behind him.

27

Miss Leighton Hughes, reporter extraordinaire, had been fired for the press release fiasco; she wasn't particularly bothered about it. She'd decided to quit anyway, at least that's what she told herself. The truth was that she'd have stayed behind that desk forever because it felt a little like working as a proper journalist again. It had all the worst aspects of the job without any of the satisfaction.

She'd walked into work and been ushered into the manager's office, where she was told to take a seat before she could even drop her handbag. There followed an uncomfortable ten-minute conversation where Leighton slowly managed to piece together the garbled sentences her manager let slip. His constant fidgeting, throat clearing, and inability to meet her eye told her that she was fired before the man could say, "I'm afraid we're going to have to let you go," which is the phrase people use because they won't say, "you're fired," as it's too confrontational.

At one point she had been given the impression that the office would have fallen apart without her, which was of course absolute rubbish, but it was expensive training new members of staff. She had been saving, slowly building up to returning to university to get a brand new degree in post-life journalism. Part of her had always expected to be given a chance at the paper, even if she couldn't stand the place.

Instead, she had been made a scapegoat to appease the Office of the Dead, who, without ever saying anything, always somehow insinuated that they demanded retribution for any mistake at their expense. Particularly if it could be used as a source of amusement; amusement was something hated by bureaucrats living or dead, but particularly by the dead who had a lot of time on their hands for sullen brooding.

The sacking had enraged her. She'd stormed out of the office and raced home so she could throw herself on her bed and sob for half an hour. When she was done, she sat in her dressing gown on the sofa eating things that were bad for her, particularly chocolates and ice cream that contained pralines, while watching rubbish television. After wasting half a day watching shows talking about the presenters of other shows, she decided enough was enough. If nobody else was going to report the real news, then she would.

So she set herself up at home. She bought herself a flashy-looking mechanised screen projecting typewriter, and read through the papers, looking for possible leads to more interesting things. The first and most obvious story to follow up was the demise of the Marquis of Muerto Lago. The papers were filled with tributes to the man, which was more than a little presumptuous, as there was still a chance he would be found and reunited with his body. Oddly, nobody seemed to want to know what had actually happened to him.

A piece on his life would be just one more in an already saturated market. It wasn't really investigative journalism the way Leighton thought of it. Nobody knew how he'd been, well—she'd have to come up with a better word—decapitated and stolen and now this chief investigator person had turned up out of nowhere.

Now that was something worth investigating. Who was the Chief Investigator? What could he tell us about the case and possible suspects? Why had nobody else reacted to the story? Why wasn't the Grim Reaper investigating? If it wasn't important enough for the big man to take a look at, then why not just throw it to the police? They'd find somebody to pin it on within hours, and they'd elicit a confession to make it plausible.

It seemed that everyone else just didn't think it was news. They were all so used to reporting celebrity rubbish they'd lost the plot. Every paper was smeared with a picture of the Marquis with other celebrities giving tribute, but not one of them gave more than a couple of lines on page seven to the mystery surrounding his disappearance.

There was something strange about the way it had been reported, and the way that this chief investigator was announced. Normally, the Grim Reaper would come out in person to solve a mystery like this. No, that wasn't quite right; the Grim Reaper came out in person to deal with a known criminal but never really investigated anything.

She smiled to herself. For the first time in a long time, she felt empowered. She'd posted her resignation to the office when she went out to buy the laptop. She'd already been sacked, but the disorganisation at the office would probably mean someone would forget. A letter of resignation would mean she could claim she quit even if she hadn't.

There was only one course of action remaining. It was time to go to the library.

She dressed in a grey trouser suit that said she meant business, but that she wasn't a corporate bitch. Over the top, she wore a long beige coat and finally, to prove that she was a journalist, she wore a small trilby hat, with a rectangular piece of card tucked into the surrounding ribbon. The card didn't say anything, but she felt it added to her credentials as a serious journalist. She bundled the laptop into a brown leather bag and set off for the library.

The library gave Leighton Hughes the creeps, yet she knew she wasn't going to be a hard-hitting investigative journalist if she bolted at the first sign of a little creepiness. She was hoping to do some research, but the biggest problem with the library— and there were plenty—was the librarians, furtive little people who were merely waiting for the day when they would adorn the bookshelves.

It was nearly impossible to get any help from them, and if they did pay you attention for longer than the three seconds it took for them to tell you to be quiet, you normally ended up with a sticker on the side of your head telling you where you'd be placed in the future. Leighton had spent every day for a month in the library when she worked for the university, but she'd had to quit when the depressing atmosphere got too much for her.

The library was the second oldest building in Gloomwood, with the first being the Office of the

Dead. Unfortunately, the library didn't have the same refurbishment system in place. Parts of it hadn't been visited by a patron in centuries, and others weren't even visited by the staff.

The central administration desk was, logically, in the centre of the ground floor. Which meant from any entrance (there were five) it took nearly twenty minutes just to walk to the main desk. It didn't matter which entrance you used; the journey was a harrowing experience.

Heads lined the corridors, and now and then a spark of what was once a person burst out of them, usually a cruel and bitter spark that refused to fade away. It didn't matter that she was prepared for it; she still felt sick by the time she was halfway. When she reached the main desk, she was in tears, but the woman behind the counter wasn't surprised. "Tissues are on the counter, love. Take a few minutes and give me a shout when you're ready," she said. Leighton was too tearful to reply. She grabbed a handful of tissues and collapsed into a chair.

Maybe she wasn't strong enough to deal with the sort of ordeal the library offered, but then most people weren't. The problem was that she needed to be; she needed to be the strongest bad-ass reporter Gloomwood had ever seen, going straight for the heavy hitting stories and ignoring all the petty celebrity snapping. Leighton Hughes, reporter extraordinaire. In years to come, people would win the Leighton Hughes award for investigative journalism. It would be Gloomwood's Pulitzer Prize. She balled up the tissues and walked to the desk with purpose.

"Leighton Hughes, investigative journalist. I'm a woman on a mission, so no time to dilly dally. I need to find your section on—"

"Oh look at you now, don't you feel a hundred times better?"

"Listen lady—"

"Now, now, calm yourself, dear. It's just the tissues making you feel like that. Take a few deep breaths and you'll feel a million times better."

"What?" She looked at the tissues and felt a pit of embarrassment welling up inside. *Thompson's feather-soft feelbetters, now infused with egoboost, making your fears, disappointments, and terrors fade away.* Feelbetters were new to the market, and she couldn't deny they worked. Bloody Thompson's, always coming up with new ways to change your world.

"Sorry about that, I was wondering if you could show me where I could find details on entries into Gloomwood."

"I'm sorry, dear, do you want historical information on Gloomwood?"

"No, it's my fault; I want to look at the records made when people first arrive in Gloomwood."

The little old lady behind the counter removed her glasses and started to polish them with the sleeve of her cardigan as she spoke. "Oh, well the electoral roll will tell you everyone in Gloomwood and when they arrived."

"Great. I'm trying to find out about one person in particular. His name's Augustan Blunt," Leighton said, bouncing up and down in excitement as the woman looked at her computer screen.

"Well now, I believe that one will be in our new clairsentience system. You can access it over there in the booth. Looks like an old typewriter. Just type his name in and all the references will print out. Just be careful with it as it can be a bit sensitive."

Leighton beamed at the woman, who seemed a little put out by her enthusiasm. "Thank you so much for your help," she said.

"You're welcome, dear. I hope you find what you're looking for," the old woman said. It wasn't genuine. She said it in a way that showed she'd said it a hundred times before and couldn't have cared less. "Now hold still," the librarian said as she brandished a stamp, and before Leighton could move, she felt sudden pressure on her cheek. It left behind a damp mark that left red on her fingers when she rubbed it. She didn't care. It wasn't the first time she'd been stamped.

She sat down in front of the clairsentience machine. The strange contraption did have the appearance of an old typewriter. It could have been mistaken for one if it wasn't for the addition of a grinning skull that sat where the ribbon would have been. Wires were attached to the back of the macabre attachment where the spine would have been when it was part of a body.

She cracked her knuckles and typed in *Augustan Blunt*. Every time she pressed a key, the machine shook and the jaw of the skull opened and closed. When she finished, she hit the enter key and the eyes of the skull glowed a deep crimson colour.

"AUGUSTAN BLUNT... SEARCHING." The skull spoke with a deep rasping voice that shook the typewriter and the desk it was sitting on. Leighton couldn't help but sigh as she waited. Eventually the eyes of the skull flashed several times and a piece of black paper with white writing began juddering out of the top of the machine.

There were four entries on the paper. Each one had a partial printout of the piece the reference came from. The first entry was from the electoral roll. It showed that Blunt was registered at one hundred and eighty-five Pale Avenue Flat 4B. It didn't give any details of his death, or when he had arrived in Gloomwood, not that Leighton had expected either. Interestingly, his registration to the roll was done directly through the Office of the Dead. apparently when he was appointed to the position of chief investigator, which meant he hadn't been registered before. Nobody not registered to vote could hold any kind of government office. As nearly everyone who entered Gloomwood took up some kind of public service position, very few people slipped through the gaps.

The next entry was the press release about Blunt's recruitment to the position of chief investigator. There was no sub-reference to a job advertisement, which suggested the role was created specifically for Blunt. Leighton scribbled notes on the paper as she read; she circled a question, "Why Blunt?" There were numerous others in the city who could have taken the position. It stood to reason that he was extremely qualified for the role, which was strange because he apparently hadn't been in the city more than a few days, and there must be thousands of things he wouldn't know. She caught herself biting on the end of her pen as she thought about it and felt it unexpectedly crunch beneath her teeth. She quickly placed it on the desk and flipped to the next reference.

It was from yesterday's newspaper in a piece about the Marquis. Blunt barely received a whole sentence: "Chief Investigator Augustan Blunt is investigating the Marquis' unfortunate demise." It was useless to Leighton, but she was undaunted.

With only four references being found about the chief investigator, she already knew that he was a newcomer to Gloomwood, and it appeared that he had somehow managed to get the Grim Reaper to appoint him as chief investigator to an entirely new department of Gloomwood's government. She couldn't help but be a little impressed. Whatever Blunt was, he was a smooth operator, clearly capable of intricate politics, and he must be massively qualified in the arena of police work and criminal investigations.

Leighton wasn't afraid of admiring the subjects of her work. She knew how to maintain her objectivity and an interest in the subject only increased her motivation. All the same, she wasn't accustomed to relishing an upcoming meeting with someone involved in a high-profile story. Of course, it might have had a little to do with her excitement at working on a proper story again after all this time.

She flipped over the sheet with the article about the Marquis and found something she wasn't expecting.

**** Office of the Dead internal mail***

For the eyes of the manager only

Top level request for the rapid delivery of one Augustan Blunt to the Office of the Dead.

Permission granted to use most direct method of transport and to bypass unnecessary bureaucracy.

Undue attention to be avoided. Do not use outside agencies.

Discretion required.

END MESSAGE

She read it twice to make sure she hadn't made a mistake, but the official secrets' stamp was on the top of the sheet. The skull had passed her a lead she should never have seen. For a moment, she panicked. She was hoping for something big, but stepping on the toes of the Office of the Dead was a dangerous game. She couldn't help thinking that it was unlikely that it had never happened before, but the fact that it was unheard of meant it was a very dangerous thing to do. The question on her mind now was what to do next.

28

Constable JJJ Johnson felt sick. He'd watched the woman convulsing in front of him for half an hour until she had thrown up the contents of her stomach. He'd rolled her over to make sure she wouldn't choke on it, not that it would have killed her, but it would have been unpleasant coughing up vomit for the next few days.

The acrid smell of vomit mixed with the stench of Oblivion made his stomach churn in protest, but he was going to have to hold his nerve. He sat on the wooden floor. His grey uniform, now powdery as dust, attached itself to the scraggly fibres. With his legs crossed, he read over the note that had been addressed to him. It was the writing of a junkie, but at some point in the past, the writer had possessed beautiful penmanship. Swooping, curling letters wove across the page, making the note something beautiful to look at regardless of the content.

Johnson had tried repeatedly to find a way to decipher the handwriting, to discover what lay beneath the facade of terrified words.

Dear Constable Johnson,

I write to you in desperation, for I fear the matter has gone beyond the reach of my meagre resources and now puts the very fate of the city in grave peril. Please heed my words while I still have the capacity to divulge this information. Those who have been given the freedom of the city hold the answers.

Beware the girl with eyes of buttons and follow the sound of the chorus, for only they can restore the rightful order of things. I beseech you, do not take these for the ramblings of a poor mad woman or a cry for attention. My role in this is small and I would want it no other way.

Yours,

Gwendolene.

From the poorly covered window on the opposite side of the room, he could see day had broken some time ago. He had spent the night staring at the letter and waiting for this woman to wake up. He didn't know why, but for some reason, he knew this was something he couldn't walk away from.

He folded the letter up once again and slid it into the inside pocket of his police coat. That name, *Gwendolene*, sounded like some kind of cleaning product, but beyond that, he was clueless. He tucked the piece of paper away carefully, fearful that it might be an important piece of evidence that he was in danger of corrupting. As he slipped it back into the safety of his pocket, there was a gasp.

Looking up quickly, he saw that the woman sat cross-legged, staring at him with eyes that didn't see. They were milky white and clouds seemed to swirl within them.

"Constable Johnson, 'tis you?" Her voice rasped.

She spoke in an old fashioned way. It wasn't uncommon in Gloomwood, since people from throughout the ages had been drifting there for centuries.

"Yes, ma'am, I'm Constable Johnson. You sent me a letter?"

'Twas I who sent for you. For how long have you watched my wretched state?"

"Not long, ma'am, but you need help."

"Kindness is welcomed, but naivety is not a virtue in those who uphold the law. I am beyond saving. Were I not, then I would surely seek it."

"Nobody is beyond help, ma'am."

"Be that as it may, you are not here to help a lost soul like me. You are here about the letter."

Johnson stared at the woman, unsure of how to progress. She was a wreck, her body riddled with rot and the putrid odour of corpse pouring off her. It was a common symptom of those who were addicted to Oblivion. It didn't concern him. He'd been around it enough, witnessed it enough, to know that the addiction was a disease. Once, a long time ago, he'd even been there himself, not that the police knew. That was his secret, but it made him empathetic, understanding of the woman's feelings. Still, he wasn't here to save her. "Tell me about the letter," he said.

"Indeed, the letter. Well now, I penned the note, so where better to begin your search. Except that I remember naught of what was written, nor do I ever expect to. I am a conduit to the thoughts of others, you see."

"Of course you are, Gwendolene."

"Hah, Gwendolene. My name is Rosalind. You see, I am not the one you seek."

"But you wrote it. Surely you can help."

"Not I, not I." Her voice sent a chill up his spine.

"Okay, maybe we had better talk about this down at the station. We have procedures for addicts, you know," he said with no malice in his voice.

The woman sat silent for a while, her lips pursed, and Johnson began to wonder if she had fallen back to sleep. Her eyes fell shut, and she rocked from side to side, gently humming a lullaby. After a minute of this, he decided his journey had been wasted, a fool's errand following a letter from a pitiful woman whose mind was addled from narcotics abuse. He had moved to leave when she cried out.

"Wait." Her voice was clear, without the rasping that had been there a moment ago. "Don't leave me here, don't leave me inside this mad woman's head."

He looked at the figure before him. She sat straight now, no longer hunched over as if her head was a burden too great to carry. "What does that mean?" he asked.

"I wrote the letter, through this wretched body's hands, but the thoughts were mine. Poor Rosalind is lost, and she is taking me with her, but first you must know it all."

"What? Who are you?"

"I am what we once were, Rosalind Gwendolene the Third, the Duchess of Hallows End."

"That means nothing to me."

"Think nothing of it; most have long since forgotten. I was the first, and so they came for me before the others, but they failed and I have hidden here since. You must stop them because now I know what will happen to us. They will come for me again before the week is over." And then she told it all, and the burden passed on to a man who was nothing but lost hope.

"Come with me. I can protect you," Johnson said.

"You can't, and you shouldn't. This thing needs to be stopped, but I am not concerned with my own existence."

29

Ralph Mortimer was having a bad day. He went to his office, where he was greeted by a memo from Neat, ordering him to report to the manager's office as soon as possible.

When he arrived there, he was told to detail everything Blunt had so far uncovered, which was, as far as he was aware, nothing. This led to another bollocking. By eleven o'clock he was perilously close to depression, but nobody survived eternity in Gloomwood without the ability to bounce back from adversity.

Instead of wallowing in self-pity, he got on with his work. He had plenty to do. He contacted a recruitment agency and arranged for four possible receptionists to interview with Blunt first thing the next day. Then he contacted the bank and ordered an account to be opened for the chief investigator. They were more than happy to oblige when he explained there would be a wage paid in by the Office of the Dead.

After that, he contacted payroll to give them the bank details of Sarah and Blunt. They kicked up a bit of a fuss about the lack of a signed contract, but Mortimer assured them the contracts were in the post. After clearing the matter up, he called the contracts department and requested standardised contracts for two temporary employees as per Neat's instructions and that copies should be delivered to payroll as soon as possible.

He'd been having doubts about the situation he was in. Blunt's previous, almost amicable attitude towards him had soured. Or maybe it was just the investigator's general attitude that he was starting to dislike. Either way, any amount of guilt for the predicament he'd helped to orchestrate seemed to have passed. Mortimer was well on his way to a promotion, and he wasn't too concerned about how he got it any more.

Everything was in hand and he was carrying on with his usual duties, which had begun to build up, when he received a phone call that ruined his day.

The call had come from the central administrator's office, from a special unit run by people who rarely left the building. Their job was simple: prevent the public from knowing what they didn't need to know. Mortimer didn't know a lot about them, but then he wasn't supposed to. Nobody was. Knowing that they even existed was enough to get a person into serious trouble.

He'd been assigned to assist Blunt for the simple reason that he knew something he wasn't supposed to. Telling somebody else would just have complicated matters, so he had become embroiled by default. Neat had to keep a low profile, and Blunt had nothing apart from the case, which left only Mortimer. In the end, he was responsible for everything. He'd be damned—or even more damned than everyone else in Gloomwood—if he was going to be made into a scapegoat if they didn't stop the head hunter.

Mortimer sighed, ran his hands through his hair,

and shook his head. He was Ralph Mortimer, so he knew he was probably going to end up looking the fool, and he'd go back to being a dogsbody for whoever would be his next boss.

The phone call posed a serious security risk, and he knew the minute he put down the phone that it was probably trouble for him. Someone had accessed the Office's internal database and seen a classified memorandum from the manager of the Office of the Dead to the Independent Soul Recovery Division, commonly known as the Reapers. It was bad news; someone out there was looking into things they weren't supposed to, and if certain things were discovered and brought into the public domain, there would be serious repercussions.

Somebody knew that Blunt had been rushed into Gloomwood and he had already been appointed chief investigator. If they discovered why, then things would turn very nasty very quickly. Everything was on Mortimer's shoulders, but that wasn't the worst of it. He knew that it wouldn't take long for the spooks to get involved.

He decided to put the phone call to the back of his mental to-do list and concentrate on more immediate matters. Next week was a big week in Gloomwood; the Changing of the Keys ceremony was taking place. As Gloomwood's answer to a centenary celebration, it gave people the opportunity to celebrate something, and the people of Gloomwood had precious little enough to celebrate as it was.

The ceremony was normally conducted by the Master of Ceremonies, but people also expected to see the Grim Reaper. When he wasn't there, the city would implode. There would be pandemonium and it didn't matter how scared people were of Crispin Neat; they would quickly decide that he was little more than a mouth-piece for the Grim Reaper.

The city wasn't run by a democratically elected government, although there was some democracy involved. The Grim Reaper was the ruler, and that was something that would never be questioned. Beneath him, there were several factions of government, one of which was the Office of the Dead. They were responsible for the maintenance of the city, the organisation of things like the streetlights, local services such as post offices, and, of course, taxes. For this reason, they were civil servants employed by the city but not voted into office.

The policy makers, at least in theory, were the mayor's office and the governor's office. Traditionally, they did pretty much the same job, and each one came from a different political party. They were voted into power every five years. It was done in a random, anonymous process whereby everyone voted and whoever got the most votes as an individual took office. There was no campaigning, at least not officially. Instead, those standing for office had one opportunity to write a case for their election. It was hoped that this would lead to a fairer political system, less overloaded with PR stunts and marketing scams. In reality, it meant little.

The traditional holders of the keys were the two people who had held government office the longest, normally the current governor and mayor. Then the Grim Reaper held a key and two people were always chosen who were not in any government office. There was a key for the leader of the largest religious group of the time, if there was a religious group, and finally the official greeter of Gloomwood, a person who had been chosen to welcome any guests from alternative lands of the dead, not that they were ever called into service. Mortimer scribbled down the list of names and was about to pick the phone up to ring Blunt when it began ringing.

"Ralph Mortimer, third assistant to the manager of the Office of the Dead, speaking. How can I help?"

"Mortimer, it's me." Blunt's voice boomed out of the receiver, and Mortimer had to hold it away from his ear. "Listen, the evidence so far points towards a child—well, not a child, but a person in a child's body—having attacked the Marquis. Sarah also thinks we might be able to find out where the Marquis is by using his body. Look, hurry up and get down here. I need to get to this body company place."

"Body company?" Mortimer said.

"Yeah, the place that he got his body from. Apparently, the body and head are linked to prevent body snatchers. Unfortunately, we've got a head snatcher, though it might still help."

"You mean Hare and Burke's?"

"Is there more than one of these companies?" Blunt asked.

"Well yes, but Hare and Burke's is the most famous, and probably the most exclusive."

"Sarah didn't say who she'd spoken to. Get over

here so we can get moving," Blunt said. There was a click, and Mortimer sighed into the mouthpiece of the phone.

30

Toe-Dee Sicofant was a born yes-man. Unimaginative, starved of attention and affection, he had spent his life crawling up the backside of anyone and everyone who would allow him access to their shirt-tails. In the end, he was framed for the murder of his boss's wife. He didn't turn his boss in, believing what he was doing was for the best. He was murdered in prison by a man with a sharpened toothbrush.

When a man in a black cape collected him and took him to Gloomwood, Toe-Dee followed quite happily. He was impressed by Willowford's scythe and how he commanded the situation, not to mention his powerful-sounding name. When Willowford left him at the gates of the deathport, Toe-Dee didn't worry too much about what he would do. He simply followed directions and kept a lookout for the next person who needed a yes-man. There were plenty of them around.

In the end, he found a perfect niche, propping up the grossly exaggerated ego of the high priest of the Church of Mankind's Everlasting, Eternal Purgatory. Toe-Dee was only too happy to take religious vows and join a small but organised unit of do-gooders who worked under the name of religion.

They collected money from parishioners and did good deeds. When Toe-Dee made the leap into the role of Grand Assistant to the High Priest, he did so with modesty and grace, and with no small amount of gratuitous brown-nosing. His ability to fawn over his superiors with a shower of compliments and adoring concurrence verged on the obscene. His appointment was met with good grace by his competitors, who saw in him not a rival but a future assistant should their day at the top ever come.

Everything was fine with Toe-Dee. He was as happy in death as he was in life. That was, of course, until he opened his master's chamber door to discover his worst nightmare before his eyes. His master was sans head, and as nobody else was higher up in the religion than the grand assistant, he was the de facto high priest. If there was ever a man born to follow, it was Toe-Dee Sicofant, and now he had to lead. The first thing he did, as any good sheep would do, was call the leader of a bigger flock.

31

In a very dark, small, confined, and strangely cosy place somewhere a conversation took place. It went like this:

"H-hello?"

"Hello. Who's that?"

"None of your business. Who's that?"

"I'm not sure anymore. I've been here some time."

"Oh, right. Where are we?"

"I have no idea. Do you?"

"Well, I wouldn't have asked if I knew."

"Wherever it is, it's very dark."

"Yes it is, isn't it?"

"Do you want to play twenty questions?"

"What?"

"Do you want to play twenty questions? It's a game."

"I know what it is. Shouldn't we be trying to find a way out?"

"Can you move?"

"Um…no."

"So..."

"Fine, fine, I'll play twenty questions. Who's going first?"

"You can go first."

"Okay, I'm thinking of something."

"Oh, I meant you can guess first. That's okay though. I'll guess first."

"No-no, if you've got something good, go ahead. Mine wasn't very difficult."

"Well, is it animal, mineral, or vegetable?"

"What?"

"Is it an animal, mineral, or vegetable?"

"I thought you could only ask yes or no questions. I thought I was guessing, anyway."

"Right... shall we start again? Or would you prefer a bit of a sing-song?"

"Just shut-up, will you?"

"That was rude..."

"I'm sorry. I'm just a little stressed. I think a little girl might have done something to me."

"Yes, she got me too, I'm afraid, although I did try to get her first."

"Really? Well, this is ridiculous. I always said there was something unnatural about people running around in children's bodies."

"That is how they died."

"Oh great, you're probably one of their sympathisers. Next you'll be telling me the Grim Reaper is always right."

"I would never say that, although he is rarely wrong."

"Whatever."

"How about we play I spy?"

"You can see?"

"I spy with my little eye something beginning with L."

"A liar? As in you?"

"No."

"Lining, as in the lining of this bag?"

"Nope."

"Oh, what is it?"

"Light. Look right above us. It's getting bigger."

"You're right. HELP, HELP! GET US OUT OF HERE! Ouch! Did you feel that? I think someone just kicked us."

"Maybe if you hadn't screamed for help like a little girl, they wouldn't have."

"Well, what do you suggest we do?"

"Brace ourselves for impact?"

"What? OUCH! What the hell was that?"

"Oh God, I'm blind, I'm blind. The Lord has cast me down even further into my pit of eternal admonishment."

"And then there were three."

32

When Mortimer drove onto Pale Avenue, he could already see Blunt waiting in front of the building. The detective wore the same coat he had arrived in, despite the fact that Mortimer had ensured there was an expensive winter-wear woollen knit coat in the wardrobe of Blunt's room. He was relieved to see that Blunt had at least bothered to change the clothes he was wearing beneath it.

He pulled up to the curb. Blunt grabbed the handle of the door and awkwardly climbed into the car. In his free hand, he carried a tray with two coffees on it. "Here, I figured you might want a coffee," the detective said.

Mortimer's eyes opened wide. "Thank you, that's very, um, thoughtful of you," he said.

"Yeah, well, I wasn't sure what I was ordering. Everything's got different names here. Well, every coffee shop has different names, but you lot—I suppose I mean us lot—don't even seem to know the name for a simple black coffee."

As he released the handbrake and pulled into the road, Mortimer glanced at Blunt and said, "I don't understand."

"Well, I got one for Sarah too. I mean, I would've got you coffee anyway because I'm nice, obviously, but in this circumstance I only got you coffee as an excuse to try three different types. Anyway, yours is the Morbidius Macchiato. Tastes a bit too, um, perfumey for me."

Mortimer grabbed the cup and took a mouthful, wincing as he felt it burn the inside of his mouth. "Well, very nice of you all the same. Am I driving to Hare and Burke's?" he asked,

Blunt reached under the seat and moved his chair as far back as possible. "Yup, Hare and Burke's Physical Manifestations Emporium. Sounds very flash," he said.

"It's just around the corner. You could've walked," Mortimer said.

Blunt nodded. "I could've, but where would I have been then? By myself at a place I'm bound to find a little bewildering. You're supposed to be assisting," he said.

Mortimer sighed. "Of course, sorry, I'm here to help," he replied.

He turned left off Pale Avenue, then took a series of back alleys until they came out on another busy road near the canal. "Waterside Park is a fancy development by the canal. Hare and Burke's are right in the middle of it. Look, just there," Mortimer said as he pointed to an archway with the word *Waterside* carved into the stone. Beyond the archway, a series of buildings, brilliant white with a huge array of windows, looked over a large pond area.

They were stopped at the archway by a security guard, who asked where they were going. Mortimer flashed his credentials and was waved through. He took the car around the pond and pulled up outside an entrance to one of the buildings. A simple silver sign on the wall marked it as Hare and Burke's Physical Manifestations Emporium.

A man in a red overcoat and top hat met the car and opened Mortimer's door. "Welcome to Hare and Burke's, sir. Do you have an appointment?" he asked.

"Ah, no, actually I'm here with Chief Investigator Blunt. We're investigating the incident with the Marquis," Mortimer said as he stepped out of the car. The man seemed satisfied with that, and he took Mortimer's keys to park the car.

Mortimer led Blunt through a set of sliding double doors and they walked towards a woman sitting behind a reception desk. The main entranceway was a huge expanse of empty space. Glass elevators moved up and down through the centre of the building, and as Blunt looked upwards, he could see people walking across transparent bridges that spanned the space around the central elevator column.

The woman behind the desk was dressed in a skin-tight white PVC suit. Mortimer swallowed nervously as they got closer.

"Like what you see?" the woman asked.

Blunt stepped in front of Mortimer as he struggled to answer.

"Yes, very nice, now—"

"It's from our summer collection—the body, I mean, not the suit, of course—available now, though you may prefer a more masculine image. Are you here to view or for attachment?"

Blunt spoke quickly. "If you'd allow me to finish, we're here about the Marquis' recent beheading and we were hoping someone from your security section could help us." As Blunt spoke, the woman's hand went beneath the desk.

Before she had even spoken, two large men arrived in matching black PVC skin suits. The woman leant forward over the desk and introduced them. "These are our male summer collection models. This one is Espirit de Luna; it's the male version of the one I am currently using. And this is Machismo." She indicated the other man, who looked like he had been on a serious steroid, protein, and weight-training programme.

Clearing his throat, Blunt leaned over the desk until his face was inches from the woman. "I want to see your manager," he said slowly and clearly.

Her smile grew slightly wider on her perfectly symmetrical and unblemished face. "Wonderful sir. Our Manager and Executive design range have been specifically created to embody the very essence of professionalism. One moment please," she said as she reached beneath the counter again and Mortimer watched an elevator shoot up to the fourth floor.

"Sorry, can I try please?" Mortimer asked from behind Blunt.

Blunt stepped to one side and said, "Be my guest. This woman seems unable to accept a simple request."

Mortimer stepped forward and looked the woman in the eye. "Ah, I see what the problem is. She's not actually a woman at all. It's a display model," he said.

Blunt stepped forward again, pushing Mortimer to one side. "A what? She's a woman. She's right there. We've been speaking."

"Well, actually you've been entering commands, and she's been responding to them according to her programming. Watch." Mortimer leant on the desk as he spoke. "Receptionist, please send a real person to discuss further."

"A real person?" The woman replied.

Blunt reached forward with a finger and poked the woman in the face gently. "So, she's not real?" he asked.

"Please don't touch, sir. It is inappropriate," the woman said.

Blunt pulled his hand back and stepped away from the desk. "I'm sorry, I mean, really I thought you were, well, ah," he stuttered.

"Yes, I heard him." She glared at Mortimer as she spoke. "I am a real person. I am also an extremely good professional salesperson. I wasn't being difficult. I was simply trying to make a sale. Now I will have Mr Hare come and meet you. For your information, sir, it is illegal to create a head of a person that could be in any way mistaken for a real person."

Mortimer looked away nervously while apologising. "I'm sorry. I thought, well, this place, it wouldn't surprise me if they could, you know? And I mean to say it's a compliment. After all, you are very attractive and so, um…"

"Thank you. I paid a lot of money to look this way," she said, turning away from them both and busying herself with paperwork.

The two men who had been standing nearby wandered back to the elevator and disappeared into it. Meanwhile, Blunt and Mortimer looked in every direction they could to avoid meeting the eyes of the woman at the desk. It didn't take long for Mr Hare to arrive, though Mortimer checked his watch four or five times as they waited.

"Gentlemen, I'm Mr Hare. I understand you are here regarding the Marquis' recent decapitation. I'm afraid that we have very little to do with the heads of our clients, and it is my understanding that you already have possession of his body. What exactly would you like to ask?"

Both men took a moment to take in the man before them. He was a towering figure, easily a foot taller than both of them. He wore a perfectly tailored charcoal-grey suit which hung off him better than it would a shop mannequin. While it was impossible to tell for sure, it was clear he was athletic and his chiselled jaw suggested there wasn't an inch of fat on him.

"I'm Augustan Blunt, and this is Ralph Mortimer. I wanted to ask you about the security system you have on your clients', um, bodies," Blunt said.

Hare clasped his hands together and placed his

chin on his pointed index fingers. "Ah, security. I see," he said. "Of course, this kind of thing is completely confidential. What kind of authority am I dealing with, if you don't mind me asking?"

Mortimer cleared his throat, before saying, "Actually, I suppose it would be fair to say the highest authority in the land. Mr Blunt has been appointed chief investigator for the city of Gloomwood by the Office of the Dead."

Hare didn't bat an eyelid. He clapped his hands together in front of him and smiled, showing the perfect teeth of a man who could afford the highest quality veneers. "And you are with the Office of the Dead?" he asked.

"Yes," said Mortimer.

Hare nodded and turned to the woman at the desk. "Ethel, call the Office of the Dead please and confirm the identities while I take these gentlemen to my office." He motioned Blunt and Mortimer to follow as he started towards the elevators and began talking. "The security system is really quite simple. We install a link between the owner and their body. It's nothing too complicated, and don't worry, Mr Mortimer. It is entirely legal and above board."

"How does it work?" asked Blunt.

"It's basic enough," he replied. "We have more advanced options currently going through our research and development process, though, to be completely honest with you,"—he looked them both up and down as they stepped into the elevator—"and given that it's unlikely you'll be a customer anytime soon, I can tell you that it's more of a money-making endeavour than any attempt to provide protection to the owner."

"How so?" Blunt said.

Hare rocked on his heels as the elevator shot quickly up to the top floor. Blunt watched carefully, but he couldn't detect any particular nervousness. If anything, he seemed to be treating them with something between indifference and a welcome distraction from his work. "I'll tell you more when we reach my office. This is obviously not something I would consider divulging to the public. I expect confidentiality," Hare said.

Blunt glanced at Mortimer, who was staring down at the floor of the elevator as they travelled upwards. "I can't guarantee it, but I see no reason why I would mention anything to the public that might damage your reputation," he said.

"I'm not sure if that will be sufficient."

"Do I look like a confused man to you, Mr Hare?"

"It's Doctor Hare and no, not particularly," Hare replied. The doors to the elevator slid open, and they walked along one of the strange bridge-like walkways, able to look through the floor to view people scurrying around below.

"Ah, well then, it must be you that's confused. I'm not actually here to help you out. Now, I'm not here to do you any damage either, but you will answer my questions because I'm investigating the kidnapping of a man. From what I understand, he's a fairly well known man as well, not that it should make any difference, but I doubt anybody here is naïve enough to imagine it doesn't. This man was a customer of yours and we have his body in custody. How would it look, Doctor Hare, if it came out that you were being unhelpful?" Blunt asked as he walked next to Hare, while Mortimer followed a few steps behind.

"Is that supposed to be some kind of threat?" Hare asked.

"Not at all. As I said, I've no intention of causing you or your business any harm at all. I want your help. It's just important to me that you aren't under the illusion that being unhelpful at all might benefit you in some way, unless you want to cast suspicion on your company?"

They walked into a Hare's office. An interior designer had put a lot of effort into making the room contemporary and sophisticated. A single piece of artwork was displayed on each of the four walls of the room. They were modern and abstract, one of them nothing more than a tiny grey circle on a black background. The desk, which sat in front of a large window, was teardrop-shaped. In the centre of the room was a solid glass rectangle, on either side of which were black leather sofas.

"Please have a seat," Hare said as he walked towards his desk. He pressed the surface, and a telephone popped up from an unseen panel.

As Hare conducted his phone call, Blunt turned to Mortimer. "So, is it common for people to get a whole new body?" he asked.

Mortimer had been staring at one of the pictures on the walls, this one of a black square with a splash of grey paint across it. "Not their whole body. Bits and pieces occasionally if they break. This place is more for the mega-rich. A whole new body, well that's more than my house, is worth even for a basic model. The ones from here would cost you millions," he explained.

"But people obviously buy them?"

"'Course they do. Everyone's dead. Got to do something with your money."

Blunt grunted. "Vanity is everlasting then?"

Doctor Hare took a seat opposite them. "It would appear you are both the genuine article. I apologise again for checking, but I'm sure you understand how important confidentiality is to us here," he said.

"Of course," Blunt said.

"Now, if I understand the situation correctly, you have the Marquis' body but not his head, correct?"

Blunt nodded.

"In which case, I'm not sure how we can be of much help. We can track the Marquis' body, but not his head. That's got nothing to do with us."

"The Marquis purchased his body from you?"

"Ah, no, not exactly. We use his body as a template for some of our other models."

"Is there any way we could reverse the system?" Blunt asked.

Hare stood up and walked to his desk. "Not that we can do. Sorry, but the system we use isn't that advanced. The best I can say is that the body will begin to react to being in the presence of the owner's head, meaning it will move about if it's close to the head," he said.

33

Neat sat at home. It wasn't often he spent an evening there, but tonight he needed a break away from the office.

His house was unremarkable by Gloomwood's standards. It was a middle terrace in a nice neighbourhood on the south side of the city. It was the residency that came with the position of manager of the Office of the Dead. The public knew, but they didn't really care. There was none of the fanfare or prestige associated with places like Number 10 Downing Street.

In front of him lay a plate with the crusts of a sandwich on it and half a cup of tea. He rubbed his hands through his greasy, slicked-back hair and walked across the room to the television. He hit power and sat down.

His favourite soap opera was on. *Ashes Town* depicted working class life in the west side of Gloomwood. The story lines were obscenely far-fetched and often just mysteriously faded out as the writers struggled to find a way to bring them back to reality, but he still enjoyed the show. The villainous Edgar Bowery had decided that he was going to stitch up Mary Swan and somehow manipulate her partner in business into selling him the local bar. It had just reached the crucial confrontation scene when the phone started ringing.

Neat picked it up and quickly buried any

annoyance as he said, "Crispin Neat speaking."

The voice on the other side of the phone belonged to Toe-Dee Sicofant, and the information spouting from the earpiece of the phone wasn't what Neat wanted to hear.

"You're sure?" he asked. "It couldn't have just fallen off and rolled under the bed or something?" Neat held the phone away from his ear as a barrage of high-pitched squealing erupted from it. "I'll send the chief investigator. Stay calm," Neat said.

He put the phone down and slumped back into his chair. After a moment's hesitation, he turned the volume back up on the television and watched the remainder of his show. The big scene was over, but it wouldn't take him long to work out what had happened.

Even as the front of his mind gorged itself on the meaningless tripe being spewed out by the box on the other side of the room, the sharp, lighting-quick mind of the manager of the Office of the Dead worked steadily and efficiently to compute the latest news. When the credits finally rolled up the screen, leaving viewers on another bizarre cliff hanger, he picked up the phone and tapped in the number to the office on Pale Avenue.

"Who's this? Ah, Miss Von Faber, yes I remember. Why are you answering this number? Forensics? Ah, I see. Well, tell Blunt and Mortimer as soon as you can that the high priest of the Church of Mankind's Everlasting, Eternal Purgatory has been decapitated." He didn't wait for an answer. Instead, he dropped the phone back onto its cradle and gave out a long, pensive sigh. "And now there are three!" he shouted into the empty room.

34

"What the hell is this supposed to mean?" Captain Sowercat waved the newspaper above his head while shouting at everyone and anyone on the precinct floor. "Some smartarse bastard has decided he's going to be chief bloody investigator, has he? Well, we'll see about this. Berkfield, where are we on the Marquis' headnapping?" He addressed a moustached man stuffing a doughnut into his mouth.

"Hmm, um, Marquis, Captain?" He sprayed his desk in crumbs as he spoke.

"Yes, remember the flash git with bags of money who's had his head nicked?"

"Well, we aren't anywhere, Cap'n, on account of you not having told us to investigate nuffink about it."

"Haven't told you? HAVEN'T TOLD YOU?!" The Captain had a cheap nose that tended to inflate and make him look like an elephant seal when he was angry. Right now, it covered most of his face. He'd arrested the man who'd been selling them out of a suitcase; the nostrils didn't work properly. He kept a drawer full of them so he could quickly replace them after arrests got particularly violent. For some reason, he always felt the need to try to head-butt people shorter than him.

"That's right guv," the mustachioed Berkfield said, oblivious to the fury building behind the Captain's nose.

"Has anyone in this entire bloody police force got half a brain?"

"Yes, guv, Constable Peters has only got half a brain at the minute. Some bastard got him with an axe. We've got the other half, but the lads have hidden it and we're having a sweepstake to see how long it will take him to find it. I've got next Thursday 'cos he's gonna find it tough as he keeps walking in circles."

The Captain's fist shook as he shouted, "Shut up Berkfield, shut up, before I beat you into even more of a trembling pile of jelly than you already are. Somebody else, please, tell me what you know about this bloody impostor into our legal system." Every uniform in the room suddenly looked extremely busy. Paperwork that hadn't seen the light of day for months flew around the room.

"Perhaps I can be of some help?" a voice asked from behind the Captain, who turned slowly to look back into his own office. Standing outside the building and peering into his window was a man of peculiarly elongated features.

"Oh, for crying out loud, no. I've got enough to deal with. I'm now going to have to deal with bloody Mandrake as well."

35

Will Noyers was an old man, older than any living man. Had he been alive, he would have given Methuselah a run for his money. However old Will actually was, though, he still looked like a child. He wasn't the only one who made the decision to remain as a child. There were even one or two who became more child-like when they arrived in Gloomwood.

Will had died at the age of about eleven. He couldn't be sure, as he only learnt to count after he died, and he'd long since forgotten his birthday. When he arrived, he had been a child, but he quickly grew up, and once he'd been in Gloomwood for twenty years, people began to ask him why he didn't upgrade his body to make him adult-sized at least. If his head had been on an adult body, people would just assume he was baby-faced. At first he'd made up excuses, and then he'd become angry, and eventually people stopped mentioning it.

It took a long time for him to realise that there were other people living with their child-like bodies. At the time, Gloomwood wasn't a very big place, but there were still a number of children around, and that number was growing. They did it for plenty of reasons, mainly financial and psychological. Will's reason was simple: you could get away with a lot more when you were a child. People saw a child and something inherent in their psyche told them to forgive, have patience. Will knew the value of this addition to his scoundrel's tool kit.

The other useful thing about being a child in Gloomwood, or at least having the appearance of a child, was the ability to become unseen. So few were they in numbers that they automatically banded together. Being children, and having the stigma that child-like appearances gave them, they held a lot of power.

The children of Gloomwood only feared two things: a law demanding they take adult form, and the birth of a child. The birth of a child was not something they actively worried upon, knowing it was impossible, but it was still dreaded the same way that people in the land of the living dreaded the monsters under the bed.

The Youth Order, an organisation that didn't legally exist, had a mandate that expressly demanded that all efforts to prevent children from being children should be fought against tooth and nail. Will, along with all the other children of the dead, were more than eager to follow the Youth Order.

Will Noyers wasn't an important person in any respect. He was pretty much the lowest rung on the ladder in all social circles, but at least he had social circles to move in. In Gloomwood, there were two things that almost everyone participated in. The first was supporting their local team. Everyone supported a football team. It was impossible to get away from it, and a major topic of conversation. The other was the support group. There were hundreds, possibly even thousands, of the things.

Support groups for the recently deceased, the long-term deceased, people who died in the 1890s and every decade since the dawn of time up to the present day, support groups for people who were addicted to support groups. There were groups for people who struggled with addictions and then groups for people who struggled to have an addiction, the support group for people who have no support group, the support group organisers support group, the anti-support group support group, the support group supporters group. If there was a reason for a group, and even if there wasn't a reason, there was something for everyone.

Will was a member of two groups. The first was for people who chose to remain in their pre-deceased forms. The majority of its members were people with child-like appearances just like Will (occasionally gods and demi-gods with odd appearances would join before quickly realising it wasn't a patch on the support group for those who never really died but still for some reason look weird). The second was for people who didn't see a problem with their criminal natures.

It was the second group that Will was attending a meeting with. He was sitting on a chair in a seedy nightclub on the west side of town with a motley crew of dead people. There was something about the criminally content that bred a genial atmosphere, especially when everyone knew that everyone else was equally criminally minded.

A large woman with a permanent smile ran the meetings. There was an abundance of her kind in Gloomwood. Normally they were avoided, but in community organisations such as support groups, neighbourhood watches, and bake sales, they were a requirement. With Gloomwood's massive support group culture, they practically ran the city.

"Okay, everyone, I see we've got some familiar faces and some not-so-familiar faces. Of course, that's nothing new here, so before we begin, has anyone had recent re-constructive surgery they'd like to tell us about? No, okay. So, as usual, let's start by having newcomers introduce themselves," she said. Then she beamed from ear to ear as she gestured to an uncomfortable-looking man covered in tattoos.

Awkwardly, he got to his feet and looked around the room. Across his knuckles, the words pan and fry were written. He was missing the second finger on both hands.

"Um, 'ello, my name is Richard Herringbottom, but people normally call me Richie Pounder on account of my preference for violent criminal acts. I'm here because I don't think there is anything wrong with my criminal nature," he said. A smattering of applause filled the room with a chorus of, "welcome Richie Pounder."

Will was sitting near the back of the room. He noted down the name *Richie Pounder* for future reference. A newcomer of his size, and predisposition for violent acts, was going to move up the ranks of criminal society, and Will was always looking for someone big and strong to hide behind.

The meeting was the same as usual. The newcomers explained why they'd joined, regurgitating the standard stories about how people were treating them badly because of their criminal natures. The fat woman talked about reaffirming their confidence centre and coming to terms with most people's unfair perspective regarding the criminally predisposed.

At the end of the meeting, there was the usual scramble for the sandwiches, tea, and coffee. Oddly, it was paid for by a collection bowl and all the attendees were always generous. There had never been a case of the money being stolen. Once things had quietened down and the meeting was definitely over, the bar staff appeared and began preparing the club for the night. Sawdust was liberally sprinkled over the floor, and the decent chairs were removed and replaced with the type designed to break easily; it caused fewer injuries.

Will found himself sitting at a table with a familiar bunch of miscreants. They were discussing the new chief investigator and, more importantly, what it meant for them.

"If you ask me, the whole thing stinks. It's just further evidence of the government persecuting the criminal element," a tall drunken man said as he was holding court over the table. "I mean… *chief investigator*. Well, chief of what, exactly? They're gonna fix the police force, and then they're gonna come after us."

A beast of a man crashed a tankard onto the table, spilling beer everywhere as he shouted, "Shut up, you stinkin' thief. Police is good. Right now, they're just ignoring us. How can we be proper criminals if nobody is going to stop us or punish us? You're only a criminal if there's a police force who actually tries to catch you. Don't you see? They's finally recognising us. Now it's all gonna work properly. I'm sick an' tired of robbin' places and the police just arrest some bystander and pin it on him. Where's my respect? I done the crime, I wanna escape the time."

"Police-loving hippy," was screamed from the far side of the bar, and the sound of breaking furniture followed. Will did what he always did in these situations: he found a small safe place and crept into it. Fifteen minutes later, when the fighting was over, he crept out to take whatever he could. Support group night was always a good night for picking up bonus swag. He always carried a big bag with him, just in case.

He was reaching for a wallet someone had carelessly dropped when a shoe landed on his wrist. Inside the shoe was a foot that, by some unfortunate coincidence, was attached to Augustan Blunt's body. "Right then, sunshine, you appear to be a thieving little git in the body of a child. Now leave go of that wallet, and you and me can have a little chat," Blunt said. Then he smiled and grabbed Noyers by his shirt before releasing his arm. "Oopsy-daisies," he said as he picked the thief off the ground.

Five minutes later, Blunt was in the back of Ralph Mortimer's car with Will Noyers, trying to get some kind of useful information out of him. "Listen, cretin, I need to know who in your little segment of society might have a vendetta against the Marquis, and you can either tell me or I'll take you down to the police station," he said.

Noyers stared out of the window at the traffic going by, a smile on his face. "Be my guest, Chief

Investigator. What exactly do you think they'll do?" he asked.

"Whatever I tell them to."

"I don't think you've met our police force yet, Chief. If you had, you wouldn't be so keen to believe they'd care about you, or about me."

Noyers reached into his pocket and pulled out a packet of cigarettes. He waved them vaguely in Blunt's direction. A lighter appeared in his free hand and he dragged a cigarette out with his lips, lighting it quickly. The pack and the lighter disappeared in a blur. "Gonna tell me I'm too young to smoke, Blunt?"

"Not like they can kill you," Blunt said, shrugging. "We're getting nowhere here, so let's go to your part of town. I'll drop you off, say thank you very much for all your assistance—in a nice loud voice—and tell people that it's honest-minded citizens like you that help us capture the low-life scum in this part of town."

Noyers took a long drag on the cigarette and blew the smoke out of the window. "What is it you want?" he asked, still staring at the streetlights outside.

"Answer the question. Who might have a problem with the Marquis?"

"Are you joking? Half the city hates that guy, so why are you picking on my people? Adults! You're always blaming the kids."

"Shut up, Noyers. You're older than I am. I'll level with you. We found evidence that one of your people was at the scene."

"No way, no way, would one of us do something that insane. Why would we want his head?"

"Well, you know what people say."

"Look, I know what people say, and calling us skull crushers or anything else isn't going to make me want to help you any more than I do right now."

Blunt grabbed the cigarette out of Noyers' mouth and flicked it out of the window. He shifted his bulk along the car seat, forcing the man-child further up. "Listen to me carefully. Who do you think might be able to give me some answers? Give me a name, or I will make it my sole ambition to make the rest of your eternity as miserable as I possibly can."

"Make whatever threats you like, Blunt, but you don't scare me. I'm not afraid of jumped-up newbies. Stop the car, Ralph. I'm getting out here, and we're even. I can't believe you actually let this ape come near me."

Mortimer slowed down to a crawl and looked over his shoulder. "Sorry, Will, but I don't know a lot of, well, you know, your kind of people, and you owed me a favour, so..." Mortimer said before trailing off.

"What? You let me off when I was nicking a bottle of milk off your doorstep. It's hardly equal to this."

Mortimer looked at Blunt sheepishly through the rear-view mirror. Blunt glared back with nothing but contempt as Will Noyers opened the door and hopped out of the car. "Noyers, who are the Youth Order?" Blunt asked.

"Really, Blunt, you think I'm going to start talking

about the Youth Order to you? Some things are worth keeping your mouth shut for."

"What's that supposed to mean?"

"I don't believe for a second the Youth Order are involved, but if they were, you wouldn't be able to touch them, anyway. You think Neat and the Office of the Dead have control of this city? Well, you want to take a trip into our part of town. There's only one law there, and it's the Youth Order. If I were you, I'd stop bad-mouthing them while you still can."

When the door shut behind him, Blunt scowled. "You said you had a contact who could help."

"I thought I did."

"How could he help? He steals milk bottles."

"Well, he's one of, y'know, *them*."

"A child?"

"Don't call them that; they aren't children."

"It doesn't matter, Mortimer. We've wasted two hours on a lead that went absolutely nowhere. What the hell is the matter with you?"

"Just trying to be helpful."

Blunt sat fuming in the back of the car. Then he shrugged. "Mortimer, have you heard of the phrase 'by any means necessary?" he asked.

Mortimer turned the key in the ignition and looked in the rear-view mirror. "Of course I have. I've been dead a while, but I didn't die in the dark ages," he replied.

"Good, well why don't you drop me about a hundred metres down the road and come back around the corner in, oh, say, ten minutes?" Blunt asked, attempting to be as nonchalant about the request as possible.

Mortimer put the car in gear and began rolling forward. "I think it's better if I don't know whatever it is you're about to do," he said without turning.

36

When Blunt jumped out of the car, he immediately disappeared into the shadows of a tall building and glanced down the street. Mortimer pulled the car away from the curb and drove off. The big expensive saloon was quiet, but a miscreant like Noyers hadn't remained a successful ne'er-do-well by chance.

The man-child stopped in his tracks, took a long careful look down the street in front of him, and then bolted in the opposite direction. Blunt immediately took chase. He'd never been a fast man in life. Not slow, of course. He'd done well to make sure he'd never been last in the pack of people, usually fellow policemen, who'd been running from whatever was chasing them. He had a feeling that being dead would mean he could keep running a lot quicker for a lot longer. It was all a matter of remembering he was dead, but not too much. Then he'd really remember he was dead and probably stop running completely.

His chest heaved. Then he remembered he didn't need to breathe. His heart pounded, and he told it to shut the hell up and stop whining—it was only around because he felt sympathy for it, not because it was needed. His dodgy knee wanted to collapse beneath him, but he reminded it that he could, at any time, have it replaced and feel absolutely no difference.

He found himself gaining on Noyers, who kept shooting terrified glances over his shoulder at the strange huffing red demon behind. It was one of these glances that provided Blunt with the means to catch Noyers. Despite his hope that he was now impervious to the state of his personal health, he knew that very soon the heart he didn't need would explode, the knee he could have replaced would buckle and collapse, and the lactic acid in his muscles, if there was still such a thing, would reach such ridiculously high concentrations that he would technically be a battery and his muscles would dissolve.

Noyers, lip trembling, eyes welling up as he looked over his shoulder, suddenly fell. Well, he actually tumbled and skipped off the pavement a couple of times like a smooth pebble thrown across a calm pond. Blunt reached him and picked him up by the back of his now-drenched shirt. Through gritted teeth, Blunt demanded, "A name, give me a name or I'll chase you forever."

Noyers was crying. "Sodding Ralph Mortimer, all I did was take a bottle of milk. I've never done nothing to harm nobody," he wailed.

"*That*, my young ancient friend, was a double negative, and I think you meant it to be."

The man-child squirmed desperately, flailing his legs, trying to connect with any part of Blunt's body that he could. "They'll kill me," he said.

Blunt shrugged. Not an easy task when you're holding someone up with one hand, something his body warned him he should not attempt again. "They won't know it's you. Now give me a name," he said.

"I don't know who's in charge, but… Bernie Spitspeckler will. Just let me go, and please, please don't tell them I told you."

Blunt dropped the man—who now appeared much more like a boy—to the ground and watched him run away. Once Noyers had turned the corner, Blunt collapsed to the ground and let the coloured lights that had been clouding his vision take over.

37

Leighton had parked opposite the address she'd found for Blunt's office and was watching the doors intently. She'd bought herself a cup of coffee and used the excursion to check the other buzzers on the building. There were no names on the buzzers, but the fourth floor had the words *Chief Investigator* written on it. She assumed he lived and worked in the building.

The rest of the building was empty, which wasn't strange in Gloomwood. At any given time, nearly fifty percent of the city was empty. Contractors had spent a lot of time building in preparation for more people arriving. It was the Office of the Dead's intention to never have a problem with space. So far, they had stayed well ahead of the game, but then most people thought too far ahead of the game. There were suburbs on the edge of the city that had remained empty for over a decade.

She watched out of the car window for nearly three hours, hoping to see someone enter the building. She'd used the time to begin work on her article and formulate plans for the paper.

Twice she'd visited a pay phone to check her messages and two of her newly recruited team had already called in to let her know they would be posting their first articles to her before the end of the day.

She planned to release her brand new paper to

Gloomwood the day after tomorrow. If it sold well, she'd be able to go after investment. If it didn't, she'd start job hunting. Either way, she knew that her story on the new chief investigator was going to be a make-or-break article. There wasn't a lot to go on at the minute. She knew she could hook people in by relating it to the death of the Marquis, but if the feeling she had was right, the chief investigator could be a healthy source of stories for the future.

As she looked out of the window, she saw a man sauntering down the street. He had the eyes of a recent addition to the city, still giving some of the unusual sights a double glance, like the woman across the street with four legs and the man who was carrying his head under his arm.

Two grown men were playing hopscotch on the pavement in front of the chief investigator's building, and the man she was watching walked straight through the middle of their game, oblivious to their looks of frustration and disbelief. He fumbled in his pocket and pulled out a key.

Leighton waited ten minutes before walking across the road and pressing the buzzer for the fourth floor. Nobody answered at first, so she pressed it a few more times. There was a crackling sound, and she heard some muffled expletives. "F... kin... bas... rd... wo... work. How th... hell... hello, hello?" Leighton shook her head. It was easy to associate the voice with the man she had seen a moment ago.

"Hello. Leighton Hughes for Augustan Blunt," she said with as much confidence in her voice as possible. When she had been alive, she had always found that with enough assertiveness in her voice, she could often wheedle her way into places that should have remained off limits. It worked especially well on men.

The intercom crackled again. "Do you have an appointment?"

She sighed. "No, but I need to see him urgently. Are you going to let me in or should I go elsewhere?"

There was a lengthy pause on the other side of the intercom and she listened to the static while she waited.

"Okay, come on up. I'll buzz you in," the voice answered. She waited, listening to more expletives. "Hang on, just a second." Eventually, the door buzzed, and she pushed it open.

At the top of the fourth flight of stairs, the man in the trench coat stood waiting. When he saw her, he raised an eyebrow but said nothing. She reached a hand out as she drew closer. "Leighton Hughes," she said. He made no effort to shake hands and instead simply nodded and gestured for her to enter the door to an office.

"Take a seat," he barked at her in a gruff voice. "What can the Department of Investigations do for you?" Leighton sat down on a leather couch that faced a cluttered desk covered in scraps of paper. The man who had let her in, the same one she had watched enter the building, stood at one side of the table. She hadn't yet seen a picture of the new chief investigator and didn't want to make the assumption that this was him.

The man didn't look like a politician. He didn't look like a policeman, either. Then again, the last policeman she'd seen had a horse's head and wore a Grecian toga. All the same, he wasn't what she expected the chief investigator of Gloomwood to look like, and she was cautious not to assume he was any more than an assistant.

"Well, Miss Hughes, what do you want?" the man asked. He was pacing backwards and forwards in front of the desk.

"I'm an investigative journalist, with the city's only real quality publication. I'm here for an interview."

"The department doesn't give interviews. It's policy."

"Really? And where is this policy written?"

"It's an unwritten policy."

"Perhaps if I could just speak to the chief investigator? The public are eager to know a little more about what's going on." she said.

"I'm sorry, but the chief investigator doesn't give interviews. What newspaper do you work for?"

Leighton hesitated. She knew this was going to happen, and bluffing was the only way through. "I work for the Gloomwood Independent, the only newspaper that actually produces news in this city."

"You produce news? Don't you report news? If you produce news, doesn't that mean you make it up?"

Oh crap, she thought to herself. She was being

toyed with and by some oaf in a cheap suit. He was well built, not in shape but not far off, and he moved like a man who was used to fighting, which was an unusual sight in Gloomwood. There weren't many fighters and what few there were tended to congregate on the west side of the city in bars and clubs that served the dregs of society.

"Fine, if you won't let me meet the chief investigator, perhaps you would like to tell him yourself that you've turned away possibly the only other real investigator in the city," she said as she stood up to leave and walked towards the door.

"Wait," the man barked. He looked like he was struggling with an internal dilemma of some kind. "What do you know about the chief investigator?"

She was surprised at the question, but knew that it was an opening. "Not a lot, but nobody knows much. I know that he's a newcomer to Gloomwood. I also know that he was specially appointed and I believe the role was created for him, which would suggest he's highly qualified. I've also had access to some sensitive information from the Office of the Dead that tells me he was brought here with some urgency, oddly before the Marquis' disappearance." She paused for dramatic effect. "Which means he wasn't really hired to investigate the Marquis. I was hoping to ask him what he was rushed here to investigate." She fixed a poignant look on her face and directed it at the man opposite her, hoping to see some kind of discomfort. She was disappointed. The man could have played poker for a living.

"My name is Augustan Blunt. I am chief

investigator to the city of Gloomwood, as appointed by the Office of the Dead and the Grim Reaper himself." He named his role with undisguised disgust, and Leighton couldn't help liking him a little more for it.

"I've never heard of your paper, Miss Hughes, and I think your theory is pretty easy to dispel. After all, the Grim Reaper already knew he wanted someone to take over. They wanted to treat me well, so they rushed me through. How often is there a brand new appointment like mine? You're making a mountain out of a mole hill," he said, pushing aside her story with such ease that for a minute she felt empty. Everything she had planned depended on her breaking a big story, and now she didn't have one.

"No need to look like that. I'll give you a story in return for your help. I'm new here, and so far everyone who has been helping me has turned out to have flaws I've been unable to look beyond. I guess I'm close-minded. As it happens, I hate the press. And the press you have here seem to be the lowest of the low. As I said, I've never heard of your paper, but I couldn't name you any others off the top of my head."

"They're all much of a muchness, barring ours, of course," Leighton muttered. She felt like she needed to contribute, but had nothing to add.

"It doesn't matter. You're a step above the rest for attempting to interview me and for staking out my premises here. I did notice you, and to be honest, that's why I climbed out of a first-story window and walked back around to the front of the building. You may want to try getting a less conspicuous car next time. For a moment I thought you were something I should be worried about," Blunt said. Leighton drove a dusky pink car that looked uncannily like a Citroen 2CV replica, although why anyone would choose to replicate one was fairly unfathomable to Blunt.

"Um, thanks for the tip. I'm sorry, what's going on? I'm quite confused. Am I getting an interview here?"

"No, you're not, but you will get an exclusive on the whole thing if you agree to help me."

"The whole thing?"

"Yes, whatever that might be, but the whole story on the Marquis' headnapping. And I can promise you he won't be the last."

"How?"

"You can't print anything until I give the go-ahead, understand?"

"How exactly will you stop me?" She was beginning to bristle. This wasn't part of her plan to become the city's most respected journalist.

"I'll arrest you," Blunt said without a hint of humour, and she was forced to nod her agreement.

38

The meeting with the snitch Noyers had turned out not to be a complete waste of time, and then he'd returned to the office to find a reporter casing his building. When she'd been so forward about her intentions, he'd been impressed. Generally he hated reporters, photographers, the whole thing, but if he'd learnt anything from his days on the force, it was to have a reporter on your side. Build a relationship and you got what you wanted put in the paper rather than what they imagined. Plus, they were territorial like wild dogs, so if he worked with her, the others shouldn't bother him as much.

He needed to eat, and eating alone wasn't something he enjoyed. With that in mind, he decided to leave the reporter in his office while she made up some kind of contract and went to see Sarah. When he returned to the office, he hoped the reporter would have had the opportunity to tidy up the mess he'd made trying to keep track of the work he'd been doing. He hadn't specifically asked her to do that, but she seemed the type that couldn't abide a messy desk.

In the lab, Sarah was working on something in a beaker, stirring it and heating it gently over what looked like a Bunsen burner.

"Hello, Sarah?" He asked quietly as he opened the door. The Marquis' body was hidden under a blanket, and Blunt was glad he didn't have to look at whatever remained.

"Ah, Blunt, good of you to pay me a visit. I was thinking I could do with an assistant in the future, if we are going to get more work than this, of course." Her voice was like ice.

"Fine by me. It's Mortimer who pays the bill. I'm just the pretty face," he said as he grinned his most winsome smile.

"The body company,"—she ignored his grin—"were less than forthcoming with any further details about their tracking system, but it wasn't a complete dead end."

For the first time, Blunt realised that she wasn't at all invisible. "You're in one piece, Sarah. Isn't that unusual?" he asked.

"I've noticed I've become more myself since I've been absorbed in a work of some immediate importance, probably out of necessity, but it's nice. Anyway, the Marquis' tracking system can't track his skull but we can use his body as a kind of radar."

Blunt looked over at the corpse hidden under the blanket, already worried at what he might see. "You just said we can't track him," he said.

"That's right, but the closer this body is to his head, the more animated it will become."

"What? Are you saying what I think you're saying?"

"I don't know what you think I'm saying, but what I am saying is this: the body will start to come, for want of a better word, more alive the nearer it gets to its owner's head."

Blunt wasn't hungry anymore. He rubbed his face and sighed. This was unpleasant. "You mean his body will start moving about as we get closer to his head. That's what that guy Hare said," he clarified.

"Exactly." Sarah waited for a response.

"He couldn't tell us how far away we'd need to be before we get any kind of clear reaction."

"About a mile."

"So you're suggesting we take the Marquis' body and drive around in circles."

"I'm not suggesting anything, but it isn't the worst idea I've ever heard."

"How big is the city?"

"I don't know."

"Roughly. I mean how many miles across."

"I know what you meant and I don't know."

"Well, think about it."

"Blunt, I've been in a museum for the last forty or so years. I don't know what's been built since I've been an exhibit. I don't know what colour is in fashion. I don't even know, if I'm honest, what day of the week it is. You very kindly reminded me of all of this before you stormed out of the building like some crusading madman."

"It's Tuesday," he said with such snarling conviction that he almost believed himself.

"Oh, well, sorry for not knowing."

"It doesn't matter. We can't do it, anyway. It would take too long. Maybe we can get the police to do it."

Sarah smiled, trying to look as innocent as possible. It was rare, but now and then she didn't mind being invisible. "Have you spoken to the police yet, Blunt?" she asked.

"Not yet, no. I better get myself down there. Do me good to be around some relatively normal people," he said pointedly.

Her smile grew bigger still as she replied, "Good thinking. Get yourself down to the central station and see what they have to say. It's in the Cremation district—Ashes Street. Can't miss it."

Blunt nodded. "I was going to ask if you fancied getting some lunch, but I guess it can wait," he murmured, and suddenly Sarah felt guilty. Setting him up for a disaster this way had been cruel and manipulative. She liked the man. He was gruff, miserable, sullen, and rude, really rude, but in a kind of grumpy teddy bear kind of way that was somehow endearing. He wasn't good-looking in the traditional sense of the word, which she supposed made him not good-looking, but that didn't mean he wasn't attractive. "Not today, I guess," she said as she shrugged, quickly shoving any thoughts to one side and remembering that whatever he was or might be, right now he was her boss and her only hope of an interesting job.

Blunt nodded, his inner voice screaming expletives. He should have kept his mouth shut. Did that count as sexual harassment? He never actually said anything incriminating, did he? What did he say?

This was bad. Bury it and move on. "No problem. I'll get a hot dog on the way to the police station," he said.

"No, don't do that, really. Don't eat the hot-dogs around here."

"Why?"

"Just don't, okay, please. Consider it a favour for me." There. She had made things even. She'd made him look an idiot, but she'd also stopped him doing something much worse.

"I've had one before, it seemed all right."

Oh god, she could never, ever, ever look at him the same way again. Anything but a hot dog, that poor man. Blunt was walking down the corridor when Sarah suddenly remembered the phone call she'd had earlier. "Blunt, wait, there was a phone call. I'm such an idiot. I completely forgot, but you'd better call Mortimer. There's been another head abduction," she said.

"What?! You only think to tell me this now? Oh for Christ's sake."

"Well, not exactly Christ, but it is religious."

"Oh no, don't tell me. Mortimer mentioned this to me already. It's what's his name, isn't it? Leader of the miserable sad, lonely, aren't we all pathetic church?"

"Um, if you mean Hugh Sullivan, high priest of the Church of Mankind's Everlasting Eternal Purgatory, then yes, it's him."

39

Mortimer had dropped Blunt off back at his office and driven straight back to the Office of the Dead, feeling stupid. He'd managed to get back on top of all his work when there was a knock at his door. He sighed and then almost fell out of his chair when he saw Neat standing in the doorway. "Hello, sir."

"Mortimer, please stay sitting. I've a couple of things I need to talk to you about," Neat said as he stepped through the doorway and pushed the door shut behind him.

There was a chair opposite Mortimer's desk, but it was very tight between the desk and the wall, which made it fairly redundant. Neat lifted it up, turned it sideways, and sat down in it diagonally, attempting to make up for the ninety-degree angle.

There was a hair out of place on Neat's head, and Mortimer found himself staring at it despite internally pleading with himself to ignore it. Neat didn't notice.

"Now, first things first. How are you?"

"Um, fine, thank you, sir."

"Good, I'm impressed. You're doing fine despite the fact that you have the responsibility of ensuring that Augustan Blunt captures the attacker of the Marquis and the head of the Church of MEEP. Have you forgotten that we are also missing the Grim Reaper?" He finished in a low whisper filled with foreboding. It was a voice he was very good at and had spent a good deal of time practising. He was even taking foreboding supplements, but that wasn't common knowledge.

Mortimer swallowed quickly before replying, "Well, I'm not doing well obviously, sir, not well at all, but I was being polite. I'm sorry, sir, Head of the Church?"

"Don't you check your messages? I told that woman you hired. Look on your desk. I left a note. Pull your socks up, Mortimer. Clearly I've made the right decision."

"Decision?"

"The spooks are now involved, Mortimer. I feel this has gone beyond anything that you or Blunt are able to deal with."

"But—"

"Shut up, Mortimer. The spooks will be investigating in parallel. Stay out of their way."

"I don't understand."

"I am speechless. What a monumental shock: Ralph Mortimer is confused. It's really quite simple. The spooks will be watching, listening, and making their own tactful investigations. Blunt is free to continue and he will, as far as the public are concerned, probably solve this crime—the Marquis, that is."

Mortimer swallowed heavily, this time trying to stay calm. "But the spooks now know about the Grim

Reaper."

"Correct."

"But sir, how can you—"

"We have no choice."

"Why now?"

"Because we are now down to only three of the most likely recipients of the keys to the city."

40

Constable JJJ Johnson walked his regular beat with the practised swagger of a Gloomwood policeman. His gait told anyone nearby that they'd better do what he said because he was hard as nails and capable of horrific violence, but more importantly, that he had a lot of mates who were even harder. They actually trained officers in how to walk like a tough guy; they called it the bad-ass mosey, and Johnson had surprised himself by finishing top of the class in moseying along. He held the force record for swaggering and could make a group of petty thieves nervous from five hundred metres away.

There was only one problem with a bad-ass mosey as good as Johnson's: as powerful as it was at scaring off the lowlifes, it was also a real slap in the face for some of the true thugs, the kind of men who downed twenty, thirty, forty pints and then ate every pint glass for dessert, the sort of people who would use sandpaper for toilet paper and owned home surgery kits. Johnson was built like a brick shit house, but that didn't mean much to men built like glaciers. When he walked out of the door of Rosalind Gwendolene's hovel, he walked slap bang into seven foot by five foot of solid lead by the name of Petal.

"'Allo, Constable Johnson," the giant rumbled. He was a demi-god through and through, not too bright, but very vain and arrogant. Worse still, he was as tough as they come and knew how to hold a grudge. Petal was the name he had chosen for himself, and nobody was going to argue: big, strong, violent, and very much your traditional righteous deliverer of vengeance and comeuppance.

"Hello, Petal. What can I do for you?"

"It would appear that you are bovvering one of my customers."

"Not in the slightest. I was merely checking in."

"Not so long ago that you was one of my customers, was it now, Triple-J?"

"Mention that again, Petal, and I'll rip your god-damn head off." Johnson enunciated this slowly and carefully.

"Well look-ee here, if the no-hoper hasn't suddenly grown himself a pair of balls. You should watch who you speak to like that, copper. Just 'cos you're with them doesn't mean I can't touch ya."

"Here we go again, Petal. It's all about you wanting to touch a man in uniform, isn't it?"

"What did you say?" The demi-god's voice dropped to a whisper, his eyes open wide and his face pale.

"Just between you and me, Petal, I think the name might give it away."

"Shut your mouth, copper, and get out of my sight before I decide to make you part of my own personal library."

Johnson shrugged and attempted to shove past

the drug dealer with as much aggression as possible. He barged with his shoulder, but the huge man didn't seem to notice him. "Um, Petal, could you move to one side please?" he whispered out of the side of his mouth.

"Sorry, see you at dinner," the mammoth whispered back, winking.

Petal was a monster, easily capable of things that were despicable, and he sold Oblivion, which was horrific. But if Johnson was honest with himself, he didn't see a whole lot of difference between himself and the big man. Johnson had been on Oblivion for a long time and it had been Petal who had sorted him out, helped him kick the habit completely. The demi-god sold the drug to those who wanted it, but he always offered to help anyone who wanted to get off it. He was really quite altruistic. Okay, so he would beat the hell out of anyone trying to sell on his patch, but at the same time, people knew that if they needed help, Petal would be there for them to solve the problem.

Johnson was the same. Was he any better because he was paid by the government instead of by the sales of Oblivion? He did the same thing. He probably didn't even do it as fairly or even-handedly. The problem was public perception, not the perception in this neighbourhood, but across the city. People saw someone like Petal and they immediately thought the worst. They spoke to him and they thought worse still because he came across as an idiot, a thug who didn't know any better, but Johnson knew him. He cared about him. They looked out for each other.

As he walked away, ensuring his mosey was at its highest level—*come near me and I'll rip your head off and urinate down your open oesophagus, punk*—he realised this wasn't a job for the police. Oh, they might come in handy, but this was really a job for him and Petal. This called for a little less bullying and a bit more thought and muscle.

41

Mortimer had driven over to the office as quickly as possible through rush hour traffic. Even when people had all of eternity to get things done, it was still bedlam at rush hour, with everyone using the conformist five-until-six-thirty slot as the time to get home.

Despite his rush to arrive, he found himself hesitating before he got out of the car. The spooks would be involved soon. Did he really want to be around when that happened? What would Blunt make of them? Would it really have any bearing on the case? Mortimer didn't think so, but then again, he'd never had to deal with anything like this before.

He sat with both hands on the steering wheel, rain pounding down on the windscreen. The sky was darkening, and he glanced at the clock on the dashboard. He'd been sitting thinking for five minutes before he finally took a deep breath and opened the door.

When he stepped out of the car, he had to leap to one side as a pink CV replica nearly ran him down.

Blunt was standing on the pavement. "Ah, Mortimer, good timing," he said.

"Who was that, Blunt?" Mortimer asked, as he stood up and dusted himself off.

"You look like you've got some news, the bad kind

of news," Blunt said, not feeling it necessary to explain to Mortimer that he'd just signed a contract with a journalist for the exclusive rights to information released by the Department of Investigations.

"Another incident," Mortimer said. "I'm here to take you to the scene." He gestured towards his car.

"I already know."

Mortimer rubbed his face with his hands. His eyes were beginning to sting. He was tired, and admitting it made him realise just how exhausted he was.

Blunt paused to check that they were out of earshot of anyone. "I need to know if we can put Sarah in the loop as well," he said. "The Grim Reaper's body is still in his office and there's been no work done by forensics. I want Sarah to go in and check it out. She can prove if it's the same murder weapon and might be able to find some little fingerprints."

Mortimer's mouth was hanging open when Blunt finished. He struggled to find the words before replying, "You can't be serious. We can't tell anyone about this. You don't understand what it means, how people are going to react. For crying out loud, Blunt, think about it."

Blunt's face was slowly turning red, but he was conscious of his temper rising. "Mortimer, I'm the chief investigator and I've made my decision. I wasn't really asking you; I was just being courteous. Now I can tell her, or you can tell her, or we can tell her together. Make your mind up now," he said.

The little man was flabbergasted. "You're serious," he said. "Fine, I'll tell her on my own, but when this blows up in your face, I want you to remember that I was against it. Neat's going to be furious when he finds out." Blunt watched as Mortimer walked into the building, muttering under his breath.

Blunt paced back and forth by the car. The rain fell from the sky like thousands of tiny parachutists who'd forgotten to pull the cord. Blunt looked up at the clouds. Bunting stretched between the streetlights. Across the street, a drunk man shuffled, holding his dismembered arm in his other hand. A newsagent was closing. A figure with two heads and six arms pulled down a roller shutter after dragging a newspaper billboard into the shop. The sign on it said something about the awarding of the keys to the city.

Mortimer returned, with Sarah in tow. Miraculously, she seemed even more whole than when Blunt had seen her earlier.

"I've told her everything, Blunt. I hope you're happy," Mortimer said. He was angry and was finding it difficult to hide behind his pathetic, drenched-puppy image.

"That depends. How're you feeling, Sarah?" Blunt asked, brushing away Mortimer's comments like they were crumbs on an otherwise spotless table.

"I'm okay, a little shocked, but okay. Glad to be part of the team that will bring in the Grim Reaper's… um… assassin?" she said. Then she looked at Blunt for clarification.

"*Assassin* suggests an ending… I think *headhunter*

will do. To be honest, Sarah, I'm impressed. Mortimer here seemed to think your head would explode, and you'd go screaming into the night."

She had a slightly vacant look, but the colour was returning to her face and Blunt began to wonder if Mortimer hadn't been pretty close to the truth. "To be honest, Mortimer is probably right. I'd take my reaction as an exception," she said. "After all, I'm used to parts of my body disappearing into nothingness and I'm still pretty shook up. Most people probably would find it tough to deal with; there'll be a period of mourning, of course. Why don't you fill me in while Mortimer drives us to see the latest victims?"

Blunt explained everything that had happened since he'd arrived in Gloomwood before Sarah's arrival, being sure to omit any of his rudeness, or the way he had died.

42

As they drove, Mortimer released the only piece of information he'd withheld in the first place. The victims were found at fourteen Hangman Drive, home to Lulu Devine, the city of Gloomwood's leading female socialite. She was the woman women wanted to be, the most photographed person in the city, including the Marquis. If it had happened at her residence, it was going to be serious front-page news.

Blunt was unimpressed. So much for keeping a low profile. It also seemed likely that since Lulu Devine was at the home of the Marquis when they went to review the previous crime scene, the extinctions were going to be related.

Fourteen Hangman Drive was an exercise in overkill. Numbers twelve to sixteen had been merged into one; number fourteen just happened to house the main front door. As they drove up, Blunt began to get an uneasy feeling. He wasn't used to dealing with high society. In the land of the living, the clients he'd met were normally middle-class businessmen, and the suspects, contacts, or criminals he met were all more used to handling pool cues than champagne flutes. The Marquis' house had made him uncomfortable, but he'd simply barged his way through the niceties. He had a feeling he might not find this as easy.

Blunt hammered on the front door with his practised policeman's knock. It was opened by a sober-looking man in a top hat and tails. "Good day, sir. Are you expected?" the man asked while bowing.

"Chief Investigator Blunt, here about the incident. My team will be joining me. This is Ralph Mortimer, third assistant to the manager of the Office of the Dead, and Sarah Von Faber, chief of forensics at the Department of Investigations." He said it quickly, but was careful to make sure the man was following what was said.

"We've been expecting you. Please come through to the lounge where Miss Devine awaits," the butler said—at least Blunt assumed he was the butler, or doorman, or something along those lines—and then he ushered them through into a side room where Lulu Devine waited.

He introduced them as they entered the room. Miss Devine waved him away and lifted herself out of an extravagant armchair. She was dressed in a long black dress with a shawl over her shoulders.

Mortimer had turned slightly pink when he saw her, but Sarah had looked like she was already bored. Blunt was once again grateful for the forensics specialist, if only so that he could be sure that the spell this woman seemed to cast over people wasn't all encompassing.

"Why Chief Investigator Blunt, we always seem to meet in such morbid circumstances, but still a pleasure to see you again," she said as she fluttered her eyelids and reached a hand out to Blunt. He took it and shook it, not realising until afterwards that she had expected him to kiss it.

"Well, Miss Devine, I am glad to see you're not

one of the unfortunate victims in this case. Perhaps before we visit the scene, you could let me know who's extinct," Blunt said, not in the mood for pleasantries.

"Certainly. Miss Dora Roberts and Mr Hugh Sullivan. They're upstairs in the guest bedroom. Mr Greaves will show you the way," she said as the smile on her face fell ever so slightly and Blunt noticed Mortimer stiffen.

"What was your relationship to the victims, Miss Devine?" Blunt asked while watching carefully for a reaction.

"Hugh was my lover; Dora Roberts was one of the housekeepers. This is a rather sensitive matter for me, Chief Inspector. That's why there was no press outside. I haven't told anyone what has happened except for Crispin Neat, who presumably sent you here. It was actually Toe-Dee Sicofant, Hugh's assistant, who discovered them. I'll not pretend the public didn't know about Hugh and I, but he was, after all, a man of the cloth, and while his religion certainly did not say he could not have relations, we still tried to keep it somewhat private."

Blunt nodded cautiously. This did put an interesting spin on things. So far, the victims were high profile, but a housekeeper, well, that was new. "Before I take a look at the scene, perhaps you'd like to clarify?" he asked.

"Fine," she said. Her smile had disappeared and Blunt realised he was seeing the true Lulu Devine. She was quite scary. "They were found in bed together, and no, I didn't know that bastard was screwing the housekeeper. I knew I shouldn't have trusted him, and that little slut was always parading around, flaunting herself in front of him. So, Detective, yes, I have a motive for doing this, but I didn't. I may be angry but, I'm not stupid."

Blunt raised an eyebrow at the vehement outburst. "You understand that this puts you in an awkward situation. After all, you were also one of the first people on the scene of the Marquis' head loss."

"No I wasn't, Chief Investigator; I arrived after he was—what's the way you put it—headhunted. I just happened to take charge of the situation as any good friend would." She sat bolt upright in her chair as she spoke.

"Okay, Miss Devine, we're going to go take a look at the scene, but unfortunately we're going to need to have a chat about all this, and I think it's best if we take it back to my office." He said it in his most reasonable voice, the voice he usually reserved for giving bad news, but he was still expecting a strong reaction and he wasn't disappointed.

"Listen to me, you jumped-up, pencil-pushing, self-important bureaucrat. You don't have any right to treat me like this, and if you continue to cast aspersions on my good nature, I'll have my lawyers take every penny you have. Do you understand?" There was venom in her voice, and as Blunt watched her get more agitated, he was reminded of a snake, or a giant poisonous spider.

"Miss Devine, I want to make this as easy as possible and keep it quiet. I've no opinion on your involvement or your personality. You can either come to my office and we can have a chat about things, or I can get physical and make a citizen's arrest on you. Of course, I will make sure the press is there for the photos. Now, I don't want to do that because it doesn't look good for me either, so I'll ask, is it really necessary?" He was speaking more quietly than he normally would, trying to soothe the woman in front of him.

Lulu Devine took a deep breath before continuing. She leaned back into her chair and smoothed out her dress on her lap. "Fine, please excuse my attitude. This is a very unusual situation. I'll agree to your request, provided we keep things quiet. This can't get to the press."

Blunt nodded before replying, "I can't promise anything, but you will not be announced as a suspect, and we won't even use the phrase *helping with our enquiries*. In fact, it's department policy not to talk about an ongoing case." Mortimer flinched when Blunt said *departmental policy*, but the detective carried on. "Miss Devine, we will not tarnish your reputation in this matter, provided you are, of course, not involved."

Her smile returned. It wasn't as vibrant as usual, but it appeared more genuine. "Thank you. There is one thing you could do for me, though," she said.

Blunt never liked it when someone asked for something in return, for something they didn't have a choice in any way, but he was prepared to listen. "Go on."

"Rip that bastard Hugh, and that little slut Dora, to shreds," she said as her smile widened. Blunt had to suppress a shudder.

"Not a problem. In fact, Sarah here actually enjoys that sort of thing." Blunt indicated his head of forensics, who gave a curt smile and a nod. "Oh, before I go through, I was wondering, given how much more about the city you know than I do, if you knew who Bernie Spitspeckler was?" he asked.

Miss Devine seemed taken aback. "Spitspeckler," she murmured, "well, it sounds familiar. One moment, please." She reached a dainty hand out towards a wicker table that sat by her side. On it stood an elegant lamp that was far taller and thinner than it needed to be. Beneath it sat a bell not unlike one you would expect to see in the reception area in many bed and breakfasts. She held her hand over the bell and then hammered on it repeatedly and dangerously heavily. Blunt watched as eventually the bell fell to the floor. Into the room ran a haggard-looking woman who immediately fell to her knees in front of Miss Devine.

The girl, who was clearly out of breath, didn't look up. Instead, she began desperately apologising. The speed at which she attempted to placate Lulu was incredible, and Blunt could barely catch a word. Suddenly Lulu silenced the girl by raising a hand in the air. "I rang the bell eleven times before you arrived, and the lamp fell off the table and broke. You will pay for it out of your wages," she said.

"Yes, of course, Miss Devine," the girl, who Blunt believed was now crying, whispered.

"Good, now why does the name Spitspeckler mean something to me?"

"Bernice Spitspeckler, head of children's entertainment for Dead Air, mistress."

"I knew that. Now get out of my sight," Lulu barked. The woman, as quickly as she arrived, was gone.

Lulu turned to Blunt and the smile that all of Gloomwood was apparently in love with reappeared. Blunt was trying hard not to appear shocked or disgusted at the treatment of the woman who had briefly been in the room.

"Well, Chief Investigator, there you have it. Bernie is clearly actually Bernice. So glad I could help."

43

JJJ Johnson was sitting at a cramped table in a small kitchen, slowly eating a bowl full of what could be described as chicken stew, and enjoying a glass of white wine. The table and kitchen wouldn't have felt so full if it hadn't been for Petal, who was sitting opposite him.

"That okay for you?"

"Lovely. Thanks, Petal. Your stew always hits the spot."

The giant beamed with pleasure. "Anything for you, cupcake," he said, as he cleaned away the dishes. "How's work then, and what on earth were you doing on my patch today?"

"Sorry about that. I was following up on a letter someone had sent me. Actually, I think we need to talk about something. The police thing, well it's not really going too well."

"Oh god, has someone found out about, well, you know, *us*?"

"No, no, nothing like that. It's just that, well, they don't do anything, you know?"

Petal's smile shifted from pleasure to the grin of someone who had just been vindicated. "Well, I don't like to say it but–"

"Don't say it then. I'm perfectly aware that you

warned me before that they were a useless bunch of fools, and yes, I agree. I honestly believed that with the support of the law behind me I'd be able to make more of a difference."

"Well, what are you going to do? Surely not let one bad day put you off?"

Johnson pushed his chair back and grabbed a dishcloth so he could dry while Petal washed. "It's not one bad day. Every day has been crap. You know what they did this morning? Covered my desk in all the memorabilia they could find for last season's relegated teams."

"They did what?" Petal roared, the china dishes in the drying rack rattling at the sound.

"Calm down, it's not as though I can do anything about it."

"But, but, I'll crush those sons o' bitches."

"They have no idea how offensive they were being, and it doesn't matter. I'm going rogue, anyway."

"Right, well, that will show 'em."

"You don't know what it means, do you?"

"No idea," Petal said as he passed a plate to Johnson and shrugged. A shrug for Petal was like watching the Great Wall of China during an earthquake.

"It means I'm taking my badge and doing whatever the hell I want in the name of the police."

"Oh, right, and that's not what the police do anyway then?"

Johnson grimaced before speaking. "Listen, the place you saw me coming out of today, well, something happened. A woman told me something. I didn't want to involve you, but I really think I need your help."

44

The guest bedroom was actually one of fourteen guest rooms. Inside, it was decorated in a typically decadent style. A four-poster bed with drapes stood in the centre of a room with a fantastic bay window on one wall and a huge roaring fireplace on the other. There was a roll-top bathtub by the window. Blunt couldn't help noticing how the feet of the bath were, for some unknown reason, the hands of a human at the front and the feet of a goat at the back. Interestingly, the bath was red.

The body of Hugh Sullivan was sprawled across the bed while Dora Roberts had clearly fallen off as she'd been attacked. There was no blood to be seen. Blunt was beginning to get used to the sight of assault without the blood spatter. It made it somehow sadder, but less violent.

"Okay, Mortimer, I want you to speak to Mr Greaves and the rest of the household staff. I want to know who was the last person to see them um, undecapitated." Blunt didn't look at Mortimer as he said it, but the little man shot off as soon as he'd been given the order.

"Sarah, you and me are going to give this room a thorough going over. I want photos. You have a camera?"

"The latest in digital technology," she said as she indicated a strange blue box about the same size and shape as a camera.

"Great. Photos of everything and anything. I'd rather have stuff that's irrelevant than miss something relevant. You start on the right side of the bed. I'll start on the left."

It took them two hours. By the end of it, they had bagged up every item of clothing in the room and photographed every square inch. Sarah had lifted footprints and taken a sample of dirt off one of the prints. They had managed to recover several pieces of Dora Robert's skull and were able to confirm their worst fears: Ableforth had taken place. At least one of the victims could be confirmed, as there was no way even the most skilled anatomy constructors could reassemble her head. Blunt searched the room in more detail and decided that her skull had been blown to pieces by a high-velocity weapon, something like a very large sawn-off shotgun.

Both the victims were naked. Judging from their positions at the time of extinction, it appeared that Sullivan was decapitated before he had a chance to move, but that Dora had desperately tried to scramble away from the killer. Sickeningly, Sullivan's body sat up and lay down again several times during the search of the room. It was a reflex action, Sarah assured him. It wasn't related to the proximity of the man's brain.

The most interesting piece of evidence fell from Dora's hands as they wrapped her body in a large black sheet. There was no such thing as a body bag in Gloomwood, and Blunt made a mental note to mention it to Mortimer if things continued. When they moved the woman's body, a ring fell from her hands.

It was a large silver ring, with a bright blue stone set into it. Blunt was careful not to touch it with his hands as he placed it in a plastic sandwich bag. "Is it unusual?" he asked Sarah.

"Unusual certainly. The blue is very vivid. It's probably expensive. Until I get it to the lab, I can't tell you what it's made of, or if it's traceable."

"It's likely it's from the attacker. Her hand was locked around it when she died. She may have lunged at the attacker and managed to pull this from them."

"Pulled it off their finger? That would be quite difficult."

"Actually, look here." Blunt pointed to the ring. There was a small scratch on the inside, where the silver shone more brightly.

Sarah looked closely. "A scratch? You think it may have been worn as some kind of necklace?" she asked.

"Almost definitely. The murderer must have recovered the chain but didn't have time to find the ring. Hopefully Mortimer will be able to find a witness to the escaping attacker."

Blunt nodded; there was a lot to take in and so far the clues they had weren't paying dividends. He wasn't being decisive enough: he wasn't following through on the clues they did have. The half-hearted attempt to get information out of the little man, Will, hadn't led them anywhere except to another name. If anything, the fact that it was a child—or whatever they called themselves—was their biggest clue. Then there was the bear, the toy. More fibres had been found at this scene and they matched the last one, but now, well, things were worse than ever.

Ableforth. He'd have to ask Mortimer why they called it that one day, not that it mattered. He'd just died, and he'd already been given a new form of death to fear.

It was clear now: the person committing these headhuntings had been targeting the soon-to-be holders of the keys to the city. There had to be a reason for it, something more than vanity. Revenge was always a good motivator, but other than the keys, these people weren't really related. They'd taken out the Grim Reaper as well. Blunt didn't know the man, but he knew enough from the statues and the tones that people spoke of him in that he was next to godliness, considered untouchable. Yet somebody had waltzed into his office and lopped his head clean off.

Blunt shook his head, trying to clear it. "Sarah, pack your things up. You and Mortimer can head back to the office, but I want to be dropped at police central on the way," he said.

"Don't go, Blunt. Those guys are arseholes."

"What? Don't be ridiculous, Sarah, they're the police!"

"You were the police once, Blunt. Think about it. Look at the people who end up here. The least they'll do is lock you in a cell and assault you. If they want to, they'll make you disappear and there's nobody to argue with them."

"I think I can handle the local police."

45

The outside of the police station was clean. That was how people described it: not the colour, which was light grey, or the fact that it seemed to have no windows, just that it was very, very clean. They didn't even use the word pristine. If the building had been a word, it would have been *blank*. Except for a small bronze plaque on the wall by a set of sliding glass doors, there was nothing to identify it as a police station.

Blunt was a little surprised at this, but then remembered that this was headquarters. It was probably not meant for the public, a bit like Scotland Yard, or even MI5. He walked up to the doors, and they slid open. Artificial light shone out and he stepped inside.

As soon as the doors slid shut behind Blunt, Mortimer, who had given him a lift, hit the accelerator and sped, keeping within the speed limit, to the end of the street and out of the police-controlled area.

Inside the building there were house-plants. They littered the reception area as if it was some kind of greenhouse, every one of them dead. Behind a large desk, fighting her way through the dead undergrowth, a woman rattled away on a keyboard faster than should have been possible.

He walked towards the desk and tried to gain her attention. "Hello?" There was no way she couldn't have heard him; he was being ignored. In Blunt's opinion, she was making a concerted effort not to look at him or anywhere near his general direction. At first he thought he was imagining it, but then he noticed that her chair, one of those typical office swivelling numbers, was actually turning further away from him by nearly imperceptible increments.

This wasn't typical of any police station he'd ever been to. They might not have been friendly, but they'd always been professional enough to point out that whoever was talking wasn't important. He didn't want to make the mistake of coming across as, well, himself, but he felt his temper rising.

"Excuse me, I'm not speaking to myself here. I'm here to see whoever is in charge. I'm the new chief investigator."

The woman still didn't speak, but she looked up at him with disinterest and placed a notice on the only empty space on the desk. *Out to lunch.*

"What the hell is going on in here? Is this a police station or not?" His frustration finally overcame him and the second he raised his hands above his head as he shouted, five policemen appeared as if out of nowhere.

"Right, you, 'ands behind your 'ead and down on the floor. You're under arrest," a man with what appeared to be a large caterpillar growing across his forehead barked.

"Ah, finally some policemen. Right, fellas, calm down. I'm Chief Investigator Blunt, here to see—" He was abruptly cut off by a swift truncheon to the gut, followed by several more truncheons until the individual blows became indistinguishable.

When Blunt eventually regained consciousness, he found himself in a cell. The fingers on his left hand appeared to be broken, and his right knee was even more reluctant to support his weight than normal.

A small hatch at eye level opened up in the door. "Prisoner is awake," a voice shouted. Blunt guessed that it belonged to the same person who was peering through the hatch.

"Why have you locked me up?" Blunt asked, being careful to remain calm.

"You will be taken to an interview room where we will tell you what you did and tell you the subsequent penalty."

"What? Surely that's dealt with in court."

"Are you being clever, sunshine? Last thing you want to do is be clever. See, us real policemen have no time for cleverness."

"So far you've made that very clear."

The eyes squinted, lines forming at their corners as their owner considered Blunt's reply. Then the metal hatch slammed shut.

46

Petal was sitting on the sofa, rubbing the stubble on his chin. "Sounds like quite the con... conun... um, problem. So you reckon we've gotta do summin' about it?"

"I don't see how we can tell anyone else without causing widespread panic. Everyone would go crazy, riots in the streets, Ableforth and mayhem," Johnson said, his hands with palms spread outwards. He stood in front of the fireplace, the electric fire up to its highest level, one of the few signs in the house that its occupants weren't as poor as their neighbours.

"Yup, you're not wrong there, but just the two of us, an' we'll 'ave to go into, well, you know where we'll have to go."

"No, where do we have to go?"

"And you're the policeman? Only one kind of person who could build a machine like that, and I should know 'cos they're as far from me as you get."

Johnson still looked confused, and more than a little surprised at himself for being outwitted by Petal, who wasn't the sharpest tool in the shed.

Eventually the big man sighed and said, "It's the little people, innit? I mean little hands, people always trying to flog them toys and that. If anyone's gonna know about clockwork and machinery to build this thing, it's them. Don't they have the watchmakers centre right next to their district?"

"Petal, that's not true. Well, I mean yes, the mall is nearby, but the rest is rubbish. Just because they're in kids' bodies doesn't mean they're elves or something. Really, I expected more of you, Petal. It's far more likely to be one of the big pharmaceutical or engineering companies. They've got all the best anatomical construction workers up there and the biological architects' head offices are there."

The big man looked momentarily ashamed at himself. "Yeah, yeah," he said. "Actually, no, you know what? You can call me a what'd'ya call it-ist, but if we're gonna be honest, I do know it. Yeah, it's a stereotype, but I still reckon I'm right. It's those little buggers. Just the other day, I watched one of them get crushed by a truck right outside. I walked back in, had a cup of tea, and when I came out he was gone, and you can bet your policeman's pension that the truck driver won't be seen in these parts again."

"What? What the hell is that supposed to mean?"

"You know what I'm saying."

"I think I do, but I really hope I'm wrong."

"They look out for each other, don't they? I mean, now and then you're walking along and you think you see a pair of eyes looking out from a sewer drain and you know, you just knows it's one of them little buggers, they're like rats."

"They're children."

"No, they're not," Petal bellowed, leaping to his feet, his powerful frame and booming voice reminding Johnson that he may be a dead demi-god, but he was still a deity. Johnson had known him too long to worry about being hit, but he was still surprised at the fury in the big man's voice. "Everyone's always saying that. It's the stupid norms' fault and now you're doing it too. What's the matter with you, Jeremiah John Jacob Johnson? You are not a norm, so don't start acting like you is."

Johnson raised his hands in surrender. "I'm sorry," he said. "Calm down. I'm sorry, it just slipped out, but you're right. I think that sometimes and it's the norms. They have this instinct to treat anything that looks like a child with some special set of rules—even the police—but do you really think they would do this? I mean, why?"

Petal had sat back down, but he was still red in the face. "Well, you said that woman you spoke to told you she was grabbed and taken to some big warehouse, and that she was carried there by a bunch of people. Well, I figure she was grabbed and pulled down into the sewer. They'd have carried her straight across to their district, and what's smack bang in the centre?" he asked.

"Oh, they've just opened that new supermarket, you know the chain—what's it called?"

"Not that. Next to it."

"Brian's Burgers?"

"Um, no, across the road."

"Oh, that place they opened. The garden centre."

"Exactly, nice big open space, but all covered up.

Bit like a warehouse, and it's got very good drainage, so they never even have to use the doors."

"Petal, that's actually a really good theory, but I still think you're grasping at straws. Why would they want to do it? How would they benefit?"

The demi-god shook his head slowly and sat back in his chair. "Triple-J, I'd have thought you would have enough insight to see that."

Johnson grimaced and said, "Have you ever noticed, Petal, that when I know something you don't, I don't make a big deal out of it and I tell you in a subtle way, but when you know something I don't, it becomes a bit of a pantomime?"

"Are you calling me stupid, Triple-J, cos' you know that's not fair."

"No, never mind. Tell me how they'd benefit."

"Well, they're the most against it, aren't they? So if they've got it, they can own it, and if they prove it doesn't work or has some kind of evil effect, then they banish it forever."

Johnson nodded and leapt to his feet. "Of course, and even if it does work, they register it as their intellectual property, and then nobody else can build it. It's brilliant. We've got to go stop them. Wait, it gets worse. They get to keep the very components that everyone would need to be able to build their own, and they're one of a kind! Come on, let's go," he said.

"You've got to be kidding. You and me against an army of those little buggers? No chance. You need to send the police in."

"They'll never listen."

"You're gonna have to make them."

"As much as I like your theory, I'm not going to be able to convince anybody that we need to make a raid on them without some better evidence than the words of an Oblivion-addled addict from the poorest and—let's face it—most insignificant district in the city. I'm not even sure myself. What do the police have to gain from going in there?"

"It's not always what you get that makes you do things."

47

He was dragged into a dim room and shoved into a chair that felt like it would snap at any moment. After waiting for what seemed to be an age, he was offered a cup of coffee. He accepted, and the coffee was thrown straight into his face. It was disappointing, but it did wake him up.

By the time the coffee had dried, a man had taken the seat opposite him. He had a nose that looked like it might have come from a joke shop. He also had one of the least genial manners Blunt had experienced since he'd died.

"Right then, Mr Big Shot, Mr I'm More Important Than The Entire Police Force, Mr I've Never Done An Honest Day's Work In My Death, think you're a big man, do you?" The man had clearly honed his questioning technique over time to near perfection. Blunt was being sprayed with just enough saliva to be uncomfortable, but it was an almost constant fine mist which meant wiping his face would begin a never-ending cycle.

"Yes, I think I'm a big man," Blunt said.

"What?" The man with the dodgy nose was thrown. Nobody had ever said that before. "Well then, big man," he recovered quickly, "I'm Captain Sowercat, and I am the head of the police force in the whole of Gloomwood, so I'm a bigger man, understand?"

"No, sorry, you've completely lost me."

"Are you intentionally being an awkward bastard?"

"Yes."

"Right, well, there's an easy way to solve that. I've five men outside who all fancy coming in here and kicking your head in. Right now I'm inclined to let them."

"I can imagine you are, because you know if I attack you first I'm going to make you eat that plastic thing you've got stuck to your face."

"What? I'm not afraid of you."

'Course you're not, Captain. You're chief of police. Are they watching through the glass?" Blunt asked the second half in a whisper, being careful to hide his face as he said it.

"You're damn right I am, you miserable little shyster," the captain said, then nodded almost imperceptibly.

"Fine, Captain, you win. What do you want from me?"

"Listen carefully, Blunt." The Captain leant forward and whispered in Blunt's ear, "Just pretend you're my subordinate in some way, please. Otherwise, I'm going to have absolutely no control over the lads. Honestly, I couldn't give a damn what you do, but I had to do something to save face."

Blunt nodded and attempted to look afraid. His acting was poor, but he was guessing the audience was more than ready to believe. "I understand,

Captain. Believe me, sir, I know my place. My department will make sure to keep out of you and your boys' way. That's not a problem. After all, we do the investigating, but it's you lads who have to uphold the law and keep the peace. Just think of what we're doing as an extension to the service you deliver to the city. I apologise for any miscommunication up until this point."

The look of relief on the captain's face was unmistakable, and he clearly knew it, which was why he made sure he was facing away from the mirrored wall. "Glad to hear it, Chief Investigator. You're free to go about your business, and should you ever need the cavalry, please don't hesitate to call us. We're on the same side, after all," he said.

The captain led Blunt to the door, all the while whispering, "Thank you so much. You have no idea how much I owe you. Anything at all I can do to help you, just let me know and we'll be there."

As the door opened, Blunt turned with a smile to the captain. "Oh, I know exactly how much you owe me," Blunt said. He stood a couple of inches taller than the captain, but the difference seemed monumental as he glowered down at the man in uniform.

Sowercat didn't even blink. He reached forward with one stubby finger and poked Blunt in the chest. "Be careful, Detective. I might have needed your help here, but you'll be needing my support in the future. You can bet on it."

Resisting the temptation to snap the policeman's finger, Blunt took a deep breath and nodded once.

Sowercat returned the nod, and the animosity dissolved.

Blunt followed the captain, glowering at the surrounding officers, who seemed to have found some new confidence. The captain left him standing in front of a man who was incredibly elongated. His head was bent forwards to prevent it from rubbing against the ceiling. He wore a brown suit that must have been tailor made. His legs were thinner than Blunt's thumbs, and the belt he wore wouldn't have fitted around Blunt's neck. His face and head were as stretched out as the rest of him, and the distance between his forehead and his chin was the length of two wine bottles stacked on top of each other. There was more than a little of the circus freak show about the man.

"Ah, hello there?" Blunt asked. He had by now perfected the art of appearing unfazed by appearances.

"Chief Investigator, it is nice to meet you." He stretched out the vowels as he spoke, making him sound like a musical instrument.

"And who might you be?"

"That is irrelevant," the tall man said. The word *irrelevant* had never seemed less so.

"I'm not in the habit of helping strangers out, so maybe you should do a little explaining."

"You may call me Tomb."

Blunt wasn't sure if it was Tom or Tomb, but either way, it didn't make things any clearer. "Is that

Sergeant, Chief, Constable Tomb?" he asked.

"None of the above. I don't think you understand the situation, Chief Investigator. My employers call me Tomb Mandrake," the man said, looking at Blunt expectantly.

Blunt looked up into the odd figure's face. "Do you have to speak like that?" he asked.

"Yes."

"Oh, for crying out loud, what do you want?"

"Come with me." The man took one long step forward and beckoned Blunt to follow him. In two long strides he was standing at a door that Blunt had failed to notice earlier. It was flush with the wall; yet another door designed to be missed by all those who didn't know it was there.

"It is best we avoid the normal police. They are not exactly friendly," he said, pushing open the door with one spindly arm. For a second Blunt flinched at the thought of the man's limbs suddenly snapping like toothpicks. Mandrake had to bend down to get beneath the door, and his body folded almost double.

"So, you are a police officer?"

"I am something outside of the normal police." He spat out the word *police* as if it was a curse.

"How outside of the police?"

"Lets us just say I am part of what most consider to be the real police. To be honest, Detective, I am here to warn you to stay out of my way. Allow me to explain."

What followed was one of the most painful experiences of Blunt's death, and that included the recent beating the police had given him. Listening to Tomb Mandrake speak was an arduous experience and one that he hoped not to have to endure again.

What Blunt managed to translate suggested that Mandrake was part of a government intelligence service. A secret intelligence service in the same vein as the National Security Agency in America or MI5 in the United Kingdom. They existed, and everyone knew they did, but little more than that was known.

Mandrake had suggested that the meeting was a courtesy, a friendly greeting much like the one Blunt had been attempting to deliver to the police, but it was clear there was more to it. There was something sinister in the manner of the conversation. Nothing was openly said, but Blunt got the message: he was being watched. The police didn't appreciate his involvement, and neither did Mandrake and his spooks. Whether this meant they were in some way involved, Blunt couldn't be sure, but he doubted it. It seemed too obvious.

The spooks had decided Blunt's investigations would make a suitable cover for their own operations, but they didn't hold the chief investigator in high regard. Mandrake's office had suffered a blow to their pride when they had eventually been told about the Grim Reaper. The organisation felt it was their case and that nobody should have been involved except them. Mandrake seemed at a loss to explain why Blunt was in the position he was in.

The freakish man ended the meeting by warning

Blunt that greater forces were at work than he understood, and that if something untoward happened to the detective, there wouldn't be much of an investigation.

The tall man disappeared into the back of a large black SUV that sped away as soon as the door was slammed. Blunt watched it leave with growing apprehension. His ruffled coat and suit were slowly drenched as he trudged down the pavement, looking for a landmark or method of transport he could use to get home.

48

The mayor and the governor had been watching the news carefully. Celebrity drivel was occasionally interrupted by the stories about the Marquis and the head of the Church of MEEP. In the longer segments, a sentence or two was spared for the Ableforth of the chambermaid, who remained unnamed throughout.

The mayor was a round little man who wore a tuxedo wherever he went and had so much gold on his pudgy fingers that it looked like he was wearing gloves. The governor, on the other hand, was tall and lean. He looked like an athlete, and for a period of the time at the beginning of his death he had played professional football, a fact that was never missed by his campaign management team.

They were chalk and cheese in appearance, but in personal ambition, there was little to choose between the two. Power hungry and in need of the public eye, the two had both risen to head their respected political parties in record time. They had then gone about making their party as close to the political middle ground as possible. It had reached the point where people couldn't tell the difference between the two policies, which suited the politicians well. The lesser opposition parties looked decidedly extreme in their political stances.

While the parties were not far removed from each other, they made a big show of the differences they did have. There was no love lost between the

Gloomwood Grey Party and the Death for All Party, but their main bone of contention was over the Gloomwood national flag. Both parties agreed it should be grey, light grey and dark grey, but neither party could agree to the order.

During the recent spate of skull thefts, the two parties had put aside their differences and both the mayor and governor were currently under guard in the most luxurious hotel in the whole of Gloomwood. The Light at the End of the Tunnel was ridiculously overpriced, far more extravagant than necessary, and strangely, despite a complete lack of visitors to the city, always overbooked.

The two political leaders had booked out the top floor of the hotel and were, for the sake of appearances, occupying separate rooms. In reality, they were sharing a double room on the floor below in the hope that they could fool whoever might be after them. Unfortunately, sharing a room was only increasing their fear and paranoia.

"What if it's somebody on the security team?" the mayor asked. He had a strange whining voice when he was frightened. If any of the public ever heard him, it would probably damage his profile. As it was, he had perfected a strong booming voice for his speeches and public addresses, which was in fact nothing like his natural voice.

The governor, on the other hand, was a man of very few words who had a fantastic voice for public addresses. Unfortunately, he wasn't particularly bright. "No, it couldn't be somebody on the security team. They wouldn't choose a job in security if they were going to chop people's heads off," he said.

"Um, good point," the mayor said. He had suffered enough time with the governor to know that sensible debate, even if it was about something the governor knew about, was pretty much impossible without a team of writers and spin doctors standing behind him or a discrete ear-piece in one ear.

"I don't want to have my head chopped off," the governor wailed in his manly way.

"Neither do I. Are the doors locked?"

"Didn't we just check?"

"Yes, but… check again."

"No, you check."

"I don't want to put my feet on the floor. What if something reaches out from beneath the bed and pulls me under?"

"Didn't we check under the bed?"

"Yes, but, well, we've checked so we know there's nothing there. We're being silly."

"Yes, we are. We should be more sensible. There's security all around us. Nobody could get through all those guards, and there's nobody in here."

"Right, we just need to stay calm and last through until Monday. Once we've made the ceremony, we'll be fine."

A light tapping came at the door."What was that?" asked the governor.

"Someone at the door?" the mayor said.

"Well, go answer it then."

"I checked. It was locked last time. You go answer it."

"No, I'll, wait, I've got an idea. Who is it?" he shouted towards the door.

From behind the door came a muffled voice. "It's security, sir. Just want to check the room again."

"How do we know you're really security?" the mayor squealed.

"Um, well, hang on a sec," came the voice from behind the door. A moment later, a security pass was shoved under the door.

The governor, some small amount of bravery surfacing, tiptoed to the door and picked it up. "It's real. Must be security, then," he said as he snapped the lock back on the door.

"No wait," the mayor squealed.

In walked a security guard carrying a tray with two dishes with silver covers on top. "Room service," the guard said, smiling as he put the plates down. He didn't bat an eyelid at the mayor's fear. He'd been trained well enough to ignore the people he was protecting. As quickly as he arrived, he was gone.

"Guess we're safe after all," the governor said. The mayor just shot the man a look of pure disgust.

49

Lulu Devine had a driver; it was customary for someone in her position to have a large contingent of lackeys, servants, and professional assistants. She wasn't quite the commercial entity the Marquis had been. She was much more of a celebrity in the traditional sense.

She hosted a talk show on the television. There wasn't a lot on except for celebrity exposé programmes and reality shows. Her show rounded up the dregs of society and delivered them to the masses as a kind of freak show. They didn't advertise it like that, of course. That would be ridiculous, and instead she pretended she was there to help them with their problems. That's why she did things like lie detector tests, and had security men who were only allowed to intervene after thirty seconds of fighting.

As well as her talk show, she hosted the breakfast show, which was basically inane chatter and about thirty tiny five-minute mini-shows about cooking, or home decorating, or occasionally calls for poverty aid for the homeless. Some segments were so short that the advertisements before and after outshone them.

She was big in the charity world, but only because it was important to be seen being a nice person. She really wouldn't bother if she could help it. Charity fundraisers were a big thing for her, and she was often asked to give speeches, which she was happy to do as she could plug her shows or her upcoming autobiography; she released one every year.

Lulu Devine had a name everybody knew and loved. She was well liked and for good reason. She put a hell of a lot of work into appearing to be a decent dead human being. It would have come easier to her if she had been a nice person in the first place, but then nice people don't really care as much about recognition.

Overall Lulu didn't have to be a decent human being; her chosen vocation required her to come across as a nice person, which meant she did nice things. So everything she did was for herself. It didn't really matter in the long run. Unfortunate people sometimes benefited, and the public hated themselves for not being nice people. Everyone was happy in the end.

Perhaps it was understandable that she was terrified of a scandal. Her livelihood depended on a certain public perception of her. If people thought she might have been involved in something like Ableforth, she'd be in serious trouble. How could she make innocent people's lives seem scandalous on her show if she was involved in a much bigger scandal off screen? Whatever had happened with her onetime lover and the housemaid needed to be wrapped up and presented to the public in a way that made her seem hard done by.

The problem was, before all of that, she needed to be interviewed by Blunt. She wasn't worried. Blunt might have been a brute who, for some reason, was unaffected by her beauty and charm, but he wasn't an idiot. She was innocent, and she wasn't going to worry about being accused of anything. She had enough power in the city to know that even Blunt would pussyfoot around her unless he knew, without a shadow of a doubt, that she had been involved. And she hadn't. It was that she was being interviewed at all that concerned her. It didn't take a conviction to turn someone into a criminal in the eyes of the press, just the slightest doubt about their innocence.

Ideas for potentially damaging headlines kept running through her head as she watched the world go by. *Lulu delivers Devine intervention. Did the starlet off the harlot?* Her fingers dug into the expensive leather seats as she swore under her breath.

She was sitting in the back seat of her car waiting in traffic. The windows were heavily tinted; she wasn't foolish enough to drive around in her well-known stretch hearse for the world to see. She kept a luxurious but fairly commonplace black Gothic 4000 for occasions where she wanted to attract less attention.

She was filing her nails and checking her make-up at the crossroads minutes from the Department of Investigations when it happened.

A lorry smashed into the back of the car, throwing her from her seat. She struggled to her passenger door. The window on her left exploded inwards and car horns up and down the street burst into life. A black-gloved hand reached in the window and yanked the door open. She dived to the opposite side of the car and had managed to roll out of the door when the gunshots rang out.

Searing pain shot up her leg as she pulled herself

out onto the road. Her driver, who had lost an arm in the collision, was at her side immediately. He pulled her to her feet, and they ran for the pavement while more shots rang out.

In shock, Lulu Devine collapsed on the pavement. She looked around, dazed, just in time to see someone dressed in a black cloak sprinting away into an alleyway off the street. Gasping in pain, she turned to her driver. "We need to get to Blunt, quickly."

50

Blunt was rudely awakened by the buzzer downstairs. He rolled out of his bed and, half asleep, hit the intercom button. "What?" he barked into the speaker.

"Let us in, for Grim's sake. Someone's trying to kill us," a near hysterical voice screamed at him.

"You're already dead," he muttered as he pressed the button to open the door. He dressed quickly and was putting on his shoes when the door burst open.

A man wearing a black hat burst into the room. He was helping a woman that even Blunt couldn't fail to recognise. "I've lost an arm, and she's been shot," the man said, there was a good chance that he was speaking quickly and hysterically by his standards, but if he was, Blunt hoped he'd never have to suffer a normal conversation with the man. His voice had less emotion in it than a greeting card bought from a petrol station. He wore a peaked hat and looked the perfect image of an elderly manservant, except he was missing an arm.

Fortunately Blunt had cultivated an ability to act in an emergency second only to paramedics and primary school dinner ladies. He lifted Lulu Devine over his shoulder and wrapped his free arm around the driver, who was rapidly going into shock.

The exertions of his meeting with the police had Blunt feeling like he had been tenderised by a three-hundred-pound chef who hated tough meat. He moved as quickly as he could down the hall and kicked Sarah's laboratory door open. As soon as he was in the room, he lay Lulu Devine down on a Gurney and found a chair for the driver to sit in.

Sarah burst into the room just as Blunt had managed to extricate himself from the driver. "What the hell's going on?" She asked, rushing straight over to Lulu Devine.

"Where were you?" Blunt was splashing water into his face as he spoke.

"I was sleeping down the hall. There are plenty of empty rooms. I thought a couple of hours' sleep away from the lab might be a good idea. Especially after you woke me up at whatever o'clock this morning," she replied.

"Good thinking, and you know I got lost," he mumbled. "Anyway, she's been shot in the leg. I've got a feeling it was by some vicious little bugger with some curved shears. Could you stitch her up? This guy's lost an arm. Don't really know what we can do about that."

As he spoke, Sarah ripped Lulu Devine's dress apart along her leg and found the wound. She reached for a scalpel and placed her hand on the leg, but the talk show host started writhing in agony and screaming the second Sarah touched her. "Calm down. I need to stitch you up," Sarah said.

"It hurts. Get off me, you madwoman. I'll sue you for everything you've got," Lulu screamed at the white-coated scientist.

"Blunt, I can't keep her still. I'll make it worse if she doesn't stop squirming."

Blunt shrugged and stepped forward, slapping the hysterical woman across the face. "Now, normally I'd kill a man for raising a hand to a lady, but experience tells me that a quick sharp shock can often help with a massive overwhelming surprise," he said, quickly stepping beyond her reach.

Lulu stared at Blunt, her lip quivering as she blinked over and over. "Y-y-you, do you, I'm, do you know who I am?" she asked.

"Yes, do you?"

"I'm Lulu Devine, and you've just earned a discussion with my solicitors."

"Blah, blah, blah, sit still while Sarah fixes your leg."

Sarah worked fast; she cut the wound open slightly and reached in with a narrow pair of tweezers. After a couple of moments, she grunted with satisfaction and pulled out a bullet. She dropped it in a metal dish and carried it over to the lab bench.

Hovering a discreet distance from the action, Blunt watched nervously as he asked, "Sarah, what's the point in doing that?"

"Hmm, what do you mean?"

"Well, stitching her leg up and getting the bullet out. I mean, it's not going to kill her."

"True, but it's going to hurt a lot, could send her delirious. More importantly, the leg will get worse and could affect other body parts. You might see people sometimes out and about who look fairly normal, but their bodies are pretty much rotten. They can crumble to dust, eventually."

"They die?"

"Not to be pedantic, but already dead, remember. Their heads remain intact for some reason, though their skin won't; they usually end up in the library. There's that, and who in Gloomwood would actually shoot bullets at a person? I'm curious. I mean, that poor woman at the last scene was definitely Ableforthed by something, probably some kind of weapon that was designed to do it. This,"—she indicated the bullet—"is not intended to do that. It appears to contain a drug of some kind, probably meant to incapacitate. However, that's not the only reason to do this. More importantly, skin and limbs are expensive and difficult to replace. While Miss Devine may be able to purchase a new pair of legs on a whim, most of us can't, and I can't comfortably allow a decent pair of legs to go to waste because of one little hole."

"That's disturbing."

Blunt watched, fascinated, as Sarah worked. Behind him there came a large thud, and when he turned to look, he realised the driver had passed out. Blunt guessed it was from the shock of the accident and decided he had to move him.

He carried the man through to another spare room on the same floor and tried to lay him down in as comfortable a position as he could manage in amongst the cardboard boxes and empty filing cabinets.

When he returned to the office, Sarah was putting stitches in the leg of Lulu Devine. "Good morning, Chief Inspector," she said with a smirk as he walked back into the room.

"Isn't it just?" Blunt stated dourly. "Well, we're both up, and she doesn't look like talking. How about telling me quickly about the evidence you've got?"

It took Sarah half an hour to explain what she'd found to Blunt. She hadn't found much, but she needed to simplify things as she explained. When she finished, Blunt stood quietly for a while.

"So, this is what we've got. More kid prints, a gun that basically blew a woman's head into tiny pieces, and another victim of the headhunter, with the same scythe or shears weapon. Oh, and a pretty ring that may or may not have belonged to the perp." He shrugged. "Not a lot more to go on, really."

"Yes, but now Lulu's been attacked," Sarah said.

"By an unknown assailant. I mean, it could have been a stalker who finally cracked."

"I suppose that's entirely plausible, but what if it is the same people?"

"Would the same people have attacked in broad daylight? I've got my doubts about that. And where were the big sharp weapons? Not to mention the gun that took the housekeeper's head. Now the ring; what does that mean?"

Sarah hesitated before answering. "Well, the stone

is very rare; it's something called gravitas blue. I'm afraid I don't know much more than that. I'm not a jeweller. There was some black fabric caught in the setting. It's, well, to be honest, it's black fabric, quite expensive, high quality, but I'm not sure what else."

"Okay, but it helps. We're looking for someone quite small, probably a child, wearing expensive black fabric. They're having a party, probably for the Changing of the Keys ceremony, and we believe they have a teddy bear." Blunt was staring into the distance as he spoke, clearly thinking aloud rather than talking to Sarah. "I have to go see Bernice Spitspeckler."

"Blunt? Do you want to interview this woman?" Sarah asked, pointing a scalpel in the direction of Lulu Devine.

"What? Oh right, Miss Devine, did you remove the head of your lover and that of the Marquis in some twisted plot to overthrow the government of Gloomwood?"

"What? How dare you? Anyway, how would the heads of that pair possibly threaten anyone?"

Blunt was about to continue. He held a hand in the air, ready to point dramatically at Lulu, but instead he paused. "How would, hmm, an excellent question. Now, do you have any idea why anyone would want to harm you?" he asked.

"Jealousy, I would expect. I am, after all, extremely successful."

"Yes, yes, well done you. Look, I'm convinced you

had no hand in this, but I would like you to stay here for a little while until we get you a police escort home."

"Well, I should think so as well, but could I please have my cell phone?"

"Feel free. I don't have it. Sarah?"

"I'm afraid it was probably left behind."

"What? This is ridiculous. You're holding me prisoner. How dare you? I need that phone. You, Blunt, get it for me now."

Blunt turned away from the shrieking banshee and spoke to Sarah. "Sarah, would you join me in my office? Oh, and bring your key."

As soon as they stepped out of the room, Blunt barked, "Quick, lock the door. That woman is absolutely mental. I don't want you going back in there until I'm back."

"Where are you going?"

"As stupid as it sounds, I'm going to get her phone. Her assailants should have cleared off by now, and it gives me a chance to see if there were any witnesses. When I step outside, lock the door behind me. I've got a feeling this isn't over."

51

At police central headquarters, Captain Sowercat was crying tears of laughter. He was perched as usual on the edge of one of his subordinates' desks, his round shoulders shaking with glee. "Tell me again," he said breathlessly.

"All right, guv. Constable Johnson called, and he said he's not coming in today because he's decided to go rogue. He said that if he came into work, you'd demand his badge and suspend him so he's not going to come in. Then he said he's going to take on the Youth Order by himself."

"Hang on, hang on, tell me why I'd demand it."

"Because he used to be addicted to Oblivion and because he's a loose cannon."

"A, haha, a loose cannon. What the hell does that mean?"

"Well, when I died, we used to have cannons on boats. If one of those was loose and we fired it, we'd have a right mess on our hands and in rough seas. That's what got me in the end. Killed by an unloaded cannon. But I reckon the rest of them drowned anyway, so it's all the same to me."

"Haha, yeah, loose cannon. That makes sense. Well, I've got a surprise for him, and for our new Chief Investigator Blunt. Thinks we're stupid, does he? Well, we'll show them. Saddle up, boys, and bring your best bludgeons and horrific, pain-inducing devices. We're gonna see exactly what these bloody kids have been playing at. Johnson thinks he knows better than the police. What a joke."

"Um, guv, you want us to go into kiddie town?"

A voice piped up from somewhere behind a stack of paperwork. "Oi, watch your mouth, you bigoted bastard."

"Sorry, Blythe. You know I didn't mean you."

Sowercat's eyebrows shot up, making him look even more like a cartoon character. "Blythe. Of course. I didn't even think of that. You can drive us straight in. Nobody will even bat an eyelid if you're at the wheel of a lorry and we're in the back. We'll be like a Greek statue."

"Sod off. I'm not running around with my bits out and some leaves on me 'ead."

"Not that kind of Greek statue, you pillock. I mean like that story about the big wooden statue full of warriors."

Blythe poked his head around the side of his desk. "Trojan horse, guv?" he asked.

"Bit early for a drink, Blythe, but I'll have one if you are."

"Nah, guv. *Trojan horse*. That's what you meant by Greek statue."

"Whatever. Blythe, saddle up."

"In the lorry."

"Yeah, in the lorry."

"It's in the shop, guv."

Sowercat paused, his nose inflated, and everyone in the police headquarters suddenly got smaller and much busier. "Fine," he said, "we go as soon as the truck is fixed, and I mean tonight. Make sure it's sorted, and as for the rest of you useless idiots, I'm going to start coming in here regularly to hold my breath just to make sure you get some sodding work done."

"Right you are, guv."

52

Blunt moved out of the doorway of the building on Pale Avenue as if there were snipers in every window on the opposite side of the street. A woman in a Victorian dress peered out from beneath a parasol with a look of disgust on her face. "Filthy drunks at this time of day," she muttered as Blunt sidled along close to the wall.

The lorry that had smashed into the back of the car filled half the street and the surrounding traffic was moving slowly, a cacophony of car horns punctuating the gentle murmur of pedestrians who saw the accident as a useful point to cross the road.

The front grill of the lorry was crushed in and the rear end of the car protruded from it as though the car was being eaten. Glass littered the ground around the vehicles and a fire hydrant sprayed water up into the air. The water returning to the ground simply merged with the rain, making almost no difference to the persistent heavy downpour.

Blunt crab walked to the car and slid into the back seat where Lulu had been attacked. There was glass on the inside of the car and Blunt rooted around in it until he found a ridiculously small and no doubt horrendously expensive hand bag. He received several cuts for his efforts, but where he would have bled horrendously had he been alive, there were now just red lines. His left hand had only been repaired by Sarah in the early hours of the morning after the broken fingers of the day before.

There was little to gain from searching the car further and he quickly extricated himself as more and more abuse was hurled his way, passers-by assuming he was the fool responsible for the traffic. Before he went back to the office, he clambered up into the booth of the lorry. Trapped between the steering wheel and the roof of the car was the crushed body of a man.

Immediately, Blunt's living instincts took over, and he assumed the man was dead. It took the man's desperate shout of help to remind Blunt of the new world he lived in. "Help, please help, I'm stuck. Don't just stare at me. Pull me out."

Wiping the rainwater from his face, Blunt deliberated over what to do. If he freed the man, there was the chance of a struggle and a small risk that the man would escape, although he definitely wasn't going to get very far. If he left the man in the truck, whoever had attacked him could finish the job. Getting the man out of the truck would expose Blunt to the attackers as well, providing them with an opportunity to kill two birds with one stone, if that was what they wanted. If that wasn't enough, he was also becoming increasingly worried about the innocent commuters who seemed to be getting more vociferous every second. There was no way to predict how long he would have before some frustrated banker finally snapped.

In the end, Blunt set to work freeing the man. It took considerable effort, and he had to stop to catch his breath twice with the exertion and once because he was gagging at the sound of the man's rib cage snapping. Eventually, he dragged the man free and back into the building, stopping on his way to pick up an arm. "Can always use an extra hand," he muttered, grinning at his own startling wit.

After banging on the door for five minutes, Sarah finally opened it. "I'm sorry, but you didn't say to open it again. You just said lock it," she said.

"Then why the hell did you open it at all? Never mind, how about you just give me a hand carrying these remains up the stairs?"

"Remains?"

"Look at the state of him. Hardly fair to call him a man now, is it? Oh, I think this belongs to the driver." He waved the arm with his free hand as he dragged the prisoner's crumpled form behind him.

53

Mortimer woke up feeling refreshed; he had a feeling that today was going to be a better day than yesterday. Then again, he had that feeling every day. It was all part of being a foolhardy optimist.

He had breakfast with his wife; they did the same thing every morning. The paper was delivered, and they split it between them. He read the sports section and the culture section. She read the celebrity gossip and the property section. They drank tea and had a leisurely breakfast, talking about everything and nothing.

Before he went to work, she helped him make sure his tie was straight, gave him a kiss, and wished him good luck with whatever was going on. The last few days she'd wished him luck with dealing with Blunt. This morning it was more appropriate than normal.

Marriage wasn't a rarity in Gloomwood, but few marriages were truly expected to last. When you have eternity, there's a lot of time for things to turn sour. Long-lasting marriages were something looked upon with great envy and not a small amount of curiosity. Mortimer and his wife were happy, happier than most, who lasted any length of time, and they'd been together since Mortimer could remember.

Mortimer was supposed to head straight to the Department of Investigations, but he decided to stop in at the Office of the Dead instead. He wanted to see what had been dumped on his desk since yesterday; it seemed like an age since he'd last been there. He arrived at his office early; the cleaning staff were still doing their early morning run. He sat down at his desk just before refurbishment started and concentrated on his work while the building rearranged itself around him.

Half an hour later, he'd successfully changed his answering machine message and replied to three letters from the public. He opened his office door and found himself face to face with Crispin Neat.

"Mortimer, what are you doing in my office?" The manager of the Office of the Dead scowled at him.

"Er, was *my* office when I went in, sir." Mortimer stepped backwards as he said it. He wasn't afraid of the manager suddenly getting physical. There was no risk of that.

"Well, it damn well isn't... oh... sorry, Mortimer. My mistake," Neat said while peering over Mortimer's shoulder. Before anything else could be said, Neat's long legs sped him away.

Mortimer didn't think much of it until he was in his car driving towards the Department of Investigations. It had been a strange moment; it was the first time Mortimer could remember anything like that happening.

The manager didn't make mistakes, and he hadn't recently missed an opportunity to remind Mortimer of his duties, or the fact that there hadn't been a significant breakthrough in the recent spate of murders. In fact, Neat didn't seem like himself at all. It wasn't just strange; it was pretty scary.

It was the first time Mortimer had truly realised just how important a man Crispin Neat was. Mortimer hadn't panicked when he realised the Grim Reaper was dead because he knew that Neat would deal with it. He hadn't panicked when he realised Blunt was going to create as many problems as he solved because Neat knew what he was doing.

The traffic lights turned green, but Mortimer didn't realise until the horns behind him woke him from his stupor. Neat was worried, he was stressed, and he was making little mistakes. If Neat was worried, then Mortimer was absolutely terrified.

He pulled up outside the building on Pale Street and, for the second time in as many days, sat in the car thinking. He wasn't a detective. He'd never wanted to be, and he was starting to wish he hadn't been asked to act as a go-between. That wasn't true. He wasn't *starting* to wish. From the moment he'd been given the task, he'd wished he wasn't involved, but now it was an intense feeling, a wriggling in his gut like a handful of maggots chewing his insides.

Pedestrians walked past, and he watched them longingly. The blissful ignorance they lived in made him more than a little envious. He wasn't happy, and that worried him. He was a happy person. Every day he woke up in a good mood, and normally, for all the crap he took, he managed to step into his house at the end of the day with a smile on his face.

He punched the steering wheel, causing the horn to beep, and was shocked at himself. Frustration wasn't something he was entirely a stranger to, but the need to take it out on an inanimate object was something he hadn't felt in a long time.

After composing himself, he walked up to Blunt's office, but it was empty. It was also remarkably unkempt, considering Blunt had moved in just days ago.

He decided to drop in on Sarah and was shocked to find Lulu Devine's body on a gurney. At first he assumed she was Ableforthed and was surprised he wasn't more upset about it. Sarah popped her head in and explained what had happened that morning, and he began to panic.

"I need to see Blunt. Where is he?" he asked, struggling to keep the near hysteria out of his voice.

"He's conducting an interview; it might not be a bad idea for you to join him, actually. The man he took in there is an absolute mess already but the mood Blunt's in... I wouldn't be surprised to be handed the guy in pieces."

"Who has he got in there?"

"Someone who was involved in this," Sarah replied, gesturing at Lulu without batting an eyelid.

Mortimer rushed out of the room, already imagining the things Blunt might have done to the man he was questioning.

He moved along the corridor, trying the doors on either side. In one room, he found a man in a black suit, holding an arm. Thinking Blunt had gone too far this time, he tried to wake the man up. When the man did finally open his eyes, he quickly explained that he was Lulu Devine's driver, and he wanted to go back to sleep. Mortimer left him to it.

As he approached the end of the corridor, he heard muffled voices. The one that was doing most of the talking could only have been Blunt. His voice held the threat of violence in it, and Mortimer wondered if he was just in time or too late as he knocked on the door and pushed it open.

Blunt was sitting opposite an angry-looking man with a scar running down his face and horrific injuries to the rest of his body. Mortimer didn't recognise him, but that didn't come as much of a surprise, as there was a good chance the man's mother wouldn't have recognised the disfigured pretzel of a human. "Blunt, what in Gloomwood have you done?" he asked.

"Let the record show that at ten fifteen, over an hour later than expected, Ralph Mortimer, third assistant to the manager of the Office of the Dead, entered the interview room. Interview suspended," Blunt said into a battered old tape recorder on his desk. The chief inspector picked up the recorder and walked out of the room, being careful to lock the door behind him.

"I haven't done anything. He was already like this when I pulled him out of the truck," Blunt blurted as soon as they'd moved away from the door. "Where the hell have you been, Mortimer? I asked you to be here first thing in the morning. We've had a serious crisis on our hands. Have you seen Sarah?"

"Ah, yes, I have. I'm sorry about this morning. I popped into the office on the way over."

"Why would you do that? You know I need you to

take Sarah down there to check the other crime scene."

Mortimer slapped his forehead. He'd dropped the ball. He knew there was a reason for being there on time, but he figured it was just his normal fear of a bollocking. Why did he pick that day to rebel against Blunt? "I'm sorry, I completely forgot. I'll take her now," he said.

"You'll have to wait until Leighton gets here. I need someone to sit in that room with Lulu Devine until she wakes up. At the same time, I've got to get on with this interview. Things are looking up, Mortimer. Sarah will fill you in. I need a cup of coffee and something for breakfast," Blunt said. He was working in overdrive. Whatever Mortimer had previously been dwelling on was shoved to the back of his mind. Blunt was on a warpath and it was infectious.

Then something clicked, "Ah, Leighton. She must have been one of the secretaries. Well, I'm glad it's sorted," Mortimer said.

"What?" Blunt asked, "Yes, fine. Secretary: that'll do nicely," he recovered quickly.

"Okay, I'll nip downstairs and get some breakfast and fresh coffee. Then I'll get Sarah to update me. Hopefully, this Leighton will turn up soon and we can get going. Looking forward to meeting her. Um, Chief Investigator, that man in there, he um—"

"He was like that before I got to him, Mortimer. I'll admit I can be a bastard, but even I'm not that ferocious."

Blunt suddenly stopped walking and looked Mortimer in the eye. "What is it you've got to tell me, Mortimer?" he asked.

"What? I never said I had to tell you anything."

"You've got something to tell me, Mortimer. I don't know what it is but there's something, and you need to do it now before it's too late, if it isn't already."

54

Leighton Hughes hadn't had the eventful morning everyone else had. She'd woken up and read the articles she'd been sent by the journalists who wanted in on her new venture. They were typed, error strewn, and crumpled, on black paper with white text.

They weren't awful, but they weren't exactly riveting either. The first piece was about the rapidly rising cost of physical maintenance. It didn't tell anyone anything new, but it was written from a sensationalist angle that would catch people's attention, and it had some quite emotional examples of individuals it had affected, with decent quotes. She sent it back to the journalist who'd written it with a note on top asking for the other point of view, i.e. the parts vendors'. It was easy to blame the high prices on the people who sold the goods, but Leighton believed it was the manufacturers who were upping the prices, and with limited competition, they could get away with it.

The next piece was pretty woeful, an article on the decline of maintenance on properties in Gloomwood. For every new building going up, the reporter believed there were two buildings going to waste and disintegrating where they stood. It might have been true, but there weren't any figures from a reliable source, nor was there a human interest angle. She sent it back with a fairly curt note pointing out the glaring flaws, not to mention one or two spelling and grammar errors that were just embarrassing.

Sports were a completely different matter. There were a lot of people desperate to get into sports writing and a lot of good sports writers had been left out as the number of papers had declined and the sports sections had shrunk. It was strange, but the majority of the football teams had their own magazines, which meant that most the fans only knew about their own club. The writer she'd contacted had clearly taken it upon himself to mix it up a little and she found that she actually had work from several journalists. The copy that had arrived with Leighton had been formatted and there were even full colour pictures.

She grabbed the phone after she read it and nearly cried with joy as she told the sports journalist, who had at first grudgingly agreed to help, how grateful she was. Typically, the journalist tried to suggest he had other offers and Leighton had to backpedal and tell him she was waiting for some other work before she decided who to make sports editor. Despite trying to keep it friendly, the desperation began to pour down the phone, and she managed to sound as if she begrudged having to give a decision by tomorrow, which was rubbish of course, but she had to keep him in check.

It was ten before she left the house, in a much better mood than she had been in for a while. As far as she was concerned, she had the sports section completed. She had a newly appointed science and technology writer, Sarah Von Faber, no less, who she had recognised at Blunt's offices and signed up. The woman was not well respected in Gloomwood, but Leighton had long been a fan. To top it all off, she was going to have a fantastic story for the front cover of her first edition. It was a pity she didn't have much else to go in the paper, but she had an idea of how to get plenty more news.

The Damned University had a ready and willing cohort of future journalists waiting for their break. She wanted to avoid the faculty members if she could. She needed vibrant minds ready to work, and the staff at the university were only a haircut away from being in the library. The students at the university were different, though. There was a healthy mix, and she didn't have to worry about them being fresh out of school without any life experience; they'd all lived their lives already. It was an entry requirement to all courses at the university that you'd been dead a minimum of eighteen months. They had entry exams for all the courses as well.

The entry requirements were the university's way of covering its back. By carefully selecting those people who were admitted onto courses, the professors could do almost nothing for the entire course of a degree, and the students would be intelligent enough to teach themselves what was required to pass the course. The harder-working ones would get better marks, the lazier, less intelligent ones would fail. It didn't make any difference to the university; they were the ones who decided what did and didn't happen.

Leighton had spent four years at the university and left with a master's in journalism. It was the second time she'd done it, but apparently her qualifications from the land of the living were considered irrelevant. While she'd been there, she'd learnt a lot about the university and how it worked, or rather how it didn't work.

After she'd visited Blunt's office yesterday, she'd driven down to the university and posted some advertisements for 'Talented Voices.' It was the kind of advertisement that students expected: vague yet promising. She posted an address for submissions for completed news stories with various warnings for unscrupulous reports and intentionally put the deadline at today, barely twenty-four hours after the advertisement went up so that only the most eager candidates would get their work in on time. That way, she wouldn't have to worry about clawing through a slush pile.

55

Mortimer felt sick. He was sitting in Blunt's office opposite the chief investigator, who was drinking something alcoholic he'd managed to pick up on his way home last night, before breakfast.

"So what I'm asking is what lies beneath the Marquis' house?" Blunt asked.

"Beneath? I don't understand what you're asking."

"He was moving, not much, but he was moving."

"Yes, oh, I see, um, sewers, well drainage pipes that lead to the canal in the city centre."

Blunt stood up, bottle in hand. "There, that's detective work, Mortimer. So, what's in the sewers?"

"Water, effluent, um, I don't know."

"Bollocks, well, someone was in there. I think that's how they got into the Marquis' and Miss Devine's homes: sewers. Nobody thinks people will be in the pipes."

"They're quite small."

"Kids?" Blunt asked.

"Children?"

"No, baby goats. Yes, *children*. Why are you being so cagey? What's going on?"

"Okay, I'm going to tell you, but you have to

promise not to react badly," Mortimer stammered.

Blunt shook his head and smiled. "No can do," he said. "Doesn't work like that. If I lose my temper and pull your head off, you're just gonna have to accept it. Now spit it out before my patience dwindles to such a small amount my body starts a charity called Patience Aid where my funny bones do stand up."

"What?"

"Tell me what you need to tell me."

Mortimer looked around the room nervously, glancing at anything to avoid eye contact with Blunt. Eventually, the silence and tension became too much for him. Maybe it was the way Neat had been that morning, but something in him seemed to click. He needed to help Blunt because he might be the only one who could deal with things with Neat out of the picture. "I think I know why someone would want these people's heads. I'm not sure and it's just a theory, but I think it might be important. I mean, it just makes sense," he said.

"Get to it, Mortimer."

"Well, I mean it's more of a myth, really, the kind of thing students at the university talk about when they've been at the Oblivion. It's about the Changing of the Keys. You see, there's this theory that the keys are actually keys to a place between here and the land of the living."

Blunt leant back in his chair, his eyes narrowed. "Okay, suppose for a second that I don't think this is bullshit. Tell me more," he said.

"Well, they say that there's a way to travel between the two that was once used by the Grim Reaper to collect souls, and if someone has the keys, they can open it up and travel back but only as ghosts."

"Well, that's very vague and mysterious. Is there any truth to it?"

Mortimer paused to bite his fingernails before saying, "I shouldn't be telling you this. I mean, this could be the end for me. If Mandrake knew, he'd…" He said it so despondently that Blunt felt ashamed of himself. "You know who Mandrake is?" Mortimer asked.

Blunt nodded, "Tall fella, bit of a Johnny Narrow—well, more than a bit of one—talks like he's got a mouth full of marbles," he said.

"Ah, yes, though I wouldn't want to be heard saying that."

"Okay, Mortimer, I don't want to make things worse, but what makes you think that Mandrake doesn't already think you've told me."

Mortimer stood up and placed his hands on the table. "There's some truth to it, Blunt. I know that much, but not much more. It's something I overheard a long time ago when I was a clerk back in the early days."

As Mortimer finished, the office door opened and Leighton walked in. "Hi guys. Front door was open." She smiled.

"What?" Mortimer and Blunt asked in unison.

"Front door was open so I let myself in."

Blunt and Mortimer both leapt to their feet and ran past Leighton, who chased after them.

56

Sarah was standing with her back to the door in the laboratory when it opened. She was stirring a mixture up that would help Lulu Devine's leg heal without a scar. Ever since she'd finished putting the stitches in she'd begun to worry about being sued. She turned to the door when she heard a strange clicking.

"Sorry, but you're in the wrong place at the wrong time, lady," a man said. He was standing in a black suit, staring at her, and in his hands he held something that looked like a gun. Lulu Devine must have just woken up as she started screaming, but Sarah couldn't tell if it was at the awful job she'd done of stitching her leg or because there was clearly a threatening man in the room. A shot rang out and before Sarah could do anything, everything went dark.

Blunt heard the shot as he left his office. He sprinted down the corridor and checked on the driver first because he was the nearest. His door had been opened, but he still lay fast asleep on the floor.

The next nearest door was the room he'd dubbed the interview room. It just happened to be one of the smaller offices on the floor. When he pushed open the door, he saw what he'd been dreading. The mangled man from the truck was gone. Blunt checked the wooden door frame. It had clearly been broken into from the outside. Splinters of wood showed where the lock had been forced through the cheap wooden frame.

He looked behind him. Leighton and Mortimer were watching him, waiting to be told what to do. "Get out of here. Run downstairs and get the hell out. Don't look back, get out and run, keep running until you're somewhere safe. I'll find you, and if I don't, you need to get to Neat. Tell him everything, Mortimer. This isn't going to end until the headhunter is found. Let's just hope it's not too late," he said.

Mortimer and Leighton looked at each other, and for a second Blunt was proud they were considering whether to stay and fight alongside him. Blunt was proud, but he wasn't stupid. "Get out, you stupid bastards, or we'll all end up like Lulu's maid," he said, mustering as much authority as he could manage. They didn't wait. This time, both of them ran to the stairs and disappeared.

Blunt tiptoed along the corridor towards the laboratory. Whoever had come in wasn't going to leave without making sure there were no more witnesses. He grabbed hold of a flower vase that someone had decided to place on a windowsill and hefted it in his hands. It was heavy enough to do some damage but would smash at the first use. Not only that, but Blunt knew that if it came to it, he only had one good hand after his visit to the police station.

The laboratory door was slightly ajar. Blunt crouched to the floor and tried to peer through the gap. He could just make out Sarah's white coat on the floor. He was already angry, but the thought of Sarah prone on the floor was starting to make the red mist descend.

He tried to calm himself, to think logically, but

before he could do anything else, he heard Lulu Devine's voice: "Oh please no, please—"

Without thinking, he reacted. As much as he hated the fake snobby cow, he was damned if he was going to sit back and wait while she was executed.

He burst through the door and dived behind a laboratory table. He heard shots as he moved, but didn't feel any pain.

"Well, if it isn't the chief investigator. Should I call you Blunt or Augustan?" a voice asked from the over the counter.

"You've screwed up royally here, buddy. Nobody comes into my place uninvited."

"Tough break, Blunt. I told you not to mess with me," the voice of the scrawny man from the interview room snickered.

Blunt looked around for some kind of clue as to what he was facing. The lab was mainly steel, all shiny and new. He looked across the room at a half-open cupboard door that reflected some of the scene for him. From what he could make out, there were three men in the room. One stood not far from Sarah's prone figure on the floor. The precarious way he was balancing against the gurney suggested he was the one from the truck, barely able to stand. Another stood by Lulu Devine, but the distorted reflection made him difficult to see clearly.

The third was creeping around the side of the laboratory table. Blunt watched the man drawing nearer. He couldn't see the culprit's face, but from the reflection on the cupboard door, he watched the man pull something out from beneath his jacket.

Rather than wait to be shot, Blunt gauged the position of the man trying to sneak up on him and launched the vase. He ducked his head beneath the counter and listened to the smashing porcelain.

"Nice try, Blunt, but you missed," a voice he hadn't heard before said. Blunt used the sound to correct his aim and threw the first thing he could lay his hands on. This time it paid off as the beaker Sarah had been using to make tea collided with the head of one of the men in the room. The glass exploded, and he heard the unfortunate assailant screaming before Blunt noticed how badly burnt his hand was.

"Okay, nobody's getting out of here without going past me. Put your weapons down and raise your hands over your heads," Blunt said. He knew it wasn't going to work. He was stalling for time. Hoping he might be able to come up with some kind of plan before things blew up in his face.

The remaining two men in the room were keeping quiet. Blunt's hopes of picking them off without getting shot himself were rapidly dwindling.

"Okay, looks like we're all stuck here, so what do we do now?" Blunt asked.

He watched as the two men held a whispered debate. If he moved fast, he could probably take one out without getting shot, but he wasn't going to get them both. Then the thing he'd been hoping to avoid happened.

"All right, Blunt. You better just come out now." it wasn't the voice Blunt had listened to when he entered the room, and it worried him. Whoever it was clearly pulled rank over the lieutenant, which was bad news for Blunt. "Last chance, Blunt, or we start making a mess out of Miss Devine here." The voice was familiar, uncomfortable to listen to, and even in normal circumstances, it would have held an undertone of malice. In the current situation, it was spine chilling.

"Mandrake," Blunt realised, "touch her and I'll be wiping your remains off my shoes for the rest of the day. It's your choice." Blunt tried to sound menacing, but he wasn't in a good position to make threats. "You sound like you're smarter than the idiot I brought in. Why don't you make the sensible move?"

"Enough, Blunt," the voice shouted across the room. "Where shall we start, Miss Devine? Shall we take your fingers one at a time?"

Blunt swallowed and then realised the key to the situation. These men didn't have a weapon that could wipe him out; they wouldn't have given him the chance to talk if they did. There was nothing that suggested the careful approach to snatching a victim's head. In fact—if anything—they were messy and unprofessional, or at the very least, not worried about being seen.

"Please, Blunt, just give them what they want. I can't defend myself." Lulu Devine's voice was shrill and panicky, but there was something in it, a message to Blunt. She wasn't the sort of woman to admit to being feeble, or to beg for help. He glanced at the cupboard door and saw what he was looking for. Lulu Devine was looking straight at the same point, and when she saw Blunt was looking, she winked. At the same time, he noticed Sarah's hand. Her fingers were lightly drumming on the floor, just enough movement to let him know she was still in play.

Blunt hesitated, then said, "Okay, I'm going to count to three. Then I'm going to come over to you. At the same time, you're going to let Miss Devine go. Do we have a deal?"

"You're not in a position to negotiate, Blunt. I'll count to three, you walk out, and we'll talk," Mandrake replied.

Blunt looked at the reflection and noticed that Sarah's palm was pressed to the floor. Lulu had balled her free hand into a fist.

"Fine. One, two, three—" Blunt dived out of the other end of the counter and threw a fist at the nearest man to him, the lieutenant. At the same moment, Sarah's body leapt to its feet and Lulu swung a punch at the other man. In the confusion, the last man standing—Mandrake—dropped his weapon. He dived towards it, but it landed at Blunt's feet. Blunt picked it up and pointed it at the man who was now on the floor, his feet almost exactly where he had just been standing.

"Now who's in a position to negotiate, you freaky bastard?" Blunt asked with a grin.

57

Leighton and Mortimer had reached the bottom of the stairs before they'd both stopped running. "What are we doing?" Mortimer asked.

"We're doing what we were told to do. I'll admit it feels wrong, though. I'm not good with authority. We should do what he said. I mean, we're not even part of the department," Leighton replied, but she smiled as she said it.

"You don't mean any of that. You're as much a part of this department now as Blunt."

"Well, I was never a good listener," Leighton replied.

"I think I've had enough of following instructions for today. You know what, how bad can being shot at be, anyway?" A feeling filled Mortimer that he barely remembered; it was rebellion. Decades of snivelling and wheedling his way through life were seemingly being washed away.

"I think the being shot at bit is actually not that bad. It's when they manage to hit you that you've got to worry," Leighton said. "Not sure if I fancy dying all over again." But she was already walking back towards the stairs.

They walked slowly and quietly, assuming the building was full of people out to get them. By the time they reached the fourth floor, Blunt, Sarah, and

Lulu had already taken down two of the men and he had the third held at gun point.

Mortimer and Leighton crept down the corridor, crouching as they went. They took it in turns to check the doors to every room. When they reached Blunt's office, Leighton opened the door as quietly as possible and poked her head around the edge.

Just as she glimpsed the boots of somebody, the door frame exploded above her head. Mortimer yanked her backwards into the hallway and she avoided screaming purely because the wind was knocked out of her.

Mortimer helped her to her feet and pushed open the door opposite Blunt's office. They both fell inside as they heard the office door being opened.

Leighton kicked the door shut and glanced around the room. They were in a storeroom. It offered absolutely no protection, and they looked at each other with their own fear reflected on the other's face. "Why didn't we just do what we were told?" Leighton asked Mortimer as what little colour she had vanished from her face.

"Not a good time to panic," Mortimer muttered. He was searching for something to use as a weapon. In the end, he settled on a long-handled mop.

Leighton, realising she didn't have much choice, scanned the room for something useful. She grabbed a can of air freshener and reached into her handbag. Mortimer watched curiously, and then she revealed a lighter. She pulled a handkerchief from her handbag and reached for a bottle of cleaning alcohol.

By stuffing the handkerchief into the bottle, she made her own Molotov cocktail. She then placed the bottle over the top of the door that was slightly ajar and lit the handkerchief.

Mortimer looked shamefully at his mop while Leighton created her trap. She then stepped back and held the lighter in front of the air freshener, ready to engulf their attackers in flames. They heard footsteps approaching and both of them retreated as far back from the door as they could. The steps stopped outside the door, and Mortimer glanced at Leighton. She was ready. Mortimer attempted to ready his mop for battle. There wasn't a lot he could do with it except point it at the door.

The door had a blind covering it, but they could see the silhouette of a figure stop in front of it. The figure reached out a hand, then appeared to think better of it. Leighton shrugged, a little disappointed, as the figure turned away. She let out a sigh, and the figure spun back to the door. She looked at Mortimer and made a face that attempted to convey an apology.

The figure kicked the door, and the bottle fell to the floor and smashed, spilling liquid everywhere, which was chased rapidly by fire. "Shitting hell!" a voice exclaimed.

Mortimer, seeing his chance, ran forward with his mop and used it as a lance. He hit the figure in the face with it and the man went down hard. Leighton was fast on Mortimer's heels, brandishing the air freshener and lighter. She leapt over the flames, and screaming, hit the air freshener button. Unfortunately, her lighter chose that moment to stop working. She had her knee planted in the attacker's chest.

"Get off me. Argh, stop spraying me, I hate pine fresh," the man spluttered. "For god's sake, woman, what are you playing at?" It took Leighton a moment to realise it was Blunt. She rolled off his chest. It took Mortimer a moment longer. He brought his mop down hard on Blunt's stomach, causing the chief investigator to ball up in agony. "Mortimer, what the hell is wrong with you?" Blunt wheezed.

58

Neat walked to the roof of the Office of the Dead and gazed across at the city. The Office of the Dead was the tallest building in Gloomwood, and the views from the top were impressive. He could see across the whole city, the domain of the dead.

In the far distance he could just make out the deathport, and beyond that the strange purple glow that made up the end of the void. He paused to take a breath before walking to the edge.

A set of stairs that led down to a door in the side of the building lay before him, and he shrugged before walking down them. He was certain they were a new addition, the building yet again following its own pre-emptive safety routines. Through the door were the inner workings of the massive clock that stood at the top of the Office of the Dead. It had never kept the time, but the design was impressive.

He climbed through the workings of the machine and opened a trap door, beneath which lay a corridor that seemed to cover far more distance than the building should have had room for. At the end of it was a wooden door with a slot in it at eye level.

He reached the door and knocked three times. The slot flew open and a pair of bespectacled eyes looked out at him. "Hello Crispin, in you come," the voice that belonged to the eyes said. Neat listened to several bolts being drawn back. The door opened, and he stepped through into a familiar room.

"Notice I locked the door this time. Your man Blunt has been getting quite physical with some of the malcontents in the city," the wizened old man said as he shuffled to his chair on one side of the table. On the table sat a chess board, the game still ongoing.

"Yes, well, employ a brute for brute force. That's the way it goes. He's getting there slowly, although I think it's taken a lot of help from others." Neat sat down in his chair and looked at the board intently.

"Well, surely you expected that. You can't expect a complete newcomer to come in and solve all your problems on his own."

Neat frowned and said, "Not my problems, the city's problems."

"They're the same thing. We both know that. You seem nervous, unlike yourself. Something bothering you?"

"I don't think Blunt's up to the task. I've asked Mandrake to get involved."

The man, who had been reaching across the board, withdrew his hand. "So you've told Mandrake what happened?" he asked.

Neat had barely glanced at the table. He nodded. "Yes."

The little man smiled as he moved a knight. "I think you've underestimated Blunt, and as for Mandrake, well, let's just say he never made it near the honours list," he said.

Neat, without looking at the table, moved a rook.

"Why hasn't Blunt come to question me then?" he asked.

"Would you?" the man asked, his eyes still fixed on the board.

Neat, for the first time, glanced at the table. "No, I wouldn't, but anyone else would."

A pawn clicked on the surface of the board. "Really, maybe you should take it as a sign of greater intelligence than you thought rather than lesser."

"You're suggesting he immediately discounted me."

"Of course, any logical course of action would have been to arrest you straight away and waste possibly days on interrogating you. Presumably Blunt saw this as a waste of his time by following the logic further and realising that you do not have enough to gain for the risks you would have to take."

Neat leant forward and moved his queen. "Checkmate."

The man leant back in his chair. "I'm not changing the list."

"Not for one second did I suggest that."

"Maybe, but for the first time in years, you have beaten me, and it's because you weren't concentrating hard enough to lose. You were too busy seeing if I would change my mind."

Neat managed a smile. For some reason, he imagined it hurt, although it didn't. His subconscious mind told him it should; he had been manipulated.

"Well done, but can I ask one more time, did you have anything to do with this?"

The man sighed and shook his head. "Crispin, what would the Master of Ceremonies have to gain?"

59

Blunt stood in his office with Mortimer, Leighton, and Sarah.

"Right, we've got Lulu Devine still in the lab. The three offices on this side of the corridor house a prisoner in each one. Lulu's driver is still asleep in a room on the other side. I want to hear your ideas. Let's have them," Blunt said, in no mood for games. He sat at his desk, waiting, with a face that hid nothing about the bad mood he was in.

"Well, we should probably interview the people who broke in," Mortimer ventured.

"Have you ever thought about going into brain surgery, or rocket science, Mortimer? Your levels of insight astound me. Of course we're going to interview the suspects, but we have four people waiting to be interviewed, including Lulu Devine, and not a lot of time."

Leighton coughed, and all eyes were on her. "Um, if we have their names, we can run them through the clairsentience machine and see what turns up. Might make the interviews a little easier," she said.

"That's the thing you used to find out about me? Actually, that is a good idea. Mortimer, you sort out someone to provide us with some up-to-date security in here. It's like working in a bloody pub at the moment. Anyone can come in when they fancy it. I want cameras in the interview rooms. The door needs to be reinforced, and nobody gets in without being checked for weapons. I don't care how you do it, but get on with it."

"But who's going to pay for all of it?"

"The Office of the Dead can pay. Get on with it and don't take no for an answer. Explain our position to Neat and if he says no, you can tell him that I quit, and my reasons will be given to the press. We are working the most sensitive case the city has ever seen and we've got people waltzing in here with guns. He's not an idiot, Mortimer, so stop quivering." He winked at Leighton as he said it.

Mortimer nodded. "Yes, sir," he mumbled before leaving.

"Sarah, how's your head feeling?" Blunt asked, genuine concern showing in his voice for the first time since the attack had happened.

"Fine, now that it's back," she replied. Her head had taken some finding. When they'd shot her, she'd thought she'd died. Everything had vanished, but moments later her vision returned and she found herself face down on the floor. Unfortunately, she also realised her body was some distance away. The gun shot had gone through her shoulder and out the other side, but as she fell she managed to decapitate herself with a particularly large and sharp blade she had used earlier on the Marquis' body. Blunt had spent twenty minutes playing Marco Polo, trying to find her head. Even now, it was held in place by some unsightly stitches that Leighton had attempted.

It had been an eventful morning and everyone's

nerves were frayed, but Blunt wasn't prepared to take a breather. "Listen, this was a desperate attack against us. If we weren't getting close to something, it wouldn't have happened. We need to find out why they were here…" Blunt stood up. "Oh God, Leighton. Before I forget, Mortimer thinks you're a secretary. Keep up the premise, please."

Leighton grinned. "Undercover work," she said. "Right, fine with me. Should I call you boss?"

Blunt frowned and pointed at her, but didn't have a riposte ready. Instead, he moved on. "Okay, I think I'll start with the gobby bastard who was clearly in charge: Mandrake. It doesn't make sense. He's a spook, he's clearly insane, but he supports the Office of the Dead. Sarah, you need to check on Lulu, make sure she's okay, and have a chat with her. Try to find out why anyone would want to harm her, and if she knows of any connection between the people who've been attacked. If she hasn't spotted the keys to the city thing, then for god's sake don't tell her. If she has, well, she's safest here." Blunt grimaced. "Bollocks, I've sent Mortimer off without asking if he found anything out from the staff at Miss Devine's." He scanned his desk, which was littered with his handwritten notes on scraps of paper. Beneath them was a report from Mortimer. Blunt glanced at it, then put it to one side.

"Okay, here's the plan. Sarah, you go interview Lulu. I know it's not your job, but needs must. Be thorough; it could be vital. Leighton, you're coming with me. We've got a little job to do, and then I want you to sit in while I interview the suspects. You won't have to do anything. It's just intimidating to have two people in the room rather than one on one. Let's go, people, we haven't got all day." He stood up and strode towards the door.

"Blunt, what's wrong with your hand? And you're limping."

"Nothing that's going to kill me."

"The police?"

"In one. Oh, and your bloody tea beaker."

Leighton and Sarah looked at each other, bewildered. Sarah managed a sly smile. "I'm going to need therapy for months after all this. Just wait until the support group hears about it."

"Just don't tell them until I've printed it," Leighton whispered.

60

Blunt dragged Mandrake out of the tiny office he'd been held prisoner in and shoved him into another nearly identical office. "Sit down," he yelled, inches from the man's face.

The prisoner squeezed around the desk and sat down. His ridiculously long legs meant that his knees were well above the edge of the table. He looked like an adult sitting at a child's tea party. Blunt pulled a seat up for himself, and Leighton sat down next to him.

"Right, this is a tape recorder. Anything and everything you say during the interview will be taken as evidence and can be used against you in a court of law, understand?" Blunt asked.

"Not really. What court of law would it be?" the man asked.

"Right, he understands," Blunt said to Leighton. "Present at the interview is Leighton Hughes, and Augustan Blunt for the Department of Investigations."

"This morning you broke into the Department of Investigations with what intention? Please bear in mind I have already had a chat with your subordinate," Blunt said without looking at the man.

"It's classified," the man spat across at Blunt.

"Right, when I bury your screaming body twelve

feet under the ground, I'll be sure to write 'classified lies here' on your headstone. I don't think anyone will rush to dig you up. After all, you and your organisation don't really exist now, do you?"

"You are messing with the wrong people," the man said, smirking. His hands were tied behind his back, and he kept shifting to try to get comfortable.

Blunt stood up and placed his hands on the table so he could lean closer into the suspect. "Who are the wrong people, you skinny bastard?" The insult was a bit obvious, but he was building up his part.

Leighton looked on nervously. She knew that Blunt was being as aggressive as possible to try to panic the man, but it still made her uncomfortable.

"You already know. I explained all this to you at the police station. Maybe you weren't paying attention." The man was grinning and staring at Blunt as if challenging him. His point wasn't completely unfounded, though. Blunt had barely taken in a word at the time.

"What was your plan here?"

"None of your business."

Blunt didn't hesitate. He hit the man as hard as he could. It would have been harder, but Blunt nearly missed due to Mandrake's height. The man fell on the floor and Blunt walked around the table and shoved him back in his chair as roughly as he could. "Try again," he said.

"We may be able to hide in the shadows, Blunt, but you are going to have to face public scrutiny about the way you've run this operation," the man said. Blunt had knocked out one of his front teeth. It fell on the table, looking remarkably like a tiny coffin.

Leighton had paled, and she stood up and walked to the corner of the room, leaning against it with one hand.

"You don't have any rights until you give me some information. That's how it works. Paperwork, you see." Blunt smiled as he sat back down.

"Fine, fine, we were here for the woman. Now release me before you have a full-scale assault on your offices."

"No, you can tell me what you were doing here."

"I just did."

"Do you take me for an idiot, Mandrake?" Blunt asked quietly and without any attempt to mask his venom.

Leighton couldn't bear it any longer, so she decided to play the good cop. "Okay, Mandrake, you can see that the chief investigator is pretty wound up right now. Why don't you tell us what was going on, and we can sort this out like civilised people?" she asked, careful to sound friendly and relaxed.

"Who are you anyway? What was your name again?" Mandrake raised one eyebrow, his misshapen head becoming all the more disfigured.

Blunt leant over the table and slapped him lightly across the face. "Don't you disrespect my colleague, sunshine. I'd hate to have to knock out the rest of your teeth. You're such a pretty fella as well." Blunt grinned. The man's face had already been ravaged by his lifestyle, and sarcasm covered Blunt's words like a silk bed sheet.

"My men will come for me soon."

"Okay, how about you tell us what you broke in for and what you wanted Lulu for? That's all we need to know. Imagine we're down at the pub. You'd tell a mate at the pub, wouldn't you?" Leighton asked, still trying to play the good cop.

"Very cute. I don't think Blunt has quite explained who you're dealing with. Perhaps my agents will take you in when they take me. They tend to treat prisoners quite poorly, particularly female prisoners. It's distasteful, but they do have to live in the shadows. Who can blame them?" The man laughed.

Blunt reached across the table and grabbed him by his shirt front. "What did I just say?" he asked quietly.

The man swallowed hard. "Don't disrespect your colleague?"

"Someone get this man a prize; we have a winner." Blunt shouted. He pulled the man across the table until they were nose to nose. Unfortunately, Blunt had to stand up to make eye contact. "Last chance, Mandrake. Start talking or forget about walking. Your choice." He pulled the prisoner up towards him and shoved him back in his seat with his palm on the tied-up man's face.

"You have no idea who you're dealing with, Blunt.

I will destroy you."

Leighton stepped up to the desk. "I've tried to help you, Mandrake, but the simple fact is that you've pissed the chief investigator off. I don't know who you're frightened of, but the chief investigator works directly for the Grim Reaper. Piss Blunt off, and you've pissed the Grim Reaper off. Do you know what happens to people who piss the Grim Reaper off?" she asked, looking at the prisoner. "They end up as ghosts, Mandrake. Can you imagine being a ghost?"

The spook grinned from ear to ear. Blunt shot a nervous look at Leighton, who sat in silence waiting for him to speak.

"Miss, whatever your name is, you are talking to Tomb Mandrake. I answer only to the Grim Reaper, and usually he prefers not to know what I'm doing. Of course, if you knew anything about what was going on, you'd know that your threats are very empty." Before he could continue, Blunt interrupted.

"Enough, Mandrake. You're not willing to talk, and you and your little gang of malcontents are used to making people disappear, so maybe I'll just show you my newfangled investigative techniques. My favourite's the tenderiser. Can you guess what happens afterwards? I'm sure Sarah can make you disappear if I ask her nicely."

"Enough of this. We're on the same side, after all. Perhaps we should start over. I think it's reasonable to say I've underestimated you and your team."

Leighton shot Blunt a look, but he didn't notice. "I

think you tell me what's going on and I'll think about starting afresh."

"We needed her head, or rather we needed nobody else to have her head."

Blunt moved to hit the prisoner again, but stopped when the man flinched. "Keep talking."

"We believe she is a target of the headhunter."

"She was going to receive a key to the city?" Blunt interrupted.

"Yes, wait, how do you know about that?"

"We can all see the importance of the people being taken out.," Leighton said, unable to contain herself any longer. "You can't believe we haven't made a link to the Changing of the Keys."

Leighton was about to continue, but Blunt looked at her with so much anger she felt like she'd been slapped. He turned back to the prisoner once he was sure she'd got the message. "Okay, why don't you tell me what we've missed and what you've got to do with it."

"Me? I have nothing to hide, Chief Investigator. Well, nothing that is relevant to this case, anyway. I am, much like yourself, a servant of this city. My goals are solely to protect. Our methods may be different, you with your brutish, in-your-face approach, and we with our more subtle methods."

"Subtle?" Blunt's tone made it clear he was less than convinced.

"Yes, we prefer people were not made aware of

some of the things that happen to put our fragile world in jeopardy." The man leant back as if he felt that excused him from further questioning.

"You know what, Leighton? I don't think we've learnt anything useful. Old, long, tall, and twig-like can just sit back and wait a while. Maybe we'll crack it ourselves."

"No—wait—there isn't time to spare. Blunt, you have to trust me. This matter can be dealt with quickly if you'll simply release me and let us take Miss Devine to safety."

"I'm not sure about any of this," Leighton said.

"The people who have been attacked: the Marquis, the head of the church of MEEP, Miss Devine, along with…" The man took a deep breath and Blunt nodded. That made perfect sense.

"They are all going to receive the keys." Blunt sighed.

"There's more." The man looked exhausted.

Blunt held up a hand. "Mortimer told me already. The keys are literally keys. Used correctly, they open a gate, or door, or something, to the land of the living."

Mandrake looked confused. "No, that's an urban legend. The only people who can travel to the land of the living go through the deathport, and travelling back is useless unless you are only visiting the dead. The living can't see, hear, feel us in any way. The keys open the door to here."

"To here?"

"That's the theory. Used correctly, the keys open the way to the land of the dead for those not yet living."

Blunt slouched back into his chair. "That's it?"

"That's it? Ah, I see a newcomer couldn't possibly understand what this could potentially cause. We're talking about birth, and with the birth of new life must come death, and so this place would no longer be a land of the dead but a land of the living. Then what happens to the dead people, Blunt? What happens to all of us?"

Blunt turned to Leighton. "Get out there and get on the phone. I want you to get a list of the next recipients of the keys to the city." She raised an eyebrow and thought about refusing. She wanted to be there for the interview, but she put aside her feelings and left.

"Okay, Mandrake, you're going to have to work with us on this. You made a big mistake by coming in here like you did, but I'm not going to let your bullshit blow this case. Who's behind all this?" Blunt turned his full attention to the man opposite him.

"That's why we wanted Lulu Devine. She was bait to draw out whoever was doing this. Do you have any idea who's behind this?"

Blunt was listening intently when he realised the man wasn't asking a rhetorical question. "We think it's the children."

"Children? There aren't any children in

Gloomwood."

"Whatever you want to call them, the short people who keep their childlike bodies."

Mandrake's features contorted into something Blunt could only interpret as a smile. "Of course, the Youth Order, that makes perfect sense. Well, Blunt, it turns out I really have underestimated you."

"So you agree?"

"Oh yes, definitely, and I understand now why you were brought here specifically. Neat is very shrewd, ingenious really." He stopped talking and looked at Blunt.

The door suddenly burst open behind Blunt and four large men in black suits piled into the room. Before Blunt could react, his face was shoved forward onto the desk with considerable force.

"Thank you for your assistance, Chief. We'll take it from here. Oh, and we'll be taking Lulu." Mandrake muttered as he walked out of the room, his black-suited officers quickly following.

61

Leighton sat behind Blunt's desk, looking at the clairsentience unit. There was something wrong about using it outside the library. A bodiless skull belonged within the confines of that ancient cemetery of the near soulless. Outside of the ancient tomb, they served as a reminder of what awaited everyone in the long run.

She held her fingers over the keyboard like a concert pianist preparing to play. She took a deep breath and glanced at the skull. "Well, whoever you are—or were—let's hope you can help."

Every key she pressed felt like a death knell, and she felt the hairs on the back of her neck rise.

She leapt out of her seat when the machine spoke. "RECIPIENTS, KEYS TO GLOOMWOOD… SEARCHING…" The tension was palpable. She held her breath while she waited for the machine to speak to her or print out some information. "RESULTS: 7,322,411. SEARCH WITHIN RESULTS?"

Relief flooded through her. Moving the unit hadn't broken it, but she still couldn't shake off the strange eeriness of the situation. "Um, yes please." She was surprised by how feeble she sounded. She typed.

"NEXT RECENT RECIPIENTS, SEARCHING…3011 RESULTS."

Leighton frowned. This could take some time. She

decided to try the first result. "How do I ask to print the result at the top of the list?"

Without her having to hit anything, the machine started typing, churning out a sheet of paper with a list of seven names. When she saw the first name, she gasped. The Grim Reaper himself was a target. She tore the sheet out of the machine as soon as it finished and bolted towards the door, stopping for a second to shout over her shoulder. "Thanks!"

As she ran along the corridor, she saw Tomb Mandrake disappearing down the stairwell at the far end with four serious-looking, suited men following him. The storeroom that had served as an interrogation room had been left wide open. Inside, Blunt was slumped over the desk.

62

"How long have we been in here?"

"Several days at least."

"Well, what on earth are they planning to do with us?"

"It's best we don't think about that. Be positive."

"And how would you suggest we do that? We've been decapitated and are being held in a bag. My face has been pressed against this fabric for days now. If the public sees me, it could have serious repercussions for my business."

"That should be the last of your concerns."

"What will my followers do without me? They'll be lost."

"There's plenty of time left. There should be more of us here."

"More? There's going to be more of us in here?"

"Well, they could use a different bag."

"There must be something we can do."

"You're the Marquis. Weren't you a god or something? Can't you do something?"

"ME! We're in here with the Grim Reaper, for crying out loud. If he can't do something, who can?"

"I was hoping you hadn't recognised me."

"Well, I wasn't going to mention it. It will only panic our friend here."

"Really? I'd of thought you would panic before the head of the church."

"Ah, that's it, I knew I recognised your voice from somewhere."

"Oh my lord, the Grim Reaper! If they've got you, then who in Gloomwood can help us?"

"Have some faith."

"Hah, and they say you've got no sense of humour."

"A gross misrepresentation."

"Let us pray…"

"Or we could play the name game."

"What?"

"Okay, I'll go first: Grim Reaper."

"Is that a T or a G? The Grim Reaper or just Grim Reaper?"

"Well, it doesn't matter. It's just the surname that matters."

"Oh, yes, quite right…"

"I can see the light."

"If you don't want to play, fine, but stop preaching."

"No, you idiot, above us."

"Oh dear."

"Ouch… oof… two? Why's there two?"

"That's bad news, isn't it?"

"Yes, very bad."

63

Johnson put the phone back on its cradle and turned to Petal with a vicious grin on his face, "Hook, line, and sinker."

"What? Do you think they'll go for it then?" The big man asked.

"That's what hook, line and sinker means. It means they took the bait. It's fishing terminology."

"I don't get it. They use nets and spears for fishing."

"And fishing lines. When was the last time you went fishing?"

"Never been. Saw them do it before I was forgotten."

"Oh well, yes, they fell for it. That was a guy from Sowercat's office pretending we were old mates and asking for more information. Ridiculous. I could hear Sowercat breathing next to him. They're going tonight. Can't believe we've had to wait this long." Johnson slipped into his grey police coat and tugged on a pair of thick gloves. "Ready?" As he asked, a loud knocking came at the door.

"Hang on. Let me get this first." Petal walked out of the little living room they shared, slipping out of the door diagonally, as his shoulders wouldn't fit otherwise. Johnson listened to a muffled conversation. Somebody was in a panic and asking for help. It wasn't unusual. People in the neighbourhood knew all about Petal and his altruism, and a lot of them also knew that Johnson lived in the same house. A drug dealer and a policeman who were both prepared to help the people nearby—they were a popular port of call for people in distress.

"Jay, we've got a problem." Petal half shouted from the door.

Johnson sighed as he joined Petal at the door. "What is it?" Standing in the doorway holding a frayed hat in both hands was a woman with whom both men were familiar. "Aunt Agnes?" Johnson asked, puzzled.

"Boys, you'd better come with me. Something awful has happened, and I didn't know who else to go to." Without hesitation, Johnson and Petal left their house and followed the little old woman down the street. It was an unspoken rule that both men had always adhered to: if Aunt Agnes ever wanted anything at all, they would help. She rarely asked, but when she did, they knew it was important.

When Petal had arrived in Gloomwood, he had been a mess, frightened and more than a little confused. It was Aunt Agnes who had found him and taken him in; the Office of the Dead wanted nothing to do with him. When Johnson had arrived, he'd been in the same state. When a hope or dream dies, they are thrust into a completely new world. Self-consciousness rears its head for the first time and they become individuals rather than a collective wish. It's a difficult time, but Aunt Agnes had taught him what he needed to know and looked after him before he knew how to do it himself.

In the ramshackle neighbourhood in the slums of the city, Aunt Agnes was more than respected; she was loved. And there wasn't a person in need that she wouldn't help, regardless of whatever they had done before.

Thirteen years ago, a boy had stolen one of Aunt Agnes' pies. When he had been found with it, the neighbourhood had been in uproar. They wanted him lynched, torn apart, and left just a head in a bin. Aunt Agnes had asked Johnson and Petal to step in and help. They did, and the boy who had arrived in Gloomwood only a day earlier was quickly given another chance. It was this sort of kindness that had left so many people indebted to her, but not a single one ever begrudged her help.

The woman led them down a deserted alleyway and when she was sure the two men were paying attention, she lifted a blanket off what appeared to be a pile of rubble. Beneath it lay two headless bodies.

"Belinda, a working girl, found them about an hour ago and came to me. She didn't know where else to go. Now I've come to you because I don't know where to go."

"Do we know who they belong to?" Johnson asked.

"I think they're Cornelius Potterson and Gloria Budge."

"The lecturers?"

"They had these in their pockets." She handed over

a purse and a wallet. Johnson opened them up and found the university identification cards.

"Why would anyone want their bodies?" Petal asked. "It's not the first time we've found a store around here."

"I don't think that's what this is. I think it's the heads that were wanted."

"Then why dump the bodies here?"

Aunt Agnes cleared her throat nervously. "They were on their way to see me."

Johnson grinned. "You? Well, that makes sense, Aunt Agnes. Even high fliers like these have to get some help in the beginning, I suppose."

"It was a very long time ago now. Actually, I asked them to visit me. I was thinking of doing a course."

It was Petal's turn to grin. "You always told me education pays dividends, Auntie."

"Stop it, boys. This isn't the time for laughter, especially at my expense. I've been through quite a shock."

"Sorry, Aunt Agnes," they both mumbled in unison.

Johnson frowned. "This isn't something we should keep to ourselves. This is something much bigger. Have you seen the newspapers?"

"Of course. I've got to give something to people to sleep on."

"The Marquis, and then this morning they were saying that religious guy." Petal was nodding as he spoke.

"Exactly, Petal. This isn't an amateur job. This is that headhunter again. I didn't think it would have any impact on us, though. Could they be related?"

Petal shrugged. "Aunt Agnes, would these two have received keys to the city?"

"Oh no, I shouldn't think so, I mean not again."

"Again?"

"Of course. When they started the university they received it, and rightly so, all the work they put in."

"Right, Aunt Agnes, you need to call the guy they've put in charge of all this, what's-his-name Captain Investigator or something," Petal said with urgency.

"Chief Investigator Blunt, Auntie, and when he gets here, tell him that the police are making a raid into the children's sector, and that me and Petal will meet him outside the new garden centre."

Aunt Agnes was nodding along. "Right, boys. I don't want you putting yourself in danger now. I expect to see you on Sunday for lunch, and Petal…"

"Yes Auntie?"

"Make sure you look out for Jeremiah. He's not as tough as you, and he sometimes thinks just because he's clever, he can get away with things he shouldn't. Now off you go."

64

Blunt came around on a gurney in the laboratory. His hand had been bandaged up and his trousers had gone. "What the? Where the hell are my trousers?"

In the corner of the room, something dropped to the floor and clattered, making Blunt's pounding headache ten times worse. "Sorry!" Sarah squeaked.

"Don't mention it." Blunt swung his legs to the floor and stood up. "But again, where are my trousers?"

"They're right there." She indicated a bench top. "How does your knee feel?"

Blunt glanced down, shocked. "Much better, actually. Thanks."

"Well, you were in a bit of a mess. I figured while you were out cold I might as well make some repairs."

"So am I roadworthy?"

"Should be. You'll need to be. Mortimer's waiting to drive you to a new crime scene. It's a double decapitation."

"You're not coming?"

"I'm going to head down with Leighton in a minute, but I need to collect a few things first. Mortimer made it sound very urgent. I was about to wake you."

Blunt glanced at the things that had fallen to the floor. The objects included one very large and dangerous-looking syringe. "I'm glad I woke up."

"Oh, your knee—it's not fixed. Well, it is, but you've still got your old one from the land of the living and it's faulty."

He struggled into his trousers. "I know. I like it," he muttered back to her as he opened the door and walked to his office. Inside, Mortimer was waiting, nervously fidgeting while Leighton was looking furious sitting in Blunt's seat.

"Feeling better?" she asked with absolutely no concern at all. "Why the hell didn't you tell me about this? The Grim Reaper's a target and you knew—"

"He's not a target, he was the first victim." Blunt cut her off curtly. "And I didn't tell you because you're just the bloody receptionist." Blunt glared pointedly at Mortimer, who appeared oblivious to the argument. "And it would have caused widespread panic if the entirety of Gloomwood had found out."

"What? A victim? You mean, oh, oh, OH!"

"Give me the list." Blunt snatched the piece of paper she'd been waving in the air out of her hands. "This is wrong. I realised why Mandrake hadn't completed his task and people were still getting beheaded. The Changing of the Keys hasn't happened yet. They're going after the people who got the keys last time. Get the right list."

Leighton smiled smugly. "You mean this list? I told you that you're not the only investigator in town."

She fanned herself with a piece of a paper.

Blunt raised an eyebrow. "You've gone up in my estimations. Mortimer, let's go. Leighton, you're taking Sarah to the scene. Just remember to keep your bloody mouth shut until we've cracked this thing, or whatever happens actually happens."

They raced down to the car without a word exchanged between them and hurried into Mortimer's car. The little man put his foot down as soon as they got in a drove like a maniac towards the scene. "What's the rush, Mortimer?"

"The people who found the body said we've got to hurry. Something's going on."

"I'm guessing Lulu is with the spooks."

"She is, but they've missed something important."

"What? What have they missed?"

"Look at the list."

"The list was simple and seemed to have been followed in order for the most part. First to go had been the Grim Reaper, top of the list. Next the Marquis, then Hugh Sullivan, head of and founder of the church of MEEP. Next on it were Cornelius Potterson and Gloria Budge, who had created the university." Blunt turned to Mortimer, who was looking very wild-eyed as he weaved through traffic, occasionally bringing them very close to being in a serious accident. "So we've got the two university scholars next. Any chance they're the victims we're going to see now?"

"But look at the last name."

Blunt did as he was told for a change. "Lulu Devine. What's the big deal? We already knew that."

"Look again, Blunt."

"Lulu Devine the Second. Well, it's a bit grandiose, but we've come to expect that."

Mortimer nodded. "Right, I know, but our Lulu Devine is Lulu Devine the Third."

"What? There have been others?"

"It's a title. It wasn't originally, and our Lulu Devine has been around for so long it doesn't really matter any more, but back then the first Lulu Devine was like a kind of princess of Gloomwood. When she grew tired of all the ceremony, she passed on her mantle to someone else. Then it happened again."

"What? I thought people here didn't normally die or go through Ableforth or whatever."

"They don't, not normally anyway, but originally Lulu Devine was like a gatekeeper. She was the Gloomwood Greeter."

"What does that mean?"

"It was her job to welcome people to Gloomwood. The first ever greeter gave it up because she wanted to help people. We're going to go see her now. She changed her name to Agnes, Aunt Agnes actually."

"What about the second one? The one that actually matters, Mortimer?"

"Went crazy, mad as a hatter. Ended up locked in

the library until recently."

Blunt was growing impatient. "Mortimer, get to the bloody point."

Mortimer stamped down on the brakes hard as the back end of the car swung out and he managed to complete a controlled slide around a tight bend. "The library sold some of its collection. That included Lulu Devine the Second."

"Who to?"

"Leighton was looking into it, but she seemed to think it was a shadow organisation owned by the Youth Order. Anyway, they made a formal complaint to the Office of the Dead. It was in my pigeon hole yesterday. Apparently they were expecting Lulu Devine the Second in the package but said she'd been damaged."

Blunt slammed a fist onto the dashboard. "Those bloody kids again. We're not going to the crime scene. We need to see Bernice Spitspeckler."

Mortimer swerved the car. He was so shocked by Blunt's reaction. "Wha—Bernice who?"

"Spitspeckler. Take us to the, oh crap, what was it called, ah yes, television, something death, Dead Air. Take us to the offices of Dead Air." Blunt was tugging on Mortimer's sleeve in his excitement.

"They'll be shut. It's quarter to seven."

"Don't be daft, Mortimer. It's television. They never stop."

"Fine, it's on the way. Stop pulling on my shirt.

We'll crash."

65

Captain Sowercat checked that his nose was properly attached and turned to his men. "Gentlemen, today we remind Gloomwood what we have a police force for. We are going to crush those that are intent on breaking the laws of our fine city."

Around the back of the lorry, several conversations continued, oblivious to the Captain's attempt at a rousing speech. "Hey, you two, shut your faces before I shut them for you," he barked at two unlucky men at the back of the lorry. The brief burst of anger made the rest pay attention for fear of suffering a public dressing down.

"Right. Here is the plan. We are going to drive straight into kiddie town with our own man at the wheel so they won't know what's hit them until we arrive. Then we are going to burst into the district and surprise them while they're at it."

"While they're at what, guv?"

Sowercat glared at the man who had asked. A bright young officer who in any normal organisation might have been going places. In the police force, Sowercat made it a personal mission to ensure these types were broken quickly and their ambitions were shattered. "Illegal activities, you absolute idiot. What on earth else? Now that bloody lost hope Johnson, clearly knew something was going on, so we're going to go in and find out what it is, using some good old policing."

"Yes sir, can I use my special baton, sir?" an overeager, long-time constable asked.

"Would that be your special long-range baton, Simmonds?"

"That's correct, sir."

"Are you sure it is not simply a gun, Simmonds?"

"Definitely not, sir. It fires small batons, sir, not bullets."

"And it won't make holes in people like bullets do?"

"Definitely not, sir. I have carried out extensive field tests."

Sowercat eyed the weapon in the constable's hand with curiosity. "You're sure it works?"

"Sir, yes sir."

"Have you only got the one?"

"Actually, sir, I brought a few extras just in case, you know."

"In case of what?"

The man looked around at his colleagues for support. "Well, in case you said we could use them, guv."

Sowercat reached forward and plucked the long weapon from the man's hands. It looked a lot like a blunderbuss with a truncheon poking out at the end. "Go and stand at the back of the lorry," Sowercat ordered the man.

With difficulty, the man clambered up and, unsteadily due to the rocking of the lorry, made his way to the other end. When he reached it, he turned around. "Guv, you're not gonna—" Before he could finish the sentence, Sowercat had pulled the trigger. The weapon made a sound like a small firework going off and the man at the back of the lorry disappeared through the rear doors out onto the road.

"Did anyone see if he was all right?" Sowercat shouted to the men.

"He's getting back up, guv," one of them said nervously while peering out the back of the truck.

"Excellent. Hand out as many as we've got. It's not like they'll kill anyone."

66

Johnson and Petal were walking confidently through the streets of their own neighbourhood towards the outskirts of the part of the city inhabited by those people who chose the bodies of children. People had long since given up trying to name the place. Every name seemed to become offensive. Johnson was trying hard to make sure he wasn't going to have any kind of mixed feelings if it came to a fight.

Petal was humming gently to himself as they walked. He never felt any nerves when it came to situations that would have terrified the average man. He was confident in his own ability to take care of himself. Even when he had come up against people who were larger than him, he had always come out on top. It was partly due to determination, but a lot to do with his natural instincts.

As they walked, Johnson realised they were passing through the transitional area between the two parts of town. Coffin Town and the unnamed area backed on to one another. The consensus was that they backed on to one another because neither one wanted to look at the other. Things were a little less poorly kept and there were telling signs that the area wasn't built for adults. The doors began to get smaller in the houses and a careful observer would have noticed that the houses, while not changing in height, began to gain floors. What might have been a three-floored terraced became a four-floored or sometimes even five-floored building.

It was getting late and the evening dusk had turned to night. The street lights that worked had come on, but most of them had been smashed or torn apart for scrap, so it was easy for the pair to remain in the shadows. Occasionally, they had to cross the street to avoid small congregations of child-like figures, but for the most part, the city seemed deathly quiet.

Johnson could feel a tingling in his bones that spoke of impending danger. A kind of sixth sense that had served him well as a policeman but had been honed long before he'd joined the force when he had lived on the streets, eking out a living through whatever means necessary.

Petal abruptly stopped walking and pointed into the distance. Beyond the roofs of the surrounding houses, at the top of a hill, the outline of the garden centre could be seen against the strange pinkish hue of the night sky. "We're nearly there."

"I'm surprised nobody asked questions about that place while it was being built. I mean, a garden centre in Gloomwood? It just seems ludicrous."

"Well, you've got to buy your twigs somewhere. They've got some incredibly real-looking plants."

"Really?"

"Yeah, I went once with Aunt Agnes. She said she wanted to add some life to her house."

"And?"

"I bought her a plastic tree and some real

deadwood with leaves stuck onto it. Looked good, but she gave them away to some lady who needed fuel for her fire."

"Oh."

"Where will we meet Blunt?"

"We'll wait across the road. Sowercat will turn up first. If he acts like I think he will, he'll already be smashing up things on the other side of the neighbourhood. He should eventually reach the garden centre. It sounds like a nice place, so he'll want to make sure he messes it up as much as possible."

"He's a vicious little bastard."

"Yeah, he is."

"And you went to work for him?"

"Not for him, for the city. *Police*man. Not Sowercat's man." He kept muttering as they walked.

"Can't believe we're going to go up against the Youth Order," Petal muttered.

Johnson shrugged. "If we don't do it, who will?"

"Sowercat and his monkeys, this Blunt fella, what about the spooks?"

"Good point. We shouldn't be stuck doing this. Should we just leave it?"

"Nah, the rest of them will just bugger the whole thing up, anyway." Petal grinned.

67

Crispin Neat strode through the corridors of the Office of the Dead, occasionally shooting a look of approval or disappointment at the few subordinates who were still in the building. He had been waiting for Blunt to turn up and try to arrest him when Mandrake called him on the special phone in his office, the phone for which nobody else had a number.

Mandrake had experienced some difficulty in securing Lulu Devine, who he believed to be the next target of the headhunter. Apparently, he and Blunt had had some kind of conflict. Neat didn't fail to notice Mandrake's less than forthcoming attitude. It was unusual. Full and complete disclosure to the manager of the Office of the Dead was something the spooks always adhered to, since it absolved them of blame.

Blunt had been more than a passing inconvenience, another sign that the man was more capable than they had originally considered. Lulu Devine was secured at an undisclosed location under guard, much like the mayor and governor were, but Neat couldn't shake the feeling that something was missing. It all seemed a little… obvious.

He decided to venture into the Grim Reaper's office. The room had been abandoned since the attack. It seemed an age away now. It was a sign of his own political prowess that Neat had managed to keep the disappearance of the Grim Reaper quiet up until now, but at nine o'clock tomorrow morning, that would all go out of the window.

Traditionally, the handing over of the keys to the city took place at noon in front of a crowd in the courtyard of the Office of the Dead. The huge clock at the top of the building would be set to chime at midday. It was one of the few times the clock would actually keep the correct time and the engineers were already working on it. A hundred years ago, five men had to run around with hammers making the bells ring to give the illusion the clock worked. Neat was determined not to have to sink as low as his predecessors.

Although the ceremony took place at twelve, people still gathered in front of the building to watch the potential recipients arrive. Twelve people were invited, six of whom were chosen to receive the keys. The Grim Reaper always turned up with the other guests. It was a tradition he had started and wanted to maintain, despite the fact that he would always retain one of the keys. Neat had once asked him why he bothered with the pretence and had been laughed at. The Grim Reaper didn't believe it was pretence. He said the day would come when he wasn't needed and he could become a normal civilian, allowed finally to leave office.

At nine o'clock tomorrow morning, there would be no Grim Reaper. Then the public would ask why and then worry followed by fear would set in. Questions would be asked, demands would be made, and then eventually people would realise he wasn't coming, that for some reason he wasn't able to.

Neat walked up the steps to the Grim Reaper's office, conscious of the sound of his own footsteps on the polished marble. The secretary who worked on the Grim Reaper's desk had quit before she'd realised what had happened. There was a cleaning lady who had begun to ask questions, and Crispin had been forced to ask Mandrake to intervene temporarily.

He pushed open the huge doors and stepped into the humble office within, being careful to shut the door behind him. Blunt hadn't solved the mystery of how someone had got into the office and past the security. Neat was curious. The office was the same as it always was, complete with the kind of paraphernalia most people associated with kindly old women. Neat smoothly sidestepped the handle of the scythe that was buried in the door and glanced at the calendar hanging beneath. It was covered with appointments, but there was nothing written on any of the dates since the incident.

As the de facto ruler of the city, the Grim Reaper didn't keep his own calendar. That was his secretary's job. Despite this, he had an odd habit of keeping a last-minute note of who he was about to see or had just seen. The calendar kept track of all of this in case he needed to refer back, on short notice, to the last time he had seen somebody.

Neat hadn't even thought of the calendar before now. It was the kind of thing that you shrugged your shoulders at and forgot about. Like learning that somebody folds the corner to mark their page in a book. It might be irritating if you spent time in their company, but otherwise, it didn't really matter. Now it was something Neat knew he had missed. If there had been an appointment, no matter how insignificant, the Grim Reaper would have marked it on his calendar. Staring out at him as if it was a massive neon sign with bells on it were the words he should have noticed days ago: 18:45—chocolate bars for the new children of Gloomwood, Susie Blunt.

His mind reeled. *Blunt*. Could it be a relation to the chief investigator? Could it be something so unheard of? He ripped the page off the calendar, being careful not to touch the blade on the scythe, and ran out of the office down to the basement.

The central administration room stretched far further than the outside of the Office of the Dead. The people who worked within it had gone home long ago. It was the workplace of the less impressive employees of the Office of the Dead, people who had been employed, more often than not, by mistake, Many of them had said the wrong thing, or failed in some vital task, and as punishment had been redeployed to the basement.

Every entrant to Gloomwood had a file in the basement. They were in the process of being uploaded to the clairsentience system, but there was always a need for a hard copy. The process of transferring them would take many years, yet and it wasn't as if the administrators were in any kind of rush.

The refurbishments to the building meant that every day the central administration was reorganised. Sometimes it helped, sometimes it confused things, but it never threw the place into disarray. It was an odd quirk of the system that the building seemed to understand the need for a kind of continuity. Either chronologically or alphabetically, the files somehow stayed in order. Neat was in luck: the files were alphabetised. He found the corridor for entrants under the letter B and began scanning along the shelves. After fifteen minutes, he'd found the BL section, and it was a further ten minutes before he located the name Blunt. There were four files. It was a relatively unusual surname, but not apparently unique. Ebeneezer Blunt had joined the city over three hundred years ago. Neat scanned the file, but it was irrelevant and unlinked, just as Phyllis Blunt—who had joined the city in the land of the living's year of 1908—had no hereditary connection to either Augustan or Susie Blunt. He pulled down their files and read through the one for Susie; he was already familiar with Blunt's.

The girl, as she had been, arrived in Gloomwood twenty-six years earlier. She was separated from her mother on route to the land of the dead. Nobody could identify quite where the separation happened or where her mother had gone, but then no-one really tried. Just like so many others who didn't end up in Gloomwood, the consensus was that they had simply gone to a different afterlife. Whether it was better or worse depended on the individual. Neat could have picked fifty children who had entered Gloomwood, and half of them would have been with their parents when they died. Half of those again would know that their mother or father had died with them, but for some reason, relatives never ended up in Gloomwood. With only one notable exception.

The Ableforths had both been in Gloomwood, for

a short period at least, and the events that unfolded showed that it wasn't supposed to happen.

Neat shuffled through the file until he found what he needed, what he hoped wasn't true, what shouldn't have been possible.

68

"Hey look, the bag is opening again. Oh, what the—"

Five heads rolled out of a black sack and bounced across a concrete floor, each ending up pointing in different directions. The last one to fall out bounced with the hollow sound of bone on rock.

"There was a man called Michael Finnegan. He had hairs all on his chin-i-gin…" The girl skipped as she sang and scooped up the head of the Marquis. "Well, Mr Marquis, you are the most handsome man in all of Gloomwood. Might I say how lovely it is to meet you finally face to face. So sorry the rest of you couldn't join us."

"Who are you? Why have you done this to us?" the Marquis squealed as the girl spun him in the air by his hair.

"Now, now, Mr Marquis. Don't you worry your pretty little head." The girl giggled as she spoke. She placed the head into a metal bowl. To the four heads on the floor, the Marquis took on the appearance of a large boiled egg in a cup. The girl spun quickly and grabbed the next head. "And you are the head of the church, literally. Let's put you next to the Marquis. You're kind of like the opposites of each other, aren't you?" Hugh Sullivan didn't even acknowledge the girl. He was too busy muttering prayers, begging for his own salvation.

She grabbed the heads of the academics from the university, pausing only briefly to lay the threadbare teddy bear carefully on the ground as she dragged them towards the huge egg cups. "Now professors, I'm sure you would both agree that two heads are better than one. In this case, it's six heads we need. Oh, I've just realised I've got egg cups for a pair of egg heads. How clever of me."

When she was satisfied the four heads were balanced, she turned to the last one on the floor, the skull of the Grim Reaper. Unable to show any emotion on his face, his empty eye sockets watched the scene unfold before him. "Hello, Mr Reaper. I'm sorry you didn't get to enjoy any more of the chocolate bars I brought you. I really didn't want to chop your head off, but my friends said I needed to."

"And who are your friends, Susie?"

"The other children, silly. Who else would they be?"

"Yes, that was silly of me. Why did they say you had to do that?"

"Because I'm the youngest, of course, I've got the key."

"But you will have to give that up eventually, anyway."

"Well yes, I know that, Mr Reaper, but I don't want to give it up for free."

"We all have to grow up one day, Susie."

"No we don't. You are not as clever as I thought

you were, Mr Reaper. You don't have to grow up at all in Gloomwood. My friends said that you were the one that allowed us to stay young."

"That's true, Susie, but what I meant was that there comes a time to put away childish things."

"You mean my teddy bear?"

"Well, that's one example, yes."

"But I can't give that up. It's going to bring us more friends."

"You can make more friends without a teddy bear, Susie."

"Oh, Mr Reaper, you're quite frustrating. I know that." She stooped and lifted the skull off the floor with both hands and carried him towards a fifth egg cup. "But I want brand new living friends to play with, and so do all of us." She placed the head carefully in the cup and stood back.

"How old are you, Susie?"

"I'm seven!"

"It's been a long time since you had a birthday, hasn't it?"

"You don't have birthdays in Gloomwood, so nobody has to grow up."

"And yet you have a cake with candles on it."

The girl looked at the cake with some confusion. "That's not for me. That's for the new person we're making."

69

Captain Sowercat and his men were ransacking the neighbourhood of the children of Gloomwood, grabbing anyone too stupid or too slow to get out of their way and trying to get information out of them. The plan to drive in and surprise the neighbourhood had worked, largely because it was nighttime and nobody was really paying any attention. In fact, so far everything had gone to plan, which was a bit of a problem because there wasn't much of a plan left.

Sowercat was trying to interrogate people without any idea what he was trying to find out. A small boy was being held by two men beneath a flickering lamp post when Sowercat kicked into action.

"Tell us everything you know about the Youth Order."

The boy desperately searched around the edges of Sowercat's bristling frame for some kind of help. "They organise a bake sale every other week at the Church of MEEP's cathedral to help homeless children."

"Are you trying to be funny? What are they planning?" Sowercat nodded at the officer holding the child's arm, and the officer dealt a swift slap to the back of the boy's head.

"I don't know. Next week's bake sale?"

"What do you do for a living?"

"I sell clockwork toys."

"You some kind of wind-up merchant?"

"Yes, yes I am."

"What? Oh, yeah, I guess you are. Tell us what you know and we'll let you go."

"Just tell me what you want to know and I'll tell you. Please, whatever it is, I'll tell you if I know."

Sowercat hesitated, unsure of where to go with his questions. He nodded to the officer who had dealt the slap to the back of the man-child's head. He released the boy's arm. "You can go." The boy scampered away, shooting furtive glances over his shoulder.

"Guv, what are we looking for?"

"I don't bloody know, do I? That bloody lost hope knew something, though. It was something big. We need to get to the bottom of it and quick."

"Um, why? We're never normally bothered."

"Because of that bloody chief investigator bastard, people are going to start to question what the hell we do for them."

"But guv, we're the police, we stop crimes."

"When was the last time you stopped a crime, you fat-arsed idiot?"

"Eh? Me? Talk about the pot calling the kettle crap."

"What? You mean *black*, pot calling the kettle black."

"Nah, I mean crap. My kettle's crap."

"Bollocks to this. What's happened here recently?" Sowercat looked around at the street. The walls were covered with fly postings, some of them aimed just at people in this neighbourhood: a children-only nightclub, kids-only cinema showings, two-for-one offers on kids' meals at various fast-food restaurants. Others were the same rubbish that covered most walls in the city: advertisements for gigs, Office of the Dead warnings against fly posting. And staring Sowercat in the face was a month-old poster for a new garden centre run by children. "There, that's new, it's big, and it's local."

"Right, guv, and what does that mean?"

"It means we're going to go get some flowers."

"Eh?"

"That was supposed to sound much more assertive and arse-kicking-like."

"Oh, right, okay, let's get some flowers, boys!" the constable screamed into the night.

70

Mortimer drew the car to a halt outside the television studio. "Blunt, whatever you're doing, please make it quick. Neat's going to tear me apart for this. We were supposed to be rushing."

Blunt leapt out of the car and ran straight through security, who were a little surprised but not moved enough to do anything about the harassed-looking man running through the door. Twenty seconds later, Blunt reappeared. "Hello, ah, sorry about that. Got a little carried away. I'm looking for Bernice Spitspeckler."

The more senior of the two guards nodded gently. "You 'av an appointment?"

Blunt hesitated. "Um, yes, I have. I'm Chief Investigator Blunt here to see Bernice Spitspeckler under direct request from the Grim Reaper." A small part of him hated using the Grim Reaper as an excuse to get things moving more quickly, but he was in a hurry.

"Blimey, the Grim Reaper, eh? Well, um, right you go, straight up the stairs. At the end of the corridor, take two lefts and then it's straight in front of you, it is." The man seemed to be staring at Blunt in awe, but Blunt didn't have time to bask in the glory of it and set off at a sprint.

The two guards watched him running down the hallway. "Wouldn't want 'is job for the world." the more senior one said into his mug of hot cocoa.

"Nah, 'specially not as Bernie's just gone out in one of the vans," the junior—and yet in appearance far older—guard mumbled. The two guards waited patiently for Blunt to return. "Hey, have you ever wondered why they always pair us up like this?"

"How d'you mean?"

"Well, you look really young and I look like I could have made the ink the Dead Sea scrolls are written in," the older guard said.

The younger one smiled. "Company policy, isn't it? Older guard and younger guard, best way to make a team, all right now."

The older junior guard pointed at his colleague. "So it's just for appearances?"

"My, my, I can see why you became a security guard. Veritable genius, you are," the man said, looking disappointedly into his now-empty mug of cocoa.

Blunt's figure appeared at the far end of a corridor and he came to a breathless stop in front of the two men. "She's... not... there," he managed to say.

The man who looked younger nodded. "My colleague has just kindly informed me that Bernice has taken possession of one of our vans, so she is not currently available. Sorry for any inconvenience."

Despite his exhaustion, Blunt could feel himself becoming agitated. "Where has she gone?"

The senior younger guard walked to his desk and

flicked through several pages of irrelevant information. "Ah now, she appears to be heading to that newfangled garden centre, ready for a live broadcast."

Blunt nodded. "And that's normal, is it?"

"No, nothing normal about that at this time of night, not for children's television, anyway."

71

Across the street from the garden centre, Johnson and Petal waited impatiently. "We should just go in there and sort the whole mess out."

"I left a message telling him to meet us."

"It's been ages."

"It's been about an hour since we left Aunt Agnes. Even if he was on his way immediately, it will have taken at least ten minutes to get there, more than ten minutes at the scene. We should be expecting a long wait. He's an investigator, Petal, not just some brute like the rest of the police." His sentence trailed off as he watched a large black saloon screech around the corner. It came to a very sudden stop slightly after where Petal and Johnson were waiting.

A man climbed out of the passenger side, pausing briefly to grab a battered hat. He shouted some kind of obscenity at the man inside the car. Whoever it was eventually climbed out of the vehicle and locked it. The two men walked towards Petal and Johnson.

"One of you two JJJ Johnson?"

Petal stuck an arm out, blocking Johnson's step forward. "One of us might be. Who are you?"

The man in the battered coat had a face that had seen too many late nights. "Chief Investigator Blunt. Which one of you is Johnson?"

Petal stepped to one side, letting Johnson step forward. "I'm Johnson, this is Petal. He's a friend. I'm with the police."

Blunt shrugged. "You don't seem much like the police I've met. You said it was urgent. If you've got any information on the recent incidents, we'd be grateful for your help." Blunt was still panting from running around the television studios. They'd only given the crime scene a cursory glance. Mortimer had actually left the engine running, but when they'd been passed the message to meet Johnson and Petal, Blunt forgot the pretence and they rushed to the garden centre.

The crime scene had been much as they had expected: two bodies belonging to people on the list, which meant things had taken a step closer to wherever they were going. Blunt had left the job of working the scene to Sarah, who would report back her findings when she returned to the office.

The message Johnson had left was something of a bolt out of the blue, but Blunt wasn't about to look a gift horse in the mouth. The children's television people were here, and they were here for a reason.

They stood in front of the newly opened garden centre. It was a huge building, unlike anything Blunt would have associated with a garden centre, a grim sight that blighted the view of the neighbourhood, which was pretty depressing in the first place. In the strange Gloomwood night, it seemed to take on a ghoulish appearance. The cut stone pillars at the entrance had poorly crafted stone birds balanced on their tops, and the shadows they cast made them look like gargoyles standing guard.

Blunt quickly assessed the threat the two men posed to him and Mortimer. He was conscious of the little man's presence, and the fact that Mortimer had been reluctant to leave the car had added to the tension Blunt already felt. The larger of the men was a frightening prospect, and as they'd drawn closer, Blunt found himself calculating the time it would take to run back to the car if the meeting turned out to be some kind of setup. He'd already known Johnson was a policeman, which had only served to fuel his paranoia that he was in for some kind of attack.

Johnson himself would have made Blunt nervous. He was muscular and lean and stood several inches taller than Blunt. The policeman's confidence in his movements suggested that he rarely needed the help of a man like Petal when it came to any kind of physical action. The larger man deferred to Johnson, but when he had moved to engage Blunt, the bigger man had stopped him. He was protective.

"Two days ago I received a letter at work from a woman. When I saw her she told me she used to be somebody else. I'm not going to lie about it; she was under the influence of Oblivion and had clearly been addicted for some time. I believe that she was a target of the headhunters and that they have her now. Chief Investigator, she was once Lulu Devine. I don't know if you realise this, but—"

Blunt raised a hand to stop him. "She was the second Lulu Devine, I understand. We've managed to get that far. What did she tell you?"

Johnson nodded. "Of course you know, sorry. I'm

not used to people properly investigating matters. I'll get to the point. The Youth Order, at least I believe it is the Youth Order, either way it's a group of once-children—"

"Aren't we all people who were once children?" Mortimer piped up from behind Blunt.

Petal's voice rumbled. "Who's he?"

"I'm Ralph Mortimer, third assistant to the manager of the Office of the Dead," Mortimer said haughtily.

Blunt felt things escalating. "He works with me's fine. I understand what you're saying, constable. Please carry on."

"Call me Johnson; I'm not a constable. I'm doing this outside of the police. I've quit."

"Good for you, you're wasting time." Blunt tried to keep the surliness out of his voice, but failed.

"Don't speak to him like that. How's he wasting time? We've been waiting for you." Petal shifted slightly and Blunt got the sudden image of an eighteen-wheeler revving its engines.

Johnson continued. "She said they were building a machine, a machine that would end the Grim Reaper's hold on everything. She was telling the truth. She was terrified but couldn't do anything about it."

Blunt nodded. "Why did she contact you?"

Johnson looked confused for a second. Then realisation dawned. "I'm a lost hope and Petal's a demi-god. We're not like you norms. The woman was a lost hope, her brain addled with Oblivion. Where else would she go? The rest of the police wouldn't have listened. The Office of the Dead wouldn't give her the time of day. There's more to this city than it appears. I know you're new, so you might not understand, but we look out for each other. She came to me because she knew I'd listen, but even then she wasn't sure. That's why she sent a letter."

Mortimer shifted uncomfortably. "She could have tried. We wouldn't have ignored her."

"It's nice that you can say that, but you don't believe it. Even if every individual believes that they don't feel that way or don't want to admit it, it doesn't stop the way things work. Mr Third Assistant to the Manager of the Office of the Dead, you may want to believe you don't think that, but the organisation you work for does collectively, and you know that. Don't beat yourself up about it."

Blunt wanted to keep the conversation on track. It was veering dangerously. "Why do they want to make this machine?"

Johnson shrugged. "Lots of reasons I can think of. There are plenty of people who agree with the idea, but there are even more who don't. Some people think they can be reunited with loved ones. Others think they are actually in purgatory or limbo and that they should be allowed to pass on to heaven or whatever you want to call those things. It's different for everyone."

"What do you think?" Blunt asked.

"I think it's a very bad thing to do and it won't lead

to anything good." Johnson seemed to make up his mind about something. He turned and looked across the street at the building. "Petal and I think they're in there, but we don't know. We're not sure about anything. This whole thing is based on assumptions and the beliefs of a madwoman. I wanted to ask you what you thought before we acted."

Blunt turned to Mortimer. "Ralph, it's probably best if you leave and pretend you weren't here. It won't do any favours for the Office of the Dead if we're wrong."

"Really?" Mortimer was genuinely surprised to hear Blunt's consideration for things other than the investigation. "No, I'm not going to go. At least if I'm here I can explain to Neat what we were doing, I think."

"The headhunter has been taking the heads of the holders of the keys to the city, and we know children are involved. We've found evidence of them at the crime scenes—" It was Blunt's turn to be interrupted.

"They are not children." Petal's voice was like thunder in the distance. Blunt could almost feel the man's voice and he remembered: the man had been a demi-god.

"For the sake of argument, let me call them sodding kids or we'll be going around in circles forever. We know that little people —" he shot a look at Petal, whose eyes seemed to burn with rage, " — were involved. Everything points to them. They're stealing heads, but we don't quite understand why. So it makes sense, a strange kind of sense, that they might need them for this machine. It's cropped up in our investigations. On top of that, we received a tip that a woman, or girl, whatever, called Bernice Spitspeckler is involved, and last notice we got she's in there. Not only that, but the previous Lulu Devine pretty much told you everything we've come to believe about what's going on. I'll go in with you. This has to stop."

Johnson nodded. "Good. We go in when Sowercat gets here."

"Sowercat? I thought you'd left the police."

"I have, but I made sure Sowercat knew I was on to something. He hasn't got any idea what it is, but he's ripping apart this neighbourhood to find out. When he realises the garden centre is new, he'll burst in there with most of the police force and start wrecking the place. He's a bully."

Blunt grinned. "You're using him as a diversion."

Johnson smiled back. "The Youth Order are a nasty bunch. I wouldn't want to go up against them, just the four of us."

"Maybe he'll do the job for us?" Mortimer squeaked.

Johnson's smile got bigger. "Sowercat's an idiot. He won't think to look around the place. If the machine is in there, then he wouldn't know what it is. Anyway, they'll keep it hidden. Petal says they use the sewers, so we're going to do the same. When he goes in those doors, we go down there,"—Johnson pointed to a manhole cover—"right beneath them and into the middle of whatever's going on."

"What makes you think it's here?"

"The woman told me she was carried through tunnels. It was Petal who cracked it." Johnson turned to the demi-god, eager for him to share in the glory.

Petal seemed less keen to speak up, but he did, albeit begrudgingly. "It's a well-known fact that they use the sewers to travel around the city so they can get in places we can't. I've seen them do it before. Sometimes they pop up out of nowhere. Most people think they just don't notice them, but they jump out of the drains quick as a flash. They try to appear mysterious and magical, but they's nothing but rats. They even wear these creepy rings that glow in the dark to see their way around."

Blunt searched in his pockets for the ring he'd taken from Sarah. "Like this?" he asked, holding it up.

Petal nodded, "Yeah, only they normally glow. It must need charging up."

"Okay, well, that explains the sewer, but why the garden centre?"

Johnson stepped in again. "That was Petal too. It's big, it has truckloads of deliveries all the time, it was built very recently, and it's got excellent access to the sewers. I hadn't thought of it until now, but if you look at it now, it looks like it was designed for the purpose."

Blunt turned to the building. "Isn't it a bit, well, it's not subtle, is it?"

Johnson nodded. "They spend their entire death

trying to be subtle, makes sense that they finally give it up when they think things are going to change."

"Very true, but if anyone asks, it all hinges on bloody Bernice Spitspeckler, agreed?"

The two men shrugged.

72

"Oh, the grand old duke of York, he had ten thousand men, he marched them up to the top of the hill and he marched them down again…" The little girl waltzed around the room singing, flitting in and out of the columns upon which sat the heads of the keepers of the Gloomwood keys.

"Do you like singing, Mr Marquis?" She paused, smiling at the head of the Marquis of Muerto Lago, who had remained silent since being placed on his egg cup.

"No."

"Well, that's not very good, is it? You'll be singing with me soon. We'll all be singing together. Oh! How silly of me. I forgot to introduce you to your old friend. Say hello, Rosalind, or whatever you want to call yourself." She reached down and lifted a head from somewhere out of view to the five watching heads. It belonged to a woman, her face contorted and twisted in anguish, her eyes gazing far away. What light there had been behind them now little more than a flickering candle.

"Lulu? That's Lulu Devine. I haven't seen her, well, I can't remember how long it's been." Hugh Sullivan gasped. "Lulu? Lulu, can you hear me?"

The woman's eyes fluttered. Somewhere within, there was a spark of recognition. "Hugh? Is that you, Hugh? It's good to hear your voice. Oh, no wait, you're a bastard. You dumped me for the next Lulu Devine. Oh dear, I'm sorry, but it's not good at all, is it? Is she here? The little girl, I mean, not that new Jezebel. Are you here, dearie?"

"Of course I'm here, just like I said I would be," the girl answered.

"Oh, and your friends? Are they here too?"

"Yes, of course they are. They're watching through the windows."

"Ah, through the windows, of course. Well, I still wish you would change your mind, but I don't get a say in it, do I?"

The little girl pouted. "Don't make me feel guilty. You shouldn't complain. It's going to be wonderful."

Professor Cornelius cleared his throat, which was impressive given that he had very little throat left. "Um, I don't want to be involved in this either. Nobody actually asked me."

The girl wheeled around, smiling. "Oh professor, you should be happy. Think of all the theories that you can prove and disprove."

The professor looked confused. "What are you doing to us?"

Directly across from the Professor, the Marquis started laughing but there was no joy in the sound. "You're the professor. I'm just a pretty face, and I know what this is. The silly girl is trying to open the floodgates and we're the keys."

Madame Budge shouted, "The keys, oh dear,

Cornelius, I told you we shouldn't accept the stupid things. Now they'll be the end of us. Keys to the city... the whole thing was a horrible idea, and look at poor Lulu. What happened to her?"

The little girl's smile grew as she skipped across to Madame Budge. "I know that; my friends told me. She went a bit loopy because she wasn't like a normal person. She used to be people hoping for something and then one day they gave up hope, so she came to Gloomwood. When she got here, everyone was very nice to her and they made her into the city's greeter, but then one day people found out she wasn't a normal person and people started being mean to her, so she ran away. Then she started taking nasty drugs because she was so sad, alone, and unhappy, and they just made her worse. It's a very sad story, but it's okay because when we all sing it will fix everything for everybody."

The Grim Reaper suddenly had everyone's attention. He didn't make a sound or a gesture, but everyone knew he wanted their attention. ***"Perhaps your friends would do us the pleasure of speaking to us before they take the next step. It would, after all, be polite."*** There was something ominous in the way he said the word *polite*, as if, even in the situation he was in, being rude to him was the worst kind of insult imaginable.

Not even Susie was impervious to the undercurrent of menace to the Grim Reaper's voice, and she stopped skipping. "Yes, you're right. It would be polite. My friends are always polite. Daddy always said good manners were important."

She walked away from the egg cups, but not before she carefully placed the woman's head on a final egg cup that sat in the centre of the other five. Their heads were all pointed towards the head as it gazed into nothingness, jaw hanging loosely.

The girl disappeared from their view when she stepped out of the ring of podiums and down several steps. They could hear the sound of a door opening and a very muffled conversation, followed closely by multiple hesitant footsteps.

"Ahem." A small boy cleared his throat nervously as he entered the ring of decapitated heads. "I am Peter. Welcome to the new headquarters of the Youth Order."

"You are not the leader of the Youth Order, Peter. Where are Rose and Frederick?" the Grim Reaper asked.

The boy looked around nervously at his compatriots, who remained in the shadows. "They're not in charge any more."

"Why? When did this happen? Nobody told us. It isn't legal without my seal."

The boy seemed to lose any awkwardness he felt. "Your seal? You're not in charge any more either. We had enough of being told what we could and couldn't do. We want to leave Gloomwood and you can't stop us."

Hugh Sullivan suddenly started wailing loudly. "Heathens, you shall be cast down. You are undeserving, and the fire shall purge you of your ill-doings. Repent now or all is lost."

"Shut up, Hugh. 'Repent now… cast down.' We're dead already, bloody religious idiots." Professor Cornelius sneered. "You'd think people would finally turn their minds to more fruitful pursuits once they've died."

The Marquis suddenly seemed to perk up. "Ah, a religious debate? Science versus faith: always a good one to break into a fight, and neither of you have bodies. This should be amusing."

"Gentlemen, now is not the time." The Grim Reaper's voice never revealed any emotion. It was as soulless and hollow as he appeared. This meant that those he spoke to read into it whatever they felt they should, and usually this meant that even the kindliest-intended comment could be terrifying.

The room fell into silence, which was eventually broken by a nervous-sounding Susie. "Shall we start the cameras? Bernice says I can say action."

The young boy in the centre of the circle seemed to remember where he was and who he was very quickly. "Yes, Susie, why don't you go and get the party hats and cake while I entertain our guests, but you better hurry. You'll want to shout action very soon." The boy was grinning maniacally. "We're all very excited."

She skipped across the circle, her every step making a loud click on the stone floor, echoing throughout the chamber. As she went, she sang, "Hickory, dickory, dock, the mouse ran up the clock."

"She sings a lot. She was singing when she cut my head off," the Marquis muttered to nobody and everybody.

The Grim Reaper's head spun. *"Actually, that was me. She put it in my head and it just wouldn't stop. I am sorry."*

The boy's grin grew. Any wider and the top of his head might have fallen off. "Careful now, Mr Reaper. No more of that spinning or we'll have to nail you in place." The boy kept turning slowly, looking at the heads in turn with his head cocked to one side. He was dressed in smart shorts and a blazer with a white shirt and navy blue tie underneath.

"You're dressed like you're a school boy," the Marquis exclaimed.

"Of course I am, I'm a child after all."

"It's so last year," the Marquis huffed.

73

Sowercat pounded at the door to the massive building in front of him. Behind him stood twenty policemen, half of them brandishing their projectile truncheons, the others holding a mixture of blunt objects in their hands. One of them, a god in his previous life, carried a wooden cudgel with lightning bolts carved into the staff. He pushed his way towards Sowercat. "Allow me, guv." He swung the cudgel hard three times at the door. Splinters flew out of it, spraying the policemen where they stood. "I reckon they heard that," the man remarked with a smirk.

The policemen waited, hopping from one foot to another, rubbing their hands together, and blowing on their fingertips in an effort to keep warm.

A sudden bang punctuated the still night and a policeman at the back of the crowd crumpled to the ground. Sowercat and his men fell as one. From his position on the ground, Sowercat whispered, "What happened?"

A policeman awkwardly climbed to his feet. "I think he knocked himself out, guv."

"He did what?" Sowercat barked, getting to his feet, his nose inflating.

The policeman who had spoken tried to back up, but the men behind him prevented him from gaining any distance from Sowercat's ever-expanding nose. "With his truncheon cannon, guv. I think he pulled the trigger by accident."

"Well, is he all right?"

"Think so, um, hang on." The rest of the policemen were dusting themselves off as the man Sowercat was talking to threaded through them and bent down to the prone figure on the floor. "He's all in one piece."

"When he wakes up, make sure he gets a good slap for being such an idiot. Now everyone be quiet. I can hear someone coming." On the other side of the door came the sound of footsteps drawing nearer. From behind the massive wooden panelling, rattling and clicking emanated until eventually a small, previously unnoticed wooden window slid open, revealing a pair of tired-looking eyes.

"What do you want?" the figure behind the door asked in an unnaturally high voice.

Sowercat bent down so he was eye to eye with the person behind the door. "I'm Captain Sowercat of the Gloomwood police. Open the door."

The eyes disappeared for a moment. When they returned, they looked annoyed. "Have you got a warrant?"

"A what?" Sowercat asked.

"A, um, warrant." The eyes disappeared for a moment and returned again. "It's an official piece of paper that says you're legally allowed to enter the building. You need to have a good reason."

Murmuring came from behind Sowercat. The policemen surrounding him were all confused by this new ruse to try to stall them. Sowercat's nose had momentarily deflated. It now looked like a balloon that had been filled but had been left to deflate again. "A warrant, that's new. Who gives out the warrants?"

"Hang on, I'll find out." The eyes disappeared again and Sowercat could just about make out the sound of whispering, but the words were too quiet to catch.

"I don't like this, guv," the policeman with the cudgel attempted to whisper, but it was a poor attempt. Gods and demi-gods were not known for being particularly discreet. It wasn't something they had ever learned in the land of the living.

Before Sowercat had an opportunity to berate the man, the eyes reappeared. "Warrants are normally given out by judges."

"Right then, who's got some paper on them?" Sowercat asked the men assembled behind him.

"I have, guv," answered the man who stood waiting to slap the unconscious man on the ground.

"And a pen?" Sowercat barked, his hand held in the air, waiting. "Come on, lads. We're police officers, and we never go anywhere without a pen and paper, do we?"

The assembled men shuffled their feet awkwardly, all refusing to look at each other or, more importantly, catch the eye of their captain. Sheepishly Sowercat turned back to the eyes in the door. "Do you have a pen?"

"Yes, certainly," the eyes said as a pen was slipped

through the window in the door.

"Thank you," Sowercat said, his voice smothered in gratitude.

The eyes disappeared from the window again and Sowercat made out two words from behind the door: "Oh bugger."

He knelt on the floor and quickly scribbled a note on the paper with the bright pink pen he had been handed, which had a clown's head on the end of it. "Right, here's your warrant. Let us in," he shouted as he stood up, waving the piece of paper.

The eyes narrowed. "I'll have to see the warrant. I don't see how you could've got it signed by a judge."

"Judges decide who gets locked up, and only me and the Grim Reaper decide that, so I'm a judge. Now stop wasting time."

The eyes stared at Sowercat. Without a word being said, they blinked three times and the window quickly slammed shut. The sounds of locks being opened and keys rattling made the men behind Sowercat stand to attention, ready to burst into action. The huge door slowly creaked open, dust showering the waiting men. As it opened, it revealed two children. One of them was dressed in a security guard's uniform. Sowercat recognised his eyes from the window. The other one wore a pair of blue and white pyjamas with a towel dressing gown and big furry slippers designed to look like rabbits.

The boy in the dressing gown stepped forward. "Why have you disturbed us in the middle of the night like this? The Office of the Dead will be hearing about it."

"Police investigation, step aside," Sowercat barked while waving his men forward.

"What investigation? What are you looking for?"

Sowercat frowned. He had no idea what they were looking for. "What? Somebody hit him quick; he's annoying me." An officer stepped forward and brought a truncheon down hard on the boy's head. He crumpled to the floor.

"Right men, tear this place apart and let's find out what the hell bloody Johnson was on about."

74

Across the street, hidden in the shadows of an alleyway, Blunt stood watching Sowercat and his men. With him were Mortimer, Johnson, and Petal. The two men from the hard streets of Gloomwood looked at ease with the situation. They were going in to stop bad people from doing something wrong; it wasn't a complicated scenario. Mortimer, on the other hand, seemed to be getting ever-increasingly smaller and more preoccupied with anything other than the situation in front of them.

Blunt couldn't blame the bureaucrat for his nervousness. He himself was feeling uncomfortable. The investigation had been pointing at the right people from the beginning, but Blunt's living-world investigative techniques hadn't been getting them anywhere. Strong-arm tactics were something he had been known for using in the land of the living: intimidation, insinuation, character assassination. There had even been some dark times when he'd considered planting evidence on a suspect to get the job done. But compared to Mandrake and his spooks, or Sowercat and the goon squad, he was positively genteel.

He allowed himself an amused grin. People had always told him he was a dinosaur with bad manners and a violent disposition. He hadn't needed to change to become a better person. He'd just had to die for everyone else to be worse.

When the door to the garden centre finally opened, Petal reached down and lifted a manhole cover from the ground. Blunt winced when he saw how easily the huge man was able to lift an object that should have required special equipment to move.

"Down into the depths of hell they strode." Mortimer's voice wavered.

"Actually, the sewerage system in Gloomwood is a remarkably clean place, which is good news for us," a voice from deep down below them shouted up. "Are you new members?"

The four men around the top of the manhole looked at each other, each one waiting for someone else to speak. Finally, Blunt poked his head over the top of the hole. "We're not sure yet. We might have the wrong place."

"This is the headquarters for the Gloomwood instruments of death support group. You must have the right place, since we're the only ones made to meet in the sewers. Normally we meet beneath Pestilence Lane, but there's been some trouble with blocked lavs above, so we've come over here," the voice replied.

"Instruments of death?" Blunt's policeman's attitude rushed to the fore. "Well now, this is unfortunate. I'm afraid we're going to have to ask you to move along. I'm Chief Investigator Blunt, and this is my colleague, Constable Johnson. We're not going to have any trouble now, are we fellas?"

There was silence for a moment, and then the voice piped up again. "But we've unpacked the tubas and everything."

"Tubas?" Johnson now poked his head over the top.

"Aye, tubas and violins, clarinets, oboes've even got a couple of trombone players and a couple of double bassists. It takes us an hour just to get the stuff down here. Come on, lads, we're not doing anyone any harm."

Realisation hit Blunt like a wet kipper across the face. "Instruments of death. You're musicians?"

"Aye, what did you think we were?"

"Never mind, we're just passing through. We won't disturb you. Just keep out of our way," Blunt grumbled before hoisting himself over the edge of the hole and gripping onto a precariously slippery ladder. "Do you play in the dark?" he shouted down into the pitch black below.

The voice shouted back up again, "We take the lights out. The humming that comes from the old electrics interferes with the acoustics. We've got some spare night-vision goggles."

Mortimer followed Blunt down the ladder carefully, but still managed to kick him in the face. When Blunt reached the bottom, he hurriedly stepped out of the way of the others, following him down. The smell he had been expecting to overpower him since the manhole cover had been removed still hadn't arrived. Instead, there was the strong odour of pine trees. He spread his hands out in front of him and found that he was facing away from a wall.

"Here you go, Chief," said the voice, now inches away from him, while something was pushed into his outstretched hands. "Just slip them over your head."

He did as he was told, and the room suddenly burst into view. Everything was tinged with a pink hue but, surprisingly, he could see almost as well as he could in daylight. "I thought these things made everything green." In front of him, he could now see a man holding a trumpet, grinning inanely. Behind him appeared to be an orchestra of at least forty people with a wide range of musical instruments. "So you're the instruments of death support group, then?"

"Yes, that's us." The grinning man nodded. "Would you like to hear a song?" The obvious eagerness in the man's voice presented Blunt with an image of a dog eagerly waiting for a ball to be thrown. It broke his heart to say no, but they were in a hurry. "Perhaps next time. We're in the middle of a very important investigation."

They were furnished with a further three pairs of night-vision goggles and quickly but apologetically made their way further down the tunnel in the direction of the garden centre. As they walked away, the orchestra they'd left behind began playing the theme from *The Dam Busters*. Blunt groaned.

75

Leighton and Sarah stood at the scene of the latest abduction sipping cups of tea that Aunt Agnes had provided and dunking delicate shortbread biscuits the kindly old woman had made.

"Looks like we've got a serial headhunter on our hands," Leighton said in an imitation of Blunt's gravelly voice.

Sarah laughed. "That's good. How about, 'I couldn't give a monkey's how you do it, sweetheart, just get your bloody arse in gear.'"

The two stood chuckling while they looked at the decapitated remains of the latest victims.

"Is he really that chauvinistic?" Leighton asked, while trying to bite a shortbread biscuit that was dangerously close to collapsing under the strain of the tea it had absorbed.

Sarah nodded. "Yes and no, I mean, he's a chauvinist. There's no doubt about that, but I think he means well. It's sweet in a kind of big, dumb animal kind of way, like a dog. You know, they can rip your throat out and they crap everywhere, but they're cute anyway, or people think they are."

"You think he's cute?!" Leighton's excitement caused the biscuit to give up, and half of it fell into the mug with a plop.

"That's not what I meant." Sarah felt herself

blushing and hoped she was going invisible.

"Oh my god, you do. You fancy Blunt. That's hilarious. Sorry, I mean, well, you've got to admit he's a bit of a head case. I mean, he's kind of charismatic in an 'I'll fight them to the death' kind of way, but really? Blunt? You could do so much better."

Sarah scowled. "Let's change the subject. What do you think of the scene?"

"Well, it looks like somebody chopped off their heads and took them away. That's the normal modus operandi, isn't it?" Leighton replied, still smiling at how uncomfortable Sarah was.

"Good terminology and yes, you're right, but there's a big difference. The attack didn't happen here, and they risked attacking two people at once."

"How can you tell if the bodies were moved? Couldn't they have happened in different places?"

Sarah nodded. "Yes, definitely, but they happened at the same time, or so near to the same time. It doesn't really matter. We can tell by the condition of the area around where their heads have been removed. Looking at the fibres and dirt on the bodies, we can get a pretty good idea of where the incidents happened, and both bodies have almost identical trace evidence."

"So the attacker is stepping up their game. What does that mean?"

"I only do forensics, so I'm not going to speculate. Blunt's the investigator. He makes the inferences."

Leighton's eyes narrowed. "Is that a dig at me?"

"At you? Why would that be a dig at you?" Genuine surprise appeared on Sarah's face before it flickered like a light bulb and vanished. "Oh sorry, I was hoping that was finally stopping."

"It's okay, except if people walk by, they'll think we have three victims now. I meant, is it a dig at me because I'm an investigative journalist?"

Sarah was quiet for a moment. "It wasn't a dig at you at all. Sorry if you thought it was. Maybe you should be thinking of what it might mean rather than arguing about the fact that you're capable of investigating."

Leighton nodded haughtily. "Right, well, I suppose it could mean the attacker is gaining in confidence, or maybe nearing the end of whatever it is they have planned. They could be taunting Blunt by proving they're not afraid of him, or they could've just taken two heads because they were interrupted getting one. No, wait, if that had happened they wouldn't have taken the head. They'd probably just have Ableforthed whoever they weren't after, like they did with the chambermaid. Actually, I'm pretty sure they weren't taunting Blunt. So far, the attacker hasn't done anything to suggest they want to engage with anyone who's investigating the crimes. So… confidence or nearing their endgame. One of the two."

Sarah's headless body walked over to the corpses. "I'll bet you it's their endgame."

Leighton placed her mug on the cobbled street and stepped forward. "Why?"

"Because we've got another shopping list here. I didn't look too closely before because, well, I didn't fancy trawling through the bins, but I recognise the writing and I'm pretty sure it matches the one we got from the Marquis, although I'd need to check."

"And?"

"Everything's crossed off it."

76

They followed the sewers carefully, avoiding the stream of effluent that passed down the centre of the long cylindrical pipes, until they stood beneath a huge vertical tunnel that Johnson believed to be beneath the garden centre.

"You're sure this is the right place?" Mortimer had already asked twice, but the others had ignored him.

Johnson turned to the little man. "I'm sure. They sell a lot of water features and the tunnel slopes downwards towards the canal in that direction." He pointed in the opposite direction they had approached from. "They need decent drainage in case the place floods due to one of the fountains breaking or something. Trust me: your lot would have insisted on it."

"My lot? Meaning norms?" Mortimer asked, angry at the way Johnson differentiated between the different groups of people in the city.

"Your lot, meaning the Office of the Dead," Johnson replied curtly. His eyes weren't visible beneath the goggles, but he kept his focus on Mortimer long enough to make him squirm. "If we climb up, we should be able to hear what's going on inside. If my information's correct, and Petal's right that this place is their base, then there'll be guards."

Blunt nodded and reached for the first rung on the wall. "I think we can handle a bunch of kids." Before he could move, Petal placed a massive hand on his shoulder and pulled him back so he could step in and take Blunt's place.

"I go first. And Blunt, they's gonna have more than just a bunch of kids up there. There's muscle for hire in Gloomwood. It ain't even expensive."

Blunt simply shrugged his shoulders and watched while Petal pulled his massive frame up the ladders. The rungs creaked under the strain. Johnson followed, then Blunt, followed by Mortimer, who made no effort to hide the fact that he was moving as slowly as he could without falling too far behind.

When they reached the top, everyone stopped. Blunt gripped the ladders desperately when something heavy brushed past his shoulder. "Won't be needing those any more," he heard Petal murmur in his attempt to be quiet. Blunt sighed with relief, realising that it was the pair of goggles the demi-god had been wearing and grateful that he hadn't released the girlish squeal that had been begging to burst from his lips. "Right," the big man at the top of the ladder continued, "I'm going to try to lift this thing and see what's going on above before we make our entrance." With a grunt from Petal, a circle of light appeared from above.

77

In the room where the heads of the six holders of the keys stood, strange things were afoot. Well, stranger things than before. A film crew had arrived and the boy who was clearly the mastermind behind the operation was having make-up applied to his face while trying to read lines from a piece of paper in front of him. In the centre of the circle stood a newly erected tall clockwork device. It surrounded the podium on which Rosalind's head sat and was connected by five long poles to the other podiums. Where these rods met the podiums, a hatch had been opened which revealed cogs and wheels that were clearly a further part of the complex machine.

Next to the column, three children were busy making preparations, oiling the various complicated cogs and valves. A fourth child, a large, round boy, was using a bellows to pump air into a balloon which was rapidly expanding.

Susie was holding the brown bear in her hands and whispering soothing words to it that couldn't be heard over the loud clanging noises of the machinery being put in place. The Grim Reaper and his compatriot heads watched the surrounding scene with growing frustration, occasionally shouting but being constantly ignored.

The man-child in the school uniform waved away the little girl who had been applying his make-up, as another boy dressed in a black suit whispered something into his ear. Whatever it was, seemed to animate the already hyperactive child even further. He waved his hands in frustration and appeared to shout at the suited boy until an agreement was reached. Around the room, the assembly work drew to a close.

The doors around the edge of the circular room were closed, but not before the sound of some kind of fracas was overheard from outside. The children looked at each other nervously as heavy bars shut the only two entrances to the room, and they were plunged into silence.

"Are we ready yet?" the boy impatiently barked at the television crew, who were being organised by a girl who couldn't have been older than six when she died.

"Yesh, yesh, we're ready now." She sprayed words as she spoke, clearly never having quite grown into the teeth she had while she was alive.

"Good. Susie, it's time to bring our furry little friend to life. Are you ready?" The boy switched personalities like a golfer switched clubs, always finding the right one for the person he was speaking to.

Susie had a tear in her eye as she stepped into the circle and found a space within the podium beneath Rosalind's head. "It won't hurt him though, will it?"

The boy smiled. "Of course not, sweetie. We wouldn't want to hurt Mr Fuzzles, now would we?" He led her away from the stage, whispering reassurances. Once she was safely deposited into the hands of waiting children, he danced over to the circle and stood facing the camera. "Well now, Bernice, time to get this show on the road."

The little girl organising the camera crew nodded over to Susie. "Are you ready to shout action?"

Susie nodded, the tears still damp on her face.

"Okay, in three, in two, in one, and—"

"ACTION!" Susie managed to shout before continuing to sob.

The boy in the school uniform suddenly became even more energetic. He moved around the stage to the cheers of the children behind the camera. "Ladies and gentlemen of Gloomwood, tonight you are going to witness the Youth Order's greatest accomplishment. Tonight we are going to bring you life. That's right. You heard me right, boys and girls. We have cracked the secret to creating life in Gloomwood. A once-in-a-deathtime opportunity to see life created once again! This will never be repeated, except of course, in repeats. I present to you the keys to the city." As he said it, he spun backwards to allow a camera on a crane to circle the heads on the six podiums.

"As many of you know, the six people here have recently undergone some minor surgery and have since been unavailable to comment on the goings-on in Gloomwood, in particular in respect to the so-called headhunter. Speaking of which, may I present Susie Blunt, our headhunter extraordinaire. She's been trained for twenty years to bring this day together for us and I'm told that a documentary is in the making. Is that right, Susie?" The boy held a hand in Susie's direction. She appeared dumbstruck by the lights and cameras.

"Yes," she said. Her voice, amplified by the sound equipment, echoed around the room.

"More on that later, but right now we're coming up to eight in the morning. Now, you may not realise this, but the keys themselves aren't the shiny keys the Office of the Dead has led us to believe. 'Oh no,' I hear you cry, 'surely the Office of the Dead wouldn't lie to us.' Well, I'm afraid we have some disturbing news. They have lied." He dropped his voice low and Bernice clipped a camera man around the ear to tell him to zoom in closer. "They've lied a great many times, I'm afraid, and not just about little things; oh no, they told us that life couldn't exist here, and you know what, we were HAPPY ABOUT IT!" he shouted and the camera zoomed away.

"We were all happy about it, but, and I must be honest, the Youth Order were especially happy about it. We didn't want real children stealing our places and confusing things. In fact, truth be known, we still don't want that, which is why we have built this, and we are creating this record for you all to see. We are going to create a new life here, and because of us, nobody else will ever be able to do the same thing. Start the music." He pointed off camera at the boy who had been pumping the huge balloon full of air.

The boy was sweating profusely. He wiped his brow and reached for a valve, pausing to take a deep breath before twisting it open. Suddenly the room was engulfed in a noise that shook the walls, and from the six skulls came a wailing sound that was both horrific and beautiful at the same time. The boy, who had been resisting the urge, suddenly began laughing wildly. "Life—we're creating life."

The central podium began to rotate as it rose slightly higher. The little girl seemed to be waving at it. She rushed over and grasped the boy in uniform. "Is that supposed to happen?" she screamed over the noise.

"How would I know? We've never built it before!" he shouted back at her, still grinning like a madman.

"Well, it's not supposed to do that!" she screamed as the podium toppled over and the head of a huge man loomed beneath.

The boy stared in shock as the pipe that was forcing air through the mouths of the six heads was severed. "My god, look what we've created, ladies and gentlemen. Look at what we've done."

Petal clambered out of the hole, scratching his head. Behind his massive frame, Johnson, Blunt, and Mortimer were hidden from the view of the cameras and most of the audience. "What the hell is this?" Blunt exclaimed.

Mortimer, attempting to be as helpful as ever, replied, "Well, at first glance, it appears to be some kind of large clockwork device that just happens to have the heads of six people who were recently abducted by the headhunter attached to it. Well done, Chief. I think you've solved the case."

"Shut up, Mortimer. Nothing's that simple. What's

Petal staring at?" Blunt stepped to one side to see around the demi-god. "Oh, Christ, what the hell is this?" he roared.

A small girl was kicking the ankles of Petal, who was doing his best not to hurt her while trying to avoid the repeated attacks. "You aren't Mr. Fuzzles," she kept shouting over and over again. In front of the demi-god, a rapt audience was watching from the other side of the room. In between them and where Blunt stood were a camera crew who were looking very agitated, along with a boy in school uniform who appeared to be absolutely livid.

"Who the hell are you and what are you doing ruining my shot at the creation of life?" the boy screamed, pointing at Blunt.

Blunt drew himself up to his full height and puffed out his chest, and just as he was about to launch into a vicious attack on all and sundry, he noticed something that knocked the wind completely out of him. On the floor, beneath a pile of broken clockwork, lay a small brown bear, one of its eyes missing. Ignoring the sounds around him, which were becoming increasingly clamorous, he reached down and picked up the small brown bear. "That's uncanny." he murmured to himself.

"Mr Fuzzles!" exclaimed the girl that had been kicking Petal, quickly forgetting her assault. She leapt towards Blunt and tore the bear out of his hands. "I'm here now, Mr Fuzzles. I won't let anybody hurt you, especially not this mean, smelly man."

Blunt felt dizzy, and then sick. The two alternated and joined forces, and just before he passed out, he was able to say, "Susie?"

78

After Blunt had passed out, Sowercat and his men smashed their way through the two barred doors and quickly dispensed their rapid form of justice to anyone and everyone who stood in their way. Petal and Johnson, aware that their work was done, quickly left the scene by going back down through the sewers before anyone could follow them. Petal closed the manhole cover before anyone else could use the same escape plan and they disappeared into the night.

The Youth Order members who had built the machine were arrested and taken down to police central, where they received rigorous and repeated beatings from all members of the force who could build up the courage to beat children. There weren't many of them, and Sowercat couldn't bring himself to do it. Fortunately, Blythe had an impressive amount of pent-up anger and energy to make up for everyone else's reluctance.

On their way through the garden centre, several members of the police had laid waste to the recording van, meaning that all video evidence and live feeds never made it outside of the building. Dead Air were disappointed that so little of their equipment could be accounted for, but the police assured them they had recovered what they could. The heads were returned to their bodies and the headhunter case was temporarily closed, with one boy and his associates sentenced to library time for an indefinite period.

When Blunt woke up, he was in the room next to his office. It was daylight. Around his bed were a motley assortment of people, most of whom he didn't expect to see. Sarah was fully visible, and she beamed when she saw his eyes open. On her lap sat the girl, who could only have been his daughter from the land of the living, playing with the brown teddy bear that had brought it all back.

Next to her was Mortimer, holding hands with one of the most beautiful women Blunt had ever seen. From the way she kept putting her hand on Mortimer's chest and whispering things, Blunt could only assume she was his wife. It explained a lot about the crap the third assistant to the Office of the Dead was able to put up with. On Blunt's right, Leighton Hughes stood with a rolled-up newspaper in her hand. Next to her were two men Blunt rightfully didn't expect to see. One of them was forced to lean forward as if he was bowing. He smiled awkwardly, still showing a gap in his teeth that Blunt had given him. "Glad to see you're awake again, Chief Inspector. We'll be in touch." Mandrake nodded before walking out, bent double due to the height of the door.

"Don't worry about him, Blunt, that's the nicest thing I've ever heard him say to anyone." Sowercat seemed more than a little uncomfortable. "I don't know how this thing turned out like it did, but for some reason you're gonna get all the credit, and to be honest, I'm not gonna resent you too much for it. I'll buy you a drink and you can explain it when you're back on your feet." The chief of police slapped the back of Blunt's hands in absence of a handshake and walked out of the door.

Leighton didn't want to wait for the others, so she stepped forward quickly and put the newspaper on Blunt's chest. "First edition and first one off the press, collector's edition if you like. Thought you'd want to see it. I'll be in touch, but not in the scary way Mandrake means." She bolted out of the door while fixing her hat.

Blunt cracked a smile. "They didn't want to hang around, I guess. Mortimer, how in god's name did you manage to get a woman that makes Lulu Devine look like a garden gnome?"

Mortimer let go of his wife's hand and leant forward. "Lucky I guess, Chief."

"I owe you an apology for being a royal pain in the backside, but I don't like giving them, so consider this an I.O.U. Now why don't you head off, and I can find out what the hell my daughter's doing here."

Mortimer grinned in genuine relief. Blunt could tell the man wouldn't be missing any of the job he'd been embroiled in.

At the end of the bed, shrouded in black, was a figure Blunt had been carefully trying not to notice, but when it stood up out of the wicker chair, the noise the seat made meant that Blunt had to stop pretending. ***"Thank you, Detective Blunt. I understand you prefer the term* detective*?"***

Blunt couldn't help feeling frightened, and he was sure it wasn't just because he was tucked up in bed in a pair of pyjamas that he was fairly sure he didn't own. "Yes, I mean, yes sir, that's right, I do. Well, whatever you like, I mean, oh Christ."

"You have a habit of that."

"Of what?"

"Blasphemy. It's almost touching in a recently dead kind of way. Your official title is now Detective Blunt, Chief of the Office of Investigations. We will talk again. For now, perhaps it is best you say goodbye to your daughter, again."

Blunt looked at the little girl sitting on Sarah's lap. "Wait. Goodbye?"

"I'll let Miss—I'm sorry, your name always seems to escape me."

Sarah, who had been listening while purposefully not paying attention, answered. "Von Faber, Your Honour, Sarah Von Faber."

"Ah yes, I'll let Miss Von Faber explain. I am sorry, but it's the best course of action. I'm sure you'll agree. Ah, and I must stress that nobody must know of this." The man in black disappeared from the room without turning around, and Blunt heard the door click gently closed.

"Hello there, Susie. It's me. Your daddy. You remember Daddy, don't you?" Blunt asked the child in Sarah's arms.

"You're not my daddy. You're too old," the girl said with a pout.

Blunt was momentarily hurt, but he tried again. "I know I'm old, Susie, but it's been a very long time. I can prove it, though. Remember this?" And then to Sarah's—and to everyone who was crowded around the door outside's—surprise, Blunt broke into song. He had a gruff voice and was almost tuneless, but the words were familiar to most of them.

"Twinkle, twinkle, little star, how I wonder what you are,

Up above the world so bright, shining like a candle light,

Twinkle, twinkle little star, how I wonder what you are."

The little girl climbed down from Sarah's lap, clambered onto the bed, and wrapped her arms around Blunt's shoulders. "Daddy!" she exclaimed.

"Hello, my little star." Tears streamed down Blunt's face as he looked across at Sarah. He knew without asking what had to happen next. "Oh, my little sweetheart, I had to come and find you, but now I've got to say goodbye."

"But you only just got here."

"I know that, but Mummy's waiting for you where you're supposed to be, where we can put all this nastiness behind us."

The girl smiled and then looked puzzled. "Why aren't you coming?"

Blunt sighed, trying hard not to sob. "I've got to stop any more nasty people from doing silly things, but I'll come soon. Don't worry."

"And Mummy will be there?" the girl asked.

The door behind her opened and the Grim Reaper

stood in it, waiting. *"I'm afraid it's time to go, little one. I brought you Mr Fuzzles."*

The girl looked frightened. "But I was mean to that man," she said, staring at Blunt's face.

"Don't worry, he knows you didn't mean it. He's going to take you to Mummy."

The Grim Reaper dipped his head. *"You ask a lot."*

"I'll know if it hasn't happened." Blunt said, glaring at the skull beneath its black cowl.

"I believe you would. You do realise she was the headhunter."

"She was innocent in life. That's how it works, isn't it?" Blunt barked. He was getting angry, and he was damned if the Grim Reaper would stop his little girl from getting to where she belonged.

"Hm, not an argument that would be wise to employ in this city."

"But she shouldn't be here, should she? I mean, I'm here, and there isn't supposed to be an overlap. She never did anything, so why would she be sent here?"

The Grim Reaper appeared to nod behind his cowl. *"A mistake was made, and it shall be rectified. However, what you ask is difficult."*

"You can't do it?"

"As a favour to you."

"A favour? I saved you. I saved this whole city."

"You were certainly present… it will be done."

79

Johnson and Petal sat at either side of the table in their kitchen, drinking coffee and listening to the radio news broadcast, trying to make sense of what had happened the night before. Some kind of furore at the garden centre was all that was mentioned. Not a word was spoken about the heads or the headhunter. Both men knew that shortly the story would be released, though neither were yet aware of the Gloomwood Independent.

On a chair at the head of the table was a pile of books: some complex textbooks on the laws of Gloomwood, which belonged to Johnson, and a few less impressive novels and easy reading pieces that Petal had purchased and spent a long time attempting to read. On top of the books, a stuffed toy was perched. A single black button marked its only remaining eye, its brown fur matted or wearing away. As they drank their coffee and listened to the radio, each of the men would glance occasionally in the direction of the bear.

"It's not my fault," the bear said, its voice gruff and defensive.

Johnson sighed. "It might not be your fault, but it's still a serious problem."

The bear attempted to fold its arms but found they were too short. "Well, how are we supposed to know for sure?"

Petal gently put down his mug of coffee and looked into the bear's eyes. "We could try to kill you," he said.

"Yes, you've said that already, but then I might die and what does that do?"

There was a thud outside the room. Johnson pushed his chair back as far as it would go and slid out from beneath the table. He left the room for a moment, leaving the bear and Petal in a staring contest. When he returned, he carried a newspaper in one hand. He placed it on the table. "Somebody dropped this with us. I'm guessing Aunt Agnes."

He opened up the paper and threw the sports section at Petal, who gratefully held it up over his face so he could avoid looking at the bear. Johnson followed suit, holding the front page in front of him and reading Leighton Hughes' first front-page spread since her death.

"Any chance I can have the funnies section?" the bear asked.

"How do you even know there's such a thing as a funnies section, and how can you talk? If you're new, as in new—" He swallowed. "—newborn, you shouldn't be able to talk."

"Well, there you go then, plain as day. I must have died and come into this body."

Johnson put the paper down. The Marquis' grinning face took up a large section of the front page. The header read, "Marquis A-head of the Game Again." "You should know if you died. You should have some idea about what happened before.

"Did you?" the bear asked.

The policeman shrugged. "I was different."

"Maybe I'm different too."

Petal placed the sports section on the table. "You're different, there's no arguing there."

"It doesn't make any sense to me. The little girl had her bear back; I saw it. It wasn't alive or dead, just a thing," Johnson said.

The bear was nodding. "Right, so I can't be the bear from the garden centre, can I?"

"You were in the sewer when we came down straight afterwards."

"Nah, doesn't make sense."

THE END

… if there is such a thing in Gloomwood.

More Gloomwood?

Get Ted Dead

All Ted wants to do is live his life. Unfortunately, he's the only person in Gloomwood who has one. He's also less than three feet tall, filled with foam, covered in fur, and has only one button eye. To make matters worse, he's lost, alone, and the inhabitants of the entire city want him dead.

As the dead start coming to life and the foundations of the government begin to crumble, it's a race against time for Ted and the members of the Gloomwood Investigator's Office. Oh, and there's the small matter of a twisted criminal kingpin with a cuddly toy fetish to deal with as well. This is no teddy bear's picnic.

Available now

You can follow the author on twitter at @inkdisregardit or at Goodreads.com

Find more Gloomwood related treats at rossyoung.ink

Thank you to everyone who has offered support as this was written and encouragement. Especially the shaman who, via dream walking, explained the culture of Gloomwood–no really folks, you know who you are.

Um… that's it…

…thanks for reading…

… it's a little awkward now…

… oh, leave a review, that would be great.

… bye then…

Printed in Great Britain
by Amazon